The Adventures of
Clark Westfield
The Smart Ones

By Tom Albright

This is a work of fiction. None of the characters or events are real. Any similarities to any events or people living or dead in real life are purely coincidental….

Table of Contents

Prologue

February 2, 2020

A cold and trembling left index finger reached through the bitter freezing rain to press the button on the call box. Another lukewarm hand, also trembling, curled up in his right hand as his wife leaned on him from the passenger seat. A nervous silence followed as Mr. and Mrs. Mackoul waited to see if the scraped metal with its aluminum speaker and flaking yellow paint could connect them with anyone. The open car window let the rain and wind disrupt the husband and wife travelers with daggers of cold, wet wisps as they waited for a sound. Then, a crackle, some static, followed by much louder static and a swab of feedback.

"Proceed!" was the word the Mackouls could make out as a garbled voice choked its way through the little metal Venetian blind slits that protect the speaker. The Mackouls glanced at each other as the ancient iron gate in front of their car drew open. Mr. Mackoul drove through the gate on what appeared to be a seldom-used trail with tire tracks in the grass but no pavement. Mr. Mackoul plowed on, the tension rising in his throat. His wife, too nervous to speak, pointed at a faint light shining through the trees. With muddy spins, the car slipped over the top of a low hill and arrived at a small house. A figure in a dark raincoat and a wide-brimmed hat stood on the unlit porch. Mr. Mackoul pulled up and rolled down his window.

"Hi, sorry to bother you. I'm not sure we are at the right pace…." he volunteered as a salutation.

The figure walked up to the vehicle, opened the door, and got in the back seat. "Drive forward on the path. I'll tell you where to turn," said the man in the back. Mr. Mackoul recognized the voice from their prior conversation. It was the same voice that had called him and told him to come to this address.

"Where is our son!?" exclaimed Mrs. Mackoul without turning around as per the prior instructions.

"You know our agreement, Mrs. Mackoul, please respect it," said the voice in the back seat. The car slipped and slid through the muddy woods at a crawl.

"Did you bring all the documents we discussed?" asked the voice.

"Yes, of course we did," Mr. Mackoul's voice cracked with the anxious dryness in his throat.

"Our agreement was that we would see our son, Greg. Where is he?" pressed Mr. Mackoul with the last shred of courage he could muster.

"Relax…," said the voice. "Greg is perfectly fine. I believe he texted you both earlier to say exactly that. As we discussed previously, Mr. Mackoul, this is a process, and you must be patient and respect the agreement while we work with Greg. This is where you will be staying." A small unlit cabin stood soaked in the rain. "Take your suitcases and leave the documentation in the car. You will both get out here, and I will bring your car to where it will stay. There is food, firewood, and a VCR with some old movie tapes. Someone will be in touch…"

As the man exited the back seat, Mr. Mackoul stood in the wet grass to confront the passenger. "We want some answers, and we want to see our son, or nobody is going any…"

Mackoul's voice fell silent as the man partially pulled back one flap of his raincoat to reveal a nickel-plated .38 revolver strapped to his waist. As his wife stood up from the passenger seat, the man closed his raincoat to conceal the gun. The mysterious stranger reached out and a leather gloved hand opened. Mackoul realized he must have wanted the car keys and leaned in to remove them from the ignition. The man took the keys and opened the trunk. He took out two matching floral patterned designer suitcases and placed them on the ground. The heavy suitcases sank into the soft mud under their own weight. A third suitcase, the kind a lawyer would roll into court containing legal files, remained in the trunk.

"That's everything," said Mr. Mackoul, pointing at the file suitcase.

"Good," said the voice from behind the open trunk as Mrs. Mackoul went to stand next to her husband.

"The cabin is unlocked, and the house keys are on the table," said the man as he got into the driver's seat of the Mackoul's car and closed the door. He started the car Mr. Mackoul shouted "Hey man… what is this? You are leaving? Where are you going with my car? Where the hell is my son? Hey! Are you even listening!!??"

But the man was not. The tires slipped in the mud a few times as the car drove off. The Mackouls, shocked, wet, cold, and worried, looked at one another, turned towards the cabin, and went inside to wait…

Chapter 1

February 2, 2022

The news felt more believable, more true, when you held a physical newspaper in your hands. And Clark Westfield still loved the powdery feeling of black ink dust working its way into the grooves of his fingerprints. There was a perfection about the week of July 4 – the sun set late with a long golden twilight, and the New Jersey summer evenings were a friendly temperature most years. The humid, soot-heavy air over the Garden State that packs a 100-degree punch usually didn't start until late July. A fleeting glimpse around the dinner table at his 19-year-old daughter, Clark could feel his gratitude swell deep inside, especially as his eyes fell on the newspaper he had folded and put down next to his plate and the empty chair where his wife Mary Lynn had sat for 20 years before losing her battle cancer. Five years had passed since their last conversation. They were five long, desolate, cold, silent years filled with the fog of grief, self-loathing, Covid isolation, self-doubt, and the deep rage only karmic bad luck could engender. But this July 4, much of that toxic emotional sludge had started to wash away. He was proud of his daughter Melody, and she had been so supportive as the father/daughter team had braved the blindness and confusion the loss of a matriarch brings that Clark even mustered a smile.

"Parents Now Missing In Boy Genius Cold Case" blared the headline. A local boy named Greg Mackoul, a seemingly rare child genius with an IQ that was off the charts had been missing for two years in a classic "vanishing." Recently, his parents had left their family home unannounced and hadn't been heard from, which had raised eyebrows. Was it grief? Either way, the Metuchen police had an open case of a missing high school senior and no one to talk to now that his parents had vanished. Now, two years after the Mackoul boy's disappearance, another high school student had disappeared from a town nearby.

"Mel, did you read the story about that kid from Maplewood who disappeared? And then also remember that kid from a few years back - right as the pandemic started and they couldn't find him? Did you hear that the boy genius's parents are now missing too? What do you think happened?" Clark asked his daughter Melody. She was a bright and fascinating young woman, and the father/daughter relationship they had cultivated over her 19 years on earth would be the envy of any father of a teen. It had been earned through the mutual dependency on one another after his wife's passing and now was deep and unshakable.

"Oh… that kid that lived on Magnolia Avenue?" chimed Melody from the kitchen. "One of my friends had a younger sister in his class, and they said he was totally weird – like super smart but weird in every other way. I think you call it Ass-berger disease or whatever?"

"It's Asperger's Syndrome, and super smart people usually have it," added Clark. "It's almost like when a brain has so much intelligence in one area like science, math, or musical performance, it can't really do anything else right."

Clark picked up the paper and began to read the article. The current missing boy, Alvin Matsumoto, was a 14-year-old with what the school principal called "extraordinary gifts" and was a National Merit Scholar, the national academic ranking that recognized high school students for their academic achievements. Alvin had gone missing two weeks ago and his parents first contacted the school and then the police, who launched a well-publicized search, fearing he may have gotten lost on his way home from school. The article stated that Alvin's parents met with the school and police, and then after a few days, suddenly stopped cooperating with police and searchers, drawing enormous suspicion before disappearing themselves.

Clark felt a faint vibration of what used to be adrenaline shock deep in his guts, knowing he was reading an intriguing news story. But the faint chemical blip was a pale reflection of the passion that used to flow freely and drive him to race to crime scenes and knock on victim's doors late at night, in the hopes of obtaining a quote, or work the crowd at repasts of elected officials. It was the excitement of the news propelling him forward as "God's messenger" -a town crier on a celestially sanctioned prophetic mission to inform the world of what was happening and what was to come. Those days - those surges out the door despite family responsibilities, those newsroom arguments with editors who didn't believe his hunches, flipping sources to expose dirty cops, infidelity stakeouts - were gone. The bulldog reporter that gave Clark Westfield's life meaning, purpose, adventure, and prestige had retreated in contempt for the world. and for news everywhere, for social media, for pundits, for 24-hour cable news propaganda factories, for podcasts, for blogs, for memes, and god knows what else was supposed to be important these days. It no longer mattered whether news was true, original, balanced, or neutral. There simply was no longer any appetite by the American people for news accuracy to be a checkpoint in a civilized society, and it terrified Clark at a very deep level.

Melody placed several steaming bowls of food on the table and called over to her father. "OK Dad, it's just you and me tonight. I made a 100% organic dinner for July 4!" she sang happily.

"We aren't having hamburgers and hot dogs for the 4th of July? Am I being punked?" Clark replied in genuine disbelief.

"No! Absolutely no hot dogs or hamburgers! Do you know how irresponsible it is to eat meat from animals that were raised on fertilized fields with a massive carbon footprint?" Melody was speaking passionately, as she was obsessed with climate change and planned to study environmental science.

"Could you have at least cooked veggie burgers or something as a nod to American tradition?" Clark asked in a joking tone but still wanting an answer.

Melody let out a deep sigh, sounding deflated in the way only a 19-year-old girl can when she was disappointed with her father. "Dad…it's time we abandon American traditions that are toxic! I made all these vegetables and they are all organic and non-GMO, and that's a better action step than perpetuating the criminal meat industry and…"

"Do you even know what any of that means?" asked Clark with genuine frustration. "Have you REALLY measured whether your passionate monologue is going to help at any practical level?"

"See Dad, this is why we are so fucked. Every person thinks they can't make a difference and then nothing gets done. If we could just rise against GMOs before it's too late…"

"What GMOs? Too late for what?? Mel…I want you to think about what you are reading and step back for a second. A lot of what you are pointing at are scary rumors that play well in the press. We have been growing and eating GMOs for decades, and there haven't been any problems," said Clark, lowering his voice as he talked further. "It just seems there are bigger problems in the world right now that need immediate attention."

"OK, but Dad…listen to me for a moment…" said Melody her eyes filling with tears. "If we don't change how we see and do everything, we are risking all of humanity's survival. How can we just allow smart people to mix and match genetics in plants with no accountability and no oversight? You realize it's not just plants, right? It's animals, too…there are genetic modifications in livestock already, and no one knows what they are, and who knows, they could be in people as well."

Mel…stop there. I'm not in the mood…" Clark said gently. "Everything isn't a conspiracy to take over the world and oppress us. That's just not how the world works in real life, only in James Bond movies."

"I think the human race is more precarious than you think Dad, and we are on a precipice with science and technology that will permanently alter humanity," Melody argued.

"Mel, I have seen humanity hang in there for quite a few challenges. You'd be surprised what we can handle," Clark chuckled. "And that part about science and technology putting us on some dangerous cliff – get in line behind Copernicus, Darwin, and all the other historical figures who were accused of creating the same risks after basic scientific discoveries.

I'm not being dismissive, Mel, but we've been here before. Humanity will do fine."

Melody felt concerned. Her entire life, her father had preached, often at high volume, about the virtue of pursuing the news as an act of patriotism. He had been a diehard 1st Amendment advocate, and some of the investigative stories he broke had made a huge impact. He would torture his family members by reciting every detail of every case and telling them "what hit the edit room floor." No journalist was more authentic and passionate about news than Clark Westfield –it would defy the laws of newsroom physics. And it was why Melody was so concerned about her father. The great crusading journalistic hero hadn't broken a major story in at least a year. His three weekly columns on the commentary of his choice had become flat, almost satirical, watered-down fluff. It was obvious to those close to Clark that he hadn't been himself for several years, perhaps as far back as before the pandemic had started and his wife passed. But this was different from personal grief - there was an existential pessimism to it that wasn't present in the immediate years after being widowed. Clark had first found solace in his work like many men who lose their wives, working twice as hard and twice as long for distraction and ultimately, survival. But the last two years Melody had watched her father at home on the living room couch, screaming at the television and the various anchors on cable news. Most people had come around as the pandemic had retreated, and it seemed the news was more vital than ever, and yet, her father seemed to sink into an even darker place of disillusionment and journalistic chagrin.

Clark tasted the vegetables Melody had sautéed. They were mediocre despite her being a great cook. He turned and grabbed the packaging that was on the counter. 100% USDA Certified Organic was stamped on the label. "What a joke…" he smirked to himself.

"What do you think happened to that other kid's parents?" asked Melody politely, changing the subject.

"Who knows? People do crazy stuff…" mumbled Clark dispassionately.

"Dad, it seems like you just don't care about anything anymore," said Melody with genuine concern. "Are you depressed? Why don't you get excited about stories anymore?"

"Mel…I didn't leave the news, the news left me," said Clark staring down at his empty plate. He wasn't ready to dissect his fundamental shift just yet so he changed the subject. "First, I've been in this business long enough to predict that this is probably some family navigating immigration issues and they just took off. Trust me, this is a non-event. And, in the impossible event that this is something much more sinister…who cares?"

"What do you mean who cares dad? That's never come out of your mouth before." Melody could sense there was something more under her father's responses.

"I just mean if it turned out to be some elaborate murder, or theft, or even spy stuff, its still a two-day story and the world moves on to the next thing. It's almost as if the news coverage packages everything with a beginning, middle, and end giving us permission to move on and not to care," Clark stared into the distance.

"Dad, can I bring up a delicate topic?" asked Melody with trepidation.

Clark rolled his eyes and sighed.

"Here we go again...," he thought. "What's on your mind, dear?" he asked.

"Well, I'm not sure how to describe it but..." Melody looked down at the table avoiding eye contact. "You just seem like you've lost your fight..." she said, her voice swelling with emotion. Clark shot her a perplexed look, though deep inside he knew exactly what she meant. Yet as spot-on as his daughter's observation was, he saw no benefit in explaining to his young optimistic daughter how he had lost his faith in humanity. That would be narcissistic and cruel, he told himself.

"I don't think you want to have this conversation, Mel," he said in a low volume evasive tone, then got up from the table and left.

There was something inherently humiliating on the twilight side of greatness. Clark Westfield had enjoyed a multi-decade career as a reporter, journalist, and author. He was known in journalism schools around the country as the example of persistence, ethics, and dedication. He brought all the major industry awards to his employer newspaper, the Newark Examiner, the largest newspaper in New Jersey. Every possible regional journalism reporting award was his— Silver Bulldogs, Westinghouse Awards, State Press Association Annual Reporter's Choice Trophies, and New Jersey Correspondents Medal of Excellence. They stood in a glass trophy case in the newspaper's reception area. Clark looked at the empty reception desk and the dark lighting in the offices behind the doors and paused. It seemed no one had bothered to come into the office for this meeting, so why should he? A voice broke the dreary gray thickness.

"Clark… how nice of you to grace us with your presence," said Elizabeth Cranford in her faux matriarchal tone. Elizabeth was Clark's editor, but 15 years younger. Clark had let her intern for him when she was a senior in college more than 29 years ago. She had started freelancing as an intern and was hired as a copy and rewrite editor immediately out of college. She had worked under Clark in his division as a right hand and protégé for more than ten years. He had taught her the ropes, looked out for her in office politics, and set her up to succeed on stories, which she did almost every time. She had worked with Clark on some of the biggest breaks of his career, most recently the investigation and discovery of a murderous ring of bereaved parents that systematically were executing opioid-prescribing doctors. She had also recently worked on a multi-year investigation that led to the discovery of Cold War bunkers in Harriman State Park in New York and a rogue CIA program that had caused a local murder. There were few people Westfield hated more than their former boss and managing editor, Sean Caldwell. Clark saw it as a mission for the greater good rather than a personal vendetta to fight him, and when Caldwell was finally thrown out of the office, it was Elizabeth who filled the chaos of the managing editor's job at Clark's insistence. Clark had abdicated his position two years ago when the paper changed ownership. Now Clark was called an "Editor Emeritus At Large " and sometimes when the layout staff wanted to tease him, they would write the tag "Legacy Columnist" above any of his articles.

Clark loved working under Elizabeth. It gave him the opportunity to keep eyes on her and assist in stories or office politics—all behind the scenes, of course. Clark had decades of contacts he provided to Elizabeth. Police captains, clergy, celebrities living quiet, private lives, CEOs, and union leaders – Clark had covered every aspect and detail of their businesses and lives. He had won over the reasonable ones, remained frenemies with some, and was a marked man with others.

Navigating that complicated weather pattern was what made Clark so extraordinary as a journalist. Now, it was all Elizabeth's. She had spent 15 years by Clark's side in the field with him introducing her to key players, teaching her how to cultivate or flip sources. He instilled in her a sixth sense that would sense when someone was telling the truth or not. When you are lied to multiple times a day by sources with an agenda, you either stop caring or you become hypersensitive to untruths, and it codifies a personal conviction. Clark was the latter, and so was Elizabeth. Whether it was a straight, bold-faced lie that they could easily prove false in their writing, like the police chief who denied being at the scene of a shooting despite video evidence, or sins of omission where relevant truths were simply left out of the conversation or obscured, they hated untruths. Years ago, a bishop had told Clark and Elizabeth the diocese had no knowledge of a predator priest's prior record, only for Clark and Elizabeth to find families in Pittsburgh to speak on the record about his "activities" that very afternoon. And it was that type of sin of omission that bothered the two of them the most, because what power players DIDN'T tell you is what usually did the most damage.

As for assignments, Elizabeth let Clark write whatever he wanted. Clark made her life difficult with the stipulation that she always found space in the print edition of the newspaper, and his pieces didn't just live online. "What are we going to do when a pulse bomb fries all our computers or a solar flare zaps the whole electric grid? I'll still have columns in the newspaper!" he would say. However, despite Elizabeth taking over the paper almost two years ago, she had yet to send Clark on an assignment. Despite the new owners being completely uninterested in the actual NEWS of the business, Elizabeth wanted to launch and break a big investigative piece. Clark had averaged at least one major investigative piece each year of his tenure and won so many awards it became a joke. That is until he won the Pulitzer Prize for investigative journalism for a piece on a local murder that had roots in Washington espionage. This was in 2019. The greatest irony was not that he exposed another example of our government behaving badly but rather that he had already been fired from the paper by Sean Caldwell, a casualty of the new ownership's need to prematurely neutralize the insubordination he was so famous for, and was the essence of the testicular fortitude that had won him the award. Clark didn't have to ask for his job back—no one even knew that paper had fired him yet, and Clark didn't care. Elizabeth, in her new role as editor, after it all went down, had just started giving him assignments and running his columns. She didn't ask anybody, and no one discussed it with her. And just like that, Clark Westfield had returned to the newsroom under the supervision of the woman he had trained to have superior skills to his own, and Elizabeth knew exactly how to use him. And not fearing any insubordination or gaslighting by Clark's stratospheric intellect, Elizabeth decided today she would give Clark his first assignment.

"There is something about the week of the 4th of July, it's a special kind of humidity," offered Clark with a smile as he appeared in Elizabeth's office doorway, which was his old office. She looked up from her computer and smiled back. Despite how much she had achieved on her own, and her remarkable independence as an editor and manager, there was a sense of security that Clark brought to the newsroom that she never wanted to grow past. It wasn't that she couldn't handle any crisis on her own – it was that Clark was living proof that you survive most of the worst-case scenarios. Clark had lived through the biggest and most tragic events of the last 30 years in world news and in his own career. He had been falsely accused, endured allegations of malice, plagiarism, bias, negligence, and every other slight the world could throw at a reporter. He had been followed and received dozens of death threats in the mail. He had been beaten up, had knives pressed against his throat, and felt the cold metal of a gun barrel against his temple. But he was still here, still looking for the next important story. Still looking for whoever wasn't telling the truth.

"Clark, I have to give you an assignment," said Elizabeth without looking up. Clark assumed she was joking.

"Politics?" Clark responded, also without looking at Elizabeth but rather staring out her office window. Silver leaves flashed as the trees swayed in the hot summer wind. "Yeah, I was thinking I would write a piece about how nothing will ever return to normal until…"

"I mean a real assignment, as in sit down and start taking notes," said Elizabeth, now looking him dead in the eyes and adding a sternness to her tone. Clark sensed the climate of the conversation shift. "I need you to do an expose series on intelligence." Her voice dipped in volume.

"Not sure you remember this, Liz," resisted Clark, trying not to bristle at his former intern giving him an actual assignment. "Though granted, you weren't my boss then, but I recently did an extended investigation into certain intelligence agencies, and I'm not exactly welcome there any longer, but okay, it's been a while since I've been to Washington and—" Elizabeth cut him off again.

"Clark, you need to follow me here…" Elizabeth slowed down her diction and made eye contact with Clark in a deep serious fashion that let him know this was something important. "I'm not giving you a generic reporting assignment intellectual columns and lengthy in in-depth investigations - as your editor that is what we agreed I would give you. So this is an investigation. But… it's going to start as a series that is going to make you look like you've lost your edge." Elizabeth paused to allow Clark to focus on the next part of what she was going to say.

"I see…. and this is supposed to make me feel good…why?" quipped Clark.

"Making you feel good isn't my job, thank god," Elizabeth said, cracking a smile. Decades of intense work cultivates room between colleagues for edgy teasing. "I need you to start off as if it were a routine feature series, and we can create some generic cover backstory like you are working with the Smithsonian or TIME Magazine or something lofty. Start out writing about the pathology of intelligence and then gradually get into the marketing of parent products like fertility and pregnancy supplements that promise smart children. Then examine the educational and learning racket and all of those conscience-gouging operations that pretend you need to go to a certain daycare to get into Harvard." Elizabeth stopped speaking as she noticed Clark was smirking. "What? What is it?" she pressed.

"Nothing," said Clark boyishly. Elizabeth wasn't going to let him off the hook on the off chance it was genuine wisdom under that grin and not Clark's Gen X pedantics. After a few seconds of an awkward, silent deadlocked stare between the two, Elizabeth spoke:

"Then I want you to draw a thumbnail portrait of what life must have looked like for that poor Matsumoto boy growing up with all that pressure to succeed," she continued. "He disappeared two weeks ago with no trace, and the police chief fears the worst."

"What does that kid have to do with anything? I think he is just a runaway, maybe an addict, maybe he met some weird girl or guy or whatever online and took off." Clark looked genuinely perplexed.

"I'm telling you he didn't take off," Elizabeth said firmly. "Apparently, this kid was in a micro-fraction of the population with his high intelligence. At least that is what the chief said."

"Liz…with all due respect, I've seen this kind of thing before."

"With all due respect?" Elizabeth shot back incredulously. "I think this is the moment when a boss is so dumbfounded by her employee's stupidity she has to actively engage in restraint." Her eyes were daggers. "Investigate the circumstances surrounding the Matsumoto kid -- find out if the parents had entered him into any smart societies where they get to show off how great they are as parents."

"Smart societies? I'm not sure I follow…" Clark inquired sheepishly.

"Yeah, you know - Mensa, National Merit Scholars, phi beta kappa, or countless branded programs for the gifted and talented students to show their elitism." Elizabeth was gritting her teeth as she spoke. Clark chuckled as he started to speak.

"Do I detect a fair amount of resentment toward the one percent whose biggest problem are likes on social media for their child's achievements?" Clark jibed. "You know I set out to teach you to be a crusader and I couldn't be more proud of where you are directing the effort." Clark still didn't see the urgency or significance of the assignment. "But Liz, so far this story is nowhere, so what exactly are you getting at?"

"Well, why not think about it and grow into that outsized mythical reputation of the great reporter Clark Westfield? Did you know your last name is used as a verb? There was a time when every public official used to live in fear of being 'Westfielded." Elizabeth let it sink in for a moment.

"And your point?" Clark realized he was being challenged and was almost cornered.

"And no one has had that fear for a while," she said slowly. "It's as if the great Clark Westfield retired and didn't even say goodbye -but here he is in front of me, trying to squirm out of an assignment. What do I have to do to get the weaponized Westfield back?"

"Liz…don't." Clark could sense she was wrapping her concern and compassion in a work conversation. "There is no rekindling the flames of youth in the furnace of investigative reporting. Not with this old bastard. Those days are gone. I'll take whatever assignment you need me to do…" His voice trailed off as he sighed and looked out the window. Elizabeth realized the rescue operation for her colleague's mental health was going to be a bit more complicated, but then shame on her for thinking anything with Clark would be simple.

"I am not trying to rekindle the flames of your early drive and passion for reporting Clark," she said in the most supportive tone she could muster. "How about we work on re-lighting the pilot light?" They exchanged a smile, and both teared up a bit. They both knew Clark was coming to the end of his career, and that after two overt attempts that saw him get fired and return twice, he wouldn't survive a third persecution from management. They also both knew that when Clark walked out of that newsroom door on his looming last day, an entire era of journalism would be leaving with him. Of course, technology had fundamentally changed journalism, and the newsroom was unrecognizable to a veteran like Clark, but there was something else afoot, and Elizabeth felt it, too. There was a malignant apathy that was robust in the college interns and cub reporters who were working at the paper, and it had bubbled up to most levels of management. Usually, that was nothing a few corporate retreats full of trust falls and cheesy icebreakers couldn't cure. But there was something more sinister underway as the advent of specialty opinionated news of 24-hour cable channels, influencers as experts, and various social media platforms had dissolved the very soul of journalism, leaving a gaping void, a virtual black hole where facts and accountability disappeared forever. Elizabeth and Clark were on the precipice of that journalistic void, and both knew the societal breakdown that loomed for a culture that couldn't agree on basic facts or principles and no longer cared. Staying on the job as a working reporter somehow gave Clark permission to forget it was happening.

"What do you really need, Liz?" Clark practically whispered. Elizabeth got up from her chair and walked over to her office window and leaned against Clark with her full body weight. It was something they had adopted as an inside joke, connecting them as loyal colleagues. Over the years, it was Clark who had always provided the support to Elizabeth as he leaned on her, but now the roles were reversed.

"Remember this?" said Elizabeth warmly in an attempt to make Clark remember what a great team they had been throughout the years. "You always let me lean on you, and sometimes I couldn't stand up otherwise. Now it's my turn, old boss. Now…what THE FUCK is going on with you?" Her tone was half-joking, but her question was serious.

"You had an assignment you wanted to delegate?" Clark's tone droned with aloof boredom as he tried to avoid his colleague deconstructing his mental health.

"OK, fine. Is that how it's gonna be?" Elizabeth leaned up against him harder pushing against the floor to the point where they both smiled. Yet under their sophomoric, loyal interplay, she saw a deep sadness in his expression she hadn't seen before. It was borderline chilling as it was so antithetical to the man she knew, trusted, and loved like an older brother. The Clark Westfield that had spoken in her high school journalism class and hired her as an intern while at Rutgers, gave her her first job, her first big breaks, her reporting awards, and now her editor position seemed gone—…vanished like those smart kids that seemed to keep disappearing. Elizabeth kept a mental memo file about Clark's alarming concoction of depression and anxiety and decided she would monitor him through this assignment and take action if necessary. She hated seeing him like this. "You know the kid that disappeared recently?" she continued, still leaning against him.

"The second super smart kid? High school kid? I think my daughter knew him from something…"

"Yes. Alvin Matsumoto, age 14, second generation Japanese born here to parents who worked as auto executives for Toyota and later Honda….? Yeah, well, nothing adds up in that case, especially with the parents MIA now. The police are suspicious they are those crazy abusive helicopter parents and they either scared him off or enrolled him in a school against his will," she explained.

"Yeah but Liz, I'm not trying to be a downer or a jerk, but… so what?" Clark's tone was professorial as he assumed his old role of pressuring Elizabeth to shape a story.

"Exactly. So what." Elizabeth waited and said nothing else.

"I'm not sure I follow.…" He still looked more frustrated than interested.

"Matsumoto isn't the story, Clark. But you already know that don't you, because you already mentally scanned his profile and realized there must be some significance to this, am I right? Use your head." She had now flipped the roles back and was quizzing Clark on where the news elements may lay. She smiled a minute as Clark waited for her to speak. His expression still didn't qualify as interested, but for now, his anticipation would suffice. "What did you always tell me since that first day you yelled at me in class?"

"I don't think I yelled at you," Clark stammered, somewhat surprised and trying to remember the day he had first met her while lecturing her 10th-grade class.

"Well, you certainly did yell at me. In fact, it was in front of the whole class. It's still the stuff of legend." Elizabeth giggled. "But that's not important. What did you tell me from that moment and every day after when I walked into your office as your protégé? You always said: "Start with the smart ones - they've always got something to hide, and if they don't, they will help you fill in the gaps." Well, the Matsumoto kid wasn't the first smart kid to disappear followed by his parents—"

"Yeah, I remember the one who did about two years ago—family name Mackoul. I think my daughter might have known him also from school. So you want a story on why adolescent geniuses wig out and then their parents disappear? With empathy in such short supply these days is this really the right story to pursue in the fight for equality and truth? Making sure the lives of the rich and educated run smoothly isn't why I got in this business Elizabeth." He may have lost much of the fire in his belly, but he hadn't lost his acerbic wit.

"I'm pursuing equality by pursuing truth," Liz shot back. "Now stop talking and let me finish. This Alvin Matsumoto boy had no friends or enemies; he was just really smart. Two years ago, Greg Mackoul had no friends or enemies, but he was also really smart. They both disappeared, and local authorities were brought in. Both sets of parents stopped talking to police shortly after their sons' disappearances, then left town and haven't been seen by anyone. And if you talk to the chief of police—"

"You know damn well I can't talk to Chief Thompson, Liz," Clark groaned. Did he have to remind Elizabeth of the history he had with the chief of police? No two men were greater arch-nemeses than Clark Westfield and Police Chief Thompson. "Plus, I'm still not seeing the news. So far, it sounds like the chess club's version of the teddy bear's picnic - a bunch of outcasts skipping town to frolic elsewhere unbothered." You could cut Clark's cynicism with a knife.

"Exactly," Elizabeth said, leaning harder and smiling at Clark He returned a look of tired frustration. "I got a call today from Connecticut from a reporter at the Hartford daily paper. Seems they had a case like this one six months ago, and there has been no progress— a local genius prodigy girl, age 15, disappeared, causing a massive search. Then, a month later, the parents are completely MIA. As the reporter was doing a six-month follow-up piece to see where the police were at with the case, she found our paper's coverage of these two cases two years apart and called me to brainstorm."

"You took a call from a random reporter and gave her backstory on work we had done here? You aren't going to last very long as an editor if you keep that up."

"Westfield, I'm the editor now, and I get to decide what to tell other papers, okay?" A faint smile softened her admonishment. "And I spoke to her and told her I would get back to her if I found anything material." Elizabeth stopped talking and just looked at Clark. He knew her long enough to know there was more to the story.

"You mean you told her you would assign an old washed-up investigative gumshoe and do the work for her?" Clark's sarcasm bordered on caustic.

"I told her that we would examine her case for patterns and similarities and get back to her if there were any. I didn't mention your name, besides, you always told us to collaborate whenever possible, as it increased the chances of finding discernable facts. But I do need you to cross reference these stories as you start covering what we will call 'smart culture'. First, find out if these are the only cases or if there are any others. The FBI has a straightforward missing persons data that is searchable. I need to know what these three youngsters have in common, individually, financially, emotionally—who their parents are, their school behaviors and reports, any sports or youth group activity, etc. I need to know why these kids went missing and then their parents soon after. Nothing adds up."

"And you want to know if any of these popular trends in 'smart culture' had a nefarious effect on these kids or their parents or both, and you want to get their parents' participation in it in the sunshine," sighed Clark. "But even if we do, and we learn all this minutiae, so what? Again, so what? Are the problems of smart rich people news?"

"Of course, not," Elizabeth retorted. "But whoever is benefitting from those problems is certainly news. Who stands to profit or gain an advantage proximity to a child genius? Many players I would presume. If a child is so outstanding that they attract attention, we have to assume there are plenty of shysters ready to step in and scam up a scheme. You always taught me that when something doesn't add up, to find out where the pieces intersect and overlay, and that is where the news is. Well, in this case, two local boys, Greg Mackoul and Alvin Matsumoto, both with astronomical IQs and genius-level analytical skills, and a 15-year-old girl genius from Hartford, Connecticut, have all disappeared in the last two years without a trace, followed by their parents. You know as well as I do there is a story under there, Clark Westfield. You really want to tell me that three hyper-gifted and talented kids suddenly missing within two years and 60 miles of each other, that you don't feel the tug? It's in your DNA, Professor Westfield… you know you feel it. You want to find out as much as I do who these kids were and where they are. And I guarantee you that the crossroad that ties these three cases together is the lid on a major story about intellectual elitism and whatever racketeering thrives on bright kids and their gullible parents. There is a lot more here, Clark, and you know it. Now, I empathize with where you are at emotionally, and I am prepared to support you with whatever resources you need. Plus, I am going to formally suggest counseling, though I know you won't do it. But you need to do this to reclaim your groove, and I've got your back. I'm telling you I will support you in whatever way you need, and I have your back, but you have to get your shit together, or I'll have to make it a formal requirement." She was trying her best to give him a version of the many pep talks Clark had given her when sending her off on a story. She did her best to look like a compassionate boss. But underneath the semblance of the boss/employee charade, she was deeply concerned that the man who had made the singular most difference in her life looked uninterested, broken, and unrecognizable.

"So…" Clark looked like a ball player on the bench hesitating to take the field. Elizabeth sighed and gave a final, loud, unambiguous directive.

"Go find the smart ones" And she got up and left.

Chapter 2

Clark felt a lump in his throat - —sixty thousand dollars? Sixty??? What could this college possibly offer worth that tuition? He kept looking at the letter from the registrar's office of Cook College at Rutgers University in disbelief as if the numbers would finally change the next time he checked, but they didn't.

"I'll bet you are happy to welcome her…" Clark thought to himself. The letter started with a text that was simple enough: Dear Ms. Melody Westfield, we are happy to welcome you to the class of 2024 as a freshman! Melody had desperately wanted to study environmental science at Cook College, which was started by Abraham Lincoln as a land grant to study agriculture and was one of the oldest and most thorough environmental academic institutions in the country. The mindset at the time was that not only did agriculture make us a better, stronger nation with its self-sufficiency, but it also gave the country some export commerce and all of the strategic advantages on the world stage with a commodity every human needed three times a day—food. Clark had gone to Cook and chose their only non-science major—journalism. However, it came with a requirement of a second major of environmental science in accordance with the mission of the school. The environmental movement had been born here, and all the old luminaries who had since become household names—Jane Goodall, Stephen J Gould, Rachel Carson, Ralph Nader—had spoken or taught or guest lectured on campus, all ringing alarm bells about pollution and industry and how fragile the Earth was decades ago. Rachel Carson had appeared to read from her seminal classic "Silent Spring," a book using the metaphor of spring frog sounds to signal the coming catastrophe of the world's natural resources. Clark had sat mesmerized at her observations as well as her courage and determination.

At the time Clark sat and interviewed Jane Goodall in 1991, ten random people on the street had never heard of global warming, fracking, or therapeutic gene modification. The campus at that time resembled an idyllic utopia where young people could rant about how the boomer generation was wasteful and how we needed an "Earth Day" mentality to take root in every politician, consumer brand, Hollywood entertainment, and most brazenly— Wall Street. Clark had gone to college with peers who saw the environmental movement as a religion. They all shared the same dogma that the earth was sacred, and we needed to preserve it, with doctrine to be written once they all graduated and started to work in the world. In the organic protection afforded in the days before the internet, such a sanctimonious mindset created an insulated Garden of Eden where idealism was a social lubricant. Guys like Clark could talk with girls like Amy Biancini for hours, telling each other how wonderful the other one was and how superb each other's solutions were before disappearing into the darkness of a green ballfield to make out, smoke pot, giggle, and then come right back out the next night to do it again. Clark chuckled to himself when he thought about how naive and self-righteous they used to be. They were all going to save the world. It was just a matter of showing up and convincing the establishment how great their ideas were, and those in high places would immediately adopt solutions that saved the planet. The Soviet Union had disappeared, and the Cold War was over. Such optimism…

But here they both sat again—Clark and his college buddy, Amy Biancini, now middle-aged adults with college-age children in the very same multipurpose room where they had seen bands like Pearl Jam and Green Day before they exploded. They sat much like they had in countless classrooms and lecture halls during their time on campus, side by side with a lined yellow legal pad between them where they both scrawled messages to one another. They had figured out this workaround in the days before texting, as it was the only way to communicate in class without making a sound.

"Seems like 1990 all over again." Amy wrote with a smiling face. Clark felt the warmth and comfort one felt when a close friend or ally had their back.

"I miss you!!!" he wrote back.

"I miss you, too! So Melody got in—congrats! She will be going to school with Bobbi!" Amy had a son Melody's age. They lived about 20 minutes from Metuchen, and Amy was a high school biology teacher. The years had been good to her—she had two well-adjusted children, the older of which, Bobbi, would apparently be attending college with Clark's daughter in the fall. She had earned tenure at the high school where she taught and won several state awards for her revolutionary curriculums that thrived in the classroom. At age 40, Amy won the Department of Education National Outstanding Teacher Award. The whole scenario made Clark feel good; it would be an excuse for him and Amy to stay in touch, and he would probably see her at whatever obligatory parent functions.

"Did I read the acceptance letter right? The tuition is really $60k?" wrote Clark on the pad between them and circled it for emphasis, making sure the pen made noise scratching the concentric circles.

"Probably. I don't know since teachers' kids get to go to state universities for free," wrote Amy, then she added a smiley face and circled it. Clark's heart sank. He had been offered a position teaching journalism after the pandemic killed several well-liked professors, but he had declined. Professor's kids got free tuition also. As Clark sat deciding how best not to berate himself, Amy wrote again on the pad:

"Wanna go play Cyclone?" She underlined the request several times. But before she could finish underlining, Clark had already started rising from his seat. He grabbed her wrist gently with his hand fully around the circumference of her watch and elegantly led her down the row of aluminum chairs and out the side door. As the sun caused him to squint, he heard Amy giggle.

"Oh my god, it's good to see you, Clark Westfield!" she exclaimed as they made a straight line across the grass toward the student center. She threw her arms around him in an exaggerated, playful manner. Their bodies had aged, but they still brought out youthful joy and affection in one another. The "Cyclone" she was referring to was a pinball machine in the basement of the student center. During their time at Rutgers, each student center and common building either had a full arcade or a few machines in each corner. The pinball machines had been there longest, and while video games had migrated onto televisions, then computers, then headsets, and finally phones, you couldn't do that with a silver ball, and thus it was pinball that remained. Clark and Amy used to leave class—the big lecture hall ones—and go play pinball for hours while talking about the world and their dreams. Amy usually had a problematic boyfriend and sought Clark's counsel, and Clark usually was writing an article for which he needed her knowledge of natural resources and biological science.

"It's great to see you again also, Amy! At least I don't have to suffer through college parenting all alone! I don't know what I'm going to do about this tuition. though… I mean, I just don't know…."

"Why not get a job here at Rutgers, and then you'll get a waiver for Melody, Clark," Amy suggested. As they entered the ground floor of the student center, he saw the familiar backlight of arcade games against the far wall.

"You aren't going to believe it, Aim… but it's still here!" exclaimed Clark, pointing to the Cyclone pinball machine in the corner. "STEP RIGHT UP! RIDE THE CYCLONE!" blared the machine. Clark and Amy exchanged smiles and found the small stool she used to stand on tucked under the machine as if they had left it there that morning. The green paint had worn away almost completely, leaving only the ridges of splintered wood.

"The stool is still here, Aim!" Clark laughed. "Guess they knew the short ones would be coming back to play Cyclone." Amy teasingly glared at him. The short ones was a collective nickname Clark had given to Amy and her three apartment roommates, who were all under 5'3. Clark's column that ran in the campus newspaper frequently referenced conversations "while playing pinball with the short one" when he was describing Amy. It was a term of endearment that reminded Amy that Clark had earned the closeness of friendship and the option for teaser nicknames.

While the years had been good to Amy emotionally, and spiritually, and physically, they had wreaked the havoc time delivers as they batter women's bodies. After two children and on the advent of menopause, Amy had taken on the weight of a 50-year-old mother of two. Yet while healthy and still very beautiful, Clark found himself staring at her ass as she played pinball, wondering what it would look like underwater next to him.

"Remember when we went skinny dipping in Alaska?" Clark asked in an effort to throw her off her game.

Hitting the flipper expertly and putting the ball in a lock position, without looking up, Amy jabbed, "How does my ass look after all these years?"

She knew him all too well. They had never dated or been romantic or had casually hooked up. They had traveled all over together in the summers between semesters and on field studies and study abroad. She had been a travel buddy, a friend, and a muse for Clark but never a lover. Clark had often wondered what would have happened if they had dated, but always stopped himself so as not to devalue the friendship they had built. He was certain that had they become boyfriend and girlfriend or fooled around, they probably wouldn't be playing the same pinball machine 30 years later as middle-aged parents of college-age children. He preferred to have her here, perched awkwardly on a little green wood step stool with fading paint, a mother, a nationally recognized teacher with an illustrious career but with the wisdom that came from raising children, and her slightly larger but still wonderful ass.

"Your ass looks great dear," Clark said and rested his chin on her shoulder as he pressed up against her. Amy leaned against him as the ball spun past the flippers and into the pit. She turned to face him, still standing on the stool, and leaned against him in a hug.

"Yeah, well, my ass needs you," Amy sighed without looking up. "So much crazy shit is happening, Clark and I'm all ground up—I don't know where to start, and I feel overwhelmed."

"Yeah, it sure has been crazy. You know, I wrote a lengthy magazine piece in 2011 when that big-budget movie Contagion premiered— I wrote that we were well prepared for a pandemic and that the 2003 shutdown of the SARS outbreak proved we wouldn't have an uncontrolled global pathogen….who would have ever thought that people could be so stupid that…"

Amy cut him off. "No, I don't mean the pandemic, Clark, because that fucked everybody up, especially teachers. I have some other shit going on right now, and I need your good advice." Her voice got lower as she spoke. Clark waited for her to continue, making sure she knew she had his undivided attention by not breaking her deep gaze.

"Clark, what I am about to tell you is really secret and could get me fired if it gets out." Amy looked like a child as she avoided direct eye contact. "I had a student with the highest NMSQT scores…" She stopped talking and drew a deep breath and paused as if waiting for Clark to say she was the worst person in the world or some equivalent.

"I'm sorry, you can keep speaking," said Clark with a smirk, not knowing if she was serious or if he was missing something. "Most teachers don't look like they need forgiveness when one of their students excels on standardized tests. By the way, what is the NMSQT again? I'm sure I did great on that one in high school."

"Let me finish. I, as a teacher, am not allowed to discuss an individual student's grades. It's as protected now as health information." Amy shook her head.

"Such bullshit…" muttered Clark.

"So I had this student get the highest score on the National Merit Scholar Qualifying Test (NMSQT), which was actually the highest score in the whole country!"

"I'd love to say congratulations, Amy, but a while back I did a big investigative series on how those standardized tests weren't just racially and class-biased but they also failed to control for the various learning styles and therefore couldn't really be used to rack students accurately, or indicate whether a school was up to standards or not—"

"Clark! I know! Jackass! You interviewed me and quoted me in that story!!!!! And that was the quote I gave that they weren't accurate indicators of intelligence, performance, or school quality!" laughed Amy.

"Oh, I see…let me get this straight…," jabbed Clark. "A couple of years back, I needed to hear your voice and wanted an excuse to call you, so I found a way to work you into one of my stories, in particular, calling out the flaws in standardized testing because your schools were particularly low, and I was showing you how to counter the pressure with a public facing posture…it actually worked…we got back in touch, you raised your profile and won a teaching award, and now you managed to raise one of the smartest students in the country who by SCORING the highest on the very standardized tests you criticized undermines your whole public persona and world view?" Clark paused, waiting for her laughter. Clark started hissing with laughter uncontrollably. But Amy's laughter never came. Amy's face didn't even crack a smile. She was still stone cold serious. "Hey come on, that's a pretty funny trajectory of events, don't you think? Don't worry….no one has to know…"

"No, Clark, it has nothing to do with any of that. I hadn't even thought of it until you pointed it out." She looked at the ground. "It's about the student that got the highest score…"

"What…. he cheated?" Clark was only half joking.

Amy sighed. "He or SHE didn't cheat. I wish. No, it's worse than that…He was having issues before the test and was very upset. Now he has disappeared. I'm worried he may have harmed himself," Amy finished. The slight mist and redness in her eyes as she thought of one of her own students was the magic matriarchal alchemy that so few in the classroom innately possessed innately.

"Right, well, that's certainly a possibility," Clark mused. "After all these years teaching, you must have observed plenty of immensely capable students who are at great risk of all kinds of problems due to their fragile psyche…"

"This boy wasn't fragile," interrupted Amy. "He had a pretty level head on his shoulders. He was practical, capable, even-tempered, and ethical with his peers. He was almost an old, calm, mature soul among thousands of adolescents in the school." Clark suddenly remembered the assignment Elizabeth had given to him about the missing smart kids.

"So let me ask you something about the smart kids," Clark said slowly. Amy turned, giving him her full attention in the hopes that would say something to calm the anxiety she was feeling. "These smart ones….do they know they are smart?"

"How exactly do you mean, Clark?" Amy stepped up on the footstool as Clark moved to let her play the machine.

"Well when you are the highest score on the NMSQT, you must know you stand out and have some uncommon ability…but I mean in the years before a national standardized test declares you the smartest high school senior in the country In the early grades and middle school – other than getting good grades, do the smart ones know?" pressed Clark. "Did you ever wonder whether their self-awareness of extraordinary intelligence was a burden or not?"

Amy chuckled. "Not in this case. That's why I'm so worried. Clark, when a child is born with extraordinary intelligence— the kind this boy had, if they manage to stay in school, they become a very different animal."

"Stay in school? What do you mean to stay in school?" asked Clark. "Isn't staying in school just about the only thing these cognitive Marvel heroes can do?" Amy's expression turned very serious.

"Well, not the really smart ones," she colored. "The really smart ones get filtered out by the 12th grade, which is why it was so rare to see such a high score."

"Filtered out how?" asked Clark bewildered. "By who?"
Amy sighed.

"Well, that's what teachers like me have always fought against—the suburban brain drain that flourishes in this country because it's such bullshit. Do you realize that when a couple has a baby now, they are solicited to through digital and regular mail countless products, apps, programs, courses, etc. that are designed to convince parents they will give their children some sort of edge? A lot of these 'enrichment programs' are actually fronts for the government to run diagnostic tests and identify exceptional intelligence. If someone is truly a genius they get drafted into a government charter school and wind up working for the NSA as they reach adulthood. The government can only let people have hypersensitive security clearance when they know what they have been doing since age 12 or younger. They need to know about their emotional patterns and whether they have a reservoir of resentment against their government. They also need to know how they will behave in a conflict and under duress, various loyalty and endurance evaluations, etc.. Then and only then are they a candidate for certain types of secret work." A silence lingered as she stopped speaking. Clark's laughter percolated the stillness.

"You really think the government is kidnapping your students?" Clark would have been genuinely delighted at this discussion back in 1992. He had spent countless hours brainstorming with Amy about huge global conspiracies involving men in black and foreign nationals. It was fun, and there was a piece of Clark that always felt if he just pushed hard enough as a reporter, someday he would find out how the puzzle pieces all fit… But that was fantasy, and it was one thing to be a 20-year-old college student when the absurdities and impracticality of conspiracy stories can be forgiven. It was another thing entirely to be face to face with a 50-year-old high school biology teacher and mother, who was swearing with conviction that it was all true.

"Clark, I know it…well, maybe not kidnapped," clarified Amy. "When I first started teaching, I was called into a meeting with the principal, some parents of a girl who was about to start in my class, and someone from the Department of Homeland Security. I was told that this girl would be in my class and go through all the normal routines and schedules of a high school sophomore, but the regular grading wouldn't apply to her, and I needed to copy everyone in the room on all assignments, grades, and class participation. I was also told that if there was any adverse situation or behavior by ANYONE around her, I was to report it immediately. The principal told me afterward that the school had gotten a sizable grant for participating in the DHS recruitment program. I did as I was told and turned in several reports to DHS on her progress. She was a delightful student and extraordinarily bright. I used to talk with her just to see if I could stump her on some things, and I never could. Then I got called into the principal's office, and he told me to stop— that somehow DHS found it disruptive. Then, at the end of the year, she came into my classroom, thanked me for being a teacher she liked, and told me she was moving away with her parents— closer to Washington, DC, somewhere in Maryland. And that was that. She moved, and no one in the school or town ever heard from her again. It was awful."

"Awful?" shot Clark incredulously. "What was so awful? A genius girl was born who was really smart, and the government saw some utility in her. I'd rather have my government recruiting homegrown smart kids and working with their school teachers and principals than doing it in secret without accountability or hiding Nazi war criminals inside NASA! We won't mention any names..." Clark paused for comedic effect, then blurted out, "Werner Von Braun! Remember? The head rocket scientist Nazi they caught at the captured facility where they were building V2's but they recruited HIM to NASA and let him build the Apollo rockets, and it was all forgotten and ok? Honestly, Amy, I'd much rather have Men In Black visiting you and engendering your cooperation regarding smart students than underground prisoner exchanges and black budgets. What exactly are you mad at?"

Amy sighed again. "Clark, I'm not mad, and I don't have a problem with her recruitment. – and yes, I agree that recruiting for smart kids is best done in the sunshine, but a school is better with the smart kids in it. A class is better with a smart kid at the front. A graduation is better with an exceptional valedictorian. It just sucks that the absolute smartest kids get drained off through various recruitment attrition, and we rank-and-file teachers get the B team when it comes to brains. And I would be calling the DHS or protesting outside their offices or going to 60 Minutes on the injustice of all this if..."

"Injustice?" Clark interjected again. "Amy, I know it hurts your pride, but if you really want to teach the super smart kids then why not apply at DHS for whatever their academic pathway is? And the government finding and recruiting smart students and creating careers in intelligence or counterintelligence —or even basic research, like climate change or computer coding – that has always gone on and frankly probably had a lot to do with the Cold War ending without any shots fired! As long as they are paying a fair wage, and there is health care and housing thrown in, and there is no coercion - —and it sounds like there wasn't— then there is ample precedent for this type of selection. So, where is the harm?"

"But Clark, that's the problem," Amy suddenly looked concerned as she spoke. She let the pinball rest against the launch plunger in the starter slot and turned, meeting Clark's gaze.

"There WAS no monitoring with THIS kid. There was no DHS staff that met with me or anyone at school. In fact, no one had any idea this kid was smart at all. He did nothing exceptional in his early grades. He didn't speak in class. His grades were always good, but so what? We all just thought he was academic scholarship material and would probably wind up in an Ivy League school on a free ride."

"So does the government need to check with you personally every time they find a kid they want to recruit into a top-secret computer coding job that hacks into Russian missile silos?" Clark's sarcasm was inflected by an underlying contempt for teachers that he hoped Amy knew wasn't directed at her.

"That's the whole point, Clark…I don't think it was the government" The pinball machine blared the gaming jingles, simulating the carnival barkers. "I may have all kinds of opinions about pulling smart kids out of school districts, but at least federal officials were courteous and predictable. Plus, they had a long-range plan of observation and interaction with teachers and administrators. This was very different. One day, this boy approached me, asking to talk after class. He told me that his parents insisted he take the NMSQT test and that he never expected to do well, let alone get the highest score in the country. He hated the attention it brought and that no one would leave him alone. He said he had been approached by some people, one of which was a beautiful woman who had subscribed to and loved his Spotify playlist. He thought this was strange because he purposely chose hard-to-find bizarre music. Anyway, they told him that they could give him consulting work, but it had to be okay with his parents. They kept finding him at school and asking if they could meet with him and his parents. One day, they offered him a ride home and waited in his driveway for an hour, but his parents weren't home."

"So you had a smart kid who was under-the-radar Einstein, was a bit self-conscious, and everyone was late to this party, so they put a pretty girl in front of him and thought some cash would work. You know normally that does work, especially on a teen computer geek. Why didn't it work on him?" Clark felt slightly impatient as he suspected his old friend's idealism was inflamed.

"I don't teach computer science, Clark," said Amy, now visibly cross. "They didn't want him to write code. He told me they wanted his insight and methodology on genetics. I had him as one of my researchers for the independent study grant on genetics in floral colors. He was the best on the team."

"I'm sorry… but you had a quiet loner who was enthusiastic about your flowers, got offered a job, and took it, and now you are upset you lost a team member."

"Flowers! Really Clark Westfield? Flowers? You know back when we were here in this very building as students you gave me the same reductionist sarcasm when we started our genetics course, and you said Mendelev should have just cooked his peas and who would care whether they were green or yellow? And I told you that genetic natural selection was the key to the evolution of all life on earth, and whoever determined the biological mechanism that selected genes would control the trajectory of the human race. Do you remember any of that?" Clark did recall some of his satirical comments about the famed genetics researcher Albert Mendelev, Amy's outsized enthusiasm for genetics exercises and Punit's squares. "Well, Clark, I think this boy had actually done it! He was hyper-precise in his equations, and his resulting plants proved all his theorems. At first, I thought it was a fluke, but then I started paying attention to his assignments, and sure enough, he was onto something. You should have seen the look I gave him the first time I realized he was accurate— talk about being emotional. I think there were spit droplets flying from my orgasmic gasps of discovery. After he showed me, I asked him if he would appear before the review board to explain his findings because he deserved the credit. Suddenly, this quiet, reserved Japanese boy got very excited and was appreciative that I had asked. I had never heard this kid make a sound, and then once I checked his work and asked him to present, he was suddenly like a talk show host."

"OK, so the kid was good at his flower science, and you asked him to present, and that turned him on. Did you say he was Japanese?" asked Clark, switching to fact-finding mode.

"Yes, he was Japanese. Two days later, it was announced that he had the highest score in the country on the NMSQT. I texted to congratulate him and got no response. When I went to find him in person that day, he wasn't in school, and I haven't seen him since. Now everyone is looking for him, and all are worried. Especially me. Something doesn't add up." Her expression was troubled.

"When did all this happen?" asked Clark. He instinctively felt like he should be taking notes.

"About two and a half, maybe three weeks ago?" Amy replied with a quizzical expression.

"What was his name?" shot Clark in rapid-fire interrogation.

"Clark, you know I can't talk about and name individual students."

"Amy, please. It's me. There is a lot worse stuff I know about you."

"Right," said Amy, looking down at the ground. "Okay. Oh, I think your paper reported on his disappearance. So I guess it's not a big deal."

"Disappearance? This boy disappeared? What was his name?" The volume of Clark's voice was rising.

"His name…?" Amy had a perplexed and vulnerable expression as she met Clark's intense stare. "His name was Alvin Matsumoto…"

As Clark exited the Rutgers Cook College campus onto Rt. 1 South in the middle of New Jersey, he tried to bask in the warm feeling of just having reconnected with an old friend— well, a "friend" in a very narrow category— who had been there for many of life's thresholds and still cared for him. His mind kept wandering as to what may have played out if he and Amy had ever dated or even gotten married. But Clark kept shutting down any sense of what might have been by repeating to himself that if they had hooked up, they never would still be friends 30 years later. But now, as a widowed man, well-weathered by life, he was fighting a more unsettling feeling of unease that no matter how much he tried to stamp down the buzz he got from spending time with Amy, he knew he would never outrun it entirely. With robot-like precision, Clark moved over to the corner of the right lane, where a small green and white sign with the NJ Turnpike logo floated above a smaller panel with arrows. Below the arrow was another panel that was slightly larger with an off-white reflective color and black lettering. The sign read New York and North, with an arrow pointing left, and with an arrow pointing right it said Trenton, Philadelphia, Baltimore, Washington DC. Clark turned right and onto the NJ Turnpike going south. Without traffic, he could be in Washington before dark. He knew exactly who to speak to about all this…

Chapter 3

There is a moment when you shut off the car engine and sit in the silence after the radio power shuts off. Before the car door opens and the bitter cold or blazing heat or driving rain present as the final insult before walking into your workplace. But every day, a majority of people hate their jobs and don't want to walk into work, and those last few seconds of car silence become moments of great reflection. In those quiet moments, usually accompanied by a sigh or a gasp, or even a prayer, people make monumental life decisions. That silence whispers rhetorical questions with no answers like "How long until I don't have to walk into this shitty job where I am wasting my talent?" and other profound challenges like "Should I stay married to this person?" or the overarching battle for a man's very soul phrased in the question "Can I live with not getting what I want out of life? Can I live with not accomplishing what I always saw myself achieving? Am I ok if this is as good as it gets?"

Lately, that silence and those questions had been more malignant with each passing second Clark remained in his car. For once one notices his quiet tormentor, it's like he is always there. Once he acknowledged this stealth, creeping malevolent solitude and the questions it brought—swirling like bats at twilight— the abyss was always right there and he was left staring into it. Clark had been peering into the edge of that abyss for some time, and when the ignition key turned in reverse and vibrations of the combustion engine abruptly subsided, the seconds grew longer, the abyss grew darker and deeper, and the exciting, fulfilling life of accolades and achievements looked farther and farther away. Now in middle age, the confidence and steady footing that made Clark such an effective reporter and a solid husband and father looked small and distant, stretched like taffy in a funhouse mirror. Clark had become a man without a mission, and some days a man without a country, and it was undeniable when confronted with solitude.

Which was why, on this day, as Clark shut off his car in the lot outside the newspaper office, he noticed that there was no abyss to be found. Mountain climbers, 100-foot wave surfers, and bungee jumper types, all deliberately put themselves at risk because of that irreplaceable thrill. It is both a physical and emotional adrenaline that comes from achieving something that includes calculated but potentially deadly risks. And as the rest of the world looks on with a baffled expression asking why someone would put themselves through such a risky and unpleasant endurance the answer was always the same: because it wasn't an option not to. That was how Clark used to feel about reporting. Journalism was an unforgiving vocation. It was tedious, humiliating, and often dangerous work. Every career reaches a plateau of familiarity and disappointment and if ignored and overlaid with responsibilities like mortgages and children, it can form a hurricane of burnout and resentment.

In Clark's case, it was simple sadness that the field of journalism and all of its nobility and honor no longer seemed important even to reporters themselves. Clark had not wanted to acknowledge the deep chagrin and discouragement he had been carrying around because that would mean that the job and profession he treated like a vocation and had won two Pulitzer awards as global recognition of his excellence, had led him to a diminished media environment where ethics seldom abound and great reporting was no longer measured because it was too hard to defend against individual people's social media. The success that Clark had achieved beyond even his wildest dreams had amounted to this—sitting in his car in the parking lot of a newspaper he had worked at since he was 21, afraid to go into work.

But today, instead of the blaring neon sign that constantly flashed messages that his best years were behind him, there was a long-missed element of genuine intrigue only a mystery story could generate. That safe anxiety of being uncertain of the facts under the surface, that obsession to know who was telling you the truth and who wasn't, and that lifelong noble pursuit to out both the criminals and heroes among us. That was what made investigative reporting so exhilarating as a job. And today, that was what had appeared as if by magic and had made the terrible depressive feelings go away. It was like a fever had broken.

***

"Hey Liz!" exclaimed Clark as he appeared in new managing editor Elizabeth Cranford's doorway. A molded cardboard tray with four depressions for drink containers held three tall Starbucks coffee cups adorned with plastic lids and stirring tabs poking out of the drinking holes. "Iced chai mocha latte with cinnamon and hazelnut flavoring right?" asked Clark mischievously.

"No," she said in a low, completely expressionless voice without looking up from her computer. "I take it—"

"Just straight black? Dark Roast if they have it?" Clark moved closer to her desk and extended his arm, holding one of the cups for her to retrieve. "Do you really think I don't know how you take your coffee? After all this time… such little faith…"

"If I recall it was usually ME getting YOU coffee so no I don't expect you to remember." The twang of resentment in her tone rang like a bell. Clark could sense something was bothering her, and he suspected it had to do with him. For weeks, he had been waiting for her to give him the "I know we are friends, but you gotta step it up" speech oozing with so much awkwardness and discomfort it could make you float out of your body and the room. As Clark mentally prepared himself for that moment and thought about how he would explain himself, it occurred to him that he was expecting it because deep down he knew it to be true. He had been checked out mentally, under a wet blanket of depression, outrunning the claustrophobic anxiety of middle age. He had gone from being spiritually committed to his chosen profession of journalism and loving the work so much that 80-hour weeks felt like adventures to having to sitting silently in the parking lot convincing himself to actually enter the building. And each day, those minutes increased..

Clark put a tall cup of Starbucks on the desk next to Elizabeth's right hand. He sat down across the desk from her, waiting to make eye contact.

"I need to speak with Professor Westfield," she sighed. Elizabeth had always told Clark that she had learned more from him as an intern than from any of her classroom professors. Clark would give her advice, answers, and insight from situations he had handled on the job, and the real-world outlook had saved Elizabeth much of the learning curve so ubiquitous in college graduate entry-level reporters. After she graduated and began work under Clark, she would often say things like "Thanks, Professor Westfield." in a whiny, humorous adolescent way whenever he over-explained something simple she could have looked up on Wikipedia. But over the years, "Professor Westfield" had been a vital resource as her career got bigger and the stories more complicated. He could count on one hand the number of times Elizabeth had actually ASKED for advice from the metaphorical Professor Westfield. Combined with her emotionless expression and intense concentration, Clark sensed it was something serious.

"Professor Westfield has office hours right..." Clark paused for dramatic effect. "Now!" There was still no expression from Elizabeth who sat trance-like in front of her computer. He allowed the silence to perpetuate for several seconds before Elizabeth finally broke it.

"Professor..." Her tone was slow and careful. "Remember the other day when I gave you that assignment about consumer genetic testing and the whole speech about what we can call the smart market?"

"Liz that was yesterday. You didn't give me a deadline, and I had to go to Melody's college orientation..."

"Relax, I am not expediting you, Clark." Elizabeth turned and looked at him. His schoolboy nervousness from being accountable to her was endearing. "I genuinely need your professorial guidance because I am having one of those moments you warned me about—the moment when you swore I would be sorry I tried to ever become an editor..." Liz turned back to her computer. Clark sat in silence watching her. Her anxiety as editor and need for his advice was endearing.

"Remember when you lectured our class? - the first lecture you gave my class when I was a sophomore?"

"Geez, Liz, that was like 1994!" Clark laughed.

"Yup! Exactly it was 1994. But do you remember what you did?" Elizabeth had no need to make eye contact as Clark knew exactly what she was referring to.

"Yeah, I gave you a hard time." sighed Clark.

"Hard time?!? Hard Time??" Elizabeth's voice was shrill. "You had me read each headline and then kept asking me, 'Where did this story come from?' 'Now where did this story come from, now this one, and what about that one??'" Elizabeth mimicked Clark's voice as if he were a chimpanzee with Down Syndrome. "And you were pointing out that each article had to come from somewhere, and some party originated the news, usually the one that benefited most from the story."

"Correct. And I asked it every time you turned in a story for the next 20 years Liz. I'm sorry I hurt your inner child but I turned you into a soldier. You sit at that very editor's desk right now because I showed you just how tough it could—"

"Clark you truly are a jackass....professor or boss or checked out old timer - if being a jackass had a trifecta, you'd win all three. I was going to THANK you for the jolt you gave me back in college and do an even deeper dive into how you restored my faith in old white guys, but you just blew that up." Elizabeth donned a cartoonish expression with her head tilted to one side as a schoolgirl would in an argument. Clark smiled and said nothing.

"Listen, we gotta be serious for a minute. Clark, I need you to talk me off the ledge." He nodded as she continued to speak. "You know that story I asked you to write about the parenting section of the consumer genetics economy? That was my way of being a wimp but really asking you to investigate a company called Crisprgen. They are a consumer genetic testing company, and I knew you would come across them eventually and was hoping you would do one of your colonoscopic investigations." She paused.

"Why didn't you just assign me a profile on Crisprgen? I would have dusted off my copy of Fletch and gotten to work." Clark was perplexed as to why Elizabeth was stammering.

"Well, I wanted to make sure that you would eventually run across their CEO and founder, a woman named Sarah Reistad. So, I called out to Crisprgen corporate headquarters and wanted to speak to their Communications VP. I was so intent on making sure you went out and profiled them that I wanted to make it as easy as possible for you." She looked at the floor, avoiding eye contact with Clark.

"OK, Liz, we are going to need to have a serious talk about why you think you needed to tiptoe around ANY of that. It's ME you are talking to! But that isn't the problem is it?" Clark could see there was more to the story. "What is it that has you so upset?"

"Well, I just got a call from our corporate headquarters in Nashville…," Elizabeth paused. If the call had come from Nashville then it was from the offices of the holding company Abscon—a huge international conglomerate that had huge multinational corporations on various stock exchanges. One of those companies owned the company that had bought the paper recently. The call wasn't from just four levels up, it was four COMPANIES up!

Clark smiled. "See! This is what I meant that day, Liz, and every day since. I don't even need to know what happened on the call to know what kind of situation you find yourself in." Clark was trying to be supportive and non-judgmental. "So what happened on the call?"

"Well, the actual Abscon CEO, Stu Zimmerman himself, told me that he had just hung up with an investor who had purchased some serious equity in Abscon, and she had mentioned our paper might be profiling her company. I was stunned! It was Sarah Reistad! She was the big investor!"

"Damn, if she is buying shares of Abscon to be in the point one of one percent of rich folk! That's hundreds of millions of dollars at a MINIMUM!"

"Clark, don't you see how fucked up this is?" Elizabeth asked incredulously.

"Yeah…yes of course. That's obvious, but who is this person with this kind of financial leverage? That's a lot of sway to come out of nowhere. Is this Crisprgen profitable?"

"Well, you can ask her yourself. We are going to see her in the morning." Elizabeth had a pained expression on her face, and Clark saw an opportunity to stealthily give her a boost.

"So, uh, Liz… Remember when you asked me to look into that missing high school kid from Maplewood?" Elizabeth turned to face him bearing an expression of disbelief. "Well, I happened to fall onto a connection the other day and it led me to Washington."

"Washington? You went to Washington on the Matsumoto kid story? Calaarrkkk…..!" Her voice was rising with boss rage.

"I went to see Kelly…" he said. Elizabeth immediately changed her expression. The Kelly that Clark was referring to was Lieutenant Colonel Kelly Pram, and she had spent decades in Air Force Intelligence and inter-agency cooperative programs. She had been a source to Clark and the paper for years; she had teamed up with Elizabeth and Clark when they discovered one of the Cold War Continuity of Government bunkers. If Clark had gone to see her then he must have had something important.

"How is she? Did she speak to you without Richie, or did he go with you?" Elizabeth raised her eyebrows sarcastically. Richie Byrne was a fellow reporter colleague who had introduced them to Lt. Pram. They'd had a long and complicated train wreck of an affair for years. It was the kind of saga where you watched a hyper-intelligent and greatly accomplished person who thrived in rigid structure, and positions of sensitive trust, like a Lt. Colonel in the Navy, completely abandon any common sense or rationale that they must possess in abundance to hold the positions they did. Richie Byrne was a Navy veteran and excellent reporter who had become adrift in a long and loveless marriage, and as his lechery ebbed and flowed, so did the state secrets he was able to coax out of Lt. Col. Kelly Pram.

"Believe it or not, she did," answered Clark. "She only mentioned his name once at the beginning when she told me not to mention him, so I didn't." Clark shook his head.

"So then, what did you guys talk about?" Elizabeth was perplexed as to why Clark would drive all the way to Washington DC to meet with a complicated informant.

"Well, I needed her to give me a tutorial on how the intelligence community finds and recruits candidates," explained Clark.

"Why is that of interest to you?" Elizabeth was trying to sound like an editor who was auditing a staff reporter's work but in reality, Clark was 10 steps ahead of her, and what would have been a supervision meeting was actually a reverse pop quiz.

"I'd love to tell you I discovered something after lengthy and grueling research, but the truth is, I bumped into an old friend who is a teacher over in Maplewood, and she actually had the Matsumoto kid as a student."

"Wow! Clark, that's great! Let's get the teacher on the record and we can do a profile piece on the missing boy…"

"I think we'll want to wait on that Liz. I haven't connected the cases yet but I have a feeling the kids we are so concerned about who disappeared that and the smart ones might be connected. I went to talk to Kelly expecting her to explain the government's recruiting process and that the pattern would overlay perfectly with the missing students, case solved." Clark paused and looked out the window.

"Good thinking, and do the pieces fit?" asked Elizabeth with a broad smile. She felt like Clark had just run a layup around her.

"Well, she explained not just the modern recruitment process but the methods that were used over the decades and it's pretty much what you would expect—screening of elementary school standardized testing, methodical collection of IQ scores, a national database of high school grades and formal organizations like National Merit Scholars and Mensa - but when I read her into the Matsumoto and Mackoul cases, she ran the names for us."

"She ran the names for you? In what? The Air Force supercomputer that has all the files of recruited spies? Clark, either she is lying to you or there really is something that valuable, and I don't want to know what you did to get her to do it…" Elizabeth made a disgusted face. "So, what branch of the military or government were they recruited into?"

"That's the thing…" Clark paused there, showing some element of being intrigued that Elizabeth hadn't seen in a while. "The government didn't recruit these kids. She checked with the recruitment teams at the CIA, The FBI, The NSA, Signal Corps, Joint Terror Task Force, and the Pentagon umbrella group, there was nothing on these two. But what is more alarming is that she was convinced it had to be the work of a competitor."

"A competitor? Like a competitive government? China? Russia? Iran? I bet the Saudis are deep into this shit."

"No, actually, a private sector actor. I guess companies like Microsoft and Apple took the Cold War playbook of identifying America's youth brain trust — the smart ones - and started funneling them to work in development along with companies like At&t, Lockheed, McDonnell Douglas, and Raytheon. Now…making sure those defense contractors and critical infrastructure companies had the best and brightest is in the interest of national security. But more importantly, plenty of smart adolescent recruits would be ineligible for a position in government, perhaps due to something like a criminal record or limiting disability, and they would be sucked up by the private sector." Elizabeth looked at Clark baffled.

"Can you repeat that and pretend ...just for a moment ...that I don't know anything about military intelligence recruiting and explain it to me?" she asked. Clark smiled to himself. When he spoke too fast or too technical, it usually meant he was deeply captivated by a topic, and he hadn't felt that way in a while.

"Basically, if you have poor eyesight, you can't serve in the Air Force, even if it's just a desk job in intelligence gathering. So, they refer you to the private sector and then they can keep an eye on you at one of these defense contractor companies. Modern technology companies have built their own ID and recruiting systems, and they compete for talent with the government. If one of the smart ones goes directly into the private sector, then Washington loses them and has to set up a surveillance plan."

"Surveillance plan? What are you surveilling? What do they care what these nerds do? Do they want to recruit them in the future?" asked Elizabeth.

"The way Kelly said it was that 'The smart ones are very dangerous.'"

"Dangerous? These missing students don't seem too dangerous. Fashion-challenged, conceited, and boorish maybe...but not dangerous? These kids never stole a pack of gum!" Elizabeth tilted her head to one side.

"Not dangerous in the traditional sense, but think of it like a loaded gun—it's only dangerous if it's in the wrong hands. Lt. Pram told me that if a smart one works in government intelligence and then leaves, the Pentagon keeps tracking them and if they wind up working for or getting too close to an adversary, they intervene. Again, we are talking about the less than one percent of humans who have an IQ four or five times the IQ of the average person. She also told me that when she ran the names "Matsumoto and Mackoul' that they definitely had not been recruited, but there had been preliminary briefings and each had a dossier file in case anyone wanted to bring them in down the road."

"OK, so it was the government that recruited them?" pressed Elizabeth. "We could do a story on how recruitment is happening in our schools and no one knows—"

"Liz!" interjected Clark abruptly. "You are missing what I am telling you: The government had identified these two kids for possible recruitment and someone got to them first and that means that some company plans on weaponizing these two geniuses and no one knows who or what for." An uncomfortable silence followed, and Clark and Elizabeth exchanged knowing glances.

"And I'm thinking Lt. Pram told you that the most likely culprit was what type of business? My guess would be weapons or semiconductors," Elizabeth mused.

"She did. There is a new field that is doing more recruiting than all others combined." Clark let a few seconds pass for a dramatic effect to swell in the room between them.

"Apparently, gene therapy. It holds so much possibility for healthcare applications that it's a gold rush at the base of the microscope lens. But if you add ancestry databases, direct to consumer wellness prevention diagnostics, and prenatal testing and counseling, you have a massive need for smart workers."

"OK, well, that's a start. Maybe we should do an expository article on gene therapy and explain how it works, etc." Elizabeth said.

"Actually, Liz, the story isn't about gene therapy. It's about how the government had viable methods for finding and recruiting smart citizens for sensitive and critical jobs and now the private sector has better search methods and is therefore getting the smartest ones first," Clark said.

"What could possibly be better than school records and standardized tests to determine how smart a person is? These are tools specifically designed to measure intelligence across huge swaths of the population." Clark looked at her as if she should know the answer then spoke in an even tone:

"Population scale consumer genetic testing…"

***

Clark felt creepy watching the high school students cross the crosswalk onto the high school campus. He had parked on the street outside the drop-off zone. When he waited for his daughter to get out of high school, he had no problem feeling at ease as the aggrieved parent saddled with the tedious trials of fathering a teenager. But today was different because this wasn't Melody's school. It was Amy Biancini's. Clark couldn't help but feel conspicuous and somewhat creepy as he waited for Amy to arrive and go into the school. As Clark had gotten ready that morning to drive to the Crisprgen headquarters and start investigating the story Elizabeth had assigned him, he realized he needed to do his homework and cultivate a good understanding of the field of consumer genetics. So here he was outside Maplewood High School waiting for the summer school AP biology teacher to appear so he could convince her to cut class once again…

A gentle knock on his car window startled Clark. He looked up into the glaring sunlight to see an elderly crossing guard smiling and motioning for him to roll down the window.

"Good morning! It's always the dads who have to pinch hit that never know where to park," boomed the crossing guard before breaking into a wheezy laugh. "Sir, you can't idle here on this street. The people whose houses we are in front of went and got all kinds of parking permits and zoning laws passed because of the high school drop-offs. -You need to park…" he motioned with his gloved hand to the far side of the school. His nose had red and purple squiggly capillaries snarled at the end from years of drinking and standing outside in nor'easters.

"Oh, I'm sorry. I wasn't dropping anyone off," Clark said. He then realized that now he definitely seemed creepy. "I'm actually waiting for a teacher—Ms Biancini."

"Oh everyone's favorite! You know she is our star, and she won the national teacher's award for science or something," raved the crossing guard.

"Yes, I know…do you know where she is?" Clark asked knowing there wasn't a chance he was going to get any useful answers out of this walking barstool in a vest.

"Oh sure, just go inside and have her paged at the office. She will come right down from her classroom. You can't leave your car here though." Clark smiled and gave him a half-wave salute before driving into the driveway right up the front entrance of the high school, where throngs of students and faculty were filing in. A dozen students had formed a circle and were looking at something in the center. They were smiling and laughing, and in the center was Amy. She was short, and it was hard to see her over everyone's head, but there she was in the middle of the group of 10th graders. Her hand was outstretched with the palm facing up. Everyone was staring at the tiny little frog that was resting in the middle of her hand.

"Genus and species…?" Amy called out, and as if on cue, a voice from the back replied:

"Pseudacris Crucifer!"

"Very good! And what is the vernacular name?" Amy called out again, smiling as she threw questions at the students who looked engaged and shockingly interested.

"Spring Peeper!" called out another voice. Amy held her head like she was waiting for more answers.

"Spring Peepers earned their name because their sounds are some of the first frog sounds in March." said a timid student in a low voice. Amy shushed the rest of the students to let the withdrawn girl keep speaking. "And the Spring Peepers were the main characters in Rachel Carson's book Silent Spring. They are the soundtrack to our environment and their silence is the warning bell." The shy girl looked down, dejected. Amy put her arm around her and then spoke to the group.

"Very good Lindsay! Gang, let's give Lindsay a solstice affirmation!" exclaimed Amy. At that point each of the twelve students raised their arms and wiggled their hands loosely while making puttering sounds with their lips. The shy girl smiled as Amy reinforced the hug. Then, all 12 students stepped into the center for a group hug around the shy girl. Amy always formed student teams in "solstice groups" of 12 to emphasize the importance of ancient people and nature's interaction with the calendar. Her students had affectionately renamed these study pods "Stongehenges" and the humor was an opportunity to dive even deeper into its significance. Every motion and detail was taken into consideration when she was teaching. Everything was a conversation starter, a question, a fact, and it was ALL fascinating and fun. She knew how to reach the shy and dejected kids, who in their adolescence, assumed the world hated them until teachers like her told them otherwise. What a scene! Clark rolled down the car window and called to Amy:

"Hey, Ms. Biancini - you have a visitor!" he called, smiling. Amy saw him and smiled broadly but afterward made a confused face, wondering why Clark was at her school.

"Hey guys, ever meet a Pulitzer Prize winner?" Amy asked, smiling as she made her way through the students and over to his car. A half dozen or so students followed behind her. She leaned on the car door and smiled at him.

"I need to talk to you…" said Clark softly.

"Well, I'm kinda in the middle of teaching a class…" Amy shrugged as she spoke, still smiling. She leaned in closer to the driver's side window.

"Seriously, Clark, what are you doing here?" asked Amy quietly while holding her smile and joyous expression.

"Hey everyone!" Clark called out to the waiting class of 12 Stonehenges. "Your biology teacher needs to be treated to a cup of coffee and donuts!" To which the dozen 10th graders applauded. One sarcastically opened the back door of Clark's car and beckoned Amy to sit down as if she were getting in a taxi. In an effort to play along with the tease, Amy sat down in the back seat, not expecting that same student to close the door while smiling at her. After which, Clark simply started driving away.

"Oh my god, you really are taking me for coffee?" giggled Amy. As Clark made a left out of the school driveway, Amy climbed over the back seat into the passenger seat, messing up her hair and causing her to blow it away from her face. "You are a man of surprises, Mr. Westfield."

"Amy, I need you to call the school and tell them you are taking a sick day," Clark said in a very serious and direct tone.

"Sure. Right. But we have to be back by 8:30 so if there is a line at the Dunkin Donuts…"

"No, I'm serious. I need you today," Clark persisted. "I have to go to Crisprgen and do some interviews. It's going to be on genetics and all that stuff you were really good at and I wasn't. So I need you to call in sick, and I'll—"

"You're serious? Clark Westfield, you just show up at my school while I am in the middle of a field practicum and want me to just cut a day of work? We are grown-ups now, Clark. This isn't pre-calc in 1991…" Silence followed, and Clark wondered if he had done the right thing or was perhaps a bit too overzealous and presumptuous showing up at Amy's school. "And…I love it!" exclaimed Amy and tilted her head back. "You are right. Fuck it! Fuck all of it! she said carefreely. "What do you need, Mr. Westfield" Amy asked coyly, pretending to be a seductive intern.

"I'm serious - Aim- you gotta call the office and say you had an emergency and they need to send a substitute. I'm onto something, and I need your science brains and ability to explain things because I have to go look intelligent in front of these Crisprgen executives. Since you are the only person who knows as much about genetics as they do, I need you to explain things to me."

"Well, today is a study hall day at school anyway, and that's why I held the field practicum outside before school officially started. Today is one of the days the school makes 900 high school students sit and stare at a wall all day and pretend everyone is enjoying the summer program. We are essentially babysitters and it's infuriating. So wherever you're going, Westfield, I'm going." Amy let the passenger's seat fall back, and she put her feet up on the dashboard. "So, where are we going?" She giggled once again.

Clark had never seen a person with such a predisposition for happiness. Amy's starting point for every situation she encountered in life was to assume it was going to be fun. Clark awoke every day and fought the feeling that he was simply managing perpetual decay and irrelevance and that the "fun" part of his life and demeanor only flourished during moments like cutting class and playing pinball with Amy— and those times were long gone.

"You know, Amy, you may be the most fun person I have ever met. Nothing ever really gets to you, and you can decide in a flash to make the most out of a bad situation. I've always told you that I find your innate happiness confounding," Clark said, trying to convey true admiration. "It's almost like if happiness were genetic, you got a few extra happiness genes." Clark shook his head in mock disbelief.

"I think happiness is genetic; I think most elements of personality are genetic, and I think you are right I got the happy gene twice!"

"OK, biology teacher, this is a perfect segway…this company Crisprgen does two main things as their services as far as I understand it. They do the mail in spit screenings and then give you a report card of what diseases you might get then they start upselling you with add-ons, etc. The other thing they do is gene therapy— - that's one of those things that I think I know what it is but couldn't write out if I had to."

"OK, where do you want me to start? And I take a little milk in my coffee." They pulled into the drive-thru lane of a Dunkin Donuts, and Clark ordered two coffees and apple fritters.

"Pretend I don't know anything," Clark said with a big smile. "Start with something basic like - what is the genome, you know…?"

"You really didn't listen at all in college did you?" she chuckled out loud. "OK, do you remember studying anything about the human genome in college?"

Clark stammered. "Ummm…sure. That was—" Amy interrupted him by making a faux basketball buzzer sound.

"BBRaaannnnppp!!!" Amy still managed to smile as her lips made fart noises mimicking a bell. "You didn't study the human genome with me in college because it hadn't been decoded in 1990! So, Clark, if you are going to be in my class, you can't bullshit this teacher okay?" If it had been any other person on the planet, this type of directive would have been the source of immense frustration, and Clark would have found them unbearably obnoxious, but not Amy. "OK, so the human genome is the genetic code that is contained in our DNA strands that are found in every cell. Think of DNA like a software or the app store for your cells with all the information needed to do absolutely everything your body must do."

"Right, so the genome is like the operating system for all the hardware in your body? Got it! But does every cell contain the whole genome? Seems like overkill."

"Yes, with a few exceptions, every cell nucleus of all types has a complete set of DNA."

"DNA?" Clark felt comfortable enough with Amy to not have to pretend he remembered certain anagrams learned in a collegiate haze of alcohol and ramen noodles.

"Deoxyribonucleic Acid…and since someone needs a refresher, DNA is a protein structure that looks like a spiral staircase, and four tags create all the combinations necessary for epigenetic function. Humans invented the binary differential between zero and one as the basis for all computer code. That was done using only two tags, while DNA uses four tags to create the genetic coding for all life forms. Maybe someday we will grow as a species to need four tags. Geez that would be wild!"

"OK Yes, I'm starting to recall all this. But why have full strands of DNA everywhere? I'm not an evolutionary biologist like you so that seems awfully space-consuming in the nucleus of a cell, and what does the word 'epigenetic' mean?" Amy smiled as Clark gave his remedial answers and asked childlike questions.

"Epigenetics simply means how a gene functions. Think of the genes like circuit breakers in your basement. If you turn one-off, a lamp in the room where that electricity is routed will turn off. Scientists have been figuring out ways to turn genes on and off, and learning how they express themselves, for centuries. Sometimes medication can do it, or diet and exercise. The most common example is in a family with a history of cancer, each member is mathematically at equal risk. But some members will get cancers and others won't, usually due to a life of prevention and early testing from which the epigenetics of the cancer are curtailed. These new consumer genetics testing companies use what has been deciphered from the genome to determine which genes you have that put you at risk for various inheritable diseases."

"Then what?" asked Clark.

"Well, then a person can use epigenetics to pre-confront health problems that can be avoided with various lifestyle modifications, such as a heart-healthy diet in families with congenital heart issues. Of course, leave it to humans to always try to find an easy workaround. Most people think they can sprinkle a little Lipitor on their Kielbasa and get away with it. One could live a general life of prevention and eat the right things but the market would never allow that kind of accountability…" Amy's voice trailed off with the tone of despair she had for the human race that had been so familiar to Clark since college.

"So that's gene editing?" Clark casually tried to clarify.

"No. Not even close." Amy chuckled. "Gene editing is exactly that. It's the rewriting of the code— the actual software of the gene to make it a different gene."

"But if we can control what genes do, then why go through the trouble of editing?" asked Clark, bordering on general confusion.

"Well, we can't control the epigenetics of every disease so we need more methods. Gene editing is actually replacing or re-writing the actual DNA code permanently." Amy stopped talking for a moment and stared out the car window. "Nah, gene EDITING is a totally different ball game, and one we have to consider through an ethical lens."

"How is it different? And why the difference in ethical emphasis?" asked Clark. He could tell Amy's demeanor had switched.

"Well, when you edit a gene, you add or subtract actual information from the DNA sequence," she said, matter-of-factly.

"And that is bad…why?" Clark was starting to feel like a talk show host without a teleprompter.

"It's not that it's bad, it's just permanent. So when the cell divides to create two new cells, which all cells do, the DNA strand that is homesteading in the new cell becomes an exact copy of the half left behind in the other cell. So any changes that happen to it before the next time it divides winds up altering all the genome in all the cells that come after that first alteration. That life form's genetic code is then permanently changed, which sounds great if you are trying to eliminate a type of cancer, but not so great if you're arbitrarily altering genes for traits that are simply undesirable. That's where gene therapy becomes more like eugenics, and there are no internationally recognized ethics for what gene therapies someone wishes to perform on themselves or their children."

"How does the gene editing process work?" Clark asked while nodding and feeling slightly more clarity. Amy smiled at the complexity booby-trapped in such a simple question. Her teacher gene always overrode all other emotions when she was asked to explain a scientific concept.

"Well, there are a few ways. Well, the DNA binding proteins that have been predominantly used for gene editing are Zinc finger proteins, Transcription Activator-Like Effectors (TALEs), and the one that will be the main tool for the medicine of the future —nuclease deficient Cas9 fusions or CRISPRs."

"Ummm…." Clark stammered.

"What do all three mean? Funny you should ask…" Amy was now speaking as if she were in front of the classroom and clearly wanted to continue without interruption. "A zinc finger is simply a small piece of a protein that has a unique fingerprint-like structure made of zinc ions that allows for precise targeting to specific genes. TALES are similar and cause the transcription of different sections of the genomic code, just without the zinc. But CRISPR… that's the cool one. It's the Thomas Edison of genomic engineering…."

"What does that anagram CRISPR stand for?" asked Clark. "Elizabeth had mentioned that Crisprgen had a team of 'expert CRISPR engineers."

"It stands for Clustered Regularly Interspaced Short Palindromic Repeats and is usually written as CRISPR with CaS-9 added. So essentially it's a small section—a chapter if you want to visualize it—and that chapter of code replaces an existing chapter of the genetic code, like swapping out pages in a book. The CaS-9 is an enzyme that helps find the right spot to replace the strand. Remember when you and I used to play palindromes in trigonometry? Gosh we never did anything in that class come to think of it…"

"Palindromes are words that are spelled the same forward or backward right? Words like civic, level, kayak, or racecar? Why would you do that with DNA?" Clark asked.

"Well, by repeating the code sequence, each CRISPR can be dropped into

the target spot. Only some will work, but it won't matter if the snippet is turned the wrong way, increasing the odds of a successful edit. More importantly, once I find a palindromic repeat that I know does something specific, I can put it in as many people as I want." Amy made motions with her hands that indicated she was cutting imaginary paper with scissors and dropping the cut somewhere.

"So, if I discover a DNA palindrome section that kills the cancer genes, then I've found the cure for cancer? Am I right?" asked Clark.

"Well, it would be a start, you would still need to figure out a few other elements. You would need the right RNA, which acts as a messenger as well as an epigenetic solution. Gene editing has always been the tool with the greatest potential to cure cancer and other major diseases." Amy nodded.

"But how do you know which genes do what and which ones need editing?" The tone in Clark's voice was similar to that of a child who watches a space shuttle launch for the first time.

"Oh Clark, I find crash lectures in bioinformatics so hot and sexy," said Amy, giggling before yielding to a body-shaking laugh. "Clark, you can't cram my seven years of post-doctoral work into a short car ride. Can you kindly tell me what specifically we are doing and then I can give you the 'CRISPR gene editing thumbnail wiki' according to Amy?"

"Alright, but this stays between us, OK?" Clark's expression got serious and Amy nodded, finding his whole arrival at her school and the subsequent trip to Crisprgen humorous, with Clark's sense of urgency endearing if not somewhat baffling. She waited for Clark to speak. "The Crisprgen Company just became one of the major investors in our paper, and they are putting all kinds of heat on Elizabeth. It's a long story, and she has no idea how much pressure they can ratchet up. I've seen this kind of thing before, and I need to get ahead of it. I'm supposed to do a story on the company, and I'm not an expert in genetics so that's why I'll need you."

"Part of me wants to be flattered and to relish the unexpected day off from school," said Amy with her characteristic partial smile that appeared when she was talking. "But the adult in me…" She started shaking her head in a No motion. "Wants to be mad at you for assuming in patriarchal default that my job was more expendable than yours." She let the silence that followed act as a muted highlighter on her last words. She didn't know if Clark realized she was being facetious, but didn't let on.

"Yeah, well, there is another reason I brought you, and you know me well enough to know that my crazy hunches start out sounding like bizarre fairy tales but ended in two Pulitzers." Clark paused for equally dramatic effect as Amy looked at him patiently. "I might have a lead on your Matsumoto kid."

"What? Really?" Amy leaned up in her seat wide-eyed.

"I have a hunch he was recruited into a job pathway for smart kids that needs off-the-charts math whizz types for niche STEM jobs, mostly computer science. I tapped a source in Washington that has access to intelligence info for the Armed Forces, and Matsumoto's name and that of the Mackoul kid had both been identified but neither had been approached or recruited. However, the people whose job it is to know about kids like this knew about the both of them."

"Look Clark, baby, honey, darling, dear, homey…whatever…don't read into this as I am actually thrilled that you've forced upon me what I will term as a mental health day from teaching, but you don't have to connect such far-reaching dots. I'm happy to just see you. After I saw you at Rutgers recently, I thought about how much I missed just taking off with you with no plans. So if it's easier to pretend we are working fine, but we don't have to." Amy looked straight out the windshield with a faintly disappointed expression.

"Aim, I'm serious! My source told me that private sector companies are recruiting smart ones faster than the government intelligence agencies, and I think Crisprgen had something to do with the Matsumoto kid's disappearance. I've never seen the kid, so you'll know what to look for and what questions to ask. Plus, you understand their core business far better than I ever will. I need you to explain my story assignment to me, and you need me to find your star student so I thought this was a win for both of us." Clark stopped talking and turned to look at Amy with a smile. Her face remained expressionless as she returned his gaze. "And…I wanted to spend time with you." Now Amy smiled back.

"OK, but Alvin Matsumoto only took the NMSQT test very recently," Amy said thoughtfully. "How would Crisprgen know his scores? And so quickly? School records are almost as protected as health records and a large private sector company would—"

"Need to pay somebody off for access to the test scores or hire an 8th-grade hacker," interrupted Clark. "Come on Amy, that's the easy part. There are a million ways to get information when you need it, especially in the digital age. Look at the stuff I've been able to find over the years; some of the stuff could land me in jail for Chrissakes! No, how they found out his scholastic profile is the easiest part of this. The question that doesn't seem to have an easy answer is WHY?"

"Hmmm…" Amy was now completely intrigued. "Maybe they want to tap the best and the brightest the way they did when companies like Microsoft and Apple started?"

"No…." whispered Clark reflectively. "That doesn't add up."

Chapter 4

A red-tailed hawk perched on a green road sign stood watch over the long grass along Rt. 70. Before Clark could point out its majesty to his traveling companion, Amy squinted and read the sign. "Crisprgen Village" was glued in white decorative plastic lettering over a green highway sign with stains from previous letters that had been removed. "Fort Monmouth" was barely readable among the powdery black mold smudges and chunks of hawk excrement.

"Clark, this is our exit. Holy shit, it's the old Fort Monmouth!" exclaimed Amy. "Remember when we used to take bird practicums down here?" She sounded elated.

"Yeah, speaking of birds, check out the red-tailed one on top of the sign. It looks like a female." Clark slowed down as he pointed up through the windshield at the motionless hawk. "You're right This is the old Fort Monmouth. I thought they were going to make it a movie studio for that horrific streaming service company…whatever. I wrote quite a few stories here. I guess I knew they decommissioned the base about 20 years ago, but there were events and hot air ballooning. It never really seemed like it had closed, it just didn't look like Full Metal Jacket anymore."

Clark drove on a sandy road through the New Jersey scrub pine. There were no signs or telephone poles or wires. While Fort Monmouth had two main entrances with well-staffed gates at the northern and eastern borders, the western side that connected with Rt. 35 was mostly woods with a few service roads. These roads had been permanently closed after September 11, 2001, but after the base was decommissioned in 2005 and then sold in 2017, the county had reopened them. As the road curved left in the dense coniferous woods, a group of small houses arranged in a development appeared through the trees. Clark realized that he had never been to this section of the base before. This was where the families of the enlisted and civilian staff lived, and the section functioned as a small town. Like many decommissioned bases that were relics of the Cold War, Ft. Monmouth had once housed thousands of people. Clark assumed that if the base had been sold, it would most likely be empty, but as they rounded the corner, he saw that all the houses seemed occupied. People and families stood on the sidewalks and yards of the small Cape Cod-style houses as if it were one big suburban block party. A large parking lot with wavy berm partitions curved a labyrinth of parking spaces.

"Somewhat squiggly parking rows for an army base, wouldn't you say?" he asked Amy.

"Sure! They don't want the families feeling like life on an army base is sterile and industrial," she replied.

"How ironic." Clark laughed. "There is a rail line here that would bring heavy weapons to the supply ship on the pier for the waiting aircraft carrier strike groups offshore. There is communications equipment and satellite antennas that make it feel like you are on the set of Star Wars. Random massive explosions were routine as they tested ordinance in the woods at all hours of the day…. but that decorative parking lot had everybody fooled, I'm sure."

"The military left here 14 years ago, and I only know of one sale of a small section of the Fort for construction that isn't set to begin for two years. So, who are all these people?" Amy asked, sounding baffled.

"I came down here once in the 90s when the base was used to resettle Kosovo war refugees," mused Clark. "But no one here looks like they have been through a war."

Amy and Clark got out of the car and stood looking across the road at the odd, yet strangely idyllic little village before them. Amy looked at Clark, shrugged, and said, "OK, let's go check it out. Let's try to blend in and pretend we live here." Her smile revealed that she was enjoying the random events of the day Clark had imposed on her.

As they shuffled through the perfectly manicured grass, they heard the roar of several people cheering and exclaiming as if watching a sporting event.. Three adults and two adolescent boys, one kneeling on one knee and holding a remote control switch box with an antennae and joystick pumped one fist in the air.

"Eat my flamethrower you sad dumpster with wheels!" the boy shouted as the grown men standing around him clapped and laughed. A remote-controlled silver dune buggy with enormous tires the size of a mailbox zipped around from behind one of the houses and zoomed right up to the kneeling boy and the men surrounding him. Clark beckoned to Amy, and they moved a bit closer to get a better look at the toy dune buggy.

As they got within a few feet of the gathering, they could see that the little vehicle the boy was playing with was made of what looked like very heavy stainless steel. The roof of what would be the driver's area was a video display screen that had data graphics running down on each side, and a video of the toy's journeys played. A 20-inch cylinder that looked like a small scuba tank was mounted across the back transom above the wheels with a gauged valve and high-pressure hose looping around to what would have been a hood ornament on a full-size car. Instead of a hood ornament though, a nozzle that looked like the pipe of a butane torch, and equally covered in burned soot, pointed forward as little wisps of smoke escaped at random from the barrel. Clark couldn't contain his fascination. Looking at the men smiling, Clark nodded his head and exclaimed, "Damn! That's quite a toy!"

"Toy my ass! That's the toy!" exclaimed the boy, and pointed to the narrow lawn space between the two houses. There, 25 yards away, was a knee-high, five feet wide pile of charred metal and melted tires. Orange flames danced between the metal shards and lines of black smoke lofted from the wreckage.

"Damn! What happened? Did we miss the plane crash?" asked Clark as he saw the burning pile.

"My Hentor scorched him!" yelled the boy. Clark realized one of the men standing was also holding a remote control box, bigger and with two joysticks. The man stared at the burning metal pile as the smell of charred plastic and kerosene blew over the group. The man reached down and extended his hand to the boy. "Nice work. You need to show me how you can hijack the signal because that was the only advantage you had." Clark didn't understand what the man was referring to as he watched the bizarre scene unfold. Then, Amy broke the silence.

"You know kerosene isn't regulation, right? Whatever maneuver you pulled off you are going to have to reproduce with nitromethane and your measurements will be vastly different." Amy knelt down next to the boy. "Can I see your box? I am impressed you generate such a far trigger signal." The boy handed the remote control box to Amy who turned it over in her hand examining it. Clark slid up behind Amy pretending to be as absorbed and got close to her ear.

"Aim…what exactly is this?" he whispered. Amy stood up and faced Clark and spoke at a volume so the group could all hear her.

"This….is a battle bot champ!" Amy patted the still kneeling boy on his head.

"And this is the defeated father who just saw his airpod vaporized." The man with the second remote control laughed and smiled. Amy smiled back. "Nitromethane wouldn't have damaged an aerial drone in the slightest;it couldn't generate enough heat to burn through that plastic. But kerosene, now that is genius!" said the man shaking his head. Amy turned to Clark to explain further.

"This is a bot battle. There are leagues for very gifted students who show an aptitude and an interest in engineering where they build robots and compete with others, sometimes on challenges like this. Usually, the loser doesn't go up in flames though!" Amy raised her eyebrows dramatically as if she were soliciting an explanation from the group. A tall middle-aged man with a confident posture moved closer to Amy and Clark, smiling as he spoke and extending his hand.

"I'm Sandro LaRocca, are you both new here?" he asked.

"Hi, no we are here for a meeting. I'm Clark and this is Amy," Clark replied, extending his hand to shake.

"A meeting? If you're on the fence then let's take a walk around, and I'll answer any questions you have and show you around. I know it seems overwhelming at first but you really can't beat it."

"On the fence about what?" asked Amy.

"We would love it if you showed us around, and yes we have plenty of questions," said Clark while nodding his head. Clark then looked at Amy and rolled his eyes in an exaggerated circular motion to indicate she should play along with whatever they accidentally stumbled into. Sandro LaRocca motioned for them to follow him while pointing to the narrow lawn between the building, where the still smoldering defeated robot lay destroyed. A grown man stood over the wreckage with a clipboard taking notes.

"This is where the center square is," he said while walking and pointing to the area inside the Cul De Sac of houses. Instead of a road, a brick mosaic courtyard created the appearance of a plaza. In the center of the circular pavement plaza were four massive heavy dark marble picnic tables. Clark saw the different quantities of chess pieces on each table. Each had at least two people seated as opponents in the game on the table. Some tables had more than one chess board and some of their seats were filled with onlookers and supporters. "As you can see, we take our chess very seriously," guffawed LaRocca. "Most of the gangs here are nationally ranked. I guess it kinda goes with the territory." Clark had no idea what he meant by 'territory,' and he had never expected a community of families to still be living on the Fort Monmouth property either. In the center of the plaza was a large metal utility pole on which a brand new jumbotron video sign displayed several names, numbers, and what looked like rankings or scores. Clark pointed at the sign and said:

"Why have a jumbotron billboard if no cars are driving by? That looks brand new. What is it displaying and why put it there?"

"Oh, that's our scoreboard. We use it for announcements and screenings, too," replied LaRocca.

"What exactly are you scoring and screening?" asked Amy. LaRocca continued smiling and slowly made his way around the edge of the plaza as another small robot zipped past them and disappeared into the parking lot.

"This is our town square." LaRocca gestured in a circular sweep. It is where the chess finals get played and since those marble tables are too heavy, we leave them in the middle of the battlefield for the robot wars. We have some blast nets that we arrange like a curtain so the bots don't hurt anyone."

"A village devoted to chess and robot engineering? Who are all these people and how many live here?" asked Amy.

"Not just chess and robots, so much more! When you build a village of geniuses things can get really weird. You should see the rocket lovers—always blasting shit everywhere. That sign is our village leaderboard. It shows the scores for the ongoing chess matches and video replays of the different bot battles. Also, if somebody makes a really big ID then we put it up for everyone to see," continued LaRocca.

"Big ID?" asked Clark.

"Yes, of a tag—a gene marker. I was lucky enough to be here the day they found one of the lung cancer genes. My mom passed away from lung cancer, and I got really emotional thinking about how children of the future won't have to be at a funeral on their 10th birthday."

"I'm sorry, can we slow down a little bit..... What do you mean by 'discovering a gene?' Why is chess so important in this village? And what section of the base is this?" Clark realized his best approach was to simply play along and ask questions.

"Oh right, you guys just drove up. I assume you got an invite and want to do some scouting on your own?" continued LaRocca warmly.

"An invite? Uh yeah…we are scouting. Wanna help us scout?" Clark made a caricature display of his confusion causing the man to laugh politely. Amy was transfixed on the jumbotron leaderboard.

"Ha! Yeah, I was the same way. When they approached us, I wanted to come down here on my own and see what it was all about. I didn't want a dog and pony show that was scripted. I wanted to wander around and see if the families here were happy and what life was really like."

"Were you in the service? Was this in order to move to Fort Monmouth? I thought they closed this section?" Clark interjected.

"Oh no, this was way afterward. It's been the Crisprgen campus for two years, and this is the old village that was built for enlisted men and officers. Now it's used for the Crisprgen recruits and their families, and I gotta say, everything is excellent. And I'd be delighted to show you around!" Sandro LaRocca's delight as he described his new place of residence was palpable.

"Crisprgen employees live here? I guess that would make sense…" Clark thought out loud.

"Not employees, recruits. My daughter was recruited in her sophomore year of high school, and she really wanted to come here. She wanted it so much that she left without us and said she wasn't coming home. We are from up in Hartford, Connecticut, and I drove down here with my wife fully intending to bring her home and get the police involved if necessary, but instead, we heard her out, let her show us around, and realized that this is truly the best place for her."

"So you and your wife just moved down here? Did you have to change jobs? That's not an easy thing to do…" Something wasn't adding up for Clark.

"Well, we just couldn't refuse the offer they made us. They gave us a house to live in so we sold our own home and got to keep the money. The one thing they ask is that you live on the base and stay here in the community on weekends and evenings. Holiday privileges are earned."

"Earned? Privileges? Why did your daughter come here and what exactly do they do here?" Clark realized that whatever they were doing on this campus with these families sounded like they wanted to keep it quiet by controlling access and financial enticements.

"This is where the Crisprgen families live. It's great because we get to be with our daughter and get her anything she needs. We honestly didn't know what to do for her at home, and I just didn't want to fail her as a father." LaRocca sounded wistful.

"What exactly is it that your daughter needs?" queried Amy, trying to prompt details that would fill in the gaps

"I still don't know the answer to that!" LaRocca regained his faint smile. "What I know is this: Everyone who met my daughter in the early grades said she was exceptionally bright and off the charts. Then after a few more years of school, we started to get contacted by state officials about how high she scored on all the standardized tests. They had her come down for the advanced testing and they confirmed what we all knew, which was that her IQ was in the stratosphere. They told us they only calculate adolescent IQ up to 170 and hers so far beyond that it couldn't be accurately assessed for several more years." LaRocca paused to take a deep sigh. "They were telling us she would need to go to a special school for hyper-gifted students and that the regular school system where we lived wouldn't take her because they wouldn't know what to do and the state wouldn't count it as satisfactory completion of the educational standards even though it was so advanced. It got really nasty—they basically said there was no place for her to go to school unless we moved to the Washington DC area, and if we didn't enroll her in the federal program in DC, they could make the case that we were unfit parents. We didn't know what we were going to do."

"So you moved here?" prompted Clark.

"Not exactly. She got this boyfriend and didn't come home one weekend. You can imagine how worried we were, and we feared the worst. Then she called us and asked us to meet her here. We came down, and she was here with the Crisprgen staff. They explained that they could actually fulfill her academic needs, in compliance with any state requirements, and she could contribute to their research here, and we would all be paid. At first, I was livid and said no way. I was mad they had discussed it with her and not her parents first. But I was a smart kid also, only they just left me in public school to waste my time. I would have given anything to live in a little community like this where I wouldn't have been ostracized for being smart. So long story short, we took the deal, and we couldn't be happier. I spend my days building the bots for the battle bot tournaments, and I'll admit I had never lost a game of chess to anyone until my first afternoon here.

The chess players they have here are outstanding. I even won the Connecticut state championship in 1985 but I get my ass kicked here."

"What happened to your daughter? Did they put her in a school?" asked Amy.

"School? There is no school here. Plus, she wouldn't have time. She does what most of the kids here do, and most days that means research up in the Hickman floor of the Helix lab. Imagine that! My 15-year-old daughter is making high six figures for a biotech company. The world sure has changed. Crisprgen told us that everything my daughter was involved with in the lab would count as academic equivalency and satisfy any requirements the state was using as leverage to direct us to DC."

"And was it true that this fulfilled the education requirements the state imposed on you?" asked Clark.

"Nope. Not even a little. But honestly, I don't care now. I can't imagine what any school could possibly do for my daughter that would be better than here. She is not missing anything. Plus, she is around other kids who are just as smart and now she doesn't feel like a freak. She really had no friends at home and forget about dating….no boy would talk to her. They were so terrified of how smart she was. She convinced the first guy she ever dated to drive her here, and they never made it to the third date."

"So what exactly is happening here? Because the way you make it sound, Crisprgen hired a 15-year-old to do Research and Development work and paid off her parents to allow it. What is she going to do without any academic degrees? I thought you said the State Board of Education threatened you with an endangerment charge," cross examined Clark.

"They did. The company took care of it. They convinced the bureaucrats that the environment here was better suited for her. And they aren't really working for the company—they are more like research subjects. They get very advanced education plans, tailored to their specific needs and strengths. They do have them do some computer code writing and some of the lengthy equations for the Passport Project but that's okay as my daughter can do those in her sleep." Clark interrupted him.

"Passport Project?" he asked.

"Yeah, the genome mapping and rollout. That's what this village is here for. Crisprgen does the consumer genetic testing where you spit in a cup and mail it to a different campus in Arizona—they have thousands of employees there. They bought Ft. Monmouth just for the Passport families. Come on, let's walk around to the left here, and I can show you around a bit more." LaRocca started to walk forward as he spoke. Clark, though distracted by how unusual the place was, absentmindedly followed him. As he turned to see if

Amy was following as well, he saw her still standing near the marble picnic table as if she were bolted to the ground. She was still staring intently at the leaderboard.

"Clark! Come over here! Look at this!" She beckoned frantically with her hand for Clark to walk back beside her. Clark turned and walked a few steps back to see what was so startling to her. Amy held out her left hand and pointed to the video leaderboard which was now showing another battle bot takedown. Along the right margin of the screen were graphics that made a rankings list.

"Look at the fifth name down…." said Amy softly.

"Matsumoto…" said Clark out loud. LaRocca turned with an expression that seemed to beckon the two of them. "Well, in Japan that name is like Smith or Jones. It's probably nothing, but let's see what else we can find," said Clark softly. Amy turned and looked at LaRocca with a very serious expression, then proceeded to march right past him.

***

As they continued through the courtyard among the small houses and dozens of people lost in recreation, Clark noticed a stone archway that rose five feet above the ground. A staircase descended from the cement square on the ground and disappeared out of sight. In the arch that formed the top of the doorway in black letters was the word "Neanderthals" in black letters on a white background. Clark smirked thinking it must have been some kind of a nickname that the army servicemen had given to that house or the people in it. A few houses down there was a second archway entrance at the same height with the same descending and disappearing staircase. This one had the same painted lettering but with the words "Cro-Magnon." Clark figured the names were leftover from the days when GIs lived in each house and likely took nicknames for their squads. He smirked to himself. They continued past more houses, each also with stone archway tunnels. The next archway was inscribed with the word "Australopithecus" and the next "Denisovan' '.

"Looks like these GIs were fans of human evolution," said Clark, attempting to be humorous. "Where do those arched tunnels go?"

"Oh, those aren't from the GIs that lived in these houses. Ms. Reistad decided to group us by our dominant pre-sapien genetic imprint, each in our own houses. The tunnels are part of the old base - they were the air raid and fallout shelters back in the Cold War, but they are great for going from your house to the Helix lab in the dead of winter when it gets so cold you can't feel your face. We are only three miles from the ocean, the winter wind whips right through here something fierce." Sandro LaRocca strode and spoke like a tour guide.

"You are grouped by your pre-sapien what?" Clark asked, not following the explanation in the slightest. Amy stayed silent and observed.

"Yeah, pre-sapien - as in the evolutionary stages before homo sapiens. You know, the earlier species at the dawn of man that went through evolutionary changes to become us?" LaRocca seemed surprised by Clark's confusion.

"Yeah, I know what the words are - I've studied evolution. So you all have groups that go by those names? I guess that's cute. Do you play intramural sports together? Are there summer volleyball games between the Neanderthals and the Cro magnons?" Clark's sarcasm wasn't generating even a hint of a smile.

"What do you mean by genetic imprint?" asked Amy with an intense stare. Clark sensed she was focusing on something specific.

"They didn't explain this to you before your child's recruitment? In the human genome, we all carry genes from the hominid species that came before us. Each person carries different amounts based on what population you were born into. It's like racial genetics but the traits wouldn't be considered race traits like skin color or height averages. It used to be predictable by geography but now with modern travel, everyone has their own unique mix. You might have more Neanderthal genes than me, I might have more Cro magnon, she might have more Denisovan," he said pointing to Amy. "We know those three early ancestors lived at the same time— roughly 100,000 to about 40,000 years ago. They also lived in the same areas— the Denisovans were farther west in Asia, but all three migrated through each other's territories, mated and offspring creating interbred family groups until about 30,000 years ago when modern man appeared as the version we are today. I haven't didn't really study evolution, so when they were explaining this to me at the recruitment interview, I didn't get it, but after being here a while it started to make perfect sense. Have you gotten your phenotype report yet? Do you know your ratios?" LaRocca's expression indicated he was expecting a simple answer that Clark or Amy should have known.

"Uh…well…we aren't exactly parents," said Clark, as he shot a smile at Amy. "I'm actually a journalist, and I'm here to write a feature on the Crisprgen company. I thought they were a consumer genetic company, and I knew they were big but I didn't realize they would have so much staff living on site."

"Oh really? No kidding! Oh well, in that case you need to interview me as a proud happy parent. I can't say enough good things about this place!" LaRocca was beaming. Amy immediately started asking questions.

"Why would they brief you on human evolution as part of hiring you? It's my favorite topic to teach and talk about, but what does that have to do with consumer genetics?"

"Oh well, they told us the early hominid genes were good markers for harvest targets," replied Sandro LaRocca matter-of-factly.

"Harvest targets? What exactly are you harvesting?" asked Amy, baffled.

"Oh, you guys didn't get a briefing on the program yet? This village here is the harvest pool. My daughter got recruited about six months ago and most of the families live here. Once they discover what they call a 'critical marker,' they will call whoever in the village that has it in their genome, and then we go up to the lab and leave samples so that they can harvest them. Sometimes it takes a few tries but once it works, they name the gene from the family it came from. Our daughter already has one— the LaRocca BRAC - 6. They never tell us what it's for, though, because they don't want to create competition, jealousy, or frankly, resentment."

"Back up a minute." Clark suddenly realized that nothing this man was telling him was in the corporate report or even known back at the newsroom. "Crisprgen moved families here and is harvesting genes from their children?" Clark tilted his head in disbelief and expected LaRocca to laugh. But he didn't.

"Yeah, well, where else are they going to get them? My daughter was in the top .1% of children born with an IQ over 170," LaRocca replied. Amy moved two steps in front of him and stood in his path to face him.

"Mr. LaRocca, let me make sure I am getting this right. Crisprgen is a consumer genetic testing company that runs spit tests from mail-in samples and provides customers with reports on what diseases they may be prone to so they can activate various prevention measures, but they have a community of families with hyper-intelligent children living on the campus. Why exactly?"

"OK, let me explain it this way. Crisprgen does hundreds of thousands of genetic profile tests every year. They have a pretty good map of the genome and they have figured out a bunch of patented CRISPR-Cas 9 procedures and are devising more all the time. So they have to recruit all the ultra high intelligence youth so they can find the material for the CRISPRs." LaRocca gently raised both hands in a shrugging motion to show he had finished his thought.

"These are all high-IQ kids, and Crisprgen is taking their genetic sequence that gave them such a high IQ and creating CRISPR patches…and they would know where to put it on the genome because they have it all mapped out.…" Amy was talking aloud to herself.

"Exactly! When a test kit gets mailed in and they see the markers they are looking for—the genetic tags that indicate the person could have very high intelligence, they look the person up and arrange a meeting with them just like they did with us. They invite them for an interview and visit, and then if they qualify, which my daughter definitely did, then they take care of the rest and we all get to live here. I got to retire early, and we moved onto the base." Clark and Amy looked at each other in disbelief.

"So…once they take the genes from kids like your daughter and make a CRISPR sequence out of it, then what? What do they do with it?" asked Clark.

"Oh well, part of the agreement is kind of a 'don't ask, don't tell' policy. I think they don't want the families to know what they are able to sell it for, which I understand. I wouldn't either, and it's probably a lot, but that is okay. They gave us an enormous financial incentive to come here and if any of my daughter's gene sequences get patented, we get the royalties." LaRocca looked very satisfied with his explanation as if it were an achievement of its own.

"Sell to who?" asked Clark slowly. Neither Clark nor Amy could believe what they were hearing.

"Well, we will get royalties when her gene sequences go on the retail market and other parents want to buy them. Right now we gave the company the rights to sell to sovereign states and corporations," LaRocca continued.

"Crisprgen built a community of super-intelligent kids and is harvesting their genes, patenting them, and selling them? To governments? And big companies?" Clark thought it sounded incredulous.

"Yup!" exclaimed LaRocca. " Ain't it great? Who would have thought, huh?"

"Great? Umm… I don't know if it's great…is it even legal? Is it ethical? How do we know who they are selling these CRISPR sequences to and for what purpose?"

"Well, it's all planning for the Reset. All hands on deck!" said LaRocca as he laughed uproariously. "As long as we are all here after the Reset, that's all I care about."

"What exactly is the 'Reset'?" asked Clark.

"Oh, the Great Reset," said LaRocca. "You know, the big shakeup—the big turning point. Whatever you want to call it, we call it the Great Reset here because it gives it a more positive spin. They will be able to explain it to you up at the Helix. Hey listen, guys, I have to go meet my wife to play racquetball. If you are all still here later after your meetings, we usually cook dinner out by the picnic tables. Come on over and hang out and meet everyone. We are making hamburgers and hot dogs leftover from the 4th of July."

"Sure. I'd love to meet your daughter," said Amy. "One last question…do all these families have the same story? Were they all invited here by Crisprgen and do they all have smart children?" Amy was trying to sound as innocent and nonchalant as possible.

"Yes, exactly, and not to sound elitist, but it's nice to be around your own kind." LaRocca shrugged sheepishly.

"OK…and do you know a family named Matsumoto? I saw that name on the leaderboard before—"

"Oh, sure! Jiro and Sukireally nice people - they are relatively new. I think they are from Maplewood or close to there?" Amy's eyes opened wide when she heard the name of the town she taught in. She glanced at Clark who shot her an equally concerned look.

"We will definitely come by later," said Clark. "If you see the Matsumotos, tell them we want to meet them!" And just like that, Sandro LaRocca turned behind a white brick house and Clark and Amy were left standing on the main concrete pathway in the middle of the village.

Amy grabbed Clark's hand and moved him off the main concrete walkway that connected the small village houses and moved them around the trunk of a huge elm tree. They stood for a few seconds, not saying anything but looking at each other. Amy leaned closer to Clark to whisper in his ear.

"Clark…" she whispered.

"I know. Don't even whisper. Who knows who is listening…" Clark looked around the lawn to see if any of the other families were paying attention to them. "Amy this whole recruitment thing is a goldmine of a story!"

"Clark, you don't understand. If the Matsumotos are here, then we have to find them and talk to them. I need to know if Alvin is okay, and his parents have to be told that everyone back home is looking for them. Plus, the school needs to know where he is and the authorities—"

"Amy, come on," interrupted Clark. "If the Matsumotos are here, then it's their intentional choice that no one back home knows about. Do you really think that a family can just pack up and disappear for no reason? They disappeared on purpose. Normally I would say there are only two reasons a family would do a disappearing act like they did—money or to hide from something, usually the law. You heard the other guy, LaRocca say they went and recruited his daughter, and then gave him a big financial incentive to come here. I bet it's the same thing - it certainly seems like Alvin Matsumoto was recruited to come to work in this genetics beehive and his parents are probably peeing themselves while laughing all the way to the bank. I'll admit it's shitty not to tell the school and it is rude to concerned teachers like yourself that go out of their way for these kids, but this is America and people can pursue personal gain in any legal manner…nothing in the constitution says you have to be polite or nice about it, just legal."

"Clark! Did you hear how fuck up it is what they are doing here? They are finding the super intelligent kids and then..—"

"Giving them an opportunity to work for an exploding private sector company in a brand new industry with fair pay? It sounds fundamentally a lot like the American dream to me." interrupted Clark.

"I don't think you realize what we just heard…They are harvesting genes,but not for agriculture or cattle ranching, Clark— for fucking people!" Amy was talking in a raised hoarse whisper but her voice was clearly audible to the people walking, sitting, and recreating around them.

"Well, I think it's an obvious natural evolution of the parenting and baby consumer industry— they sell everything under the sun so you can give your kids an edge these days. They even make little speakers with straps to fasten around a woman's pregnant belly so the wack job moms can play Mozart to the fetus they actually have schlock research to say it makes kids smarter."

"Clark—" Amy tried to stop him from talking.

"Amy, with all the mechanisms that are being researched, developed, and sold under the umbrella of smarter babies, is it any surprise that there would be a gold rush in the consumer genetics industry for these smart crispies, or whatever you called them?"

"CRISPR," said Amy, sounding slightly annoyed. "Clark, your logic is deeply flawed because there is one major difference between a CRISPR snippet and every single other nootropic product on the market."

"OK, and other than being more expensive, what is it?" asked Clark. He was somewhat surprised at how upset she seemed.

"The difference is that once you install a CRISPR section and it attaches successfully, then you PERMANENTLY change that DNA, and the person's genome...FOREVER! You now have essentially altered the biology of a person and there is no going back!"

Clark thought for a moment. "So…then how is it different from plastic surgery, or a sex change operation?" Clark smiled faintly, still not quite as bothered by all of it as Amy.

"Clark, you if anyone should understand the urgency here" Amy looked at him intently. "Let's say they identify a CRISPR section that really does appear in the genome of geniuses, then what?"

"I would think that's a pretty cool discovery as it would unlock a lot of mystery about people—"

"Clark you jackass! You and I took a whole two-semester study on Charles Darwin's Origin of Species and what was the tagline that you presented in your final presentation?" Amy was surprised he didn't see the immediate peril in the situation they had stumbled upon.

"Well, I said essentially, that according to Darwin, the evolution of life as a concept wasn't part of a grand design but rather a random outcome of being in the right place at the right time. Essentially, all life evolves in relation and in reaction to its environment, circumstances, weather changes, predators, etc. but it's never intentional, and all of it adds up to random chance. Those life forms that have traits that help survive all these circumstances will be the ones that survive through the various changes and the genetic tweaks over the millennia are reactive to finer and finer details. Then I told the fable of the lucky cockroach," said Clark smiling.

"Right…the lucky cockroach. As everyone knows cockroaches have been around for hundreds of millions of years and survived all the major changes and extinctions that affected all other life. Through it all, somehow that cockroach survived. Not out of intent or great planning, but simply because their natural history was luckily suited for major temperature changes, ice ages, volcanoes, and meteors. But not all cockroaches survived—just the lucky ones with just the right epigenetic markers that helped them last through the environmental transitions. Those that didn't have the genes that gave them an edge died off."

"Right…what is your point?" asked Clark gently. He could tell she was driving at something.

"My point is that whoever figures out which genes the cockroach needed to survive all of the major changes across geological time would have an edge over all the cockroaches. In essence, it would be a superior cockroach, and it would have the greatest advantage over all the others." Amy explained further. Clark looked pensive and then spoke:

"But only the lucky cockroaches would even know about it," said Clark slowly.

"Exactly," Amy nodded as she spoke. "And those lucky cockroaches would have control over all the others, deciding who gets the best chance at survival and who doesn't."

"And they wouldn't be accountable to the other cockroaches." Clark finally understood Amy's point. If a species somehow found a way to improve itself or increase its chances of survival, how would there be a fair process to ensure equal access and determine which individuals were eligible and which ones weren't?

"OK, look, there will be plenty of time later to deconstruct the ethics of this place," said Clark looking around again. "But we only have one random parent telling us their own experience here, and we don't even know if that LaRocca guy was telling the truth or just bragging. He could be down here fencing stolen copper wire for all we know." Amy shot him a look of pained disbelief. "Aim, I have to go and meet the founder for an interview, and Elizabeth is going to meet me at the main building. Why don't you walk up with me, and we can ask if the Matsumotos are here and you can go see them and…"

Amy interrupted Clark as she stared across the walkway ata picnic table where a Japanese couple sat across from each other.

"No need. I just found them," As Amy spoke she was already walking towards the picnic table to meet the occupants. Clark followed after her, smiling. While the ethical issues they discussed were concerning to him, finding the parents would put Amy back at ease and that satisfied him greatly. It also meant his former student, now editor, Elizabeth, was going to be blown away when she realized Clark had found the missing family in less than two days.

Amy walked up next to the middle-aged couple and started speaking.

"Hi, I'm Amy Biancini, I'm an AP biology teacher from Maplewood High School. Are you Mr. and Mrs. Matsumoto?" she asked kindly but directly. Mr. Matsumoto stood up to shake Amy's hand and bowed in customary Japanese style. Mrs. Matsumoto lowered her head in a respectful bow. Clark smiled at both of them and stayed standing as he figured the boy's former teacher, Amy, would be the better one to start the conversation.

"Oh yes, Mrs. Biancini. Alvin told us how much he liked your class. We are so happy you are here and part of the Passport Project," said Mr. Matsumoto in a cordial and respectful tone. Amy looked at both of them for a few seconds.

"Is…Alvin here?" asked Amy inquisitively. The Matsumotos looked at each other silently, then Mr. Matsumoto spoke as his wife looked away.

"Yes, but he is busy during the day. We don't get to see him much. He is usually up at the Helix lab. I should have realized that of course you would be involved with the Passport. I wish we had known— Alvin didn't tell us, or we wouldn't have been so difficult. We are so happy you are here." Mr. Matsumoto smiled slightly as he spoke and had a look of genuine relief about whatever it was he thought Amy was involved in. Clark nudged Amy to play along and with their long history together, she knew exactly what he was indicating. She immediately introduced him.

"I'm sorry, this is my old friend, Clark Westfield," said Amy as she moved a step back to allow Clark and Mr. Matsumoto to shake hands.

"Hi, Clark Westfield, nice to make your acquaintance," said Clark observing the couple up and down. "So this Passport, eh? Quite a project, right?" said Clark, sounding like a used car salesman. He was fishing for information with transparent prompts so Amy would play along. She immediately knew what he was up to. It was a prank they had pulled hundreds of times on all ages of people in all kinds of places. Once they had pretended to be a couple expecting a baby and went shopping at Target, engaged a salesperson, and tried to convince him that they were going to be the first couple to give birth in space. But Mr. and Mrs. Matsumoto simply stared politely at them and smiled, remaining silent. Amy jumped in.

"Yeah, that Passport Project. Of course, I'm glad I'm involved," offered Amy sheepishly, but there still wasn't a sound from the Matsumotos just silent smiles.

"So, I know why I love it but just out of curiosity, what is your favorite thing about the Passport project?" asked Clark, raising his eyebrows in an exaggerated expression coaxing them to speak. Amy shot him a look and shook her head. The Matsumotos continued smiling, then turned to look at one another before Mrs. Matsumoto spoke.

"The extra time," she said smiling.

"Ah yes, the extra time. Gotta love the free time," rambled Clark, trying to pry out a few more details as best he could. "So you are happy with the amount of time that's available here?" he continued. Mr. Matsumoto spoke this time.

"Yes, it's wonderful, now that we are comfortable and we know Alvin is safe," Mr. Matsumoto gestured with his hands toward Amy as he spoke. "We didn't know what to think, of course everyone wants more time, so we thought we would wait and see. We didn't know if it was fair to ask for more time or if it best for Alvin, now with Ms. Biancini here, everything now OK!" His broken English turned into a smile. Clark took two steps back and pointed to the ground, indicating Amy should step over. He leaned down to whisper in her ear so close he could smell her lemon shampoo.

"OK, this is going nowhere. I have an idea…why don't you stay here with these two and let me go find where my interview is supposed to be. See what you can get them to tell you about this passport thing, and I'll come back and get you in a little bit." Amy was already nodding before Clark finished speaking.

"Ok, well, nice meeting you both!" Clark waved in a big sweeping motion as if he were washing a window. "Why don't you brief Ms. Biancini on the Passport Project so far…you know…pretend she is the student for once and see if you can get it right, and then after, she can quiz you."

"Clark!" Amy shouted with a scolding look. She turned to whisper in his ear. "Goddammit, Clark! It's bad enough you are so horrendous at fooling them but do you have to be so damn cheesy, too?" In the spaces between the words, Clark could hear her breathy laughter. "Do you know where you are supposed to meet Elizabeth?" Amy asked. Clark nodded.

"She said we would meet at the Helix lab, which a couple of these families have mentioned. I hope I can find it. I'll text you when I do."

High above the tree line at least two miles away, Amy saw a round structure that looked like a massive water storage tank with the height of a 14-story water tower. But inside the open cylinder was what looked like a twisted ladder or a spiral staircase that made the entire building look like it was twisting in shape.

"I found it," said Amy, pointing to the massive spiral staircase building. "See that building that looks like a giant strand of DNA?" Clark looked at the odd structure. Mr. Matsumoto, smiling consistently, nodded, pointed, and spit out two words:

"Helix lab!" he said, confirming Amy's suspicion that Clark's appointment was in a building shaped like a DNA strand, and off Clark went.

Chapter 5

Central and southern New Jersey are made up of a flat coastal plain. A moist sand makes up the dirt, and scrub pine and cranberry bushes create one of the largest contiguous forests on the Eastern Seaboard. Ft. Monmouth, now the Crisprgen campus complete with its self-contained little village, was at the northernmost edge of what had gradually become the Pine Barrens. It was through this flat, hot, humid environment that Clark trudged on a shoulder-width path through the dense underbrush. He could feel the New Jersey mosquitoes quietly draining blood from the back of his neck just under his hairline. More than once, he stopped to flick off a crawling dog tick. The iridescent brown, thumbtack size dots had eight spindly legs that remained tucked under its body as it clung to his clothing until the frenzied flicking started. Then those multiple legs waved and bent and moved all over as the tiny creepy crawlies scrambled for the nearest dark crevice. Clark hated ticks. But learning the mysteries of what was happening in the Helix Lab superseded any arachnophobia. Clark told himself he was running late and would do a quick tick-check in the men's room when he got there.

Clark took out his cell phone to text Elizabeth that he was on the way. He kept moving in the general direction of the lab building that rose above the trees, which seemed to be between one and two miles away. "The average person can walk three miles in an hour," Clark thought to himself. He told himself that if he walked twice as fast as he could, he would possibly walk a mile in 12-15 minutes..... but he would be soaked with sweat if he jogged in the July heat by the time he reached the lab. "On my way, walking, less than 20 out." He texted Elizabeth. He noticed that only one bar indicating the signal reception showed on his cell phone screen, yet the message still seemed to have made it through. As he got within one hundred yards of the building, he suddenly came upon a chain-link fence 12 feet high and topped with three lines of barbed wire. The fence just ran through the woods horizontally, parallel to the lab building. Clark had found his destination and was very close, but had no idea how he would get over the fence. He looked down at his cell phone again, but still, there was no response from Elizabeth.

Clark decided in the interest of time he was going to have to scale the fence if he didn't want to be more than 10 minutes late. As he swung his left leg over the 3 lines of barbed wire that angled outward at the top of the fence, he felt the seam of his pants catch one of the spurs. The fabric ripped slightly, and he realized he was stuck as he yanked his leg away, almost losing his balance from the painful sting of rusted metal scraping his leg. The gash on his leg was on his inner thigh in the flashy part where the seam of men's briefs would be. He could feel a small trickle of warm, sticky blood. If he looked now, it would only delay him, and it didn't feel at all serious.

He sat atop the fence, apprehensive about breaking his 52-year-old ankle should he choose to jump. As he sat and thought, he had a clear view of the building he was headed towards—the Helix Lab. This building was essentially a ten-story monolith that looked like a spiral staircase. He could see that each "step" in the spiral staircase architecture was separate and distinct. Each was the same length and shape, and each had a letter of the alphabet on the face. of each "step." As Clark stared at the odd structure, he realized that while each level had a large letter at the end, there were only four total represented. The letters A, C, G, and T were scattered seemingly in random order. Adenine (A), cytosine (C), guanine (G), and thymine (T) were the base nucleotides that made up all DNA structures—the very software code that made life in the universe. It was surreal seeing something that had seemed like sacred, arcane scientific knowledge reduced to marketing signage serving a for-profit company. Clark smiled to himself. "Leave it to the humans to reduce profound super-science to a cheesy branding utility," he thought.

He landed on a bed of pine needles with a soft thud, forceful enough to cause him to fall down on one knee as shooting pains engulfed his foot and ankle and shot halfway up his shins. "Fuucckk!" Clark gasped. In the silence on the sandy floor of the woods, Clark remained crouched, holding his ankle with both hands and grimacing towards the Helix Lab. Suddenly, a voice floated above the birds, insects, and distant highway noise.

"Need a hand getting back on your feet?" rang out crystal clear from a female larynx. Clark wheeled around to see who was speaking. In doing so, he shifted his weight on his sprained ankle, causing the raw bone bruise pain to surge again. The pain was so strong he lost his balance and fell over on his side, and curled up in the fetal position. He shut his eyes tightly, waiting for the pain wave to subside. Whoever the voice came from would have to wait.

"Oh no! Are you ok? Stay still. I'll help you up," said the voice. Clark did not move, not because he wanted to follow instructions from the disembodied voice but because he simply couldn't stand up yet. He heard the crunch-crunch sound of light footsteps on dried pine needles and could tell someone was walking around very close to him. Once the footsteps stopped, he turned his head to see whoever it was but no matter how he turned he couldn't seem to catch a glimpse of the woman from whom the words had come.

"Who is there?" Clark croaked. Saying anything in this position put a unique strain on his vocal cords making him sound like he was lifting something heavy. Finally, a foot appeared in his eyesight. It was bare flesh with beautifully painted blue paisley toenails. A gold strap separated the big toe from the next one and wrapped around the ankle forming an elaborately woven sandal that crossed a pattern halfway up the shin. It was an elegant and well-dressed foot. Clark rolled on his side slightly to see who it was attached to, but in the blaring mid day sun was blinded by brightness that shot swabs of blue color, blocking any image. He wrestled his head around and blocked out the sun with his hand. He could make out the silhouette of a woman who seemed to be wearing a flowing white gown. He could see the dark silhouette of her feminine physique, the curve of her hips, and the tapering of her legs. As he squinted, he realized she had knelt down beside him. Clark smelled a faint perfume - not overbearing and not something normally found in the woods. It caught him by surprise, and he tried to identify the scent—lavender. Beads of sweat streamed down his forehead. When his eyes adjusted to the direct sunlight, he saw a beautiful young woman with strawberry blonde hair, her warm face, and feminine blue eyes smiling at him. She leaned down close to his face as if she were about to whisper in his ear.

"Hi.." she said in a breathy seductive voice.

"Uhh…hi…," Clark grunted. Her smell, her tone of voice and her pulchritude combined with her utterly insufficient footwear for strolling through the woods of an old army base baffled Clark, who could only lay there trying to collect himself. He felt a pang of despair when he realized he would almost definitely be late for his interview.

"We can stay down here as long as you like," said the woman as her warm breath poured into his ear, causing tiny goosebumps to appear on his skin and making time stand still. Clark almost didn't want to move at all as he realized the unexpected eroticism of the moment.

"A beautiful woman who smells good is whispering into my ear in the middle of the woods…" Clark paused for dramatic effect and shifted his head to finally make eye contact. "Why not stay down here all day?" Clark was being half sarcastic and half flirtatious. It had been a very long time—many years pre-dating his wife's death since he felt like flirting with any woman. Reflecting deeper, he realized he couldn't remember the last time he had even felt a pang of attraction towards a woman. After a certain age, especially if a man is widowed, he starts melting off testosterone like the Greenland Ice Cap during climate change and stops noticing 90% of attractive women. The remaining 10% of hyper-attractive people that rise above the rest only cultivate resentment and despair among graying men that they are no longer in the game or on the hunt. It's like the universe was teasing his battered psyche, reminding him of something beautiful he could never have. That was how Clark had seen the world for the last five years; lost, aimless, slowly decaying, hateful, and angry that the world had kept moving as he lay metaphorically and, now somewhat literally, in a ditch, broken. Clark had been a pale reflection of his former self until that very moment, lying there on the pine needles with a sprained ankle in the July heat when he made eye contact with this woman. Who could she possibly be?

A gentle thin hand wrapped around Clark's. The woman's hair blew in his face as she interlocked her fingers with his. It could have been for support but it felt more sensual. Clark felt like time had suddenly ground to a halt. He answered the urge to speak as a way to distract him from this odd anxiety.

"Uhh, thank you for helping me. I was looking for the gate, and I was running late so I thought jumping the fence would be a good idea. I'm not 12 anymore," Clark stammered then chuckled.

"You are younger than you think," said the woman, her eyes locking with Clark's. "Put your arms around me."

"I'm sorry?" asked Clark, surprised.

"I'm going to help you up. Put your arm around my shoulders and lean on me, and I will help you stand," she smiled as she spoke and flashed a flirtatious smile. Clark did as she asked. As he put her arms around her, he felt an electric yet calm alertness.

"OK. Don't try to put any weight on it. Put your weight on your good leg and me, and we will just hobble back ok?"

She took the first step to demonstrate, and Clark matched her stride like in a three-legged race at summer camp.

"Wow. What did I do to deserve this?" joked Clark.

"You're one of the smart ones, Clark," said the woman. Clark jumped as if a birthday party balloon popped.

"How did you know my name?" he asked, suddenly feeling a caffeine-like rush. "I didn't tell you my name." Clark stopped walking and the woman turned to him. With their arms around each other, she was about three inches from his face. She looked directly into his eyes with a kind, calm expression which gave way to a giggle.

"Ummm…" she flirted teasingly. "It's right on your little notepad that is sticking out of your shirt pocket, right here." She tapped her finger on the top of the leather-bound news pad that his daughter Melody had gotten him when he turned 50. It was a high-end, leather-bound sheathed newspad with his name stenciled in gold. When she was little, Melody always wanted him to read her notes from his news pad that he carried everywhere, and this was a permanent reminder of those carefree inquisitive years. "It says, 'Clark Westfield. Pulitzer Prize Winner and world's greatest dad." The woman laughed again. Clark sighed and felt foolish for being so suspicious, but there was a randomness to this situation in which he suddenly found himself that didn't add up.

"Wow, congratulations!" she said with a big smile.

"Thanks…that was when I was a young reporter."

"No, I meant on the dad part. That's the achievement," said the woman warmly. Clark didn't know what to think. He felt slightly disoriented, his ankle was burning with pain and this woman who had shown up right at the moment he fell in the woods was utterly captivating. No one had said that he was a great father since Mary Lynn was alive.

"Yeah, thanks. My daughter made that for me," said Clark. "She is a great kid."

"I bet she is since she has a Pulitzer Prize winner's genes," said the woman looking directly into Clark's eyes.

"Yeah, right! Genes," Clark said out loud, slightly taken aback at the emphasis she had put on the word "genes." "Look, you are really helping me out here, but I need to get to something called the Helix Lab, and I was trying to cut through here because I think it's that building through those trees." As Clark pointed, the woman spoke.

"Yes, I am taking you to the Helix Lab; it's right past this curve." As she spoke, they rounded a mound covered with oak trees, which opened to a manicured grass area. 50 yards into the grass stood a gleaming silver and black glass wall that was the start of the massive Helix Lab. The two trodded on closer to the building as Clark caught his breath. Once his breathing was even, he spoke.

"Hey, what is your name and why were you on the other side of the fence when I jumped?" Clark panted.

"I wanted to make sure you found the Helix Lab," said the woman matter-of-factly.

"You wanted to… How did you know where I would be or where I was going?" asked Clark.

"Well, aren't you supposed to meet Ms. Cranford here at the Helix Lab?" asked the woman with the same matter of fact cadence.

"Umm yeah, but how…" Clark muttered.

"I knew you would be headed towards the Helix Lab so I came to find you and walk you in." The woman looked at Clark as if she expected him to say thank you.

"Yeah…but how did you know I was going to be jumping the fence in that spot? This is a huge army base." Clark stopped walking,wanting to know who he was speaking with.

"Our drones found you," she answered.

"Your drones?" asked Clark.

"Yes, our greeter drones. When someone has a meeting we send them out and when the guest drives onto the base they guide them in. They were with you over in the village. I'm so glad you got to see our families and talk to some of them," continued the woman nonchalantly.

"You were spying on me? Those drones were yours? Who the hell are you?" gasped Clark.

"Hey, Mrs. Reistad! Oh no! Clark, are you ok?" Elizabeth Cranford hurried up the walkway towards them. "What happened to the two of you?"

"Hey, Liz. I sprained my ankle and this weird lady here was in the woods spying on me with drones and well, here we are…" Clark said sarcastically while smiling sheepishly to let the woman know he was joking. "Seriously, I was trying to make it to our 1 PM appointment to interview that founder or CEO lady—the crazy one that's all over you— at the Helix Lab," continued Clark, pointing to the building. "I sprained my ankle jumping a fence in the woods and this woman helped me back. She still hasn't told me her name" Clark turned towards her indicating he wanted an answer.

"Clark…" said Elizabeth trying to get Clark's attention.

"OK, I'll ask again Who are you?" Clark sounded slightly frustrated.

"Clark," said Elizabeth. "Meet Sara Reistad—she is the founder and CEO of Crisprgen and runs the base here. She is also now part of the family of businesses that include our newspaper. Elizabeth's tone was slightly scolding. Clark smiled, hoping a sheepish look and a laugh would be enough to mitigate him not recognizing the industrial celebrity and backhandedly calling her weird. But as he turned to launch into an acrobatic mea culpa, Sarah's warm eyes locked with his again and it stopped him instantly. He gazed back. He hadn't looked at a woman who looked back at him in that way since he MET his wife. Clark was smitten with a slight sense of unease. But a man crawling out from the dark depths of grief often willingly ignores any cautious apprehension in order to move toward any hint light. Sarah Reistad was a new horizon.

She met his gaze five inches from his face silently, for several seconds and then drew a big smile.

"Hi," she said with a breathy giggle.

"Hi…" said Clark, barely audible.

Elizabeth stood looking at the electricity between the two of them with mouth agape and shook her head.

***

The security entrance to the Helix Lab was elaborate and intimidating. Large plexiglass cylinders had scanners that zipped around like revolving doors firing off TSA-grade x-ray images of anything inside. Clark instinctively started to empty his pockets, removing his cell phone, then realized he was still supporting himself on Sarah Reistad tucked under his shoulder looking like a drunk prom date. Five security guards stood in front of the airport-style scanners and stared directly at Clark and Sarah. A tall woman in a metallic purple lycra body suit who was carrying an iPad-like a clipboard walked out from behind the scanners. She had a concerned look on her face and made a beeline for Sarah.

"Ms. Sarah, are you okay?" she asked, not acknowledging Clark or Elizabeth who stood three feet behind them. Elizabeth craned her neck to get a better look at this odd woman who was aloof and robotic in her movements.

"I'm perfectly fine, Allele," said Sarah Reistad, chuckling and gently moving Clark's arm over her head so he could stand normally.

"Do we need a de-con unit? I have one ready upstairs," continued Allele.

"Decon what?" blurted Elizabeth, And Sarah laughed while shaking her head.

"Leave it to my Allele to be ready to fix any challenge—even evolutionary ones," said Sarah joyously.

"Umm,hi. I'm the one that's actually hurt," said Clark softly and sheepishly. As soon as he finished speaking, Allele turned abruptly, almost on one heel, and walked briskly back behind the conveyor belt scanner, never making eye contact or acknowledging Clark or Elizabeth. "I guess I won't be needing a decon unit then, either. OK, well, thanks anyway," Clark said, his voice rising in volume to indicate his frustration as Allele sped away. He turned to Sarah with a look of confusion and said facetiously:

"She must have been a spectacular restaurant hostess." .

"Oh well, this particular Allele has instructions to take care of only me. Let's get you something to wrap that ankle and something to drink," said Sarah. "But for that, we will need a different Allele," she said and then broke into a joyous full-throated laugh. Clark and Elizabeth looked at each other, trying to process the bizarre scene and strange individuals that came with it. Sarah led Clark through the large metal detectors and security station without asking him to empty his pockets, or checking him in any other way. The five security guards stood expressionless and motionless as Sarah led Clark and Elizabeth into the first few yards of a corridor and stopped at a doorway on the right side. Instead of the door opening, the wood grain and surface suddenly changed, becoming translucent, then foggily transparent, and finally crystal clear,. Rather than swing open like a normal door, the door evaporated into thin air. Clark stopped, hesitant to walk through the doorway at first.

"What just happened?" Clark asked, pointing to the threshold.

"There was just a door right there. Right?" asked Elizabeth, equally perplexed.

Sarah walked three steps through the doorway and twirled around to face them. "Hmmm, was there a door? I didn't see one," Sarah teased, sounding like a 10-year-old performing a magic trick for her parents before laughing once more. "Ms. Cranford you thought you saw a door…we all did… but what you saw was a holographic projection from these micro LED halogens here in the door jam." Sarah ran her finger along the molding of the doorway, showing four black dots that were recessed holes where a tiny hologram projector was installed. "Isn't this cool?" Sarah Reistad's smile was epic and unstoppable.

"Cool? Yeah, I guess it's cool." Clark thought aloud. "Seems damn expensive though. We could go to Walmart and get a combination bike lock and a plywood door, and I'll save you thousands of dollars. If you have this technology, why are you wasting it on a conference room door?" Clark further mused, and Sarah predictably offered a fresh laugh.

"Oh, we didn't spend anything. Those hologram doors were already here when we moved into the base. The old Fort Monmouth had these installed in the '70s," explained Sarah matter-of-factly. "We just left them in place because they are so cool!" There was a carefree childlike quality to her inflection. "Sit down over here." She motioned to a couch against the wall that ran the entire perimeter of the room. Clark hopped over on one leg and fell down on the couch. He leaned back and stretched out his leg. Elizabeth stayed standing, and Sarah knelt in front of Clark as if she were going to examine his ankle.

"So you are my 1 PM interview?" Clark said, looking up at the ceiling as Sarah pulled a chair from the conference table and gently lifted his leg to elevate it. Clark winced as the stabs of pain ebbed and flowed when his leg found a comfortable position to bear its weight.

"Ms. Reistad, we can reschedule the interview if you like. We have plenty of flexibility. And Clark, you can rest while Ms. Reistad and I sit here at the conference table," chimed Elizabeth. Clark shot her a look indicating he wasn't fond of that idea.

"Ms. Reistad, your rescheduling options are 2 PM today, as well as 3 PM, 4 PM, and 5 PM," interrupted Allele robotically as she suddenly appeared in the doorway, making eye contact only with Sarah.

"Hi Allele, I'll just sit down over here. Don't worry about me." Clark held his hand high above his head and gave a flutter wave to add to the sarcasm. Allele still didn't look at him. "What is *with* her?" Clark thought to himself.

"No Allele, we will be fine doing the interview now. I cleared my afternoon so those empty schedule slots were actually reserved for this," Sarah smiled as she spoke, keeping her eyes on Clark. Elizabeth, seated at the conference table, looked at Sarah kneeling before Clark and thought that rather than her looking at her lead investigative reporter on assignment interviewing a major business tycoon, the scene looked more like the cover of a dime store romance novel. She cleared her throat and broke the silence.

"Ahem," gurgled Elizabeth. "Sarah, do you mind if we record this interview?" she asked, removing an old microcassette recorder from her purse and placing it on the conference table. Sarah Reistad turned and looked directly at Elizabeth.

"Allele was planning to take you on a tour of the campus and our laboratories, Ms. Cranford," said Sarah Reistad. At that particular moment, Allele turned her head abruptly and made eye contact with Elizabeth for the first time.

"Ms. Cranford, please come with me," said Allele, without any expression on her face. She held her head as if she were waiting for a response. Elizabeth turned to Sarah Reistad, looking perplexed.

"I can go on a tour later; I think I'll stay and help with the interview," said Elizabeth sternly, looking straight at Sarah Reistad to let her know she wasn't going anywhere.

"We can postpone the interview. I'll stay here with Clark and get his ankle feeling better. We have an urgent care clinic here on the base, and I can have some of the staff come over here and take a look. Please go on the tour with Allele, in the interest of time." Sarah smiled smugly as she politely asked Elizabeth to leave. Elizabeth didn't know what to think. The woman who was her interview subject also was a major corporate stakeholder at her newspaper company with access to all managerial supervision levels above Elizabeth was clearly trying to manipulate her lead reporter in a flirtatious way, and it bothered her at a visceral level. As she sat calmly choosing her next words, Clark caught her eye and tilted his head and bobbed it towards the door in the common gesture people use when they are telling someone what direction to go without using their hands. Elizabeth was infuriated and attempted to let Clark know with a gaze of cold steel only an angry black woman could manifest. Clark glared right back and then turned his eyes toward Sarah as if to say "Go ahead. I've got this."

"Hey Liz, I need a minute here and since I'm not going to be able to stroll around the campus, you're going to have to be our eyes on the tour," said Clark, purposely exaggerating the strain in his voice. Elizabeth realized there was a reason Clark wanted her to leave them alone. On any other story assignment, this would have been immediately obvious, and Elizabeth wouldn't have thought twice about being insulted by Clark's suggestion. But at the moment, she didn't know if Clark was acting out of brilliance or lust. But ultimately, she trusted Clark and had spent her career obeying his instructions, and he hadn't been wrong yet. But today was different. There was a very strange vibe in the air inside this mysterious Crisprgen company, and most significantly, Elizabeth hadn't seen Clark this alive and animated since long before his wife's death. This odd woman had made the sound of Clark's pulse deafening, and Elizabeth knew she had to yield.

"Fine. Good idea. I'll go with Allele and come back later. You get Clark's ankle treated and I'll be in touch." Elizabeth was expertly capable of being rational, but that didn't mean she couldn't simultaneously be ice cold. Clark gave her a frustrated look as she stood up and abruptly walked over to the doorway where Allele still stood motionless. The two of them disappeared from the doorway, and Clark and Sarah Reistad were left alone in the conference room as the holographic projectors turned back on and the entryway returned to the lifelike image of a real door. Clark looked at Sarah, who remained perfectly silent as she looked back at him. He couldn't tell whether she was waiting for him to speak, and he wasn't quite sure what to say. But there was a warmth to this silence that he saw no need to disrupt. Sarah started to remove Clark's shoe and was gently touching his foot and ankle while watching his face to identify the pain spots.

Clark needed to get information from Sarah as well as explanations on some of the issues he had discovered with Amy back at the village, but he wasn't as aggressively worked up as he usually was before a typical investigative interview. Instead, he felt butterflies in his stomach and an intensely growing attraction to Sarah Reistad He found his awkward-sounding voice.

"That's uhh…that's really nice," he said quietly. "You have a nice healing touch." Clark couldn't believe he just let that cheesy line escape his mouth. He braced for embarrassment, prepared to blame his flirting on the intense pain of a sprained ankle. But he was met with Sarah's warm smile and deep eyes again.

"Thank you, it's the Neanderthal in me," she said quietly. Despite no one else being in the room, both Sarah and Clark were whispering.

"Oh, OK." nodded Clark. "Then please don't club me to death, and I'll have a wooly mammoth sandwich." Sarah erupted into laughter so hard she sat back with her butt on the ground and took a moment to let her posture be consumed by the shaking guffaws. Clark had not made an attractive woman laugh in a VERY long time.

"Quite the opposite!" replied Sarah. "Most people don't know that Neanderthals were loving and cared for one another during sickness or injury and they also buried their dead. In fact, most of our romantic skills come from the Neanderthals, as they had a brain structure that produced much more Oxytocin than Cro Magnons." Sarah smiled as she finished speaking. "Let's go to the top of the Helix shall we?" Sarah grabbed Clark's arm and put it around her shoulder once again before hobbling him towards the door. Immediately outside the conference room door was an elevator that he hadn't noticed on the way in. In the elevator there was a crutch leaning against the back wall, and an index card taped to the front that said "For Clark Westfield."

"Oh good, your crutch is here," said Sarah as she hopped Clark into the elevator. Clark grabbed the crutch and immediately started to lift his arm from Sarah's shoulders as he stood up straight and balanced himself on the support. Sarah pulled his arm back down over her shoulders and looked up at him with her beaming smile. "Not so fast," she whispered. Clark could have assumed she was flirting with him, but was she?

The elevator soared upwards. There were no buttons on the inside and no way to tell how many floors the building had. He felt a slight altitude pressure in his ears, the kind you felt in New York City skyscrapers. As the elevator hummed higher, Clark realized he had no idea where they were going or what the plan for the interview and tour was. However, he absolutely loved being in the elevator with his arm around this beautiful enigmatic woman for however precious few seconds he had in this spiritual reprieve. He looked over at her, and she met his gaze and smiled as if she knew what he was thinking.

"So where are we?" Clark tried to ask where they were going, but Sarah put her finger to her mouth in a shushing motion, indicating to Clark that he shouldn't speak. The door opened and a hot wind hit their face. They stepped out of the elevator onto a shiny stainless steel floor with a 360-degree open view. There were no glass windows, just open space. They were at the top of the Helix Lab tower building and the elevator shaft was the central support for the giant building. The shaft had dozens of steel cantilevers resembling steps on a spiral staircase. Each one was a different floor and served a different function for the lab.

Each side of each floor had signage in the hallways with a corresponding letter from the DNA sequence, which determined whether one worked in an A, a C, T, or G DNA base name.

But the top floor where Sarah had taken Clark was more like a rooftop with only a partial covering. There was no furniture in the space they stood. Just, wind, sun, steel, and a panoramic view of Ft. Monmouth and the Atlantic Ocean off in the distance.

"Quite the view, isn't it?" asked Sarah with her arms outstretched. She spun around very slowly like a whirling dervish, and Clark just stood and looked at her. He felt utterly fascinated by this odd woman.

"So what is it you actually do here at Crispergen? I know you do standard simple consumer genetic reports, but it seems like a much bigger operation. Seems like there is a lot of money generated that is making everything work down here and you seem to be using the old base housing for dozens of families which means a lot of overhead. Also, I spoke with a few of the residents. They seem to like the company and enjoy living here, but in learning that they were recruited and paid generously, That all adds up to significantly more expense. And this beautiful building must have cost a fortune. Is the consumer genetic business that lucrative that it could offset all these costs or do you have a strategy and date to become profitable? I would imagine that biotech investors are an antsy bunch." Clark stopped talking. Sarah hadn't interrupted him, she simply smiled and listened wide-eyed and that had managed to grind the famous Clark Westfield interrogation locomotive to a halt. Her demeanor and effect were both very unusual. She was beautiful, warm, and friendly, yet her mannerisms were awkward and oddly timed compared to most people's behavior..

"Oh Clark, you are asking all the wrong questions," sighed Sarah charmingly.

"I am?" countered Clark. "What questions should I ask?"

"Well, I have no desire to talk about the business," said Sarah softly. "You all get it wrong…so wrong…you focus on the wrong things…always." Sarah was babbling to herself that Clark didn't quite know what to make of her pacing and repeating phrases in what looked like an imaginary conversation.

"Tell you what, can we go back downstairs and I'll sit down? I'll ask all the right questions, I promise…I just need to sit though," pleaded Clark. The bright sunny rooftop and the hot summer breeze were uncomfortable and distracting. To get any meaningful answers out of Sarah at all would take total focus and aplomb. Not because Clark had not encountered strange evasive geniuses who had trouble making sense, but because he knew there was an elephant in the room:

his sudden, unexpected, and somewhat inconvenient attraction to Sarah Reistad, and it seemed mutual. The story was too important to Elizabeth and her career for Clark to be asleep at the wheel. He owed her as much— he hadn't trained her professionally to eventually be his boss, only to fall down on assignment in a splattering of teenage boy attraction. Yet, Clark felt a faint undercurrent of suspicion that he couldn't explain. He sensed Sarah knew it, too, but she was completely absorbed in making sure Clark saw and wrote the story she needed him to write. Romantic feelings, especially when they appear as daybreak after several years of nocturnal grief, are the most inconvenient and uncontrollable variables a reporter could encounter. They killed stories and got guys fired. Clark knew this from personal experience. And he couldn't help having a bad taste in his mouth as he thought about the way Sarah had shooed Elizabeth out onto the tour. He would have to square up with Elizabeth later.

They hopped back into the elevator, and Clark braced himself for the long ride down, but instead, the elevator descended only one floor, and the door opened. There were no buttons inside or outside the elevator, and Sarah could sense Clark was trying to figure out how it was controlled and how she had selected a floor. The doors opened to a spectacular room that was the entire floor. All the walls were floor-to-ceiling windows. They were just below the roof in what would be the top penthouse area of most tall buildings. This was

Sarah Reistad's office, but it had a studio kitchen area and dining room table on one side. A king-size bed was in one corner. In the middle of the room were several odd pieces of furniture. An oversized square velvet ottoman, a small couch shaped like a pair of human lips, and a giant wedge covered in purple velvet that looked like a ramp made up the collection. Sarah led Clark over to the large purple ottoman that could seat a basketball team and motioned for him to sit down. He sank into the soft fabric with a sigh of relief. Despite the ottoman being gigantic, Sarah sat so close to Clark that the weight of her body dipped into the depression Clark had made with his seated frame, and they found themselves leaning against one another side by side. Clark could feel her body warmth through her flowing white gown and the curve of her hips against his. If he didn't speak soon this was going to get awkward very quickly. He turned to her and said:

"Tell me the right questions to ask, Ms. Reistad. I want to know who you are and what makes you tick. Also, I have a bunch of notes from earlier, and a few things came up…" Clark stopped speaking as Sarah simply looked at him expressionless. "Sarah, what is the Passport Project?" he asked. Her eyes lit up.

"I'm so happy you got to spend some time with our resident families," she said.

"Yeah, nice people. Several people we met talked about this Passport Project, and they all seemed to be working on it here," Clark qualified. Just then the elevator door opened, and Allele marched in like a robot trudging through snow. She had a tray with a Dixie cup and a syringe. She sat down next to Clark and picked up the syringe in her hand. He looked at her curiously and without asking, Allele took Clark's hand, stretched out his arm, bent down very close to the skin, and inserted the small needle into the back of his hand. Rather than jump, Clark turned to Sarah, amused and confused, and said, "What exactly is she doing?" as blood filled the glass barrel. Allele took the first vial off and replaced it with the second, which immediately began filling. "I need an ace bandage and some ice, not a blood transfusion," said Clark, trying to be humorous.

"Almost done. Don't worry, everyone is nervous the first time. No matter what you hear or how this goes, there are solutions, always remember that!" Sarah's eyes lit up excitedly.

"Done what? What solutions? Seriously, why is she drawing my blood right now?" As the question escaped Clark's lips, it suddenly dawned on him how strange, and slightly rude it was to take someone's blood without asking first. However, Clark had put up no resistance or said anything though.

"Oh, don't worry. We are sequencing your genome quickly, and then afterward, you and I can talk about the results. It will be the best way to demonstrate what we do here and what the Passport Project is," explained Sarah.

"I didn't ask you to sequence my genome, Sarah," said Clark, suddenly slightly more aware. "Actually, I've deliberately avoided services like yours because I worry about where my data will wind up. I'm not sure I believe consumer genetics are above reproach, Ms. Reistad. Assuming I'd give up my genomic information is a presumption on your part." Clark was more annoyed than he sounded, but something about Sarah's presence kept a blanket of calm over the vibe. Allele finished drawing Clark's blood and stood up with no expression.

"Thank you, Allele. Bring it back when you are done," Sarah said to her.

"No, don't do anything. Don't run my genome. Please don't bother because I'm not giving you my permission!" Clark looked at both of them trying to show that he was adamant about not having his genome sequenced while still sounding calm and friendly.

"Oh, but we don't need your permission, Clark. Don't you think various parties have sequenced your genome already without you even knowing?"

"No, not really," replied Clark. "I've never gone to any of those services, and I've certainly never told anyone to go get me my genome report."

"That's what you think," said Sarah. "Would you even know? Allele took your blood, and we are talking about it, but what about the saliva on your water cup downstairs? We could have gotten your sequence off those cells you left on the lip of the cup. How do you know that every time you gave blood, even a finger stick, a healthcare professional did not sell your medical record with your genomic sequence to the highest bidder? They could have a complete predictive status report on your entire pathology, congenital conditions, and overall health. They could do whatever they wanted with it, and you would never know."

"Well, I suppose you are right, it's certainly a possibility, but yes, I'm sure that hasn't happened," said Clark. He was starting to feel frustrated that Sarah was somehow avoiding the direct questions he wanted to ask her. "Frankly, it sounds like a conspiracy theory that came out of the anti-vax camp."

"Ok, let me put it another way." Sarah tilted her head as if she were in deep thought. Clark discreetly reached into his pocket and took his phone halfway out, he deftly typed in the security code, opened the voice record app, and hit the red button. Sarah might be less guarded if she didn't know she was being recorded. "Let's say you are the captain of a ship—a big ocean liner, and you suddenly see a distress call to a small island where 100 sailors are stranded, and you go to pick them up." Clark nodded out of courtesy but didn't see where she was headed with the analogy. "But you can't have anyone on board that currently has or may develop high blood pressure. What would you do?"

"You ask everyone their blood pressure and the ones with a high reading stay behind," said Clark in a matter-of-fact tone.

"Yeah, but no marooned sailor is going to be told they can't board the rescue ship. They would just assume kill you and your crew rather than be left on the island. You can't put your men at risk like that, so you would have to test them without them knowing, then select the appropriate ones." Sarah looked pleased with the explanation she had given.

"What, and then send another ship for them down the road? I'm not sure I follow," Clark pressed.

"It doesn't matter if there was a future rescue ship or not. My point was that you could only take healthy people, and it would still be hard for them to survive, so only the strongest would make it," said Sarah.

"OK, so the strongest survive. Darwin is calling in his copyright royalty on that phrase," jabbed Clark.

"No - in fact, it's the exact opposite of Charles Darwin's theorem of the survival of the fittest," said Sarah, seeming pleased at Clark's engagement and references. "Charles Darwin proved that species can genetically drift and evolve into other species and life forms as they adapt to their environment. Those with genes favorable to the circumstances survive, and those without, die. Simple, but there is no conscious decision on the part of the species that is adapting. It's simply the luck of being in the right place at the right time."

"OK, what does that have to do with the island and why you took my blood?" asked Clark.

"Because that's the Passport Project." Sarah smiled broadly as she made the declaration. Clark shook his head as if he didn't understand.

"Darwin's theory of evolution wasn't driven by choice—it was driven by circumstances. The Passport Project *is* the captain and crew determining who will be permitted on the rescue boat and who won't based on their potential survival strength revealed by their genetics."

"So the Passport Project decides who gets rescued and who dies on the island? I see. And other than a backdrop for a bad dystopian movie with Kevin Costner playing a mailman, how does this resemble real life?" Clark's sarcasm was cracking through. "I mean who would get to decide that? What government would have the assignment?"

"No governments are involved, and it would be up to the people," Sarah said very seriously. "Once we finalize the Passport sequence, it will be elective for those who qualify."

"When you are finished? You sound like you are doing this already," said Clark, surprised.

"Well, we have been working very hard and we hope that by next year—"

"Wait! You're serious? So what is it exactly that you are doing? I thought this was a consumer genetic testing company that told you if you had genes for baldness or eczema or some other harmless bullshit. When you say 'Passport,' a passport for what and for whom do you need it?" Suddenly Clark felt slight goosebumps and, as the energy heightened energy in the air between them. Sarah's expression changed from one of warmth and flirtation to one of rigid seriousness.

"Crisprgen is a consumer genetic testing company, yes. We've collected samples from more than 2 million people so far around the world. We have the largest gene library of anyone."

"Gene library?" interjected Clark.

"Yes, it's a database of all the genomes that we decoded for our customers. Obviously, we were able to identify very specific alleles for all kinds of pathological markers, not just diseases. And we know we will have to create standards for the Great Reset, and that's the Passport Project," said Sarah seriously.

"The Great Reset? Someone mentioned that back at the village. I played along like I knew what they meant, but what exactly is the Great Reset?" asked Clark.

"The Great Reset is the moment we fall from the great historical precipice on which our world is teetering. Come on Clark, I don't have to tell you. We can't feed or care for half of the 7 billion people already on the planet. The few resources left that are allocated to serve the wealthy in a few highly developed countries and will certainly be depleted soon. Climate change will prevent us from fishing and farming, leading to a global famine. Entire continents will endure person-on-person violence as people kill each other for food." Clark grimaced as she continued speaking. "Another scenario is a military escalation that doesn't even need to use weapons of mass destruction. A few large-scale regional conflicts and proxy wars, combined with China's desire for global hegemony and Russia spiraling out of control as a failed klepto state with nuclear weapons, would make the risk of a third world war a likely scenario. Do I need to go over what a global pandemic would do this time around? Covid had a kill rate of about 1% at its most deadly. Look at how people panicked, look at the resentment and mistrust the pandemic exposed from misinformation and political posturing. There won't be a coordinated sensible response next time— it will be outright pandemonium with crazy paramilitary groups fighting over everything. What would that world look like if the pathogen had a kill rate of 90% like Ebola?" Sarah looked more and more serious as she spoke.

"Wow, you really know how to cheer a guy up," snarked Clark. "You forgot the asteroid—you know the one Bruce Willis got to ride and Aerosmith got to sing about? If you are making an Armageddon shopping list you gotta throw the asteroid in there." Clark was pleased with his wit and smiled, but Sarah kept a look of steel and found none of it funny.

"My point, Clark, is that there is a convergence of all these crises and challenges happening at once. The human race can't help itself when it's still fighting over resources, religion, and politics. And there is simply not enough time. Do the math. There is no way that at least one of these major crises doesn't unfold in the near future and reduce the earth's population by at least half, maybe more."

"OK, so you are the ultimate doomsday prepper? Why do you need a passport for this joyous event?" asked Clark trying to make sense of it.

"Because whoever is left should be the strongest and the best. In everything - mind, body and spirit—all of which are determined by genetics. This is the human race's opportunity to branch off. So we have the catalog of traits for each gene in the genome. We have discovered and logged variations and trends on specific alleles for all the major chronic diseases, mental health disorders, and musculoskeletal features. From all that information— from all those millions of genomes that we have sequenced for our customers, we will determine what the ideal genomic sequence for happiness is after the Reset. Those will be the humans in whom we will invest the remaining resources as the reset starts. In other words, Darwin would be impressed that we are charting our own genetic course and you have to *earn* your way forward through the evolutionary tree." Sarah finally smiled. Clark was stunned. He didn't know what to think.

"Umm,…ok.. so first question… is when you say 'we' will determine the passport criteria, do you mean the government? Health care professionals? Who?" Clark glanced down at his phone to make sure it was still recording.

"Well, it's a global network of concerned individuals. It's not state-sponsored," said Sarah evasively.

"Oh right. So it's rich folks trying to preserve their privilege through the evolutionary fork in the road to ensure whatever new species they become is still wealthy?" said Clark bitingly. Sarah tilted her head and thought a minute, not realizing Clark was being sarcastic again. She gave him a serious answer.

"Hmm, If Crisprgen masters germline therapy, a person's genome could be manipulated. This would bestow an advantage like longer life to the individual and their children. Those palindromic repeats would enhance the patient's genome. Initially, it will be expensive and would probably only be available to wealthier people who then tend to pair up with other "enhanced" individuals. This would eventually lead to a new species of humans. An improvement on Homo sapiens the same way we were an improvement on the Neanderthals, who were an improvement on the Cro Magnon who were an improvement on the Heidelbergensis, and so on. This process is started artificially by tinkering with genes, but reinforced, consolidated, and accelerated by cultural and socioeconomic differences. So yes, it will be the wealthier humans that can afford the Passport."

"You can buy one? I don't understand," Clark was barely able to speak he was so stunned by Sarah's description of creating a new species of human.

"Well, once we finish the passport genome criteria, to get one you would have to pay for however many CRISPR therapy procedures you need to meet the requirements. But once you did then you would have your Passport," she said. Clark looked down to make sure his phone was recording one more time.

"OK, just let me get this straight," Clark said, as Sarah nodded in anticipation.

"You are a retail consumer genetics testing company that is researching the genomes they sequence to come up with the ideal genome that would serve as a passport to get you in a privileged clique of rich people who can afford to take a luxury cruise instead of enduring the apocalypse? Then over time, by definition, those rich survivors with their genetic enhancements would become a different species than the humans we are now?"

"Excellent summary Professor Westfield!" Sarah said joyously. "And because we can manipulate the genome in a living person, it will only take a few generations to genetically drift into another species. In nature it takes many millennia, but with deliberate gene editing, this will be just a couple of births away." Sarah sounded like she had discovered the cure for cancer.

"Good god!" muttered Clark. "So how do you anticipate what genes we are going to need down the road in the future?"

"Well, we are focused right now on two—the two qualities that we know we will always need to enhance as long as we evolve." Sarah paused. "Longevity and intelligence. Those are the two most important things for our life form, now and forever. So, we have the Hayflick lab where we study how to extend the life of cells. We are making great progress. And we are recruiting and hiring people with hyper-high intelligence to identify and cultivate their genes."

"Cultivate? You are cultivating genes for intelligence here?" asked Clark incredulously.

"Yes, and for longevity! Isn't it great?" Sarah was gleeful. Clark felt sick to his stomach.

"And these intelligence genes…the individuals you harvest them from…would they happen to be high school kids?" asked Clark.

"Yes! They make the best associates. They are unencumbered by family and career, they understand the urgency and the promise, and being so young, they have the most to gain from the Passport Project succeeding. They are also likely to have the most need for it. And in exchange for the genetic snippets we identify and collect from their genomes, we will compensate them and their families. They are, after all, giving the human race a life jacket."

Clark thought a minute wondering if what he just heard was legal, ethical, moral, or even a good idea at all. But there would be plenty of time for examining that. For now, the infrastructure of this company Sarah Reistad had built had caused great disruption in his community, and he had just discovered why. He had also discovered what had happened to the missing high school students and their families. He had his story.

"So….." Clark looked right in Sarah's eyes. "You've got the smart ones…"

***

Chapter 6

Elizabeth Cranford glanced down at her phone for the third time in ten seconds. Still no reply from Clark. She had texted him five times asking him if she could return to the Helix Lab where he was still with their interview subject, Sarah Resitad. But no message had been received in return. There were even three dots to indicate a message was being prepared to send through, yet they vanished with no transmission. She turned away to be as inconspicuous as possible from her escort tour guide, Allele. The tall stern woman had mannerisms that were robotic and sterile. Her mouth hadn't cracked a smile since Elizabeth was introduced to her an hour ago. Clark's voicemail picked up on the first ring, indicating his phone was either off, engaged, or forwarded directly to voicemail. It also meant that Elizabeth had no idea whether the company founder and CEO and her mentor and star reporter wished for her to return or not.

Clark had been strong when his wife died. His widow Mary Lynn had been very good to Elizabeth over the years. She had earned a metaphorical big sister status in Elizabeth's life cast of loved ones. She had never told Clark how Mary Lynn had taken her aside and assured her that Clark thought she had everything it took to become a great reporter when she was a rookie. Elizabeth also never told Clark to just what degree his late wife had helped her with dating scenarios and other matters in which women needed the support of other women. And when their scumbag managing editor Sean Caldwell began showing up on her jogging route every morning and later on her doorstep one night, it was Mary Lynn she had called first. The next morning, Clark's widow had appeared at the office with the explanation that Clark had left his lunch on the counter at home. She then walked into Caldwell's office, shut the door and blinds, and emerged less than 60 seconds later. She had breezed past Elizabeth's desk on the way out and simply said: "Situation solved." Caldwell never spoke to her about anything but work after that day and at a fraction of the previous frequency.

Clark had confronted her death with his fierce spirit and accepted the reality of her last months. As far as being widowed was concerned, Elizabeth had seen Clark try to slay that dragon as well with his usual unflappable toughness and stoicism. She had looked after him in his grief by becoming friends with his daughter Melody, and now and then stepped in as a big sister or surrogate mother. As an archetype, Clark was the "Thoughts and Feelings" version of the Marlboro Man —silent, dignified, confident, introverted, and aloof while dying a slow lonely death inside. But no amount of Pulitzers or Peabodies or blockbuster stories could mitigate the crush of grief even a tiny bit. It had been a long cold winter of bereavement that had lasted several years. That is until today.

Elizabeth hadn't seen Clark smile freely or laugh organically since the day Mary Lynn had called her to tell her about her circumstances. She had called Elizabeth before she told Clark anything about her illness to shore up his support network, anticipating he would internalize the pain and never speak of his suffering. Mary Lynn had been correct. But over time, Elizabeth had broken through and managed to help Clark process some of the more difficult elements of watching one's spouse die. Elizabeth and Clark spent many moments in the basement stairwell of the office as Clark sat beside her catatonic or sobbing. Whenever he was missing around the office, she knew where to look and there he always was. Many times she would walk down the stairs and simply sit next to him. She never spoke, the only sounds were the sporadic slurpings of his sobs. Elizabeth never told anyone of those many visits to the stairwell, and she and Clark had never acknowledged them to one another. And that was okay between friends of their nature. The deepest devotions can't be put into words most times, and the deepest acts of love can be completely unspoken.

So earlier today when Elizabeth saw Clark with his arm around Sarah Reistad, it had stopped her dead in her tracks. When she had seen the electricity between them, she knew immediately that Clark's long cold winter of grieving had come to a thaw. But whether Clark had truly met and connected with someone who brought back some of his old self or whether he was being manipulated by a brilliant CEO with an agenda, well, that jury was still out.

"Excuse me, Allele?" said Elizabeth, trying to get the odd woman's attention. "Allele?" called Elizabeth again. No response came as Allele simply stared off into the distance as if she were looking at something far away. Elizabeth moved a few steps closer to her. "Hi, I don't want to interrupt you or whatever you are doing here but I am going to go back to the Helix Lab and check on Clark's ankle," she said, though she believed Allele was not listening to a word she was saying.

"The Leopard Six drone has a two-second lead on the flying chariot. It will have to make up almost two seconds on the clock if it is going to stay on the leaderboard," Aelle said without moving her head or looking in Elizabeth's direction.

"I'm sorry?" said Elizabeth, slightly confused. "I'm not sure what you are referring to, but I want to go back to the Helix Lab, so if you could just tell me which of these access paths lead back quickest, I could just show myself." Elizabeth realized communication with AlleleAllele was somewhat futile, though it wasn't apparent why. She turned and picked one of the three paths that led away from where they stood and began to walk.

"It's the leaderboard report from the drone race playoffs happening in the village," said Allele, loudly in her robotic monotone without moving her head and still staring off into the distance.

"How can you see through the trees? Where are you even looking? What leaderboard?" asked Elizabeth confused as she peered to see what Allele was referring to. She saw nothing.

Somewhat baffled, Elizabeth walked back a few steps towards Allele and stood about three feet away. She noticed that her right ear lobe had a black wire protruding from it that looked like an electronic device. On the top of her ear, she noticed something the size of a Q tip that she thought must be an antenna, perhaps for a cellular phone ear bud. Elizabeth realized she must be hearing something from that device and ignoring her. She turned and strode down the closest path.

She heard Allele's footsteps behind her trying to keep up. Elizabeth walked faster. Soon Allele passed her on the right side, her smooth lycra body suit rubbed against Elizabeth as she whooshed by. "Please follow me," rang her robotic cadence. Elizabeth smirked to herself. "Sycophants are always the little weirdos who can't cut it elsewhere." she thought.

"Hey Allele, what is it like working for Ms. Reistad?" called Elizabeth to her guide who was now walking briskly five steps ahead. The path was winding through the thick scrub pine of the Ft. Monmouth base. As they rounded a curve and Allele continued to ignore Elizabeth's questions, they came before a large chain link fence. It was double the height of most conventional hurricane fences and had several strands of electric cattle wire that seemed to crackle with livestock-grade electricity. Above the electric fence strands were several rows of razor wire. They were at one of the main entrances to the base. A guard walked out of a glass and aluminum phone booth and walked towards the two of them.

"Oh, we aren't at the lab. How do we get to the lab, Allele?" Elizabeth let out a sigh as she spoke, indicating her frustration.

"I only have instructions to take you to the exit, Ms. Cranford," said Allele as she bowed her head.

"OK, but I need to go to the Helix Lab," said Elizabeth slowly, trying with everything she had to still sound polite.

"I'm sorry, Ms. Cranford. I'm instructed to bring you here," she said without looking up.

"Allele, you know I have a meeting with Mrs. Reistad for an interview and my colleague…er…senior reporter is waiting for us. Did someone tell you to bring me elsewhere?" Elizabeth had a suspicion in her gut that she didn't want to acknowledge. But deep down she suspected that Clark had outmaneuvered her once again and ensured his romantic trajectory could continue uninterrupted. Just then the security guard spoke.

"Hello. I have instructions to open the gate for one civilian exit." He held up a clipboard and flipped the top two sheets. "An Elizabeth Cranford. Is that you, ma'am?" He asked and looked up at Elizabeth. She reflexively nodded with a look of astonishment on her face. "Ok, come with me, and I'll roll back the gate." Elizabeth stood stunned and turned to look at Allele.

"So, to be clear, was it Mr. Westfield that sent through the gate opening order?" asked Elizabeth looking at both Allele and the security guard. Allele looked up at Elizabeth with a quizzical expression on her face.

"Who is Mr. Westfield?" she askedAllele, sounding bewildered.

"Interesting…" Elizabeth thought to herself. And just like that, she turned and exited through the gate, leaving Ft. Monmouth with Clark and Sarah still in the lab.

***

It's an inherently uncomfortable moment when another person gazes into your eyes, and you haven't the faintest clue as to their motivation. Clark sat trying to collect himself as his interview subject, Sarah Reistad simply stared at him with a warm smile in complete silence. Clark wrestled within himself as to why he was so reticent to accept her warm attention as benign. He told himself that it must be grief's toxic echo that called out to widowed men when they met a gaze as inviting as Sarah's. He knew deep down that in order to truly heal and move on with his life, he would have to eventually allow himself to be enchanted by a woman like Sarah if fate brought them to the same point in the universe. And here he was. Yet, that mythical, elusive, storied point in space-time where he had the opportunity to consciously climb up another stratum on the grief pyramid was a much more confusing juncture than he had anticipated. Sarah was turning on his nerve receptors and causing hormonal secretions in Clark's brain, which hadn't happened in years. All of Clark's self-talk in those dark moments when he didn't know whether he would drive home or off a bridge had predicted and prepared him for this precise instance when a woman's gaze would appear like a Spring thaw - and yet, under all of it was a nagging feeling of unease. Clark kept feeling that underneath her warmth, her gorgeous presence and aura was metaphorical yellow police tape ribbon beyond which lay something sinister. But for now, he convinced himself, there was no reason to break her gaze.

"How is your ankle?" she asked Clark, who was seated on a sprawling couch.

"I'm..umm, my ankle is fine…getting better, thanks." Clark felt clumsy speaking around her. There is something in the pathology of the adolescent-grade crush that causes the muscles of the jaw and mouth to tense up, making it hard to speak clearly and causing voices to squeak. "So, can we get down to business for a moment? I need to go through a formal interview with you, and I'm sorry my ankle distracted us but can we—"

Sarah interrupted him.

"Clark, we have all the time in the world. Ask me anything you wish." Sarah said warmly and flirtatiously. Clark caught himself and mentally found his journalist's cognitive reconnaissance antennae. It was a technique he'd had to perfect over the years when he found himself drawn to an interview subject or a source. It wasn't unusual, and Clark knew deep down when he was attracted to an interview subject that he couldn't be objective whether he acknowledged it or not. He decided he would question her rapid-fire style and purposely sound prosecutorial.

"OK. I am going to ask you a list of questions, rapidly. I would like you to try to give one-sentence answers and if it's alright with you, I'll record it. Many times when I do a profile—"

"You run a few questions or all of them in a gray box on the side of the article." Sarah interrupted him. "I've read your profiles Clark,, and I like how you work and how you see the world. That is why you are here to write about me. Plus…I trust you." Clark was now bewildered by the flattery Sarah was bestowing on him. She was reinforcing it too much, too often. She wanted something and somehow Clark knew it would be too good to be true if it were only him and nothing else.

"Oh,..well thank you. Umm, maybe we should wait for Elizabeth to get back." Clark suddenly remembered his editor had walked off on a tour more than an hour ago.

"No, we don't have to wait for Elizabeth," Sarah purred. "Start your tape recorder." Her eyes were still transfixed on Clark's.

"OK. What do you do here at Crisprgen?" Clark said with a serious tone.

"We sequence genomes so our customers can design their epigenetic future," Sarah replied.

"OK, and to someone who doesn't know anything about genetics, why is that useful?" Clark coaxed.

"Well, when you know your genome then you know how to manage your life, your response to disease, and your susceptibility to all kinds of things," replied Sarah matter of factly.

"And when you say "manage" do you mean remove some bad genes and insert good ones?" pressed Clark.

"Yes. That is called a CRISPR procedure. We take a DNA sequence with genes we want and insert it like a film splice edit over the genes we don't so that a person has a beneficial change in their genome." Sarah smiled, seeming to be pleased with herself.

"So you essentially provide people with the DNA they need and that helps avoid any mitochondrial disease?"

"Correct."

"Hmm, and what about the DNA they WANT?" Clark suddenly felt alert and on edge.

"They can have that too. Patients can obtain any number of CRISPRs for many things from hair color to height to IQ," Sarah said.

"Aren't those traits already present at birth? How would you change those things in a grown adult?" Clark pushed.

"We would use a harmless virus, like an adenovirus, to safely infect a person. It would be invading each cell nucleus but it would be carrying the CRISPR sequence we gave it instead of anything harmful. Think of it like hijacking a bus, then when the bus drives inside the football stadium, it empties out and the people from the bus immediately convince everyone in the stadium to change sweaters. That's a crude model for how we would change an adult person's DNA. The snippet is carried into the cell, it attaches to your DNA at precisely the right spot and replaces the existing DNA code, changing the genome of that cell and everyone that comes afterward/ Not all things will be changeable. Height, for instance, seems like a long way off. But we simply don't know all the variables." Sarah finished speaking, softly.

"So it's not just for disease prevention? You just admitted that you are attempting to enhance human beings." Clark felt this was the moment the entire vibe between them was about to change. The warm, friendly flirtatious CEO would undoubtedly now be aware that there was no such thing as a softball interview with the great Clark Westfield, no matter how long she stared into his eyes.

"Yes, that's exactly what we are doing," she confirmed, smiling.

"You are enhancing human beings—adult human beings?" Clark clarified.

"Yes. And our embryonic stem cell engineering will give us our first babies soon. I can't wait!" Sarah rubbed her hands together as she flashed an exaggerated smile.

"You are going to design babies?" erupted Clark, completely surprised by the revelations and somewhat disturbed by Sarah's giddiness.

"Yes, but we are going to do it the right way. And I don't know if 'design' is the right word, but I think it's more accurate to say we simply enhance their genome," Sarah said, still looking pleased with herself.

"And what does that look like?" said Clark in a trepidatious whisper.

"It will look beautiful." Sarah looked out the window with a faraway look in her eyes. "You know, we are only two or three generations away from having enough of the genome optimized in order to branch it off entirely and separate it in a safe population to preserve and multiply it. Then the Passport Genome will be protected."

"Branch off? You mean the Great Reset everyone keeps talking about?" asked Clark.

"Yes," she replied,

"And those with the Passport Genome will be the only ones left after this reset?" Clark now sounded frustrated. The whole thing seemed like an evil genius plot that a seventh grader would have written in an English class assignment.

"Well, not necessarily as it will all depend on what causes the reset. Those individuals with a Passport Genome will have the best chance of surviving, but others will survive, depending on what and where something happens. But Clark, in one or two generations no one will want to live their life with their original genome. Why roll the dice when you don't have to? And why suffer through the adaptations of your family ancestors, which are now deficiencies? Even if they can't afford an entire passport genome, most people will need or want enhancements."

"And what will happen to everyone else who doesn't decide to do CRISPR gene editing?" asked Clark, somewhat apprehensive about what the answer could be.

"Well, they will remain behind as the sapiens," replied Sarah matter of factly.

"And what will happen to those with passport genomes?" asked Clark.

"They will take the fork in the road!" Sarah exclaimed gleefully. "They won't go anywhere, they will just have only their homo sapiens genome with its localized traits from the population they were born into to rely on during whatever events that wind up affecting the planet—real or human-made." The tone in Sarah's voice sounded like she thought all of this should be obvious to Clark.

"And the enhanced humans…the ones with the passport genome?…they will branch off into a completely new species?" Clark had been telling himself all along that this was just an idea born of science fiction and megalomania, but deep in his gut, he felt that faint and utterly terrifying reality could be true.

"Exactly. Just like Homo Erectus forked into Homo Boediensis and the Neanderthals branched off and the Denisovans branched off after that, causing the evolutionary tree to eventually spin off Homo sapiens." Sarah sat and spoke like a Sunday school teacher. "And soon that will happen again." Clark felt a pit forming in his stomach.

"Yeah, but all of these ancestor groups in our species didn't just appear and reappear in a puff of smoke. It happened over hundreds of thousands of years," hissed Clark. "These species and groups all encountered one another, they interbred, they competed for food, and they certainly mixed their genes. Why do you think you have the right to leapfrog the evolutionary process or create your own fork in the tree?"

Clark felt himself gritting his teeth as he felt the return of his existential rage for people who thought they were God.

"Oh, Clark, how alpha male and Sapien of you!" Sarah giggled. "Men are funny. You all need such order… such linear progression…such clear binary parameters." She turned to look out the window again. "You see it as leapfrogging Darwin's divine flow chart of how the human race needed to organize itself. That's the Sapien part. The Sapiens survived because of their analytic aptitudes and ability to solve problems with objective math. You could say it was the Sapiens that invented science…or the Sapien gene was necessary for science to even appear and evolve. But the Neanderthals… they were the emotional ones. I have much more Neanderthal in me, and I see it as saving lives. My genetic evolutionary tradition drives me to help my peers and my community as much as I can—nobody is leapfrogging anything. The Neanderthals created extended families and eventually villages. They cared for their sick and elderly. They buried their dead and they likely believed in an afterlife. That's why I'm happy to be a Neanderthal." Sarah smiled at him provocatively.

"That sounds like the rationalization of a drunk paleontologist." Clark was now frustrated and Sarah's nonchalance about creating a new branch of human evolution and the idea of designer babies bothered him at some level. "So you think you should go ahead and do this? Who gets to decide what's in the passport genome? You? Me? The Government? The Church? Sonny Bono? Seriously, Sarah, what…the…fuck?"

"Why does it have to be up to anybody?" Sarah challenged. "Why not leave it up to the individual to chart their own fate? In the future, genomic modification will be common for multitudes of reasons. It will be the ultimate tool for self-determination. You will be able to chart your own course and manifest whatever destiny towards which you are spiritually driven. It's the ultimate empowerment of the individual." Sarah assumed her hypnotic gaze again as she finished speaking.

"Designer babies are empowered? You are talking about children….I assume you mean parents would be the determining authority for their children, right? How is that empowering and not simply treating children like livestock? Will we get to create star athletes and merit scholars?" Clark challenged back sarcastically.

"What would be so different from the decisions parents already make regarding their child's welfare? Every single detail of a child's life is managed and cared for by the parents, who are acting in the child's best interest in order for it to survive. Now they just have more tools." Sarah's tone of voice hadn't ebbed and flowed with Clark's rising emotion. In fact, she seemed even calmer and more at ease looking deeper into Clark's eyes with every passing moment.

"Yeah.. So…what if you give your child Kobe Bryant's foul shot gene and the kid winds up hating basketball? Then what? How can you possibly say that?" Clark was careful not to raise the volume of his voice as he was trying to sound as pointed as possible. But every time he put forward a question that intentionally revealed his suspicion and editorial bias, Sarah remained unflappable and unaffected.

"Ms. Reistad, let's stop a minute and examine a few macro issues," Clark said slowly adjusting his tact.

"Ms. Riestad?" Sarah purred sarcastically and smiled. "Is this the formal Mr. Westfield all of a sudden? Clark, I'll answer anything you ask, and I'm available to you in any way you need. No need for the sudden formal posturing." Her flirting had now become egregious. Clark could feel the juices in his pelvic floor responding to the romantic overture. This hadn't happened to him since long before his wife died. He dug deep in his guts and found the journalistic willpower to override the romantic chemicals she seemed to be intentionally manipulating.

"OK, Sarah. I'll play it straight with you and cut through your rather transparent seductive evasiveness," said Clark, deliberately trying to annoy her enough to cool off the flirting. She simply smiled back with no change in her expression. Clark spoke slowly.

"You have a company that solicits average people to pay you to turn over extremely private and compromising information about their health and their genetic capabilities. You have them sign terms that allow you to do anything you want with that info in exchange for some tidbits about what their genes reveal. You then take the genes that are advantageous and sell them to others who desire those traits at what I assume is a steep price. You are compiling information and technology that would give any person or group of people an advantage over the rest of the human race and then selling it to the highest bidder. I assume you are seeking a patent on this Genomic Passport and by proxy, deciding who gets it and who doesn't. You are doing this with no Internal Review Board, which would be a checkpoint for the ethics of this process. To my knowledge, you don't have any government oversight or accountability to any professional association like the AMA, yet you incentivize entire families to uproot their lives, and withdraw from their communities and schools with debt relief and promises of some utopian payoff after some doomsday caper fantasy." Clark paused and let silence fill in between them. Sarah's expression remained warm and unaffected. "You don't have to be a medical ethicist or an ACLU attorney to spot the problems with this scenario. Do you think I came up the river on a bicycle?" Clark had let his emotion swell as he was speaking. Hearing himself frame it out loud gave him faint pains of anger that he hoped would cut through the romantic tension between them. Sarah gazed at him for a few seconds, completely unbothered by any awkward gaps of silence. "Do I have it right, Ms. Reistad?" Clark reached deep inside himself for his warrior investigative reporter voice.

"Well, more or less, yes, you do," smiled Sarah, completely unapologetic. "We do, in fact, have an internal review board, but they are confidential and clandestine due to the nature of the work."

"Of course they are…" Clark snarked back. "I assume I won't be able to interview them, but I'll need to know their names."

"Perhaps someday," sighed Sarah. "I'll intuitively know the moment I can actually trust you and then many of your concerns will be assuaged. Until then, I'm simply going to have to work harder to show you how much the potential for good outweighs some of the messy details that encumber all kinds of scientific discovery. You do realize we aren't just saving the human race from impending extinction, we are actually creating an evolutionary Homo sapiens 2.0 that will be better, faster, more compassionate, virtually disease free, and very, very smart. We need to do this with urgency, Professor Westfield, because with the way the world is headed and as systems collapse, and as the environment dies and the inevitability of feudal wars, that is what will be required to survive the tragedies on the horizon. You know this to be true deep in your soul. You can feel it. I don't need to convince you." Sarah's tone was hypnotic, and Clark could feel part of himself agreeing with her. "But you also know that as the global problems cascade into mass suffering, the humans that survive will be the ones who plan ahead and have enough intelligence and fortitude to navigate the horror. And the ones who survive must also be the ones to rebuild the global society, and we both know the only ones who can do that will be the smart ones." Sarah sounded like a mother calming a child who had just lost a pet. "And Clark, we also both know that you fit that criteria," she said flatteringly. Clark felt exposed, like he had just stepped out of the shower. He also knew she was right.

"How do you know I'm smart enough to rebuild the Earth?" Clark quipped sarcastically. He didn't want to give the impression that he was buying any of this.

"Oh Clark!" Sarah returned to her most seductive pose. "We may be meeting for the first time today, but I feel like I have known you my whole life." Sarah then stood up slowly, drew a deep breath, and then started walking slowly toward Clark, who was still seated. "I've been reading your reporting and your columns since I was in high school. You even lectured in my journalism class once. Your interpretation of the world was foundational in forming my outlook and purpose."

"How flattering," Clark quipped in a deadpan tone. He was feeling slight wisps of anxiety as Sarah encroached further on his personal space while maintaining eye contact.

"But that isn't how I know, that's just my emotional attachment to how your brain works. We have an Artificial Intelligence program here that scans the published work of journalists like yourself and other public figures. It was always my hope that if there were ever to be a profile written about me or any of my work, that you would write it. I wasn't surprised when we ran a scan on you and it returned results showing that you have an extremely high IQ and analytical skills. But you don't need me to tell you that you in fact are one of the smart ones. You've always known that, haven't you, Clark Westfield?" Sarah crept closer and sat on the ottoman where Clark was resting his bruised ankle. He could feel Sarah's aggressive flattery needling through his best journalistic armor and wisdom. Surely, she must have an agenda…

"So are you hoping to default me into writing a hagiographic piece by telling me how intelligent you think I am? You're smart enough to know you wouldn't be the first and it would never work." Clark challenged.

"Of course not. I have nothing to hide, and I speak the truth. How is that ankle?" Sarah gently took Clark's foot in both hands, rested it on her knee, and rubbed his instep ever so gently. While it was obvious that Sarah was trying to manipulate the interview, part of him loved every second of what was happening. He was exhilarated by the surge of oxytocin and dopamine she was unleashing. At the very least, it temporarily diffused years of emotional darkness and residual grief. He would write the story that he had discovered and tell the truth. But for now, what was the harm in rolling with it a little longer? As long as he kept on track with the questions, he was prepared to let Sarah try as hard as she wanted to win him over through affection— whether real or imagined. After all, he was only a mere Homo sapiens.

"So with all of this investigation into intelligence, where does Alvin Matsumoto fit in the equation?" he asked, hoping to surprise her with the question.

"Oh, Alvin…" Sarah launched a huge wistful smile and nodded her head as if Clark had just mentioned her teenage rock star crush. "Alvin is such a wonderful boy, so unique, so dedicated—"

"So you know him? Is he here?" shot Clark, excitedly.

"Of course I know him and yes he is here. Would you like to meet him? He is here in the Helix Lab." Sarah was still unaffected and joyous. Clark felt like he should have been surprised that Sarah had immediately admitted to recruiting Alvin Matsumoto, but then he realized that if Sarah wasn't hiding anything, then she would have no reason to hide him either. Perhaps the news surrounding this intense woman and her company lay in their ideology and not secretive illegal logistics. But could Clark be harboring a not-so-small desire for Sarah to be an enigmatic figure with whom he may simply disagree on ethics rather than someone who was human trafficking in geniuses? He knew there was. The ease with which she answered about the Matsumoto boy was comforting, which meant this beautiful, smart woman who was flattering Clark and causing all kinds of chemical reactions deep in his stomach just might be a light at the end of grief's long tunnel.

"Yes. I would definitely like to meet him." Clark said softly. "Let's go…"

Sarah stood up from where she was seated, fondling Clark's ankle while still smiling, and stretched out her hand somewhat seductively.

"Take my hand, Clark," Sarah whispered softly. Clark felt a needle of anxiety sear through his spine.

"No, thanks. I can get up by myself. I have to learn how to manage on my own, otherwise what am I gonna do when you aren't around?" he said, adding a slightly awkward laugh. The extension of her hand gave him a jolt of nerves. He waddled around on the chair taking his foot off the ottoman and managed to stand up. It was then he realized Sarah had put his crutches on the other side of the room, and to get them, he would need her assistance, which meant putting his arm around her shoulders again. But something in him was holding him back. Instead, he gently put his sprained ankle foot forward and delicately put weight on it. He winced at the pain. It hurt, but he could manage to step forward carefully. Sarah's eyes lit up with sheer unbridled childish delight, and she clapped her hands closely and quietly in exuberant approval. Clark knew if he put his arm around her now and smelled her next to him again, he would permanently lose any objectivity he had left in the story, and he needed to see that Alvin Matsumoto was okay first.

Sarah walked beside Clark making sure he did not fall until he finally conquered the ten steps to his crutches.

"Look at you Superman!" sang Sarah teasingly. Clark turned and grinned sheepishly.

"Yeah, I'll get there." Clark sighed. "Where is Alvin?"

"Right this way!" Sarah chirped, still beaming. She gave a little hop and turned herself around in the air like a ballet dancer,, and started to sail down the corridor. Clark pumped his crutches and immediately entered a cloud of Sarah's lavender perfume as she continued onahead. It was intoxicating as she seemed to be getting further and further ahead and going faster with each step. Was she running ahead on purpose?

"Can you catch me Clark Westfield?" she called down the hallway and disappeared. Clark, out of breath at the far end stopped and stared down a dark opaque corridor and tried to catch his breath.

Who the fuck was this woman!?

Clark hobbled to the end of the hallway and saw a set of glass doors to his right. He turned, and before he could take a step, the glass panels drew open with a sound like a pressurized gas being released. He crutch-stepped through the doors and the ceiling suddenly opened, revealing a 360-degree view of the entire Ft. Monmouth. They were on another flange of the Helix architecture. Each of the flanges in the Helix Lab was its own open space, like a spiral staircase, and all were bordered on all sides by windows that made up the walls of the building. The building was absolutely stunning. Upon entering one of the floors in the Helix and seeing the complex and beautiful open space surrounded by the view of the Atlantic Ocean and the NJ Pine Barrens, one had to stop and simply stare.

"What the fuck have I gotten myself into?" Clark thought to himself.

At the end of the cantilever flange by the glass circumference was a desk with several computers on it. In a decorative bamboo chair sat a Japanese boy. He was in a baseball cap, gray jeans, and gray denim jacket. It was Alvin Matsumoto. Clark drew a deep breath. Sarah was nowhere in sight. Clark hopped on his crutches toward the end of the flange. He realized he was actually very high up on a narrow concrete walkway, and the height perspective with the crutches amplified his anxiety. He approached the desk which also had a bamboo facade.

"Hi…" muttered Clark. Alvin didn't acknowledge Clark as if he hadn't heard him. "I'm Clark Westfield. I met your parents earlier, over in the village and they said you would be here. I am also a friend of Amy Biancini, your teacher?" Clark said a little louder. The boy turned and looked up at Clark with glassy eyes.

"Yes, hello. You know Ms. Biancini?" he asked, smiling.

"Yes, I do, very well. She is here, do you want to see her?"

"Yes! That would be wonderful! Why is she here?" asked Alvin. He seemed genuinely surprised. Clark whipped out his cell phone and texted Amy: "911! Get up to the Helix Lab 9th floor— I am with ALVIN. Get here fast! Weird shit is going on!"

"Oh well, we actually wanted to come see you and find out how you were doing. I guess Amy, er, Ms. Biancini hadn't seen much of you after you won the National Merit Award, and she wanted to catch up." Clark sensed he should try not to raise any alarm. Just then, his cell phone buzzed with a text from Amy. "I'm in the lobby, getting in the elevator with this Sarah Reistad?" Clark realized he wasn't going to have much time alone with Alvin. His cell phone buzzed again "Does she run this place?" read the text from Amy. Clark put his phone down.

"Alvin, I met your parents earlier," offered Clark. "And I think Ms. Biancini is on her way up." Clark knew he had to move quickly if he was going to get any honesty out of Alvin Matsumoto before Sarah got off that elevator with Amy. "Hey… listen…Al…your parents seem lovely and they also seem pretty proud of you and the work you are doing here. But let me ask you something,are you happy here? Is this somewhere you want to be?" Alvin tilted his head and seemed surprised at the question. Clark made another attempt. "Well, it just seems you were really on a roll back in Ms. Biancini's class, and then you and your parents moved here pretty quickly. Was it because you wanted to? What made you decide to come live on the base and work with Crisprgen?" Clark had learned over the years that open-ended questions were more revealing than leading with binary facts. Non-leading questions were the verbal equivalent of a Rorschach test. Alvin made a confused expression and began to speak.

"I was hesitant at first. It was a very confusing time. After I won the NMSQT award, I started to get contacted the very next morning by all kinds of places. Some schools wanted to recruit me, and a few private companies called and said they had genius track positions with huge signing bonuses. Microsoft was one of them, and another was a giant Chinese computer and telecom company. One sent a package to the house with brand new iPads for the family, and the next day a flatbed truck pulled up in front of my house and unloaded a car! The keys and title were in the mailbox!" he laughed slightly as he described the vehicle.

"No way! Who sent you a car?" asked Clark.

"I don't even know— I never drove it. I didn't even sign the title. It was a brand-new Cadillac Escalade, which I would never drive because of its carbon footprint, and then we moved here, so it's still right where I left it." He chuckled again.

"Let me get this straight. You had an anonymous recruiter send you a brand new Cadillac Escalade just for being smart— something every high school junior in the country would wish for— without asking for any commitment, and you won't drive it because you are worried about fumes?" Clark was genuinely incredulous at the reality of this boy refusing the car. "Times have certainly changed," he muttered to himself.

"Yeah, well, I might have eventually driven it if I'd found out who sent it but there was no time," said Alvin nodding.

"What do you mean there wasn't any time? You moved here about three weeks later, right? Had you already planned that with your parents?" asked Clark.

"Oh no… I knew Ms. Reistad already, and she had always told me about Crisprgen. And—"

"How did you know Ms. Reistad?" interrupted Clark.

"Oh, she wrote to me on Reddit and WhatsApp when I was in 7th grade, and we would talk about calculus and then eventually genetics. There aren't a lot of people who love calculus and computer science as much as I do, and she kinda introduced me to genetics and the genome, and how the genome will be critical to all science going forward." Alvin

Matsumoto spoke perfect English with no accent, however, the timber of his voice and natural inflection revealed his Japanese heritage. "So I had a little group of a few people around the world that liked all this weird science, there were about five of us, and Ms. Reistad kept the group together and managed our Zoom calls and virtual meetings. We were using regular video chat but I got bored so I wrote a VR program so we could all use gaming headsets, that way we could feel like we were all in the same room much better."

"Wow…very impressive," muttered Clark, smiling. "You know at my age and intelligence bracket, I consider a productive afternoon getting the leaves raked." Alvin smiled slightly and seemed confused by the joke. "So is that where Ms. Reistad asked you and the family to come to Crisprgen?" Clark pressed further.

"Oh no, I didn't meet her until after I won the award, and then Ms. Allele met me one day when I was out at the GameStop and asked if I wanted to have coffee. We drove down here, and I met Ms. Resisted in person for the first time...but I knew her from the group.."

"And when was that?" Clark was taking mental notes and fumbling for his newspad. While he was a true old-school bulldog that used the classic spiral pads, he was also modern enough to reach down and start recording on his cell phone again.

"Oh, actually that was about six months ago. I have been here ever since." Alvin's expression changed from levity to a downcast frown. He looked at the floor and seemed outwardly sad.

"Well, did you not want to stay? Your parents moved here with you, so was it them who wanted you to stay?" Clark asked gently.

"Oh no! I convinced them! Yes, they are here. They joined me shortly afterward because I recruited them, and Ms. Resistad said they would be enrolled in the Transcendence project so then I felt like I had to stay," Alvin sighed.

"What is the Transcendence Project, Alvin?" asked Clark slowly.

A voice answered from just under Clark's ear.

"The Transcendence Project is a large trial study we have going on here that will let Alvin's parents and others live a very long time, perhaps four or five times the length of our current lifespans. It's named Transcendence because they will transcend death, or at least the expected longevity on the calendar of our understanding…" said a breathy female voice. Clark turned around to see Sarah standing so close to his shoulder that he brushed against her breast as he turned. She smiled. Next to her was Amy Biancini, her face bearing a lukewarm look of concern.

"Alvin!" exclaimed Amy as she skipped over and threw her arms around his neck.

"Hi, Ms. Biancini!" gushed Alvin boyishly and rose from his chair to bow. Amy caught him in a hug. Sarah looked at the happy reunion and then resumed her spacey smile looked at Clark.

"Wow…that's so beautiful!" whispered Sarah with a starry-eyed look. Clark realized his candid time with Alvin was over. Clark looked Sarah dead in the eyes.

"Sarah, how exactly does this Transcendence project work?" he asked sternly.

"Oh, Clark! I'm so glad you asked. Did Alvin tell you we got his parents involved? For the Transcendent project we use a CRISPR snippet that will cause you to produce more telomerase. By doing that, you extend the life of a cell—it can divide much longer than its normal Hayflick limit and that extends its lifespan, and that means your lifespan, too." Sarah beamed with joy as she spoke. "We opened a trial and we were able to enroll Alvin's parents as a thank you to Alvin."

"A thank you?" Clark said, baffled. "Wait, back up. You have invented some genetic hijacking process that grants eternal life? And what do you mean by a thank you to Alvin?"

Sarah turned and called to Amy and Alvin. "Hey, you two! Come join us. Clark just asked about the study and the Transcendence project, and I want us all to experience hearing its description together." Sarah was like a cult leader in her stance. Her faraway starry gaze, her flowing robes that seemed to still accentuate her figure, her long flowing hair, and the spacey, sing-song overtone of her voice gave her an oracle-like aura. An oracle with a secret, Clark thought to himself. Amy stood up and made eye contact with Clark. He nodded in response, and her eyes bulged slightly, indicating that she felt something wasn't right. Clark could tell what Amy was thinking, and it was exactly what he was thinking.

Sarah made eye contact sequentially with all three people the way a politician works a room. But she was dreamy in her expression and looked more like a boardwalk psychic.

"We at Crisprgen have identified a gene edit that lengthens the life of a cell, thus extending the human lifespan. If humans are going to live longer, they will need a host of other genetic edits that keep their bodies working, fight off disease, and maintain optimal cognitive performance. We are developing the Passport Project for these people. They will take the human race forward and carry with them the optimal genetic sequence of perfection in body and mind. They will carry with them hundreds of years of wisdom from life experience, thus being able to make better judgments on resource management and species demarcation issues. Alvin is one of the spectacular humans who is letting us harvest his intelligence gene groupings. It's brains like his that we want in future people. As part of the compensation for Alvin's contribution, and because he deserves their support in the coming decades, we have agreed to enroll his parents, and the parents of all of those contributing intelligence sequences to the study. This is the beginning of the fork in our next evolutions. Clark Amy… you are looking at the last of the homo sapiens." a tear ran from the corner of Sara's eye and down her nose. She was beaming with pride, and looked each of them in the eye again sequentially, delivering a warm smile.

Clark stayed silent for a minute. He looked at Amy. She had a horrified look on her face. She looked at Clark with her mouth agape.

"So…" Clark glanced down at his phone to make sure it was still recording. "You are harvesting the genetic codes from the smartest young people and you are promising their parents extended life to sign over their kids' brains?" Clark was stern in his delivery, but Sarah just smiled.

"Well, we don't TAKE anybody's brain, Clark; we just copy the coding so future people can benefit from their collective intellect. The company is doing this in all kinds of health areas where we are harvesting the best in class genetic sequences—immunity, cardiology, musculoskeletal structures, and all areas of biochemistry. I just like to be here with the smart ones." Sarah giggled and put her arm around Alvin.

"And this evolutionary fork in the road? You're planning a new species, aren't you?" said Amy in a prosecutorial tone. "You're even creating a new fork in the road of Ram Dass' evolution of consciousness!"

"Yes! Are you an anthropologist? Amy, that is EXACTLY the miracle that is happening here!" Sarah's eyes filled with tears.

"You're deliberately forking off evolution after raiding and pillaging all the good genes from the population and leaving the rest of humanity behind to kill each other over religion, oil, and politics, aren't you? And you are proud of this?" Clark was beside himself.

"Why wouldn't we be?" Sarah asked gently. "It's a way to ensure that those who survive the unavoidable coming collapse of natural resources and the geo-political world order are, in fact, the best and wisest humans...enhanced humans that is... to rebuild a manageable population."

"So you've totally given up on the planet...you are identifying the optimal genetic sequence for every area of life, especially intelligence, and creating a designer genome that will separate the humans with that new genome from us ...our current genome."

Sarah nodded. "And it will also have genes from Neanderthal, and Cro Magnon, and Austrailapithicus, and every genome that came before as the best and the brightest of those species survived and eventually morphed into the next species in the evolutionary chart. They did it with blood and sweat, pain and suffering and disease, and it took hundreds of thousands of years. Those who carry forward won't have those challenges or those sufferings. Those who carry on will have the challenges of managing 8 billion people through the collapse of the biosphere and the collapse of all infrastructure, which will ensure famine, disease, and suffering. That will start regional wars and societal collapse. Those will be ethically challenging and terrifying in ways today's humans and prior humans could never comprehend." Sarah's expression was one of sadness.

"Right…and you are doing this with no oversight from the government or United Nations or I don't know…the fucking Vatican…somebody…anybody! Why do you get to decide who goes forward and who gets the best genes?" Clark's tone was piercing. Sarah just gently smiled at him.

"You know… I've asked myself that same question," Sarah said wistfully. She was unflappable, and it fascinated Clark. "I guess you can call it fate, or luck, or simply that the smartest people who figure this out should be the ones making the decision. I guess where Oppenheimer went wrong was when he let the government own his discovery. We all saw what happened next. Do you really think you could get the disparate factions of the world, all its political territories, cultures, and religions to agree on anything remotely like this? It's irresponsible to put this discovery to that kind of chance…of being corrupted or simply lost or in the wrong hands. After many sleepless nights thinking about your exact question, Clark, I have come to the conclusion that we are responsible for our own discoveries, and that we must take heed from history to learn how a discovery of this magnitude can play out. I have also had the spiritual epiphany that I am to go through with this." Sarah exhaled. Clark didn't know what to think. There were valid points in her perspective. The news of this would be globally impactful if it were successful. However, whoever would engineer this massive upheaval of humanity probably should have more to qualify them for the job than just a "spiritual epiphany".

"Well...at least you thought about it," Clark said sarcastically. "And while you have a point, it doesn't mean there shouldn't be a little more sunshine around what you are doing."

Amy glared at him. Then she turned to Alvin.

"Alvin...is all this true? Did you agree to come here and participate in this gene harvesting? And did your parents get compensated with enrollment in the telomerase test project - this Transcendent thing??" asked Amy in a serious voice.

"Yes. The Transcendence Project," replied Alvin.

"And you are ok with all of this?" asked Amy.

"Yes. Absolutely. It's a way for me to give back to my parents and reward them with more time, and I am humbled and honored to contribute my DNA to future humans."

Amy looked perplexed but shrugged and said, "OK, well, I guess congratulations. We miss you at school, and I'd love to have you drop by sometime so that we can go look at the flower hybrid garden you planted last year."

"Yes, I'd like that." Alvin bowed slightly in salutation. Amy smiled back then turned to Clark with an abrupt change of expression.

"OK, well, SaraSarah, thanks for everything. Good luck with the fork in the road and uh, Clark and I have to be going now." she shot a piercing look at Clark.

"We do? Oh, yeah ok." Clark sensed Amy was about to explode with rage, and he was feeling his heart pounding. He needed to get away from Sarah's hypnotic charisma and his attraction to her and process what he just heard and everything he had seen on the base so far. Where the fuck had Elizabeth gone? She needed to see and hear all this. Amy walked over, grabbed Clark's hand, and put it over her shoulder to help him walk, the way Sarah had done previously. Clark immediately felt grounded. Amy felt real, down-to-earth, tangible, sensible, and safe. As he turned to say thank you and goodbye to Sarah, she met his gaze, and he hesitated to speak. She said nothing but walked forward and kissed him gently on the lips. It wasn't a lustful passionate kiss—rather it was more of a new-agey, affectionate, could be a European greeting kind of kiss, but longer than an American peck and definitely not common in a professional setting.

Clark said nothing. That was the first time he had actually touched another woman's lips since closing Mary Lynn's casket. Time stood still for a moment.

Amy yanked Clark forward, and he stumbled. She glared at him.

"Seriously?!?" she barked at him. Clark felt dizzy.

Amy and Clark got on the elevator and the doors closed. Clark leaned against the back wall and exhaled deeply. Amy leaned against the opposite wall and looked at him.

"Clark…" said Amy with a pained look on her face.

"I know…" said Clark.

"You don't know Clark…You fucking don't know…" Amy was almost in tears. "She is gonna get away with this… She is fucking going to get away with this…"

"What makes you say that?" asked Clark.

"Because…" Amy sniffed and a fraction of a tear escaped the corner of her now bloodshot eyes. "She's already got YOU..."

***

It had been a very long time— several years— since Clark Westfield had found himself in the office after midnight, with the only sound in the room coming from the tapping of his keyboard. His green glass desk lamp illuminated his immediate workspace with soft yellow light, the only light in the newsroom other than the blue glare of computer monitors flashing screen savers and ads. Clark wasn't tired. He lived for this. To be in the newsroom at this hour didn't mean he was meeting a deadline but rather that he cared about what he was writing enough to get it right and shape it stylistically. When a story was important, it deserved that much attention, and Clark was overjoyed that the tense, nervous feeling in the pit of his stomach and his slightly elevated heart rate had returned after an eternity of grief-induced emotional permafrost. He felt alive again. In addition to the nervous excitement of preparing a breakthrough story, there was an additional frequency broadcasting emotions, one he hadn't felt in an even longer time. He couldn't stop thinking about Sarah. There was something so odd and space cadet-like about her demeanor, a whimsical exterior that harbored an uncommon intellect. Her cadence and general affect were also unusual— she seemed to smile with every word she spoke, creating a hypnotic oratory ambiance that you wouldn't think to interrupt. She was completely unfazed by any question or challenge he had thrown at her. She didn't appear malicious or negative in any overt way. Clark knew his attraction to her would compromise any objectivity he hoped to retain for a story. That, and the simple discomfort of allowing romantic feelings to bloom under the heavy snowdrift of grief from being widowed had made it easy for him to leave yesterday.

Amy had been acutely disturbed by his flirtatious rapport with Sarah, so much so that she hadn't spoken much on the way home. Clark had asked her what impression of Sarah she had formed, but Amy only gave evasive one-word answers and avoided eye contact. He told himself that Amy was mad at a problem that didn't exist. Despite an attraction, Sarah was still the subject of a story, and Clark was still a reclusive widower, so there was nothing to be jealous of. Plus, they had been lifelong friends and knew each other deeply, but were always squarely in the friend zone. Clark had watched her date dozens of jerks and eventually marry one, divorce him, marry another, and divorce him too. He saw his attraction to Sarah as more inconvenient than problematic, and he would tough it out like a bad cold the way he had always done when he met a new, exciting woman who was unavailable. But Amy's emotional turbulence, if indicating some attraction on her part, would be a seismic game changer in Clark's life. Between the two of them, he was being reintroduced to the human condition's infinite jest - the fallibility of the heart to launch indiscriminate and nonsensical attractions at even less appropriate targets at the most inopportune moments. Crushes are like sitting in wet paint. you don't realize it until you are completely soaked. There could be no greater source of discontent in a man's mind, no greater driver of disastrous decisions and behavior and no greater distraction from one's work, and well… he just couldn't have that.

After he dropped Amy off at her car still parked at the high school and said an awkward goodbye, he had driven straight to the office. He had texted Melody he would be working late and all was well. Late had turned into the pink light of the morning sky, but Clark had yet to even crack a yawn. Clark knew when a story was important and would get a big reaction when published. He knew what he had heard Sarah explain. He also knew that several times in his career he had dove into an issue, and through his expository writing and investigation, had educated and enraged his readership to take action about various matters in the community. He had reported on the opioid crisis and lack of police compassion, the absurdity of paroling a child murderer, a clandestine government program warehousing seeds for a post-climate change planet, and a vigilante hit squad of assassin clergy harbored in the Vatican. Each were multi-month efforts that caused other media outlets to follow, eventually leading to sweeping policy changes and accountability. Those stories tapped into a very specific type of adrenaline— one that didn't flow often. For a reporter, this special premium-grade adrenaline was like rocket fuel mixed with fentanyl, and Clark lived for it. He hadn't felt that amphetamine surge of motivation in a very long time. It was an elusive moving target, and Clark knew that when it started to flow, it was futile to do anything but drop everything and yield to its chemical and psychological properties. And in that heightened state of journalistic mania where Clark presently found himself, he could forget his lingering bereavement for his beloved wife, the imminent twilight of his own career, and all but certain departure of his daughter Melody to college and then adulthood. Once again, finally, the newsroom was where he felt above life's chaotic fray.

The silence of the newsroom immersed him in a vortex of clarity. It was like an intellectual "clean room" where all outside contaminants were eliminated. An engineer at NASA would be stymied by oxidative chemicals, bacteria, and debris from the outside— a newsroom is contaminated by opinions, bias, religious beliefs, and most importantly. the journalist's life experience. Clark knew perfect objectivity was impossible but he never ceased to aspire and at least try for the ideal. With regard to the story Elizabeth had assigned him, he knew what needed to be written. To simply turn in an expository "gee whiz" style science piece about interventional gene therapy would have satisfied his green editor, but it would have been an enormous disservice to the readers and the community that trusted him to tell them what was important. Well, they used to anyway at least...

Clark attached a summary page at the top of the article he had prepared. This would give his editor the core principles that she needed to retain the key points as she made various edits. What needed to be written wasn't necessarily what Clark wanted to write. It's amazing how moral outrage can be watered down when the chemicals of romantic attraction attack with a vengeance. But Clark had done a lot of things over the span of his career that he didn't want to do that had surprised, hurt, and even ruined human subjects which he had grown to care about. It was part of the job, and he had been here before. His memo to Elizabeth read:

SUMMARY: Crisprgen—a private company that most people didn't know existed was finding and recruiting the smartest youth, the kind of smart that happens in one in ten million births, and paying them to freely sign over their genomic sequence, which was responsible for their intelligence. They were offering the promise of life extension to the parents, moving the families onto a decommissioned Army base in Monmouth County, New Jersey. They were then having the recruited smart ones work on what they were calling The Passport Project, which seemed to be the defining and patenting of an ideal or perfect genome that future generations would have as their DNA. This would eliminate most diseases, and make humans bigger and faster with the intelligence found only in .01% of the population. The resulting group of "super" humans would be so superior to current humans that it would cause them to branch off from modern Homo Sapiens in the evolutionary chart. Over time as the unsolvable problems of the globe cascade into an inevitable dystopian hellscape of famine, pandemics, and war, the current populations of Homo sapiens, or today's "people" would be reduced in numbers to the brink of extinction. Then, those who had been part of the Passport Project would carry humankind forward as a new species. As a way to fund all this, Crisprgen would also isolate and patent genomic sequences for specific traits and qualities such as immunity to congenital diseases or emotional and cosmetic attributes, and sell them to those who could afford the CRISPR procedures. That was the gene therapy. Crisprgen, and in particular their odd CEO Sarah Reistad, had created this mission and developed it without consulting a government agency or any sovereign nations, any ethics authority, professional society, or even religious leaders. It was all driven by a mysterious hyper-intelligent woman with unusual emotional timbre and absolutely no accountability. END OF SUMMARY.

Clark breathed a sigh of relief as the room brightened from the pinhole streaks of the morning sunrise. It was 6:45 AM, a time of day when the toughest neighborhoods looked peaceful and the ugly landfills of New Jersey's Meadowlands glowed with their golden Phragmites reeds. It almost made you forget the toxic pollution, dioxin, and heavy metals that had been buried just a few feet under the rolling mounds that caused New Jersey, especially the Newark corridor where Clark's newsroom was, to have the highest cancer rate in the nation. Clark was very proud of his story; it felt like he had some of the old fight back. And he knew that most people upon hearing about the CRISPR technology for the first time would react with a moral outrage and slight panic, setting in motion the necessary checkpoints to properly evaluate the work of Sarah Reistad and Crisprgen. At the very least, Clark was warning the public about some of the ethical forest fires they weren't noticing. But it would also mean that Sarah would likely resent Clark for his criticism and probably not speak to him again. Well, at least she had defrosted his damaged heart and soul, even if the feeling was short-lived. The difference with this story, though, was that every time he had written the truth before and alienated a source or subject which careened into a Paramore, he had always had Mary Lynn to come home to and they were easily forgotten. Now that wasn't the case.

Clark heard the ding of the elevator arriving on the newsroom floor. For as long as he had known her, Elizabeth had always arrived around 7 AM every morning. It was an attribute that let her stay fiercely organized and ahead of the pack. Usually, she arrived immediately after her morning jog and showered in the small gym on the first floor. Clark watched as she emerged from the open steel elevator doors. He could hear the faint metallic sound of the music seeping through her earbuds over the silent empty newsroom. She was in black athletic leggings stretched to her precise contours and her cell phone was logged tightly in an elastic pocket. She didn't notice Clark - she wouldn't have a reason to expect him, or to look in his office this early. Any time Clark was in the newsroom at 7 AM, it was because he was sleeping on his office couch after working too late to drive home, or like today, was still up from the night before. Elizabeth marched directly into her office and began toweling off the beads of sweat on her forehead and chest. She removed a pants suit from a hook on the back of the door. She began to pull down her pants and started to change her clothes, assuming no one was in the office. Clark turned his chair to look out the window and give Elizabeth the courtesy to change her clothes privately.

He stared out the window for several minutes, finally feeling the exhaustion of being up for more than 24 hours straight and falling into a trance-like state, alternating between satisfaction and faint disappointment. If Sarah had excited him so much, then that meant there would be others…right? There was no need to worry about alienating her he told himself. She had made him realize he was back in the saddle after all, and that felt confusing to him. What would Mary Lynn have said? She would have asked why he hadn't gotten back out there sooner. The satisfaction of turning in a story that he felt was important wasn't enough to offset the churning in his mind or the ripples Sarah had caused in his psyche. Sleep was going to feel miserable.

"Am I catching you doing the punch-in clock of shame?" said Elizabeth's voice from behind him. "That's where the morning walk of shame ends and becomes the work day of shame. I know you didn't get up this early on your own - did you even go home?"

"Umm… no, not at all." laughed Clark as he wheeled around to face her. She was standing in his doorway in a perfectly pressed pants suit. One would never know she had been jogging just 20 minutes prior. In her left hand was a paper clipped stack of pages that was Clark's profile story on Crisprgen. In the other, was a full coffee mug that Clark had given her in her early years. The handle had sequential spheres painted red and the outside surface of the mug had real protruding shark's teeth glued into the clay. It represented a mantra that Clark had taught her as a general principle:to be a good journalist, you need three things: a set of balls, a set of teeth, and lots of coffee.

"So…you seemed to hit it off with Sarah Reistad pretty well," Elizabeth said. Her face had a judgmental smile.

"Yeah, she is mesmerizing, and not entirely in a good way," he replied wistfully.

"Clark, I haven't seen you as engaged with anyone since Mare got sick." Elizabeth's tone turned warm. "If I didn't know you better and if I didn't think it would help you in the long run, I would have been very mad at you for that stunt you pulled."

"What stunt?" asked Clark, bewildered.

"What stunt?" Elizabeth raised her eyebrows. "I gotta hand it to you, Westfield, having Allele escort me out of the park was a master stroke on your part. I may be your editor but are you always going to remind me you are one step ahead of me?" Clark looked at her baffled Elizabeth continued with a slight shrug. "I'm not mad, I bet spending the night with Sarah probably did more good than harm."

"What? Excuse me…I didn't have you escorted anywhere, and I didn't spend the night with anyone. Why do you think I had you escorted out? I was waiting for you up in the Helix Lab and you never came back so I had to go through with the interview. I figured you just went home."

"You didn't have them take me out to the gate and then to my car? For real?" Elizabeth cross-examined.

"Liz… I didn't have anyone do anything. I didn't sleep. I dropped off our genetics consultant…"

"Genetics consultant? Who the hell is the genetics consultant?" interjected Elizabeth.

"Oh..right…uh.. I brought a biochemistry teacher with me, who teaches genetics so I could understand what the fuck they do at Crisprgen. We don't have to pay her, and you can talk to her if you want. Also, she was Alvin Matsumoto's teacher, who we found working in the lab, by the way."

"Alvin Matsumoto is at Crisprgen!" exclaimed Elizabeth. "Do his parents know?"

"Yes, they are living there too. You have no idea what we found. It's a really sophisticated and complicated situation over there. Read my story and then I'll fill you in on the details."

"So, they are reaching out to local families and employing them?" asked Elizabeth.

"No. Not exactly. Liz read my story and that will fill in the blanks. I'm going to go hit the restroom and then go get coffee in the kitchen. You want more?" She nodded, and he took her balls and teeth mug from her hand. "Sit down and when I get back let's discuss," he said. Elizabeth smirked at him.

"Umm…ok. But then come see your editor in her office when you are done." Elizabeth said, jokingly invoking her rank now that she was Clark's editor.

Several minutes later, when Clark returned with two full mugs of coffee, he found Elizabeth in her office, seated at her desk leaning back in her chair reading tnhe last page of the story. He strode in and took a seat opposite her.

"What the fuck is this Clark?" Elizabeth asked, sternly waving the pages of the story.

"Yeah, I know…the response is going to be massive," he replied with a satisfied smile.

"Massive?" Elizabeth shot him a piercing look. "We can't run this…" she said looking down. Clark stayed silent and leaned his head to one side, patiently waiting for her to explain why.

"First of all, I'm not sure our readers would believe it - even your readers," Elizabeth snorted. "But I think you must have this wrong, or your old man paranoia from one too many Clark Westfield adventures has you defaulting to global conspiracies and catastrophes when I think they are just an innovative company in an area of science that is new to you, and you don't understand."

"What?!? Liz, did you read it? They are doing this already…the missing smart kids are there, and they are harvesting their genes!. How can that be a conspiracy theory? It's happening!" Clark was slightly annoyed at Elizabeth's inability to see the gravity in the story.

"Really? A fork in human evolution? Clark, give me a break…," she scoffed.

"Those were Sarah Reistad's exact words! I recorded everything! It came right out of her lips!" His voice was starting to rise.

"Yeah - don't make me listen to a recording and embarrass you further," Elizabeth pressed. Something in her wanted to put her editorial foot down. "This is what I think Clark…" She stared straight at him. "I think if I listened to those recordings, I would hear an explanation of long-term genetic research that is about to become a major economic driver in our area and have big implications for all kinds of healthcare. But I think you hear that Crisprgen is some James Bond-style company of evil geniuses that wants to take over the world. And I don't think it has any resemblance to reality because I think that woman Sarah got you all hot and bothered. And I am saying this next part with love…we've known each other a very long time…I think she came on to you really strong, and you found yourself swept off your feet a bit because your guard was down as a widower. I think it bothered you and your reaction was to write a hit piece maligning her."

"Are you truly serious?!?" growled Clark. He was beside himself.

"Perhaps, I need to remind you that Sarah is a major shareholder in the parent company that owns the company that owns our paper. I'll also remind you that she asked for you to interview her and write the profile. Do I need to explain why we can't publish a hit job on a major investor who is the darling of corporate? But either way, I think she got under your skin and this is your ego reacting. I can't run this." Sarah sat back and waited for Clark to speak.

"You're right Liz. We do go way back. We go so far back that I never in a million years thought you would be the one I have to fight on this.Who the fuck do you think you are to question my ethics and invoke my grief…? My, such a short memory for all the times I got you out of jams whether it was the professor you were sleeping with in college or countless fact checks you botched on MY stories. But you're the editor now aren't you…? Well…good for you, since I'm sure you think you deserve it too." Clark had lowered his voice to a vicious whisper.

"What do you mean? Is your retort that I shouldn't be an editor now? Clark, we know each other too long to fight like this…" Elizabeth realized she may have overdone it a bit in her remarks."

"You're right Liz. We do know each other a long, long time. So long that you better understand how deep this next part goes…" Clark leaned over the desk to get as close to her personal space as possible. He gritted his teeth and stared piercing daggers of blind rage into her eyes. "GO FUCK YOURSELF!!!"

And just like that, Clark got up and left.

Elizabeth sat silent for a moment. There went her hero, whom she had just accused of poor ethics. Clark had been more than a boss and professor to Elizabeth. He was a surrogate brother and sometimes father, a friend, a teacher, and on occasion, a wingman. It was true that he had saved her job many times. He had covered for her when she was a young reporter and made mistakes. She had also found out many years later that he had sandbagged a colleague of hers when they were up for the same promotion. There was nobody equivalent in her life to Clark. And that is why she told herself that any relationship worth its salt will have its conflicts. If you care for someone deeply, arguments are unavoidable, right? It just took this long to happen between her and Clark. Plus, she further told herself she had seen him grit his teeth like that before….right?. No..she had never seen his teeth like that. But he would get over it …he would have to. Plus, if he were in her position, he would do the same thing. He had flagged her many times when she got too close to a source to be objective, and he had always been right. But she was right too, she reflected. Sarah Reistad had found her and personally asked for Clark, claiming she was a fan from reading his columns for decades. And Clark simply couldn't handle the interest of a woman he found attractive - not yet anyway. That all added up for Elizabeth. Sarah Reistad controlled a huge swath of the parent company, and this was Elizabeth's first opportunity to make an impression. She couldn't fuck this up. She needed to show a powerful woman leader like Sarah Reistad that she too, a black woman who had risen out of poverty over gender and race imbalances and additional obstacles was in charge of the newspaper. Most importantly, Elizabeth figured Clark Westfield was the kind of reporter that could alienate all kinds of business relationships with his reporting— relationships the paper and its parent companies needed. As a senior editor, Elizabeth had a responsibility to see the big picture. But her re-assuring self-talk still had the tempo of her anxious heart rhythm, fast erratic, and out of control. She kept picturing Clark's teeth as he told her to go fuck herself….No, she had never seen him like that…

Her cell phone vibrated and rang on her desk, blasting the ringtone "My Cherie Amour" by Stevie Wonder. It was a Connecticut area code. She answered.

"Hi, Elizabeth? It's Jodi Applegate from the New Haven Register Tribune. I need to speak with you for a few minutes.

Is that okay, Liz?" The voice on the other end was the reporter who had called Elizabeth a few weeks ago about a missing student with genius-level IQ.

"Hi Jodi! Great to hear from you. I have so much to tell you!" said Elizabeth.

"OK, well, I have something to tell you too but..." Elizabeth cut her off.

"Let me go first..." she interjected. "We found the two students that had disappeared, and they didn't exactly disappear. They are working at a local biotech company that recruited them. I just visited..."

"Crisprgen?" said Jodi.

"Yes! Oh, so you know? My reporter found the LaRoccas there too. I guess they got hired as well. We were going to do a story on..."

Jodi Applegate interrupted Elizabeth. "The LaRoccas are dead. They were killed this afternoon in an automobile accident on Rt. 95." She paused.

"Oh...that's terrible..." whispered Liz.

"No one knows where their daughter is. And there were no other cars involved."

"So what are you thinking is so interesting about this?" asked Liz. The tone in the reporter's voice sounded like she was suspicious of something.

"Well, I spoke to the LaRoccas yesterday. We talked for a long time and they told me about moving down to New

Jersey at the Crisprgen campus. They told me the reason they took the offer to relocate so abruptly and sign their daughter into the work program was that they were promised some enzyme—some supplement that would extend their lifespan." Elizabeth felt an inexplicable chill run down her spine. Applegate continued:

"So this stuff is called TA-65, and they were promised one of the gene therapy procedures..whatever…the CRISPR I think they called it... So those two things made them believe it was okay to contract with them and let their daughter work there in an accelerated research position."

"OK, so are you thinking there is any fraud or malfeasance in that? Sounds like they are just making a pretty expensive biotech gamble," countered Elizabeth.

"Yeah, but at the expense of their daughter?" retorted Applegate.

"Expense? There isn't a welcoming pathway out there for their daughter's intelligence category, and Crisprgen, whose work I'm familiar with. The company and the work they do - seems like a good fit. But I don't understand what it is that you are concerned about. Talk to me one reporter to another. I won't counterpoint." Elizabeth coaxed. She felt that something was on Jodi's mind.

"Yeah, so you know about this Passport Project?"

"Yes, I do. It's interesting and visionary, but I also wonder if it's where lofty ambition meets scientific hubris and shareholder fraud." Elizabeth chuckled to make it obvious she was kidding.

"Yeah, well, I have been trying to find their daughter and see how she is handling everything so I asked the police where she was. They said she was taken back to the campus where her family had moved - I assumed he meant Crisprgen. they said they met two staffers who arrived at the police station the night of the accident and when the police asked who should have custody of their daughter who was 16, they showed them a legal proxy that was a custody addendum to the LaRoccas' will. It said the company would have custody and guardianship of their daughter…" Jodi Applegate stopped talking for a moment. Elizabeth could no longer deny that she was innately uncomfortable with the entire Crisprgen operation, and this didn't help.

"They own her, Liz! They fucking bought her!" hissed Applegate.

"Yeah.. umm…can you come down here for dinner, or first thing in the morning? I have a colleague I need you to meet and the three of us need to talk. We may have some access inside that could get you your interview with the daughter."

Elizabeth felt sick. Everything this reporter said fit perfectly with what Clark had found and affirmed his alarm bells about the company. - and instead Elizabeth had questioned his integrity out of fear of being corporately vulnerable.

"I'm on my way," said Jodi Applegate as she hung up the phone. Elizabeth sat staring out the window as the rain droplets started to patter. It wasn't that she didn't believe Clark or share his views on the questionable ethics of Crisprgen, it was just that life would be a lot easier, and her job would be alot more secure if she didn't green light his story. And it also wasn't that she was suddenly turned around by Connecticut reporter, Jodi Applegate who was suspicious about the custody clause in the LaRoccas' will. It was simply that IF the New Haven Register Tribune ran a story that was a deep dive into the murky guts of Crisprgen and the Newark Examiner didn't because Elizabeth didn't want a headache, then Clark would definitely never speak to her again, and he would be right. She didn't know what the deal was at this high-tech dumpster fire of a company, and she didn't want to know, but she had to. She owed it to Clark…

***

Chapter 7

Clark stared down at his cell phone. The text he had sent to Amy Biancini earlier that morning still had no response, just the generic tag "delivered" which told the user the miniature supercomputer had done its job. It also told this user that the woman to whom the text had been delivered, in this case, a lifelong friend with whom he had recently had a superb and inexplicably awkward encounter, had no interest in speaking with him. At least not yet.

Clark hadn't slept at all. The one woman that he felt comfortable enough with to be emotionally vulnerable after the death of his wife was upset with him for reasons he didn't understand. The other woman in his life with whom he felt comfortable being professionally vulnerable and thought of as an unshakable ally had thrown out his story in deference to the powers that be back at the paper. Normally, Clark would navigate each scenario delicately, approaching each woman to deconstruct the friction as he had countless times over the years of knowing both. But this time, there was a third woman—Sarah Reistad, who seemed to be an aggravating factor at the center triangulating the feminine conundrum in which he found himself. Clark acknowledged to himself his intense attraction to Sarah, which seemed mutual, at least on the surface. Clark also reluctantly acknowledged to himself that for the first time since the death of his wife, he had been swept into a full-blown crush towards this mysterious Sarah, igniting that elusive, combustible biochemical combination that made the human race propel forward and the world go round. You know - that full blown bio-pharmaceutical alchemy of surging dopamine and oxytocin that stops a grown man in his tracks and makes him do incredibly stupid things? Yes, that surge was happening. And Clark knew, at least part of him anyway, that there was nothing that could be done to stop those mysterious liquid brain compounds from flowing or control their volatility. Further complicating love's toxic flood, was the fact that because it was the first time it had happened since the death of his wife, it came with the side effect of him feeling like he was guilty of some sort of betrayal. Intellectually, he knew it wasn't and that it even sounded stupid to say out loud. But emotionally, there simply was no avoiding it. As Clark lay awake in bed last night, drifting in between delirious sleep and incoherent exhaustion, he found himself rehearsing what he would have said to Mary Lynn if she were still alive and waiting for him when he got home. He defaulted to thinking how he would try to describe Sarah without raising suspicion, and how he would go about a completely normal routine and try to forget the whole thing, only to abruptly realize that she was long gone and there would be no need for explanations. Normally, when the ghosts of grief reared their seductive heads, Clark found solace in his work as a reporter where he could tell himself, authentically, that he was pursuing truth. But that escape route was blocked as he was in a major conflict with his editor as well as his technical advisor and biology teaching friend. It seemed like the only road forward, the only inviting pathway, was to get to know Sarah further. If he did so, the attraction would simply wear off like it always did. No matter how beautiful or wonderful a woman seemed on her surface, it was always a matter of time before he noticed why his beloved Mary Lynn was better for some reason. With some women that took longer than others, but it never failed. A few more conversations, a few more hours with this narcissistic enigma, and he would find a point where he felt total contempt for her and be free of the albatross of his crush. After all, he was a grown man and had dealt with these chemical hurricanes hundreds of times, sailing through unaffected by whatever woman was at the center – so why should Sarah be any different? Plus, he certainly wasn't about to sit his daughter Melody down and explain to her that he had met a woman and started dating and that the season of mourning her mother, his wife, was officially over. Melody wasn't ready for that, Clark told himself. Neither was he.

And so he sat in his car convincing himself, thinking in the prose of a hero's journey, but more than occasionally glancing down at his cell phone to see if he had received any return texts from either Amy Biancini or Elizabeth Cranford. He didn't want to be around the office. It would probably lead to an ugly confrontation with Elizabeth. It would be a while before his red hot anger at her for sandbagging his story wore off. He didn't want to be around his house where he would likely be avoiding his daughter while being constantly reminded of his late wife. And he certainly couldn't show up at Amy's high school again—at least not until he had smoothed things over for whatever it was that had made her mad at him. And that is how his car came to rest on the gravel shoulder of Rt. 34, diagonally across from the main gate to the old Fort Monmouth, which was now the Crisprgen headquarters and campus.

The twisting cantilevers of the Helix lab rose above the tree line behind the 12-foot fence with rolls of razor wire at the top as Clark sat in his car and stared. In that building was a mysterious seductive woman that seemed to have appeared in Clark's life like a tornado, wreaking havoc on the delicate balance of work and personal relationships he had taken so many years to build. Tornadoes, especially those with a Y chromosome, were to be avoided. He was old enough to know better. But there was something magnetic about the whole package. It wasn't just Sarah's hypnotic tractor beam gaze, but the equally magnetic hold she had over the families that she had recruited to the old army base and those who worked with her in the Helix Lab. Yes, Clark was intensely attracted to Sarah, but he told himself those were boyish emotions, and he couldn't let it affect his story. He chastised himself internally. There was something under the surface that wasn't right about what was going on here. Clark just needed to find something tangible to prove it. And that was why, he told himself further, the responsible thing to do was to revisit his sources for a fact check. Besides, Elizabeth hated his story anyway. He practically would have to start over, he told himself. Sure. That was legit. And just like that, Clark started his car, the tires slowly crackling across the gravel and chipped asphalt pavement of the shoulder, and crept up to the main gate of the old Fort Monmouth, where a silver sign read "Crisprgen WORLD HEADQUARTERS—Your Passport to the future." As Clark pulled up in front of the gate, he noticed there was no guard in the booth, or an intercom he could use. But as he sat looking around figuring out what to do next, a scraping metal sound penetrated his ears combined with the rusty creaking of a chain wrapping around large metal gears. The gate was opening. Without thinking any further, he shifted the car out of park and drove in.

***

Melody Westfield knelt in the dirt with the tomato plants that Amy Biancini had brought over. They were her home variety of Jersey tomatoes and had won all kinds of agricultural prizes. They were completely impractical for industrial agriculture scale growing as they needed extremely precise fertilizer elements and were hypersensitive to changes in temperature. Melody enjoyed spending time with Ms. Biancini, whom she had known her whole life. She was easy to talk to and had an uncanny familiarity and understanding of young women Melody's age. With her mother now gone, this was a gap she was happy to let Amy fill, even if it was temporary for the morning's random visit.

"Thank so much for the tomatoes, Amy," said Melody as she knelt in the moist dirt. "I was going to ask my dad to call you and see if we could get any for this year since it's now the week after July 4th, and I don't know if there is enough summer growing season left to produce the big ones we always get with your plants." Melody looked down sheepishly.

"Oh, don't worry These have half the required growing time of the accelerated hot house tomatoes that flood grocery stores," replied Amy. "So your father didn't say where he was going, Mel?"

"No, like I said, I woke up and he wasn't here this morning. And I don't think he came home last night because our door alarm would have logged an entry, and there wasn't one."

"Do you think he got up early and went into the office?" asked Amy.

"He slept in the office," interrupted a third voice from the lawn directly behind the two women who were kneeling and gardening. It was Elizabeth Cranford. "Do you know where your father is now?"

"Hi Elizabeth!" exclaimed Melody. "It's so cool you stopped by! We were just planting Ms. Biancini's tomatoes. She has bred all these different strains and won awards. She is a genetics wizard!"

"A genetics wizard?' Elizabeth cocked her head and extended her hand to Amy. "I could use a genetics expert to talk with right about now..." she said offhandedly.

"You mean about Crisprgen?" shot Amy. Elizabeth looked at her surprised.

"Yes. I'm sorry, but how do you know Clark and what did he share with you?"

"Clark and I have known each other since we were 17 years old. He needed a genetics expert for some research for a story, and I went with him out to Ft. Monmouth yesterday to see what the company did. How do you know Clark?" asked Amy.

"Oh! You're the expert he was referring to. I've also known Clark since I was 17, only he was much older," Elizabeth said with a laugh. Melody smiled. Amy did not. "Clark is my mentor, and I worked for him up until last year. Now we work together..."

"Elizabeth was dad's student, then intern, then staff writer, now she is his boss!" interjected Melody. Amy's eyes squinted.

"So you're Elizabeth Cranford…" she said. Elizabeth smiled. "Clark mentioned that you were supposed to meet us at the Crisprgen campus yesterday. We must have missed each other."

"Yeah, well, it seems I wasn't as needed as I thought," said Elizabeth sarcastically.

"Neither was I." muttered Amy. "Are you sure he slept at the office? Or did he just show up in the morning?"

Melody looked at the other two women perplexed.

"No, he definitely spent the night in the office, but just like Clark, he didn't sleep and finished writing and turned in the story he brought you to help with yesterday." sighed Elizabeth.

"Oh cool! Did he quote Ms. Biancini or at least use some of the background she gave him?" sang Melody.

"Not exactly…" said Elizabeth softly.

"Shocking," said Amy deadpan. "Did he talk about the sexy genius in charge and how the angelic intellectual is going to save humanity by creating magic with the gene patents she is using my students to mine?"

"Nope," said Elizabeth, realizing from Amy's cold sarcasm that she had a similar resentment towards Clark being enamored with Sarah Reistad. "At least, that wasn't the story he turned in."

As the three women stared at one another in silence, Elizabeth knew she had made a mistake judging Clark's story and motives so harshly.

***

"How is your ankle feeling, Mr. Westfield?" The voice of Allele startled Clark. He had found a parking spot under an elm tree just across from the Helix Lab parking lot and sat there for a few seconds before going inside. He hadn't seen anyone walking up to his vehicle and wondered how such a tall, slender woman in a crimson lycra body suit could sneak up on him so inconspicuously. She stooped at a slight angle, looking at him intently expressionless waiting for him to answer.

"Umm…it's ok, thanks," Clark said, perplexed.

"OK, good. If you can walk on it, I'll escort you inside now," said Allele robotically. Clark was bewildered. He hadn't told anyone at Crisprgen or elsewhere that he planned to stop by.

"So… Do you always stand in the parking lot waiting to greet visitors?" quipped Clark. Allele's facial muscles didn't twitch. "OK, Allele, honey… baby…darling… What do I have to do to get a smile out of you?" He was only half joking.

He was beginning to wonder if Allele was somewhere on the autism spectrum.

"I do not have any instructions to smile," Allele replied as she marched straight ahead. Her reply seemed odd to Clark so he taunted a little further.

"OK…I hereby instruct you to smile.." he said, thinking this would generate at least a smile, or perhaps even a chuckle.

"I only receive instructions from Ms. Reistad," declared Allele as she continued walking without turning.

"Sounds like you are missing out on a lot of fun," Clark joked further. What could possibly be this odd woman's problem? He thought to himself.

As they entered the enormous glass lobby of the Helix Lab with its cathedral ceilings and gigantic spiral cantilever floors, he paused at the metal detectors and began to take his cell phone and keys out of his pockets to place them in the plastic basket. However, before he could place anything into the basket, the glass gate panels sprung open with the sound of compressed air escaping. Allele walked through and motioned for him to join her.

"Thanks for the no-hassle entry, Allele. It's almost like you were expecting me!" Clark joked. His odd chaperone led him up to the second floor, where they made a drastic turn from the elevator exit to conform to the complicated architecture. Allele stopped in front of an ornate dark wood door.

"Ms. Reistad instructed me to wait for you to arrive and to bring you here," she said, beckoning for Clark to step into what looked like a very large conference room. Instead of a big conference table, maroon plush furniture ordained the middle of the room. There were several large couches and three humongous dark maroon velvet bean bags in the middle of the room. Clark stepped inside and Allele closed the door behind him. Despite the Helix Lab being mostly glass and having extraordinary amounts of natural light, this room was oddly dim and full of shadows. A floor to ceiling window was in the center of the far wall, and the wall to Clark's left had a set of double doors made out of the same ornately carved heavy dark wood. He didn't know if anyone other than Allele even knew he was there, and had no intention of waiting in an empty dark room. As he looked out the window at the tree tops swaying in the breeze, he suddenly smelled lavender and felt two warm gentle hands cover his eyes. He knew immediately it must be Sarah.

"Guess who?" she whispered with her mouth right up against his ear. Clark felt a pang of adrenaline and the rush of sexual attraction. She smelled wonderful.

"I can't imagine…" he replied, playing along.

"Hmm…maybe it's your salvation?" said Sarah playfully, immediately maneuvering around Clark so they could face one another. She was smiling like a schoolgirl who had just pulled off a prank.

"Hi…" stammered Clark. He suddenly realized that not only did he not have a clear purpose for being on the Crisprgen campus in the Helix Lab, but he also hadn't given any thought to what he would say as to WHY he was there. "Ummm, I figured I would stop by and…well, I need to fact check a few things." He didn't sound believable even to himself.

"A fact check? I see," teased Sarah. "Well, I'm glad you came, even if that is just your lame excuse so you could see me again," challenged Sarah with a smile. She was 100% correct, and Clark felt disarmed. There was no hiding the fact he had shown up unannounced for a fact check that could have been done by phone and was usually done by a third party at the paper. But Elizabeth had asked him for a re-write, so fuck it, he might as well start over. Plus, he knew he couldn't navigate his attraction to Sarah undetected much longer. "What facts can I help you check?" Sarah said softly slowly, taking both of Clark's hands and leading him over to the big velvet couch. Clark felt a lump in his throat. It was the perfect storm of attraction, suspicion, curiosity and attraction all wrapped up in guilt because she was the first woman since Mary Lynn towards whom he felt these emotions. It was all too much so Clark defaulted to the only mechanism he knew how to deploy when emotions got too murky - unrestricted brutal honesty. He struck a serious tone.

"Sarah, I didn't really plan on coming here, at least not for a fact check," he said. Sarah looked at him as if she already knew exactly what he was going to say.

"That much I know," she said smiling. "So why did you come here? I know why, but I wonder if you do…" She sat down and lay back on the couch seductively.

"You do?" he replied, raising his eyebrows. "I'd love to hear it."

"OK --Well, I think there is an obvious attraction between us, and you are hesitant to get involved with the subject of a story, especially when you aren't sure how you feel about the work we do here." She paused for a moment. Clark tried not to look surprised or let on that she had nailed it. "And not only am I completely confident and proud about what we do here and the conviction with which I approach my work, I also happen to think that you are worth any explanation you require to understand what we do here and why."

"Something like that," muttered Clark. He was somewhat disarmed by Sarah's directness and was unaccustomed to being the evasive party in an interview.

"I guess my issue, Sarah, is that you seem to have discovered and perfected something profoundly important out here, something that could help millions of people, and you don't have anyone or anything watching over it to make sure it's used properly." Clark found himself searching for words and stumbling into oversimplifying the issue.

"I understand," replied Sarah, still smiling. "Would you feel more comfortable if we were a nondescript, unknown government office under the NIH or the CDC that no one ever heard of? Do you really think there would be more accountability and safety deep inside the anonymous government? Let me show you something..." Sarah took Clark's hand gently and led him across the large room to a set of heavy double doors made of dark carved wood. She opened one of the doors a crack, revealing a large ornate conference room. Clark could see there was a large conference table with a dozen or so chairs containing well-dressed adults. He looked at Sarah, who stood smiling.

"There's a meeting going on in the next room," Clark said softly. "Is this a meeting you need to be in?" he asked. Sarah shrugged.

"I think we both should go in, and you should just listen," she whispered.

"Why? Who is in there?" Clark whispered back.

"That's our Board. They are the Directors that oversee all of the Crisprgen business—our corporate forecast, our long term strategic planning, our investors..." Sarah had a pleased expression on her face. "You are welcome to speak with any of them. I'm happy to introduce you."

"Maybe another time…" Clark stuttered. He was somewhat taken aback that Sarah had deciphered all his misgivings about her work and offered him access to their Board of Directors. Suddenly, he felt an odd journalistic paralysis. He was uncontrollably attracted to this odd beautiful woman whom he knew represented everything he had tried to expose in his journalism career—corporate greed circumventing the public good. But with Sarah, it was even deeper and more sinister. Her arrogance about the smart portion of the human species breaking off seemed fundamentally problematic, and yet Clark couldn't resist the hypnotic pull she seemed to have over him. But Elizabeth didn't seem to care about any of the ethical issues he had pointed out in his article, so why should he? Fuck it, he thought. And as he stood there turning the professional and emotional burnout over and over in his head, he felt Sarah grab his hand and pull him into the boardroom.

"Hi everybody!" she exclaimed in a happy voice. Clark almost lost his balance as she pulled him into the board room. "We have a very special guest with us today. This is Clark Westfield, a reporter with the Newark Examiner. He is writing a profile about the company and our work."

Clark stood and looked at the faces around the table. There were seven people seated. One woman at the opposite end caught his attention. It was Lieutenant Colonel Kelly Pram. She was dressed in civilian clothes, a tan pantsuit and an off white blouse with a cameo brooch. She met Clark's gaze fiercely and he realized immediately he probably shouldn't reveal they knew one another. Sarah began introductions.

"So this is Mr. Al Gamper, CEO of the Guardian Venture Capital," she said pointing at a middle aged man in the first chair at the table. "And this is Joseph Bordo, he used to be deputy commissioner at the FDA before starting Gentec Pharmaceuticals. Next is Virgilio Alomar, he founded and runs Advanced Materials Science." The next person seated was Lt. Col. Pram.

"And this is Dr. Katherine O'Halloran, she is a doctor of education and has done the most postdoctoral work on human hyper intelligence of anyone or any university. If it has to do with the smart ones, you call Dr. O'Halloran!" Sarah held out her hand for an awkward high five. Clark locked eyes with Lt. Col. Pram. She gave him an icy stare and shook her head slightly in an inconspicuous "no" motion. Clark realized she must be working under an alias.

"Good to meet you…uh… Dr. O'Halloran." He tried to signal that he wouldn't blow her cover, but still tilted his head to one side to indicate confusion and smile slightly. Pram shot him - a dagger-like look. Sarah continued introducing everyone around the table. The CEO of the largest silicon chip maker, Sing Ho Ma was next. His company in Taiwan not only made 80% of the computer chips used in the US, but

Clark had read a profile on him that revealed only he knew the actual engineering patent specifications for the latest generation of computers and that if he were to die, no one would even know where to look for them. Next to Sing Ho Ma was Michael Benevento, a young entrepreneur who while at Harvard had created the largest social media platform in the world – Lookbook - which had over 2 billion users. Benevento's company had also spun off half a dozen additional social media platforms for everything from news to dating to fashion. He claimed it situated him in a place where he could spot trends, and thus was an influencer expert on popular culture and a staple on entertainment talk shows. Next to Benevento was Harris Dade, CEO of the largest oil company in the world. He wore a white cowboy hat, a brown suede sports jacket and deep brown embroidered cowboy boots. Sarah finally got to the end and introduced the last person at the table.

"This is Karen Carmer, she is the founder and CEO of Valiant Healthcare, the largest…"

"The largest health insurance company in the world…." Clark interrupted, finishing her sentence. "Yeah, Valiant, of course, you have hundreds of millions of members and you're the umbrella company for each state chapter."Clark said it in such a way where it sounded like an afterthought.

Around the table sat some of the most important and powerful captains of every industry on the planet— energy companies, giant health, health insurers, a social media tycoon, and in the middle of all of them, was a U.S. Army intelligence officer that Clark had known for years and used as an expert source when he was setting out to find the then missing Matsumoto kid. They had met in Washington the prior week when Elizabeth originally assigned the story. At that meeting, Clark hadn't mentioned any of the missing students' names and Lt. Pram hadn't asked. Yet here they both were. But more importantly, at a table where multiple powerful figures sat was an Army intelligence officer working under cover. Clark felt sick. It was a towel tightening rush triggered by stress chemicals that makes the colon shake and quiver and usually sends one running to the nearest toilet. Lt. Pram in the middle of this table confirmed Clark's worst instinct that he had fought not to indulge— that there was something happening at Crisprgen that warranted the clandestine scrutiny of Army intelligence. It really was as deep and serious as he thought.

"Clark is a reporter whom you've all heard of. He has two Pulitzer Prizes and has had a column in New Jersey since…when did you start Clark?" Sarah turned and asked him in front of the table.

"Uh…, too long ago." Clark tried to joke but it just made him more nauseous.

"Clark is going to be writing a profile on Crisprgen, and he has been interviewing our star student recruits, their families and our staff and..well, lets let him tell us. What have you been doing Clark, and while we have this fabulous group of board members and founders here, is there anything you'd like to ask them? Be careful everyone, you may be quoted!" Sarah turned with an exaggerated expression to the table gesturing with her hand. She then turned and smiled at Clark, prompting him to speak. Clark was completely caught off guard.

"Hi…nice to meet everybody." Clark had to keep a clear, cool head. "Sarah is correct, I'm writing a story about your company, and I have had the pleasure of meeting the families who live here— you know— the parents of the kids whose genes you are harvesting." Clark felt himself slip as he said it. These were important lofty folks who likely wouldn't appreciate sarcasm, especially about their own company. But to Clark's surprise he was met with smiles and nods. He suddenly realized he could turn to Lt. Colonel Kelly Pram, or in this setting Katherine O'Halloran, to steer the conversation. "Um… ma'am in the back… did Sarah say you are a doctorate of education?" Kelly Pram nodded. Clark took it as a signal to continue. "Well, maybe you are the best person to ask. Do you think recruiting smart kids and harvesting their genes to create a genetic passport to the next branch of human evolution is a good thing to do?"

Clark had gone for the jugular. He wanted to know why she was here.

"I do, Mr. Westfield. In fact, I have a model family that I'd like you to meet, maybe when the board meeting is over later this evening. I could walk you out to the village and introduce you." Clark read her invitation loud and clear. He nodded.

"Sure, Mrs., uh, Dr. O'Halloran." Clark smirked. "I'll meet you at your convenience, or shall we say…"

"5 PM Sharp at the Neanderthal Hall in the village." Pram finished for him. Clark nodded. He then turned to Sarah.

"Listen, I don't want to take up the board's time and it looks like they are in the middle of a meeting, so uh…I'm just gonna go." He motioned towards the door. Sarah met him with her soft gaze and took his hand, turned to the table and said in her dreamy voice:

"Sorry all, I will be going to show Mr. Westfield more of what he came to see." She then turned and led Clark by the hand through the big set of double doors into an adjoining ballroom size section. They ascended a spiral staircase at the far end and arrived in a large bedroom. The walls were covered with a plush red velvet. The furniture were Victorian style couches of deep red velvet. Draperies covered the walls with even more velvet fabric. All of the velvet was a deep red. In the middle of the room was a bed shaped like a circle. It looked like a cat house in Amsterdam.

"Gee… I love what you've done with the place," Clark said facetiously. "What exactly is this room for?" he asked while looking around.

"This is my fuck room," said Sarah, looking him dead in the eyes with a sinister smile. She stepped closer into Clark's personal space. She grabbed both his wrists and led him over to the bed. They both stood against the edge of the circular bed with the plush black shag comforter. Clark felt like a rag doll. He knew what was about to happen. His inner journalistic vocation told him he should simply leave and go downstairs, but he hadn't touched a woman since he held his dying wife's hand. Sarah pushed him down on the bed and he lay flat on his back. She straddled him like a horse and sat on his pelvis and hips with all her weight. She said nothing.

"You are overthinking this, Clark," said Sarah seductively. "You remember I told you that Neanderthals were equivalent to Cro Magnon? The two blended ancestral species are Homo Sapiens. They just had slightly different talents that when combined, created the Homo Sapien branch. The Neaderthals were the romantics. It was their genes for love and desire that drove them forward. They persisted through passion. I told you I have a high percentage of Neanderthal genes, right? Well, I do…and they want you so badly right now…" Sarah leaned down and kissed Clark's neck. This was exhilarating. She undid his belt and slipped her pants off.

"Ok… just try not to grunt like a Neanderthal…,." he joked out of sheer anxiety. Sarah playfully slapped Clark on the face. She then made some grunt noises and both of them laughed. This was a joy that Clark had not felt in decades. He paused for a moment. In his mind, he imagined a hallway with his wife Mary Lynn at the far end. He waved goodbye to Mary Lynn, and she smiled and gave him the thumbs up. Clark felt several tears run down his cheeks. He then felt Sarah's warm sticky genitalia and forgot all about it. They fucked for hours…

***

Around midafternoon, Clark lay in the bed, with Sarah in the spoon position. The contours of her shoulders, back and hips fit perfectly in the crescent he made. This wasn't normal afterglow… this was something different. Their love making had been intense. Sarah fucked like a machine—never tiring, never losing a rhythm, and always sustaining whatever position they were in until Clark wanted to move. She seemed to pull an emotional intensity out of thin air, which in turn caused Clark to be even more intensely attracted and infatuated with her. She was beautiful, but knew exactly how to unleash a raw and almost bestial sexuality. Clark had only one experience in his life that was close in intensity, and it had been before he had even met Mary Lynn. Usually after sexual acrobatics on this scale, the average man, Clark included, would fall into an exasperated breathless pile and immediately get up to make a sandwich or take a nap. Most women, especially after sex this messy, would retreat to the bathroom to shower. But neither moved. It didn't feel messy. In fact, it felt like a unique perfection that happens only a few times in life. Clark didn't want to move. Ever. Strangely though, he didn't feel tired or thirsty— in fact, he was ready to go again.

"Umm, did you happen to replace my genes so I no longer have a refractory period?" he whispered in Sarah's ear.

"We can start again… I'm not tired!" said SaraSarah as she quickly flipped Clark onto his back and straddled him like a horse again.

"No…I mean yes…I mean…wait." Clark's head was spinning. Even back in college, he didn't recall having this kind of stamina. "You're pretty incredible. I mean, FUCK Sarah! You know I've been feeling like an old sack of shit lately, especially in the bedroom. Well, since Mare died, I haven't really had any exercise…" He smiled sheepishly. "So, you are pretty goddamn talented here in the sack— would that be your Neanderthal genes at play?"

Sarah giggled. "That's exactly it! We cavewomen can fuck like beasts, can't we?" Clark thought for a moment she was being serious. "But yes, there are genetics at play here, and yes, my Neanderthal surplus benefits me. It's a bit of a blessing and a curse…" she said, teasing. Clark laughed and tickled her ribs in a jabbing playful motion.

"So how do you explain me? I haven't been able to go twice, let alone all afternoon, since long before I turned 40," Clark asked, somewhat rhetorically.

"Well, that's the TA 65. It really brings back a lot of the youthful confidence and stamina," said Sarah. "Yeah, with the telomerase supplements, the sexual self gets reset at the age when we had to procreate adolescence to mid-30s. Remember those romantic years? Well, you are back at the starting line now." Sarah turned to him and smiled. Clark was confused.

"Starting line? Wait, what? What is TA 65? Is that a chemical or a hormone or something?" he asked.

"TA65 is an enzyme that is a telomerase activator. It basically tells your cells to keep long telomeres and to keep dividing. After you've been on it for a while, this is one of the many things that starts to feel awesome again. There are other things too, but I don't want to spoil the surprises." Sarah gently kissed Clark on his forehead.

"OK, but I haven't been on it…" said Clark, shaking his head slightly.

"Oh yes, you have," said Sarah playfully. She simply looked at him and was silent.

"What..is it in the food I eat, like is it in beets or something? Because I hate beets…" Sarah giggled and grabbed Clark's arm at the wrist. She turned it over gently so he could see part of his elbow. On it was a small circular flesh-colored sticker the size of a quarter. The material was very thin and Clark could barely feel its texture because it had adhered to his skin.

"What the hell is that?" He was slightly taken aback. Sarah just kept smiling at him.

"That's your TA 65 transdermal patch. I put one on you the first day you got here when you had the sprained ankle. It has been on there ever since." She looked like she was giving a child a gift.

"It's practically dissolved into my skin…I can't get it off…what the fuck? What is this?"

"Yeah, the transdermal doses dissolve. You'll only have some residual color for about two weeks. The TA65 is an enzyme so it goes right from the gel glue on the patch into your skin and capillaries."

"You gave me a dose of TA 65?? You gave me your experimental drug and didn't tell me?" Clark was extremely bothered that she would give him anything without telling him or asking.

"Well, you feel great, don't you? It's not an experimental drug. It's been around a while. It's been used since the 60s as a life extender for the wise people we need to keep living longer. It's been given to many people over the years. The average lifespan increase is 10-15 years, and as it got refined, that got longer and longer. We are at a point now where we have people living past any age records, and we have to decide if we should keep their identity or get them new identification.

No one will believe their real birthday. By the way, that is what gave you your Olympic sexual performance just now." She stopped talking, smiled and got behind Clark and held him in her lap, and he leaned against her like she was a lounge chair.

"You gave me this stuff? That's not okay!" Clark looked up at her and was completely enthralled by her deep blue eyes. "But I feel really fucking good…so…"

"I needed you to feel this. If I had offered it to you as a trial you never would have done it. It's my gift to you. Clark, you deserve to feel young again and you are one of the wise ones we need to keep around longer. The world is better with you in it, and as the Great Reset starts, we will need your wisdom through the painful transitions. I'm sorry, I know I should have asked you, but I also wanted you to feel this… here…with me…" She kept their gaze locked. Clark felt goosebumps and butterflies in his stomach. Fuck! He felt alive again. In fact, he was falling in love again… This woman had just brought him out of the dark forest of grief.

"You can give me whatever you want," Clark whispered as a tear ran down his cheek.

"So…how long does this last? Till tomorrow I hope?" asked Clark. Sarah giggled.

"No, about a month, and then you can take another dose and as long as you are on it, you're preventing senescence—

or cell dying so your body will simply keep reinventing itself. You won't start to age, as you won't really add any years."

"So…having sex with a Neanderthal woman is the fountain of youth…" Clark mused out loud as he stood up and laughed a bit. "I'll take it!" He turned to look at Sarah who lay seductively on the bed on her side with one knee pulled up halfway to her chest. "I'll take it," he said again. Clark smirked and looked around the room. "Umm…where is the uh, restroom…? I have to—"

"Pee?" asked Sarah. "So do I. Also, the board members will probably wonder where we went, and I need to speak to a few. Don't you have to meet Dr. O'Halloran at 5 PM in the Neanderthal village? Why don't you head over there, and I'll see you around?" Clark had completely forgotten about the meeting he had set up with Lt. Col. Kelly Pram as she masqueraded as Katherine O'Halloran. Sarah grabbed a black silk robe with ornate pink flowers and a gold lapel, and tied it around her waist. She turned to Clark, threw her arms around his shoulders and kissed him deeply.

"Uh…so after I meet with Lt…err Ms. O Halloran should I come back here or?…" Clark suddenly felt like it was the end of a first date, and he needed to understand what to expect next while wanting to resume this fucking marathon with Sarah as soon as possible.

"Sure. I'll be around," said Sarah as she kissed him again. And just like that, she turned and bounced out of the room, pausing for a brief moment to turn around and look at Clark once more, and then she vanished behind the red velvet curtain that concealed the door. Clark felt like he had just jumped over a waterfall and told himself not to think and just go find Lt. Col. Kelly Pram.

***

The Crisprgen Village seemed like a small, happy neighborhood. In front of some of the multi-family houses that previously housed thousands of troops were picnic tables with two or three men sitting and conversing while other couples sat having dinner. If one didn't know better, it would be easy to think this was simply an archetypically clean neighborhood usually found on military bases. Clark walked in the direction he could remember best. He walked past the first few houses with their gaping emergency tunnels. He recalled that they all had been renamed after human ancestors in evolutionary order—Ardipithicus, Australopithecus, and Homo Erectus. He stopped at the Neanderthal house and looked around. His cell phone buzzed and a text with a blocked number came through. It said: "Walk into the Neanderthal tunnel." He figured it must be Lt. Col. Kelly Pram. Clark walked into the mouth of the tunnel; its walls were the corrugated steel pipe that was a good 12 feet in diameter. Clark let his eyes adjust to the lack of light and started to look around for a light switch. Finding none, he opened his cell phone and fumbled for the flashlight feature. It was barely enough light for him to see where he was walking. He walked ten yards inside and came to the top of a cement staircase that looked like it connected to something much deeper underground. It was cold in the tunnel, like a refrigerator compared to the July heat outside. "This feels against my better judgment," he thought as he descended the staircase. It was even colder at the bottom with so much humidity that he could feel the chilly damp condensation forming little beads of liquid on his forehead and temples.

"For a man with afterglow, you are showing up pretty clammy on the thermal camera," said a voice in the corner. Clark could barely make it out, but dimly lit in the corner was a large metal desk. He could make out the figure of a woman seated, and the colors and graphics of a thermal camera app illuminated her facial features. It was Lt. Col. Kelly Pram, or Dr. Katherine O'Halloran, depending on your location.

"Can we turn on the lights, Kel?" Clark asked. Something inside him told him whatever he was about to hear and discuss with Lt. Pram was going to diminish that feeling of bliss a guy gets when he has just fucked a girl who was out of his league. No matter what men may say, that only happens once or twice in each man's life…

Lt. Pram turned on the lights with a loud click. They were in a large room with a concrete floor and cinder block walls. Military boxes of various sizes were stacked from floor to ceiling. Stenciled in yellow and black letters of classic military flint were the general contents of each. Some were marked food rations, boots, or cold weather protection. Several of the boxes were labeled "salt". A door at the far end had the words "Radio Room" stenciled at eye level.

"What's with all the salt?" remarked Clark, turning around 360 degrees.

"What's the one thing your body can't live without and that you need to preserve food?" answered Lt. Pram. Clark nodded. Of course…salt.

"Katherine O'Halloran? Really Kel? You make such a nice Irish spy. What's with the thermal camera?"

"I had to make sure there weren't any listening devices. This app has a debug function," she replied. She rested the thermal camera attachment of her iPhone on the table.

"What is this? A crawl space for a nuclear holocaust?" Clark asked, looking around.

"This is Lieutenant Col's Pram's command bunker that she designed back when she was a sergeant on this base in the 1970s. I actually designed the house bunker as one of my assignment projects required for advancement. God, I was so naïve…" she explained, looking around in admiration.

"Well, you built a beautiful bunker, Colonel. I love what you've done with the place," jibed Clark. "You military jerk-offs really were fooling yourself the whole time thinking you could win a nuclear war, weren't you?" Clark waxed philosophically.

"I sure as shit didn't," shot Col. Pram. "Why do you think I took a right turn into intelligence? I designed lots of places like this one, Westfield. One day as I was stacking boxes of salt, I had a moment of clarity that no amount of salt was going to protect me and this was all one big psy-ops to keep us all from deserting. Fighting has always been pointless—mutually assured destruction is a suicide pact. We either find a way to live together or we all go. That worked for 80 years and that's why there was no nuclear war. I realized that there was only one thing that mattered - working to prevent one, and that's what I have dedicated my military career to. Probably at the expense of what most normal people do and experience in a lifetime," she mused.

"Richie says hi by the way," Clark said without looking up. He'd had enough of the nuclear war and peace martyr act.

"Clark, you need to know what you are dealing with, and I need to know why you are here." Pram's tone suddenly got serious. Now she had Clark's undivided attention.

"Yeah…I need the same from you. You go first." he pushed back.

"I'm here under deep cover, which you will not ruin because Sarah Reistad is raising a threat and going rogue," answered Pram. "Clark, we can prevent a nuclear war, and we have successfully done so for almost 80 years, but life on

Earth as it is now is completely unsustainable. There aren't enough resources and the gap between the haves and have-nots is deeper than at any time. Nation-states don't matter anymore because geopolitical borders mean nothing in today's technologically connected world. The world will fall into two categories— the hyper-educated and healthy, and everyone else who will work to feed them. That's a powder keg with no happy ending. Now that we are all connected and share all the same knowledge thanks to the intellectual level playing field the internet provides, how long do you think the average population is going to tolerate it?"

"So when you say threat, are you talking about an uprising?" Clark asked.

"Yes, exactly. It's already happening. What does the alt-right criticize and hate the most?" she asked rhetorically before answering her own questions. "Intellectual elitism. Why? Because the educated and wealthy make the decisions for everyone else. At every stage of human evolution, the smarter apes were better off and the rest of them noticed."

"Yeah, but so what - then they just evolved into the next stage," countered Clark.

"Do you think that happened with a going away party? Or do you think they drew straws?" barked Pram sarcastically. "The smart ones had to be isolated so their genetics would remain concentrated. That means they were separated by disease and natural disasters, and there would have been grave and mortal fighting between family groups for resources. That's what is already happening today. The next fork is coming. But it won't unfold over a vague 20-30 thousand years this time. This time there is a perfect storm of catalysts that are going to force the next separation of the smart ones from everyone else. Anthropologists have known this since the 1970s and our military has been planning for it. The government has always kept a list and curated files on the smartest living private citizens. In the event of a catalyst such as, say, a war, a pandemic, a level 10 solar flare, a meteorite strike, the anticipated political and societal collapse, they would be rounded up and protected so they could be part of the rebuilding. Of course, we did this through a network of information assets, participating universities, etc. In the 70s, we started using computers and that let us manage these people— the smart ones— efficiently, secretly, and better. But it also let us calculate probabilities."

"Let me guess…you wrote a program to determine the probability of a war breaking out?"

"Yes, you've seen these probability programs before. But they can't run all scenarios. Every single one of them said that there would be a situation so big and grave that it would force only the smartest and most prepared humans to endure. I don't mean the blast or the cold winter or something acute. As time goes on, for multiple generations to thrive in whatever is left of the world, they will have to be the most intelligent of all of humanity to solve the new problems and challenges of whatever remains along with new profound technology." She paused for a moment

"Yeah, I know…only the smartest survive and go forward and those traits wind up in our genome," said Clark. "But if you have been planning the holocaust after party, why are you interested in this place?"

"Because your new girlfriend has two things that she discovered here that she hasn't turned over to the Pentagon, and we think she is going to disappear with them," answered Pram.

"She isn't my girlfriend," said Clark, sounding like an 8th-grade boy. "What two things?"

"She is your girlfriend, Clark, admit it. I know you just spent the afternoon squinting in orgasmic bliss. Don't worry, it's a good thing because we need you in there," said Kelly matter-of-factly.

"You need me in where? Who needs me? Who is 'we'?"

"We,' as in YOU, are now working with the Pentagon Joint Intelligence Units. Sarah Reistad was recruited by us when she was 8 years old. We practically created her. She was one of the first children that was infused with early gene therapies. Endocrinologists will tell you that she has contributed more to their field than any living research subject. Men say she defies the laws of physics in the sack.

That's her Neanderthal gene surplus," jibed Lt. Col. Pram with a smile.

"Yeah…I can vouch for that…I figured you guys would have eyes on her, or at least this project but I never thought she was an agent." Clark sighed.

"She wasn't an agent!" exclaimed Kelly. "She was our research subject and we also used her hyperintelligence to help plan out contingencies. Turns out she was also a brilliant genetics researcher. She's been harvesting genes from smart kids and creating a master genome. It's a highly classified and secret project, but she isn't an agent. She is under contract with us however, which means we see and own everything she does with the understanding that she could adapt it for civilian use in the private sector someday and hold the patents."

"So instead of giving you the genome for the day after the nuclear war happens, she is selling it through Crisprgen…" Clark's voice trailed off as he thought out loud. He knew Sarah was complicated but he would rather not learn she was a treasonous criminal.

"Very smart, Westfield. You really can figure stuff out," said Pram.

"But so what? Why don't you just handle it and tell her she is in breach of contract or seize the lab or something? You guys are the fucking military and your scientist is hiding her discovery and you mean to tell me you don't have at least a dozen protocols for this kind of situation?"

"Yeah jackass, we have protocols. And the one we find ourselves in says that we have to secure two critical discoveries and associated technologies before we shut her down. She won't get anywhere if she tries to take off or disappear but what we need is stored on digital servers, and we need to make sure she doesn't destroy them. That's why I am here undercover, and that's why we need you. You are on the inside, now literally, and can help us a great deal." Lt. Col. Kelly Pram checked to see Clark's expression and let him digest what he heard.

"What does she have that you want?" he asked. "What did she discover?"

"Well, there is one genome she has been harvesting from one of her recruits - the kid's name is Greg Mackoul." Clark nodded as Pram continued. "Well, Greg has a gene sequence that if it's captured for CRISPR procedures and inserted in people, it will cause the evolutionary fork to happen in one generation."

"You mean this Mackoul kid has the last link in the intelligence genome Sarah is creating to cause the genetic fork in the road, leaving humanity as we know it behind and evolving into this new species, which will be very smart, very healthy, and very long living humans?" asked Clark.

"Among other traits she has harvested, yes. And only she knows where this kid's CRISPR segment is. We have the rest of the ideal genome already sequenced, that's not a problem.

She gave it to us. But she is keeping this last snippet from the Mackoul kid, and thus the key to humanity's next evolutionary branch. And well, we just can't have that." Pram finished speaking and looked at Clark to see his reaction.

"Ok, so what does any of this have to do with me?" asked Clark. He was starting to feel queasy.

"You need to find the Mackoul boy and the CRISPR snippet she harvested from him for us. Do it with her. Romance her, she will let you meet him. One thing about Sarah is that she is very childlike when it comes to love. She has an uncomplicated innocence to her and has cooperative, straightforward relationships that are very genuine. The Neanderthals truly knew how to care for one another. Whatever emotion she is showing you is real, Clark. It's not in her genetic nature to do otherwise." Clark swallowed hard.

"What's the other thing she has that you want?" he pressed.

"We've been using an enzyme called TA-65 since the 60s. It extends life - at first for only 3-5 years, but now we are up to an average of 25, and some even longer."

"Yeah, I'm familiar with TA-65," said Clark, looking down. "She stuck some transdermal patch on me and uh, let's just say it works."

"She gave you some? Oh, so you probably had a surge of sexual stamina which explains your lateness." Lt. Col. Pram said dryly. "Yeah, that's the stuff. The patches are low dose.

The longest lasting is the injection, which lasts more than a month. This has been sold to the very elite and also provided free to our list of smart ones."

"So why do you need it if you already have it?" asked Clark, confused.

"We need the CRISPR sequence that makes your body make it permanently. You can take it by injection but the moment you stop you immediately go back to aggressive aging. If your DNA instructs your cells to keep making TA65, then you won't age. But, you need the genetic sequence to do it, and it has to be CRISPRd in, through a simple injection. Sarah has found that sequence also and she hasn't turned it over to us. If she is giving you doses then you can get it out of her."

Clark was more dejected than stunned. He felt it seemed too good to be true on the way over. No woman with that amount of electrical energy and hypnotic magnetism comes without baggage. But for just one afternoon, it had felt like he was alive again and not a sad, aging depressed widower.

"So, Westfield, we need you to help us on this," said Lt. Col Pram, rising from her chair.

Clark shook his head in disappointment and disbelief. "Come on Clark, what's wrong with having a little fun while you are chasing down one of the biggest stories you've ever discovered? You've always admired cartoonish James Bond type spies who laid while they are stealing secrets and saving the world."

"That's not it Kel…," said Clark, sounding dejected. "I know there are a ton of ethical complications with all this, but my newspaper isn't the least bit interested in reporting them, so I figured I would pay a little more attention to Sarah and find out what makes her tick. This afternoon was the first time in a long time

… that I didn't feel like a stranger wandering through the world. It's like the sun finally came out after the long cold winter of losing Mare." Clark began to swell with emotion, and he could feel his lower eyelids getting heavy with what were about to become tears.

"Look, Clark, the last thing I want to do is burst your bubble here, especially if it's helping you transcend the grief and depression you are living through, but that is the TA-65 working. It's like an emotional reset that suppresses the negativity and turns on the feel-good chemicals. As it wears off, you start to feel emotions like you are feeling now. Heads up! You are going to come down twice as hard and twice as miserable so prepare for a shitty afternoon," she cautioned.

Clark could already feel the elation he felt back in bed with Sarah starting to bleed out in a slow drip. He didn't know what to think. When he looked up, Lt. Col Kelly Pram was gone. She had disappeared down the dark tunnel on the far side of the room that led to other tunnels and god knows where else. He sat alone in the bunker for a few moments and then turned and with heavy steps, made his way back to the Helix Lab.

As Clark approached the main entrance to the spiral building, his head was spinning. He didn't know what to think about everything that Lt. Pram had just told him, and he didn't even want to. This captivating woman, the one pinhole of sunlight that he had found just a few hours before, was not only too good to be true, but she was a risk to national security. But what to do about it strategically and ethically was of no concern to him as the door swung open, and Allele held it as she greeted him. Clark's only concern at this moment was to fend off the creeping malaise which felt like bereavement and depression in freefall as the TA65 began to dissipate in his bloodstream.

"Ms. Reistad is upstairs in the Fuck Room waiting for you," said Allele robotically. Clark kept walking as he nodded in response. He then paused realizing that he had no idea where in the bizarre building the said 'Fuck Room' was. As he stood for a moment to get his bearings, Allele marched past him with her odd horseback-like gait. "Please follow me," she said, without looking in his direction. They ascended the grand spiral staircase that wound around the central elevator shaft to the second floor where they continued down a long hallway. Several left and right turns revealed a very tight small spiral staircase in the far corner of the room. The circumference of the hole in the ceiling at the top of the stairs couldn't have been more than 36 inches, almost too small for a man of Clark's size to squeeze through. He turned to look at Allele who returned her usual far away, unfocused stare then simply pointed to the hole in the ceiling at the top of the stairs. Clark made his way over to the wrought iron steps. He could barely fit his whole foot on the largest part of the triangular stairs. As his eyes adjusted to the red light in the small room above, he could see the circular bed with the satin sheets. Sarah lay seductively on the bed and greeted him with a warm, sexy smile. Clark felt a pang of excitement, which quickly dissipated back to the burning despair that seemed to bubble higher with each passing moment.

"So… let's resume shall we?" Sarah whispered and giggled.

"Sarah, we need to talk. I'm not feeling so good," Clark said as he sat on the edge of the bed with his back towards her. He felt her arms around his shoulders and then her breasts softly pushing against his back. She leaned down and kissed him on the neck and put her mouth very close to his ear.

"I know what you are feeling. The comedown is always a drag," she whispered in his ear. Clark nodded. "I'm going to give you another dose of TA-65, and let's stay here a while. Let the world turn without you for an evening, Clark Westfield. You've earned it. All the problems and all the details churning in your beautiful head can wait. Right now I just want you to relax and let me take care of you." Clark leaned back in her arms and fought the feelings of despair and disappointment, knowing that not only had he completely destroyed any ethics and objectivity related to the story he was supposed to be investigating, but that whatever was happening in this scarlet red Fuck Room was going to be ended by the Pentagon once the final genome snippet was found. Instead of a limitless horizon of romantic possibility, Sarah Reistad, though brilliant and beautiful, was yet another dead end in Clark's purgatory of depression and grief.

"Give me whatever you've got," Clark managed to choke out without his voice breaking. Sarah gently took his hand and stretched out his arm. She slipped a latex band around his arm two inches below his elbow and tapped on the inside of the elbow joint. She then looked deep into Clark's eyes and delivered her warm and seductive smile. Clark felt a small sting on the inside of his arm and found it difficult to break Sarah's intense gaze. When he could bring himself to look down, he saw her hand deftly plunging a large syringe which she had inserted into his vein. He raised his eyebrows.

"No sticker patch this time?" he asked as the warm surging flood of Oxytocin washed over him. This was bliss…

"No, trust me. This is better," said Sarah. And just like that they lay down on the bed and didn't leave that room…

Chapter 8

The hiss of the fine New Jersey pineland sand was the only sound in the car as Elizabeth Cranford drove with Amy Biancini sat in the passenger seat. The two women had sensed an urgency they couldn't explain. Sarah Resitad had tripped both their radars, each for different reasons.

"Hey Amy," asked Elizabeth. "You've known Clark a long time, right?"

"We met when we were 17 when we moved into our first college dormitory. He was two doors down, and he had a pet iguana," replied Amy, wistfully smiling through the warm nostalgia of a simpler, more innocent time in their lives.

"And? Why was that a point of attraction exactly?" asked Elizabeth, sarcastically.

"Oh, because I did too!" laughed Amy.

"You both had iguanas as pets? Are you serious?" asked Elizabeth with a tone of disbelief.

"Well, yeah," Amy replied. To a biology teacher and animal lover pet reptiles weren't the least bit unusual. "But you know Clark, he loved pet reptiles and we had our iguanas for years. I had one in the classroom until last year."

"Sounds like you two were made for each other." Elizabeth smirked. Amy felt herself pause at the remark. "Listen, Amy, you are a scientist and a teacher so maybe you can explain to me some of the guts of this gene stuff. I am worried about Clark with this; he was really fired up when I told him we would temporarily be sitting on his story the other day. I've never seen him like that. Of course, it's been tough since Mare died but there was something else about the story that came from very deep within him. He seems genuinely shook about the existential ethics of all this. So let me ask you— is it as serious as he thinks it is? Is there a corporate tycoon harvesting geniuses to create a master genome and spin off a branch of humanity into the next species? Is that really fucking possible?"

"It's been possible for a while, it just hasn't accelerated because all the science, technology, and know-how wasn't in one place under one roof," replied Amy.

"How so?" asked Elizabeth.

"Well, the genetic scientists were academics or part of government institutions. The pharma industry drove discovery in the private sector like it always has by funding research though not in a uniform way. But it's been possible since we decoded the genome in 2003. The reason it's accelerated so rapidly lately and is finding commercial use now is because we have more powerful computers and global networks to share information, practically in real-time. Throw in some venture capital money and you've got a Frankenstein in the shape of a DNA helix. At that moment you, newspaper editor, are the last link for widespread adoption and designing the next phase of the human race."

"I'm the link? How so?" asked Elizabeth, perplexed.

"Well, your newspaper will first tell the sanitized version and skip covering the massive shift in equality that will immediately activate as the privileged start their gene therapies. But your paper will also provide massive amounts of raw longitudinal data about the thoughts and habits of your subscribers that are collected as they select which articles to read, who to follow on social media, and what comments they leave. That will be cross-referenced with information from the consumer and financial companies that are owned by the parent company. Then that will refine the targeting of the gene collection to a hyper-precise level, revealing which traits from which groups are optimal, ultimately designing better and better genomes, or ones for specific purposes. Your newspaper, by bringing Sarah Reistad on as an investor, is providing her with both an unlimited repository of human subjects as well as AI tools to filter and select whatever she is looking for."

"So this is some real shit then, huh?" remarked Elizabeth.

"Yup and you're neck deep in it," Amy chuckled in a friendly way. "Listen, Clark always talked about you, and I feel like I know you. He was so proud of you, and he thinks of you as somewhere between a daughter and a younger sister. He always said how smart you were, and he also said you had a conscience. Now, I have to be very direct with you. Both of those things need to be true because how you handle this news and this merger is going to impact whether this tectonic shift in human evolution happens. Elizabeth, you have to understand what crossroads you are at." Amy let a silence fall over the car as she finished speaking.

"I'm starting to get it." Elizabeth sighed. She felt sick to her stomach. She had only been on the job one week, and she had already alienated her mentor and closest friend, and utterly collapsed when it came to ethics. "So in essence, our paper would be recruiting, curating, and providing massive amounts of information on individual people who—"

"Who then get their genome decoded by Crisprgen under the guise of preventive health care, but in reality, are surrendering virtually all aspects of their private life, circumstances, and capabilities to a company with no accountability." Amy finished Elizabeth's sentence.

"So, I kinda fucked up here and I owe Clark an apology," Elizabeth thought out loud.

"Clark will forgive you," Amy said softly. "But you gotta make it right by telling the truth in your paper and running his story.

"It sounds more like I need to stop this merger..." Elizabeth mused further.

"Liz," said Amy quietly. Elizabeth nodded attentively. "How long is Clark's assignment on profiling Sarah Reistad going to take?"

"Well, not very long. We want to run the story in next month's first Sunday edition so a piece this long has to be done two weeks out. I'd say about a week. Depending on how things shake out. Why?"

"Because I'm worried about him too," answered Amy.

The car came to the end of the packed sand road and the scrub pines cleared, revealing the large parking lot that was adjacent to Crisprgen village. As the two women got out of the car and stretched after the long ride, Elizabeth looked over at Amy.

"You know, Amy," she said in a friendly tone. "Over the years, Clark always talked about you too." Amy smiled without turning or making eye contact and kept her thoughts to herself. "He may need a lot of saving right now, and you and I may be the only people who are going to know how to do that." Amy nodded and looked at the ground.

The two women approached the circular Cul De Sacs of Crisprgen village, trying to be as inconspicuous as possible. At the many picnic tables sat a few random people and one or two families. Amy led Elizabeth to the area where she and Clark had met with the Matsumotos. As they sat at the picnic table, two drones whizzed by them at eye level and a small car robot, the size of a football sped with a whirring sound around the vast empty parking lot, making a figure eight around Elizabeth's car several times. The small car was much faster than any toy a parent would buy at Walmart for their child, and because it was so small, it created the optical illusion of moving at lightning speed. They sat watching it, not saying anything for several moments. Then, the car made a direct beeline towards the picnic table where they were seated. It zoomed closer and closer until it found the wheelchair indentation in the sidewalk and zipped up on the grass, stopping right at Amy's feet. Elizabeth turned and looked around the side of the table. Amy bent down and saw that taped to the top of the car was a folded piece of notebook paper with the words "Follow me!" written with black magic marker. She grabbed the note, lifted it off, and handed it to Elizabeth.

"I'll bet you anything this is Clark's clever way of being funny," she said. "Looks like this little car wants us to follow it." Amy nodded in return and chuckled. The two women rose from the table and began to follow. The little droid car puttered along in front of them leading the way. It led them past several houses named after different phases of human evolution until they got to the Cro Magnon house. The car stopped, almost as if to make sure they were following it. It reversed two inches, turned sharply and abruptly, then moved toward the large adjacent tunnel opening and zoomed through the gaping stone archway entrance into the blackness.

Elizabeth looked at Amy and shrugged. Amy paused a second and then began to follow the car inside with Elizabeth only a few steps behind.

The pitch-black interior of the Neanderthal tunnel was heavy, damp, and considerably cooler than the raging New Jersey summer heat that hung like a curtain over the entrance. Single drops of water from the mossy condensation on the ceiling caused random echoes near and far in the bunker chamber. Amy stood in silence. The car had disappeared. She fumbled for her cell phone flashlight to give her some bearings.

"What is this place?" asked Elizabeth a few feet behind Amy. Her voice echoed in the cavernous stone room.

"This ...is an emergency air raid bunker and long-term shelter. Every base had one after World War 2 and there were regular drills where the troops in the house— from infantry to enlisted officers— would seal themselves here for a week at a time to simulate a survival plan for a nuclear attack. If we look closely, we should be able to find phone lines and other electronics so one base could communicate with another. They were wired in groups. This is where the internet was devised and birthed," rambled Amy. As she spoke a faint gray - amber light appeared along the opposite wall 20 feet in front of her. Standing there against the wall with a terrified expression on his face was Alvin Matsumoto. His thin waifish frame adorned a wrinkled oversized golf shirt and Khaki trousers. Amy stopped dead in her tracks. In his right hand was a remote control with a long collapsible antenna and in his left hand he held the drone car that had delivered the note to Amy and Elizabeth asking them to follow.

Amy walked up to Alvin and said nothing for several seconds. On his face, she could see a deep-rooted anxiety. It was the same troubled expression she had seen when he came to see her at school in the days before he was recruited into Crisprgen. She paused in front of him saying nothing. Their eyes met and Alvin's filled with tears. Elizabeth broke the silence.

"Amy, is this your student Alvin Matsumoto?" asked Elizabeth. Amy nodded and extended her arms. Alvin fell into her embrace with his eyes tightly closed. "Hi, you're Alvin, right? I'm glad we found you, I'm Elizabeth Cranford, and I work with Clark Westfield, the reporter who you spoke to a few days ago back at the lab." Since Alvin was locked in a comforting hug from his former teacher, Elizabeth simply gave an exaggerated and extended wave. Still neither he nor Amy spoke, and Amy began to guide him gently out of the dark corner and walked him a few steps to a large cargo box painted Army green with the word "Long Term Rations/Potassium Iodide" stenciled on the side in faded white paint. Amy sat him down on the large crate like a mother tending to a child who had scraped his knee.

"So, Alvin, a lot of people were worried about you when you got your job here. We'd love to talk to you about your experiences so far," said Elizabeth in a warm invitational tone. Amy, however, could see that her former student was troubled.

"When we spoke the other day in the Helix Lab you had to be careful because Ms. Reistad was there, am I right?" asked Amy, cutting right to the chase. Alvin nodded and wiped his eyes.

"Clark said he had a good talk with you and that you were pretty happy working here and that they have given you some pretty good financial arrangements," chimed Elizabeth further. "If you were being guarded because you were in front of your supervisor, then any discussion we have here today can remain completely private and confidential." Elizabeth was doing her best to establish a rapport of trust with the clearly troubled boy. Amy looked at him with nurturing compassion.

"What's going on, Alvin? We are here to help," she said warmly, still holding one of his wrists. Alvin looked at Elizabeth then back at Amy, then glanced at the darkness that disappeared down the tunnel exiting the back wall as if to see if anyone was coming. Elizabeth felt she should say nothing else and let him speak.

"Ms. Biancini..." he choked out amid half a sob. "I've been having some trouble here at work. The other day when we met in the Helix Lab I couldn't talk about it because Ms. Sarah was there.”

“I sensed something was wrong,” said Amy as she held his wrist a bit tighter. “What kind of trouble, Alvin? Are you having problems with her?” If Sarah Reistad was mistreating any of the recruits and she could get them on the record, she would have a bona fide legitimate reason to dislike her as well as an opportunity to expose her. This would give her back her student, and perhaps, Clark.

“No. It's not Ms. Reistad. I can't find the last snippet in a CRISPR sequence that we need for the completion of the Passport.” He looked down at the floor ashamed. Amy attempted to comfort him, sensing there was more to it.

“Right. OK, but Alvin, you know complicated problems take time,” she said. “Plus, you told us the other day that you have been working on this for years even before you moved down here and went full-time with Crisprgen. You’ll get it. I have total faith in you. Is someone putting pressure on you? Have you discussed it with your parents?” Alvin looked up and met her gaze.

“I can’t tell my parents,” he stammered. “I can’t fail them.” He looked down at the floor again.

“Why would you be failing your parents?” asked Amy, leaning her head to one side inquisitively. “I’m sure they are proud of you, and they are benefiting from the anti-aging experiment that you told us about…Transference or something. I think you are too hard on yourself."

"It's the Transcendence project," he corrected Amy. "And if I'm not able to devise this last section of CRISPR code then they won't be enrolled." He was clearly troubled. "It's all my fault. If I hadn't been so enamored with Ms. Reistad they wouldn't have had to move here and leave our house and…"

"When you say enamored, is that reciprocated by Ms. Reistad?" asked Elizabeth in the gentlest way possible. Alvin looked down at the floor again with a shameful expression.

"It's hard, you know," he said slowly. "Nobody makes you feel good about being smart. Your whole life you feel like a freak because you understand more than everyone around you. Your peers make sure you feel like an outcast and that you aren't welcome. She was the only one who knew how to help me through it. She did that with all of us in our group. I don't know how I would have gotten through school and everything growing up without her help."

"When you say 'us', do you mean the group of middle school children she got together who were all geniuses like yourself?" asked Amy.

"Yes, exactly. She found us and connected all of us. It was like she understood how hard it was for us to try to make friends. She is smart, too, so she could totally relate." He paused to take a deep breath. "So, we started doing bits of this project, decoding small bits of the genome here and there when I was in the 8th grade. I loved it. Then when I won the award, she told me that private interests would never stop bothering me and it was like a target on my back. She was kinda right—no one would leave us alone."

"I remember, Alvin. You came and spoke with me about all the solicitations you were getting before you left school," added Amy.

"Yeah, I did. Then Ms. Reistad said we were going to have an in-person get-together with everyone in our work chat group, and she picked me up at school and brought me here. I met the others - Hannah LaRocca, Greg Mackoul, and a few others."

"You mean the other smart ones?" interjected Elizabeth.

"Yes. The smart ones. That's what she called us. It was the first time I felt like I could really talk to any of my peers. I loved it. I was so stressed out about everything so I stayed a few days; my parents were really worried. "

"That's when everyone at school thought you were missing and had been kidnapped," added Amy. Alvin nodded in affirmation.

"So, Ms. Reistad brought you here and didn't tell your parents?" asked Elizabeth.

"Yeah, but that's OK. They were stressing me out also. They kept telling me I had to choose a research university and to work in computer science. When I pushed back, they started saying they were going to send me to live with some family members back in Tokyo. Then Ms. Resisted explained the Passport Project and offered me the job."

"And what else did she offer you?" asked Elizabeth.

"She said if I worked here on the Passport that she would bring my parents here and give us a house, and double my father's salary if he left his job. He loved working so that wasn't going to convince him."

"So what finally convinced them?" asked Elizabeth.

"The Transcendence Project," Amy answered for Alvin. He nodded.

"OK, but if you aren't happy with the arrangements or the work isn't your cup of tea why not just leave? What kind of obligation are you under to stay?" Elizabeth asked matter of factly.

"My parents are too happy about the Transcendence Project. Also, they have started dosing on TA-65 and they feel like they found the fountain of youth. I can't take that away from them, not after all I've put them through," said the Matsumoto boy dejectedly. "Plus, they only get the CRISPR when I've completed the passport genome. That's the only contingency Ms. Reistad put on our contract."

"Ok, well, you will figure it out. You always do. You are a really smart guy, Alvin," Amy reassured him. "Remember what we always said in my AP genetics lab? Just take your time and the science will reveal itself?"

"Yeah, well, Hannah and I calculated and the one last CRISPR snippet that we need could only be carried by one in 20 million births. That means there are probably less than 20 people in the entire country who have the right palindromic repeat to complete the Passport," he said.

"Geez… How in the hell are you supposed to find that person? That's next to impossible." Elizabeth wondered out loud.

"We've been scouring through hundreds of thousands of consumer genetic tests to see if it turns up. I thought it would have turned up by now. I got a text message from Hannah the day you met me at the lab that she thought she may have found the precise sequence, but now I haven't seen her since, and she isn't answering her phone. When I asked where she was, Allele said she had been reassigned to a different workstation off-site." Alvin's voice rang with a timbre of anxiety.

"And you haven't spoken to Hannah since Monday?" Elizabeth asked. She shot Amy a look who reciprocated with her own expression of concern.

"No, and I went to find her parents who are really nice people, and they aren't here either." Alvin Matsumoto looked down at the ground.

"Alvin, were the LaRocca parents promised the Transcendence Project inclusion as well if their daughter had completed her work on the genome?" asked Elizabeth as gently as possible. Alvin nodded.

"Yeah, we all were. Mackoul's parents too. I just don't want to let anybody down." sighed the troubled boy. Amy looked at Elizabeth without saying anything. She was unaware of the phone call Elizabeth had gotten from the reporter at the New Haven Register.

"Alvin," Elizabeth said slowly and delicately as she could. "The LaRoccas, Hannah's parents, aren't coming back."

"Why not? You know them? What happened?" asked Alvin, perplexed and anxious.

"There was a car accident," replied Elizabeth softly.

"And we are going to help you find Hannah," added Amy. "We are here to help you…"

***

Clark lay with three-quarters of his body lazily stretched out on the red satin sheets of the circular bed. The upper quarter of his body, shoulders, and face were draped across Sarah Reistad's lap as she sat cross-legged, holding Clark in her arms. Sunlight streamed through the floor-to-ceiling windows in bright unbroken beams. Bits of dust danced in the white-blue light as it angled to the floor of the Fuck Room and its red interior. But at this moment, this scarlet red chamber of bliss was much more than just a Fuck Room. In fact, as Clark lay in Sarah's arms and looked up into her warm eyes and at her ever-present baseline smile, he realized that what was a

Fuck Room to her was a threshold out of the hellish coldness of grief for him. It had been perhaps decades since Clark had lay blissfully on a woman's lap letting the endorphins and feel-good brain chemicals work their magic. Sure, he and Mary Lynn, his wife of over 25 years, had enjoyed plenty of blissful moments over the tenure of their marriage before her death. But as any long-time married couple will bear witness, those chemicals that cause the euphoria, the obsession, and the baseline smile worn at the very soul are long dissipated as the decades accumulate. Sure, they are replaced by bonding chemicals of mutual respect and gratitude, made stronger with thickening agents like shared parenting, property ownership, and personal growth. One could even argue that these were the hallmarks by which many people measured nuptial merit. But no person who has experienced the enigma of love would say that any of those noble factors outweigh the sheer intensity, passion, and powerlessness of those early moments of mutual desire and attraction. The most combustible chemistry, of course, occurs when a physical attraction becomes further augmented by deep intelligence, at least for Clark. Sure, different personality types can find the explosive power amplified by other traits— sports, musicianship, artistic expression, economic independence, but for Clark, it was intelligence, analytic fluency, and a woman's ability to reason. Clark's beloved late wife Mary Lynn had possessed all three in abundance. So did Sarah. Clark had gone through life knowing these traits were rarely prevalent in any person, proving the enduring truth of his youthful mantra that pretty girls are found everywhere from the beach to the pages of magazines and everywhere in between but the "the smart ones are hard to find." And for that very reason, Clark didn't want to move from this moment of fleeting perfection. Crossing into this euphoric dimension was something he had long accepted may never happen to him again. And yet, here he was in the arms of this beautiful woman who claimed to be mostly a Neanderthal. And for just a moment, he was able to suppress the cognitive churn of how she had shattered his sense of ethics and professionalism and told himself that he didn't care where she fell on the evolutionary chart, or that she had managed to disarm decades of hard-earned journalistic prowess. She was worth it and so was the long and winding road he took to get here. The sun had returned to his soul after a long, cold lonely winter.

"Tell me what you are thinking," he asked softly as Sarah's breasts gently rubbed against his forehead. She looked down and widened her ever-present smile and spoke softly.

"I'm thinking how much I'm grateful to have met you and how you can be part of where we are going. And I am thinking that I understand your reticence and trepidation," she replied. "And I can wait as long as it takes for your enthusiasm to evolve." That wasn't exactly what Clark expected to hear. Sensing his deflation she leaned down closer to his face and added: "And by waiting, I mean patiently making love to you right here for as long…as…it..takes…" she said, kissing him intermittently between each word with playful emphasis. Clark lost himself in bliss again. The fundamental problem with romantic bliss is that as it increases, so does one's vulnerability and exposure, regardless of the degree. Clark closed his eyes and resisted the urge to speak, but he could not.

"Sarah, if you are going to talk about gratitude then allow me to go first." Clark kept his eyes closed as he spoke. "I really didn't think this would ever happen to me again." He drew a deep breath.

"What would happen?" prompted Sarah.

"I didn't think I would connect romantically and intellectually with a woman ever again," he mused thoughtfully. "So thank you for bringing this stranger in from his cold, wandering purgatory."

Sarah kissed his forehead. "I sense a 'but' coming," she said in a whisper. She was even more intuitive than Clark realized. And just like that, his vulnerability eclipsed his rational protective shroud.

"But… I did something else I never thought would happen again." Clark opened his eyes.

"You got involved with a subject of your ethnographic reporting and can no longer be objective. It bothers you at a deep level because your journalistic integrity is one of the only things that still seems real to you in this bizarre cruel world. I understand," she replied, looking at him intently. It was like she was reading Clark's mind, and it triggered an alertness. He sat up from her lap and turned to sit opposite her on the bed.

"Yeah…you could say that…" he said guardedly.

"You wouldn't be a good reporter if you didn't, and you have built your career and ascended to excellence by consciously making an effort not to do exactly that. It's admirable." she reached out and touched his face as she spoke, running her hand along his cheek. Clark was mesmerized. "That ability to prioritize integrity means that you take the truth very seriously," she continued. "It's one of the things that make you such a beautiful man." The last time a woman of any consequence had said anything remotely similar to him was in the very early days of his courtship with Mary Lynn. "I understand your trepidation and your immovable quotient of morality and fairness, believe me, I do. But another thing that makes you so beautiful, Clark, is that you have a superior intellect and higher IQ than anyone that was in that boardroom yesterday, and I include them in decision making about my company."

"I seriously doubt that's true." Clark assumed she was simply dishing out some flattery as cover.

"Come on, Clark, do you really think I asked that you be the reporter assigned to profile me and our sacred mission here because I picked a name out of a hat?" Sarah said playfully. "I have several AI engines that can calculate a person's IQ and intellect by analyzing writing samples— of which you have ample quantity from your reporting career—and I ran an outcomes report of your entire portfolio in each engine. They all reached the same conclusion—you have an IQ that exceeds at least 160 and you have the reasoning capability of IBM's Watson." Clark didn't know what to think.

"So, you were checking up on me, and I passed the machine test?" he said sarcastically. "Why were you interested in the first place?"

"The work we are doing here is extremely important," said Sarah. Suddenly she had less of her usual default smile and a slightly more serious expression. "The news of what we do will have to be handled by someone who can not only grasp the concepts but who also has a deep and insightful understanding of how the public consumes and understands information. I reviewed all the top working journalists, all the Pulitzer Prize winners, the Peabody Award winners, the Nobel Laureates, and you were head and shoulders above the pack."

"Well, I guess two out of three ain't bad." Clark chuckled. "I never won a Nobel, Sarah."

"I know!" she exclaimed playfully. "But who cares? You still score higher than those that have! You, of all people, know how political those awards are. But it doesn't matter. I have your life and career diagnostics to use as criteria. I also have some AI tools that reviewed every article you've ever written to identify characteristics and assess general intelligence. You are in a class by yourself there, Clark. You are certainly one of the smart ones."

Clark stayed silent for a few seconds. On the one hand, Sarah's review of his life and whatever other diagnostics she was referring to —whether they were medical or student records—were invasive and unwelcome. But on the other hand, usually only Clark knew that he was most often the smartest one in the room. Now this mysterious woman who he had spent all night fucking also knew. Was that a good thing or a bad thing?

"When you say you needed someone to report on your work…I'm a journalist, not a PR exec," Clark said defensively but softly.

"I know," giggled Sarah. She hopped off the bed and grabbed him by the wrist. "Come on, I want to show you something!"

She led Clark out of the velvet red Fuck Room and down the spiral staircase to the elevator. They sailed into the compartment as the door closed and Sarah pressed the button for the 13th floor, the highest one in the building. She pushed Clark against the far wall and kissed him passionately. He was elated. He had forgotten what it felt like to be attracted to someone who was attracted to you in return and being able to act on it. He felt alive for the first time in…years! And while the whole scenario was embedded with a million red flags, for now they could all wait.

The elevator opened at a floor that seemed like a rooftop deck, with a partial glass ceiling. They were on the very top of the Helix Lab. Much like a rooftop sitting area in a luxury apartment building or a swanky bar in New York City. The area had weather protection and 360 degree views of the base and nearby ocean. Rows of luxury outdoor furniture consisting of couches, lounge chairs and what looked like a huge bed were arranged geometrically. The space between the floor and the glass canopy had decorative potted trees - banana trees with huge sweeping leaves, large fica trees with braided trunks that had been allowed to grow incredibly higher than any Clark had seen in a mall or upscale office building. There were long flower beds that were made of waist high decorative marble and exotic plants of every type. It was beautiful, but exposed.

"This is gorgeous," Clark said as he looked around. "What do you do when it rains?"

"Oh, it doesn't rain," said Sarah, looking out into the broad view.

"Oh, you've got that under control too?" said Clark as he moved behind her and put his arms around her and held her, swaying slightly.

"Yes, we have a magnetic signal that creates a curtain of static electricity. The rain gets repelled by the charge," she said matter of factly.

"Yeah, they use that principle to keep the rain off the windshields of airplanes," said Clark. "But there is a pane of glass, here it's just air. You have no walls, a few droplets might bounce off, but a good thunderstorm wouldn't repel the rain, it would just attract lightning by offering a static charge." Clark was wondering out loud.

"Correct," said Sarah as she lay her head back on his chest. "Since when is attracting lightning a bad thing? Maybe we could use a jolt now and then," She said playfully.

"This woman even harnesses lightning…what the fuck am I getting into here?" Clark thought to himself. Sarah abruptly stepped out of Clark's embrace and turned around to face him. She looked at him and smiled then ballet stepped in a circle in an exaggerated fashion until she was behind him and put her arms around him from behind. It seemed playful but slightly odd.

"Are you going to give me the Heimlich maneuver?" asked Clark dryly.

"It is I that must hold you, Clark Westfield," Sarah whispered in his ear. "You are in my arms for now, dear."

She had no idea how correct she was. Clark was transfixed by the moment, a beautiful view, a beautiful woman holding him, and both in a halo of afterglow of marathon lovemaking. Yet deep down, he knew he had a job to do and this moment, no matter how perfect, was transient. Despite letting the moment simmer for a while, Clark found his reporter teeth and was determined to finish the story he had been assigned. The only bad stories he had written in his career were the ones where he got too emotionally involved with the subject or source. This one was starting to feel like the topper. He needed to regain some sense of control over the situation, and part of him hoped that if he asked the hard questions, he would discover that Sarah was simply misunderstood and ahead of her time and nothing nefarious was happening at Crisprgen other than some aggressive recruiting and ostentatious work contracts. Lt. Col. Kelly Pram had put the fear of God in him with all the talk about Sarah being able to accelerate the evolutionary fork and how Sarah was being cagey with her Pentagon supervisors. Lt. Pram had never led him astray, though, and she needed to know where this missing CRISPR-Cas 9 snippet from the Mackoul kid was. Normally, he simply would have turned and asked a very pointed question. But Sarah needed to be handled differently, perhaps, in a way that could preserve or at least protract their budding romance. Whether she was truly a threat to the state, as Pram had suggested, Clark would take his time finding out.

"Sarah, what else is needed before this great fork in the human evolutionary road happens and future generations will be a different species?" he asked as unassumingly as possible. She squeezed him tightly.

"We have everything we need, Clark," she whispered in his ear. "So do you, Mr. Westfield." Her response was somewhat confusing.

"Really?" asked Clark, more inquisitively. "You have everything for the Passport Project?"

"Yes, we sure do. There is one CRISPR Cas-9 sequence we've discovered that is so rare and so powerful that if a generation of babies were born with it in their genome, they would represent a distinctly different species," she said with a spacey gaze around the room. Clark knew the missing DNA sequence she was referring to must be the section belonging to the Mackoul kid that Lt. Col Kelly Pram had told him about in the Neanderthal bunker.

"So, what's the last link that you need for the human race to make the next evolutionary branch? Is it one person who just suddenly has whatever that next genome is?" Clark was fumbling and trying to find a non-scientific way to ask about the Mackoul boy.

"Well, normally you'd be right. One day an individual of a species is born with a genome that varies so much it makes it a different species. This happens routinely after years of genetic drift and branching subspecies," Sarah sang. "But we are deliberately creating that genome to be the next species, and the last CRISPR-Cas 9 that will make the jump is from my favorite smart one of all! You've got to meet him. I let him stay up here, and he works over behind that planter." Sarah pointed to a huge stucco planter several feet wide and 15 feet long, filled with shooting bamboo ten feet in the air.

"Yeah, I'd love to meet him," said Clark softly. But part of him didn't want to find what he was looking for. It would force him to confront his feelings about Sarah and reconcile them with however this was going to play out. He felt a lump in his throat. Sarah gently took his hand and led him across the sprawling open air penthouse floor. In the corner behind the massive bamboo planter was an enormous crystal desk that was shaped like a triangle wedged into the corner. On it were six or seven massive computers and one side of the desk had a row of what Clark thought must be servers. The front of the desk had a four panel monitor. Each section was the size of a 55 inch flat screen television. In front of the middle monitor was an office chair in which sat a male with his back to Clark and Sarah. He was staring intently at the middle monitor. His hair was curly, and he was of slender build and had dark middle eastern skin. One of his shoes had a support prosthetic sole that seemed to compensate for his legs which were different lengths.

"Hey Greg, honey," Sarah whispered as she walked closer. The young male in the chair turned around. Sarah put her arms around him and he fell into her embrace. She held him tightly. There was something odd about the intensity with which they were hugging. Sarah turned to Clark with the boy's head resting against her chest and with her arms around him. She smiled.

"Clark Westfield, meet Greg Mackoul—the smartest boy ever born! Greg Mackoul is the smart one that will lead the next human species. It's his DNA that completes the Passport." Sarah was speaking softly, and Greg's eyes were closed. Clark felt a pit in his stomach. He had to play this right. The U.S. government was looking for this kid, who Sarah had sequestered, and he was the person with the unusual sequence in his DNA that made him a hyper-genius. So smart in fact, that when combined with all the other optimal traits Sarah had harvested, the babies born with that passport genome would be a new species of human. And Clark was standing in the middle of the intersection of all this. Clark stepped a few feet closer to the two geniuses locked in their maternal embrace.

"Hi…I'm Clark Westfield," he said, extending his hand. Greg Mackoul turned to look at him and gave him a friendly smile extending his hand for a shake. He rose up out of the chair and stood up respectfully. He looked about 17 years old, thin and bony like most teenagers before their adult adipose tissue sets in to give them an adult frame. His face was warm and inviting, yet under his expression Clark sensed a hint of intangible desperation. His handshake was solid, not firm or limp. Clark tightened his grip on Greg's hand in a veiled signal of solidarity. Greg's hand tightened also in reciprocity.

This is something Clark did as a technique with critical news sources. The tightening of the grip would usually force eye contact during which Clark would give a confident and reassuring nod. Much of the trust signals between two human beings are unspoken, subtle optics and gestures which invoke an emotional trigger of security. It was what had made Clark such a good reporter, and how he had flipped hundreds of important witnesses and sources in his decades on the beat. Greg Mackoul, squeezing his hand in return, meant to Clark that he had something of value to tell him, and perhaps a bridge could be built between the two. Sarah looked at their extended handshake and a slight smile grew on her face.

"Nice to meet you, Mr. Westfield," said Greg Mackoul softly. "I've read your work, especially your investigative series on the opioid doctor's murders."

"Well, Gregg, I'm impressed!" Clark said lightly. "I'm somewhat of a dinosaur in modern media so knowing that a bright young person your age read anything I've written makes me feel relevant and young again!" Clark chuckled.

"I have some notes on the opioid epidemic I'd like to share with you, and I also gamed out some intervention techniques and extrapolated them on a longitudinal population scale that I think if you just publish, could lead to widespread adoption and a drastic reduction in overdose deaths. Do you have a minute to look now?" Greg said robotically. Clark was a bit taken aback that not even his editors or any of the public health officials he had interviewed for his "Murdered Doctors" series hadn't sat down to share any notes about long term solutions. Yet here was this 17-year-old smart kid who in a seemingly random meeting was offering a public health tool kit. Clark sensed something under the surface.

"Sure, I'd love to hear anything you've got an opinion on. God knows I had enough stories of grief from parents who lost children but not many ideas on how to reverse the crisis."

"I understand," said Greg. "But you never found out who murdered the doctors did you?" This question hit Clark with the jolt of an electric shock. Several years ago, Clark had witnessed a girl die of an oxycontin overdose at the Pt. Pleasant boardwalk and that had kicked off a long investigative series about the underbelly of the opioid epidemic in New Jersey and the murder of several of the prescribing doctors. Clark had determined, through dogged investigative work with Elizabeth exactly who the perpetrators of the murders were, yet had never reported it out of fear for his personal safety.

"I'm impressed," said Clark intently. "I wrote that series five years ago— that would make you 12 years old at the time. You were following a daily newspaper series at 12 and extending your reading on the topics?"

"Why wouldn't I?" asked Greg looking perplexed. Clark realized that a genius of his caliber was probably reading everything possible as a toddler. After all, Mozart wrote his first opera at age 3. Before Clark could answer, Sarah interrupted.

"See, I told you he was a smart one!" She hugged him again and a smile grew on Greg's face. "Boys like Greg have no need for Wikipedia. That's why human beings like him are so rare. Greg, tell Clark about your work here." Greg smiled at Sarah and turned to Clark with a more serious expression.

"Well, we are creating the ideal genome so the humans of tomorrow will be best adapted for the changing conditions and catastrophic events and challenges of the coming years. In global changes of the past, the isolated human populations that had traits that gave them advantages for survival were the only ones to make it through various evolutionary challenges. We can identify all of the traits necessary for humans to meet the challenges of climate change, food scarcity, pandemic diseases, and innovation needs and combine them into one genome," explained Greg with nervous pride.

"And of course, this ideal genome that will become the Passport will have the genetic contents for the most intelligent humans currently on the earth so they aren't inadvertently lost when these crises start to cascade and trim various populations' numbers. That's why Greg is so critical. It's his CRISPR-Cas9 snippet that will set them apart," said Sarah, smiling.

"And that is what will make these humans with the passport genome a separate species." Clark thought out loud.

Sarah nodded with a smile of ecstasy. Greg remained expressionless. "So will these new passport humans or whatever you are going to call them, be able to reproduce with the current 7 billion other humans walking the planet?" Clark sounded sarcastic but it was a legitimate question. Sarah giggled and gave Greg a gentle shove on his shoulder prompting him to answer.

"Most certainly, Mr. Westfield," Greg answered, dryly. "Several early versions of the human species existed at the same time before the last ice age and regularly interbred and shared genetics. Eventually, the population with the ideal combination were the only ones to survive a huge global event about 40,000 years ago, which most likely was an abrupt and acute climate disruption caused by either a super volcano or meteorite strike. The species to emerge from that moment in history are today's modern homo sapiens and they still carry DNA from all those prior versions of our species." Greg stopped speaking.

"Tell him about those early homo sapiens," said Sara, running her index finger along his forehead in a slightly erotic and creepy way.

"The homo sapiens to emerge from whatever that event was 40,000 years ago had certain distinguishing traits— they seemed to have developed a written language and drew on cave walls to share information about food sources and hunting techniques. This was pivotal because it was the moment that humans became able to learn through communication and root knowledge memorization rather than experience. It also meant every individual human didn't have to have the same minimal skills or strength for survival. It let our species transfer knowledge among population groups and divide specific labor tasks among individuals. This meant nomadic family groups were now a civilized society, and we have been developing those skills ever since." Greg Mackoul sounded like the voiceover narration track for a Discovery Channel documentary.

"OK, I get it," replied Clark, trying to sound nonchalant and unaffected. "But the changes you are talking about took place over a period of tens of thousands of years. This Passport Project you are building will change our species genome in one generation. Don't you think an evolutionary change that quick will have massive unintended consequences?" asked Clark.

"Oh Clark, it's been happening for thousands of years already," said Sarah. "Think about the differences between the rich educated class and those humans who are still living in family tribes in undeveloped countries. Can you really say they are equal when it comes to knowledge and survival potential? Our species discovered agriculture only about 12,000 years ago, which then established the concept of modern trade and economics by about 10,000 years ago. Since that time the differences in populations have been separated not by natural phenomenon like earthquakes and ice ages, but by class divisions. A certain sliver of humans who fall on the economic abundance end of the spectrum have more food for ideal health and immunity, more knowledge for innovation and problem solving, and thus more incentive for self-defense and preservation," said Sarah matter of factly.

"Right…so the rich have always been better off, more educated and better fed. And the healthy smart ones are most likely to survive whatever may happen—that's not exactly a breakthrough discovery." Clark felt the sarcasm in his tone as he heard himself bringing Sarah's esoteric doctrine into everyday practical language. "And over thousands of years, this would have created a natural new branch of human evolution but because you have figured out the secrets of the human genome and how to manipulate it, you are going to do this in one generation. Is that really a smart move? I'm serious - just because you can do something doesn't mean you should…just ask Oppenheimer!" Clark was setting out an ethical trap for Sarah and it was the only thing that could transcend his feelings of burning lust and attachment. Greg answered.

"You are correct, Mr. Westfield. An evolutionary change that abrupt will have many unintended consequences. But the cycle of problems humanity is about to enter will drastically impact and reduce the human population to possible extinction level numbers, likely in the near future. If we leave it up to cosmic luck that the remaining humans have the necessary genes to survive, then odds are they won't. Knowing we have the ability to help ensure humanity's survival means we have the responsibility to step in and help. The new species of humans that will result are a necessary outcome of this intervention. It's either do nothing and watch 90% of humanity disappear after suffering disease, war, famine and climate change, or do our best."

"To stack the deck…I get it," interrupted Clark.

"But there will always be knowledge we need from that disappearing 90% and there will be genetics that will be of use, which is why we are also developing the CRISPR-Cas 9 to permanently create the effects of TA-65 on the length of cell lives," explained Greg.

"So, you are saving a couple well-deserving or really wealthy people to bring along with you on this new evolutionary fork?" Clark jibed. Hearing the entire doctrine and long range plan again was starting to sound more and more foreboding. Sarah nodded and explained further.

"No matter how excellent the new Passport genome is and no matter how well it prepares humanity for the coming challenges, the collective knowledge of the past must be preserved. Those who have made huge societal contributions, discoveries, or advanced philosophers of logic must join the new branch. We have been keeping some precious minds alive since we discovered TA-65 in the 1960s, and now that we have discovered the longevity CRISPR-Cas9, we can preserve their knowledge indefinitely by eliminating the Hayflick limit of their cells." Sarah looked absolutely elated as she was talking while Greg remained expressionless.

"So you are granting eternal life to the worthy?" Clark muttered.

"Well, we are eliminating senescence," Greg corrected. "Big difference. You can still die of other causes like a disease or infection that we haven't covered in the new genome. You can certainly be injured in the traditional sense and die in a car accident. You can be poisoned, die of hypothermia, etc. What we know about the CRISPR-Cas9 is that by preventing a cell from reaching senescence, you eliminate the process of aging and all the associated health problems, allowing you to live for a very, very long time. Think of it as going from a seasonal rental to a 99-year lease on a piece of property that keeps improving. And as for the worthy, we see it as humanity being simply dependent on those humans that can solve problems and bring peace to the world. Those people should be kept alive, and we will need their perspective on the changes that will be happening because they will have lived in the old world and will know how to avoid various problems. It's like keeping some key employees at a company after an acquisition because of their institutional knowledge of the corporation and the industry. In this case, those that fit all that criteria—"

"Are the smart ones…" interrupted Clark, finishing Greg's sentence. Clark felt slightly sick as Sarah stood their beaming. "OK, thank you for the detailed explanation but what specifically is it that you do here, Greg? What are all these giant computers here overlooking the beautiful old Fort. Monmouth?"

Sarah answered before Greg could.

"I'm glad you mentioned the Fort. Do you realize, Clark, that this Fort used to train men to kill each other as well as destroy entire civilizations?" She was talking in her dreamy, flowing sage voice again.

"Yeah, I know. It also protected my family and every other American family and also planned to rescue and rebuild if we were ever the ones being destroyed," Clark countered. "We still exist as humans and as a nation because forts like this kept the world in a peaceful balance, and I and millions of others were able to sleep at night as a result."

"You are correct. In fact, the control center for New Jersey's Nike missile battery was here, ready to defend against a Soviet launch of ICBMs. But now we know better and instead of trying to build the bigger, smarter bomb, we are collecting our knowledge for preservation and changing our species into a smarter, more peaceful version, hopefully eliminating the need for forts just like this." A tear escaped Sarah's eye as she was talking. Clark asked his question again.

"Right, I get it. What are all these computers that you are working on here, Greg?"

"Oh these?" Greg pointed to the several huge desktop tower computers and the racks of servers. As he was about to answer Sarah's cell phone rang with a ringtone that sounded like an emergency alarm. She immediately fished it from the pocket of her flowing, lacey robe and looked at the screen which was flashing an alert message like a strobe light. Her face changed, and her smile disappeared for the first time since Clark had met her.

"It's Allele!" she said as she frantically typed a message. As the return text chimed its tonal arrival, her eyes widened. "Allele needs me. Guys, I have to go. I'm sorry. Clark, stay here and get to know Greg. Ask him anything you want. Greg, Clark is a trusted confidant and is a new addition to our inner circle so please treat him as such." And with that she twirled around quickly and darted off with precision like a fighter jet and disappeared into the waiting elevator, leaving Clark Westfield alone face to face with Greg Mackoul. Greg gazed at Sarah as she exited and slowly turned to face Clark after the elevator had disappeared.

"Mr. Westfield, these are the computers that have been scanning all the genetic samples we receive from all the sales of the Crisprgen consumer tests. When they find a desired anomaly, it's cataloged so we can go back and retrieve it if we need to."

"You mean if you see a genetic series or a specific gene that you want, like, say, for musical creativity, you go back and call the person and then bring them in to harvest the DNA?" asked Clark.

"Oh no," answered Greg. "There is no need. We already have the DNA in the sample they've provided. We just retrieve the vial out of cryogenic storage and snip out the sequence for a CRIPSR." Greg smiled proudly.

"And what about the person it came from? The donor? Don't you need their permission?" asked Clark, somewhat baffled.

"Oh, no need for that either," Greg continued. "The terms in the permission waivers they sign allow us to harvest whichever genes we want. It's like they are making a donation." Greg smiled.

"Good lord! Do you really think the millions of people who are turning in their spit samples for consumer genetic tests know that some of their genes can be part of a master genome that is going to create superior humans? Don't you think you should give them a little credit or at least tell them?" Clark challenged. Greg's face changed.

"Well, that's not how Ms. Reistad works," he replied, looking down at the floor.

"So Sarah specifically wants to keep the harvesting a secret from the donors?" Clark asked, sensing something under the surface.

"Ms. Reistad believes that if the donors knew, it would cause chaos with lawsuits and entitlements, even patent issues. She also makes sure that most of the people who have been CRISPRed into the Transcendence Project are unaware as well." He sounded sad as he spoke.

"So you aren't telling the people to whom you are granting eternal life? Clark asked, baffled. "Why on earth not!?"

"The TA-65 activates telomerase, but you have to keep dosing unless you get the CRISPR-cas9 to cause your cells to produce it on their own. Ms. Reistad says it's important that we do not tell people who we gave the CRISPR-Cas9 of TA-65 because, well, Ms. Resisted believes that it would cause some of the recipients to go rogue with their own agenda and others would resist or even try to opt out. But these are the records of everyone who has been given the CRISPR. There are a lot of people dosing on TA-65, and at some point it's going to be a commercial product and a recreational drug. But once they stop they will age aggressively," explained Greg Mackoul.

"Opt out like, kill themselves?" asked Clark. Greg nodded. "So you are changing people's DNA to keep them around to educate the future superior race you are engineering and they don't even know? Don't you think they are going to get a clue when they outlive all their relatives and loved ones?"

"Well, some know. A few even live over in Crisprgen village. But you are right, we should tell them but that's not my decision. The dosing is the same - both can be injected but the CRISPR-Cas 9 version of TA-65 is embedded in a harmless adenovirus that attacks your cells. It doesn't hurt you at all but as it thrives in your body as an efficient virus, it delivers the DNA map—the scissors that snip the proteins out and replaces it with the palindromic repeat. These ledgers have the record of everyone that has been enrolled in the Transcendence Project already, and these ledgers are catalogs of every DNA sequence that we have used for a CRIPSR-Cas9 and where it came from, and which ones are definitely going in the Passport genome." Greg pointed to several stacks of oversized bound hardcover binders. "Of course, we have all the records in a database on these servers but I'm keeping a hard copy and also several hard drives in case…"

"In case what?" asked Clark, sensing Greg had a significant reason.

"In case of any emergency—a massive power failure or if we are attacked, robbed, etc." Greg shrugged.

"Do you think you are going to be attacked?" Clark wondered if this was a moment where he should be honest with Greg and tell him that Lt. Col. Kelly Pram was looking for him.

"Well, with the names in here that have been drafted into Transcendence, hell yeah!" Greg lit up in an animated fashion.

"This is a shortlist of the most rich, powerful and most important intellectuals across all sciences, industries and government," said Greg. Clark thought for a minute. A book containing the names of the most powerful people in the world who had been given a virus with a DNA edit contained in it to extend their lives…now that was a story! He felt his heart race. This was why Clark had chosen to be a reporter all those years back. It wasn't for the scoop. It was to be the only guy holding the line by delivering news about issues and situations that directly affected the population. His mentor Steve Miller called it 'God's Messenger Syndrome,' and Clark knew that it was rare when God's Messenger got to deliver news that might actually make a beneficial impact or affect a positive turn of events. Every journalist in the world lays awake at night dreaming, rationalizing, and cursing that their choice of career was actually a vocation for that very moment. Some never find it. Clark had found it a few times and knew how rare it was.

"So, Greg…. buddy," Clark drew a deep breath. "Can I see who's in the books? Open it up…" Clark knew this could be a meeting ender. Instead, Greg Mackoul gave a slight shrug and turned and handed one of the ledgers to Clark. It was an academic binder with a leather cover with embossed gold letters in the center reading: "Transcendence Inductees 2016-2020"

"This has been going on since 2016?" Gregg nodded.

"Yeah, but I only got here two years ago and there were only about a dozen names. It took a lot longer back then and they had trouble with the CRISPR installations. I discovered a more efficient way to do it." His face didn't look prideful or boastful but rather sad. Clark opened the ledger. It had about 15 names per page in tables that contained basic information. He tried to read some of the names - immediately he saw Bill Gates and Neil DeGrasse Tyson. The rest he didn't immediately recognize because they were scientists and economists that he would be able to identify in a few clicks but not recognize off the top of his head. He flipped to the next page and the next until he got to the last. The last two entries had information, but instead of names had a number code: ByTor2112 and Snowdog2112. One was listed as a caucasian male and the other a female, both aged 50.

"Who are these last two entries? They don't have names," said Clark, indicating the two numbered entries to Gregg.

"Yeah, those two…Ms. Reistad doesn't want them to know," Greg shrugged.

"What? What the fuck? Why would you give someone a genome altering procedure that grants them eternal life and not tell them? What the fuck sense does that make?" Clark was starting to boil. The whole thing was starting to sicken him. The selection of people for a passport, the harvesting of genes from unknowing people and the taking of good genes for yourself? It was like a goddamn carjacking of the evolutionary chart! What the hell had he gotten himself into with Sarah? He decided to level with Greg.

"Greg, listen, we gotta talk and it's really important." Clark looked Greg dead in the eyes. "This whole lab is part of a CIA development site for contingency planning. It's a long story but they are looking for you - apparently you're the last piece of genetic material they need to complete the genome and—"

"And Sarah won't tell them where I am," Greg cut in. "Yeah, I know. Sara told me and Lt. Col. Kelly Pram from Army intelligence told me."

"You know Col. Pram?" asked Clark incredulously. "How? And does she know you are here?"

"I was recruited by Col. Pram when I was 14. I came here two years ago when she installed me here. When Sarah sequenced my genome, she realized that I had the last snippet of whatever they needed. and she hid me up here. I'm sure that Col Pram is looking for me. I don't care if you tell her where I am." Greg sounded indifferent.

Clark was churning— this didn't make any sense. Kelly Pram had told him distinctly that they couldn't locate the Mackoul kid but here he was on the top floor of a building in which she was masquerading as 'Kathleen O'Halloran, the board member.'

"When did all this happen? When was the last time you saw her?" asked Clark.

"About two weeks ago. She was here the night we made the discovery of my CRISPR-Cas9. That was when Sarah realized it was the one they needed. She didn't tell Col. Pram and then she told me that we were going to complete the Passport genome ourselves and start the process without Col. Pram or any of the Army folks that are always here." Greg shrugged again.

"Ok, so after that Sarah hid you...? Where? Up here?" Clark looked around at what would have been a terrible hiding place.

"No, there are tunnels and secret bunkers all over this base and she has the keys to some of them. I've been sleeping in there." Greg sounded beleaguered.

"OK, but I think we need to go find Col. Pram. She is looking for you. I have known her a long time, and she knew I was working on this story, and I think it's really important that you loop her back in. It's the government we are talking about, you aren't exactly going to be able to hide from them." Clark persuaded.

Just then there was a rhythmic buzzing. Greg's cell phone was getting several texts. He looked at the screen and said "Oh no, my parents are texting me. They are saying to come to the Crisprgen Village at once that it's an emergency!" Greg began to stand up. Clark didn't know if he was genuinely receiving an emergency text from his parents or if he just wanted a way out of the awkward position Clark had put him in with his invasive questioning. But there was no way he was going to let Greg Mackoul out of his site.

"OK, if it's an emergency I'll go with you," said Clark as he stepped closer to Greg. Greg nodded.

"OK, I know a shortcut. Let's go," Greg replied.

Greg led Clark to the elevator, which took them down to the ground floor. Greg was silent and so was Clark. He needed to think. He needed to process the magnitude of what he had stumbled into. He needed to bury the euphoria of his romance with Sarah. He needed to get to Elizabeth and tell her the size and scope of story they were into. He needed to find Amy and tell her…what exactly? Something… And somewhere inside, he felt he needed to save this kid's life. "I hope God is happy with his fucking messenger." he thought.

They walked briskly up the path towards the fence Clark had climbed when he sprained his ankle. At the gate, Greg produced a magnetic card tied to a string on his belt that scanned the gate to open. He and Clark continued at a brisk pace that was testing Clark's still healing ankle. Clark panted trying to keep up. As the path wound around various sized buildings and troop obstacle courses with tire runs it came to a scrub pine forest with thick underbrush. The heat of the New Jersey Pine Barrens hot summer sand was like a microwave beamed at Clark's chin. They crashed against the spiny leaves on either side of the narrow cut path. Soon the trail came to a clearing and they were in the backyard of one of the small houses in the cul de sac of Crisprgen Village. Greg Mackoul marched on. It was here that Clark noticed Greg's uneven walk because of the prosthetic attachment to his shoe. As they crossed into the front yard and into the street, they could see a small group of people about 50 yards down at the end of the block. Clark and Greg walked up to where everyone was standing. He recognized Elizabeth and Amy.

"Hey! Guys! Amy! Liz!" Clark panted. The women turned. They gave a slight look of surprise. Then Clark saw that in the center of the gathering of people was Mrs. Matsumoto. She was wailing and crying in loud, unlistenable shrieks. Tears were gushing from her wrinkled Japanese cheeks and she was speaking in indecipherable fragments of her native language. She was waving one arm and pointing in another direction. "What's wrong with her?" Clark said between breaths.

"Clark! Thank God we found you." Amy rushed up to him. We just got here, and she is really upset at something but no one is going with her or looking her in the eye. This is really fucking weird," whispered Amy.

"Well, let's go see what she wants. Somebody go with her. Let's all go with her—you me Liz and Greg." Clark turned and pointed to Greg Mackoul.

"Clark, I gotta find my parents. I'll be where you found me if you want to talk again," said Greg with a worried look as he turned and trotted off. Clark sighed and turned back to Amy.

"I can't lose that kid, Amy. You don't understand," said Clark. Amy tugged at Clark's arm and walked forward tapping Elizabeth on the shoulder and the three of them walked up to Mrs. Matsumoto. Amy took her hand. Mrs. Matsumoto immediately turned and tugged her in the direction of one of the houses. Clark and Elizabeth followed. Clark glanced at Elizabeth with a look that said he knew this was going to be upsetting, whatever it was. Elizabeth looked back in unspoken agreement. No woman wails and cries like that without a terrifying reason. She led them straight to the Neanderthal House and straight towards the mouth of the bunker tunnel. She stopped and stood at the entrance to the tunnel and wailed sobbing. She pointed inside the tunnel into the darkness but wouldn't go any further. Clark, Elizabeth and Amy looked at each other and realized whatever was upsetting her was at the end of this tunnel. The three walked forward and felt the cool dampness of the wet cobblestone walls. A droplet of water sounded with an amplified echo. They inched slowly down the tunnel allowing their eyes to become accustomed to the temporary darkness. A light was on just around the curve. They walked towards its source and entered the chamber where Clark had met Kelly Pram, and Amy and

Elizabeth had been earlier. As they rounded the corner, they heard a woman weeping. There on the floor on her hands and knees curled up into a ball and weeping uncontrollably was Sarah. Her shoulders were shaking as she sobbed. The three looked up and there, hanging from an iron water pipe that ran along the ceiling, was Alvin Matsumoto with a belt around his neck that he had used to hang himself. He was slowly twisting in suspension and his face was distorted and a dark purplish color. He was dead as a doornail.

Chapter 9

Melody Westfield stood at the top of the stairs in her split level four bedroom home. She had heard her father come in late last night around 11. She had heard him get up and walk down the stairs as the sun was coming up. Sometimes he would watch television in the front family room when he couldn't sleep. After her mother died, Melody would come downstairs in the morning and find him sprawled out in the recliner, exhausted from the insomnia that comes from profound loss. Some mornings she felt it looked like grief had physically assaulted her father and left him bloodied on the sidewalk. But Melody had heard him go downstairs when the morning light was bringing its orange glow— about 5:45 at this time of year. At least he had made it through most of the night. As Melody got to the bottom step and turned the corner, there was the chair…empty.

She paused and turned to go into the kitchen. As she crossed the floor, she could see the back porch that was enclosed with enormous greenhouse style windows. Her father was sitting in a metal folding chair that you, the familiar, boring, beige, uncomfortable kind found in bingo parlors and cafeterias. His back was to Melody, and he was sitting rigid and staring straight ahead out the back window. He sat in total silence. Melody sensed by his stillness that there was something wrong. The last time she had seen her father sitting so still and staring out the window was in the two years following her mother's death. But today no one had died… at least no one she knew.

"Hey dad…good morning," said Melody softly as she walked up behind him. Clark remained motionless. Melody waited a few moments. Perhaps her father had hit a grief patch, and he was working through it in his familiar method.

"Dad?" Melody said again. Still no answer came. She grabbed one of the large wicker porch chairs that looked like a warm weather recliner and slid it on the tile next to her father's beige metal folding chair. Mel knew not to keep pestering him. He knew she was there, and now seated beside him. He would speak when he was ready. She knew it wasn't personal. This was how grief worked.

After several moments of silence, Clark spoke softly. "Are you ever worried about the future, Mel?" After many moments like this in the aftermath of losing her mother, she had come to realize that the more the severity of the grief pang that flared, the more existential her father's mindset became. Melody shrugged.

"I try not to worry," she replied gently. "Usually that means not thinking about the future at all." She gave an audible chuckle. "My generation can't afford to..." The chuckle fizzled into a sad sigh.

"If you had the opportunity to improve your whole biology, overall health and how smart you were, would you do it?" Clark asked his daughter opaquely. Melody didn't understand the context of the question, but she knew to take the discussion seriously.

"Yes, of course. What's on your mind, dad?" Melody sat down beside him and stared forward out the window.

"Even if it meant no one else could? If only a certain amount of people could have the new technology to better their health, would you still do it?" Clark asked distractedly.

"Well, sure, I guess. Isn't that already the case? Health care isn't equally available across the globe. Neither are vaccines or nutrition or diagnostics or surgery. I don't think it would be any different than it is now," replied Melody. Clark thought for a moment. That made perfect sense. Health care wasn't equally dispersed throughout the world, hell even across America there were huge disparities in access to care between rich and poor, black and white... So, what was he so hung up about? True, Sarah and Crisprgen were widening that gap with the Passport Project, but in the big picture that was inevitable whether they contributed to it or not. Today's world was moving much too fast, and at least Sarah was trying to do it right, Clark thought. Yet no matter how he tried to reconcile her grandiose plant to create a fork in human evolution with smarter, healthier people with divergent DNA, the anxiety still bubbled in the pit of his stomach. It was an intense, uncomfortable sickness that seemed to simply sit there and ooze shaky vibes into his gut. It wasn't the Passport Project that had him so stirred up.

"Mel…" said Clark and took a long pause. His daughter turned to him in polite silence. "I miss your mother…"

Melody nodded.

"So do I dad.So do I," said Melody softly.

A raw melancholy mist hung in the air between them. Suddenly a rhythmic knock on the porch storm door broke the heavy tension. Clark continued staring straight ahead as if he hadn't heard a thing. Melody looked over and in the lower third window of the door, a man was standing below the steps. leaning around from the side. It was Richie Byrne, a friend and colleague of her father's. Mel got up and walked over to let him in.

"Hi Mr. Byrne! Why are you standing on the grass and not on the steps?" Melody laughed as she greeted him. Richie then swung a leg over the bottom step and stood upright as he ascended the other two stairs to enter the door.

"Never stand directly in front of a door if you don't know what's going to come out of it," he boomed. He was a big man with a solid stocky build. "They teach you that in the Navy." He chuckled and extended his hand to Melody in an exaggerated handshake. "Wow, you are getting really big there, little girl!" Melody gave him a warm hug.

Richie Byrne had worked with Clark at the paper for the entirety of Clark's career. He ran the national desk after spending a few years on the Washington beat. Before becoming a journalist, he had served in the Navy onboard a nuclear submarine in the 1970s and 80s at the height of the Cold War. After 10 years below the waves, he emerged and started to work as a reporter at the Newark Examiner. To start, he had covered the Pentagon, and as an ex-Navy officer, was able to shake loose some significant story breaks—the ones that had put their newspaper in the ring as a flagship paper among regionals and as a national contender. When Clark had been at the paper five years, Richie was promoted to editor and they had worked together on countless stories. He had stayed on after their mutual mentor, Steve Miller, had been forced out in a merger a few years back. Richie had served in the Navy with Lt. Col. Kelly Pram, though neither ever divulged any significant details about their work in that time other than to drop ambiguous phrases like "we dealt with something like this back in the day" or other moments of knowing recognition on a complicated subject. After Richie had long left the Navy, he had maintained a relationship with Lt. Col. Pram. She gave him insight, background and anonymous source material which helped him break even more stories. They had careened into a sordid affair a few years back, and it had destroyed Richie's marriage. Clark saw him as a big brother and professionally as a wingman. Richie saw Clark as a non-judgmental source of solace and support who reminded him of a younger version of himself, even after close to 30 years of working together. Richie finished hugging Melody, who he had known since her birth, and sat down next to Clark. This was a familiar ritual for the two men in this exact spot, as Richie had been a constant supportive presence in the days after Clark had been widowed. Often the two men would sit on the porch for hours at a clip, sometimes only commenting on disconnected observations, a baseball score, a blue jay chasing smaller songbirds from the feeder, a comment about a mutual colleague. More often than not, these sessions of long sitting were simply two men in one another's presence, and no one spoke at all.

"I'll get us some coffee," said Melody loudly, backing away. Behind her father and out of sight, Melody made sure she had Richie's attention and pointed to her father like a busking street mime and then made hand motions symbolizing tears streaming down her face to indicate to their guest that her father was feeling sad. Richie nodded that he understood and sat down. Melody left the porch and went into the kitchen, out of sight and out of earshot.

Though always welcome, Clark didn't know why Richie had shown up at his house. But, in an overt gesture of loyalty Clark got right to the point.

"Hey Rich," grabbing his hand for a shake without looking at him and still seated. "Kelly came to see me." He needed to tell Richie right up front that his former mistress had sought him out and enlisted his help. Clark had never had a mistress, but if he did, he would want to know if his friend and colleague was suddenly working with her. That was basic bro code.

"I know. That's why I'm here," Richie said. That didn't surprise Clark, in fact it was somewhat comforting.

"Did she tell you to come see me?" asked Clark, still looking straight ahead. "You know she is masquerading as a board member at this genetic company; she is calling herself Katherine O'Halloran."

Richie chuckled. "Really? That was her mother's maiden name," Richie thought out loud.

"So, you are seeing her again?" asked Clark, still looking forward.

"She finds me when she needs me," Richie said nonchalantly. "Listen, we gotta talk." Now Clark turned and looked at him. There was a comfort in the warm expressive face of an old friend, but also an undercurrent of urgency from the fact that he had shown up unannounced. Clark knew it must be connected to Crisprgen, so he cut right to the chase.

"What the fuck am I involved in here, Rich?" Clark sighed.

"What? Does that Neanderthal you are fucking have your head spinning?" Richie laughed uproariously. Clark scowled in disapproval. He hated lowbrow locker room talk between men, especially if he were emotionally invested in the woman being discussed. Melody stood in the threshold of the doorway to the dining room and kitchen balancing a tray with three coffees. She paused for a moment.

"Rich, this is the first woman to get into my head since…"

"Since Mare died," Richie finished his sentence for him. "I get it. You don't have to explain."

Melody stood silently eavesdropping. This must be why her father seemed so out of sorts.

"Clark, you gotta realize how you are being played here," said Richie in a low voice. "This project has been in development since the 60s."

"You mean the Passport Project?" asked Clark. Richie nodded slowly.

"Yeah, and if it gets out and into the marketplace—"

"Marketplace? Kelly told me the issue was that Sarah Reistad was keeping the missing link genius from all the spooks down at the Pentagon—the last smart one, the Mackoul kid. What do you mean 'marketplace'?" Clark really didn't want to hear whatever Richie was going to say next but he knew he needed to.

"It's both. By hiding the Mackoul kid and whatever genetic sequence she harvested from him, she puts the Crisprgen Passport ahead of the official version being prepared in Washington, and well, we just can't have that…" Richie explained.

"Geez, Richie. You are still playing spy versus spy with Kelly? What do you need me for? Why not do what you intelligence operatives always do and get Sarah to cough up where he is. Use some enhanced interrogation methods. Bring her to Gitmo, inject her with sodium pentothal for Christ's sake. Why do you need me?" Clark challenged.

"Because if she completed sequencing the Passport Project genome with the Mackoul kid's DNA, then she is going to sell it to the private sector, and we will have no way of telling who is enrolled in the Passport Project and who isn't. Essentially, she will have control over which humans fork off and diverge from our current Homo sapiens species and who doesn't. Also, we know she has been selling the CRISPR for the Transcendence Project—another rogue move on her part. Clark, your new girlfriend may be one of the greatest threats to national security since the Rosenbergs." Richie was calm in his delivery. Melody's ears perked up at the word girlfriend.

"Jesus, Rich…are you a reporter or an agent?" Clark asked sarcastically.

"I'm the same as you, Westfield," he replied. "I'm a reporter who was asked for help by my country's intelligence team. We are in the same boat here, pal," said Richie gently.

"Yeah…but you're fucking the Navy intelligence woman, which is why you're helping," Clark said in a biting tone.

"Well, you're fucking the woman she is asking about, so we are even," Richie shot back. Melody suddenly felt like there was sour milk in her stomach. She had heard enough for now. She always knew the day would come when her father would start seeing someone. She could learn the details later. At that precise moment her surging pang of grief would need to be dealt with in the bathroom. Clark heard her sock-muffled quick footsteps patter across the hardwood inside, and he knew he was going to have some explaining to do.

"Rich, I can get you the Mackoul kid. I'm already on it," Clark said softly. "But once I do, what is going to happen to Sarah?"

"Nothing," replied Richie. "Once we have the Mackoul kid's CRISPR then she is irrelevant. I understand she has totally hooked you in, her Neanderthal gene surplus makes her emotionally magnetic and charismatic. But we also need the records of who she has implanted with the Transcendence CRISPRs."

"OK, and when you've got all that, what happens to her?" asked Clark.

"Why? Are you thinking you are going to have some May to December romance with Sarah Reistad? Think again, buddy…" Richie laughed slightly.

"Rich you don't understand…She was the first woman since Mare that reached me at any level," said Clark softly.

"Of course she was. So what?" Richie prompted.

"What do you mean so what? I didn't think I'd feel anything for any woman ever again. And now…"

"And now you want to lay down your kingdom for her?" interrupted Richie. "Clark wake up. You are a few years out from your wife's passing. At some point, the grief recedes just enough for you to start opening yourself to other people, romantically. You are at that point of inflection and along comes a hyper-genius who happens to also be a really hot chick, and she has a vested interest in manipulating you and getting you to write the story she wants to tell as well as access to your newspaper so she can control the public conversation while simultaneously harvesting data from your subscribers and their reading patterns and social media accounts so she can harvest more CRISPR gene sequences and hoard them from the intelligence agencies that funded her entire operation. Sorry, Clark, but you are being stroked, big time. It happens to all of us." Richie folded his arms and let the uncomfortable statement sink in. Clark continued to stare forward, expressionless. The two men sat in silence for several moments.

The doorbell rang. Clark remained unaffected as Richie's head tilted slightly as he recognized the sound. Melody's light footsteps could be heard pattering across the hardwood floor followed by the clacking of the deadbolt. Melody opened the door and there on the steps stood Amy Biancini.

"Hey! Ms. Biancini! So great to see you!" chimed Melody. Amy hadn't set foot in the Westfield house since the repast for Mary Lynn Westfield several years ago. Amy's eyes lit up when she saw Melody on the other side of the screen door.

"Hi Mel! Sorry to pop over unannounced but I wanted to make sure your dad was here when I arrived, so I chose this ungodly hour," said Amy smiling as Melody gently pushed the screen door open. "You've got to catch me up on all the wildlife you've seen while hiking. Any ringneck snakes since our last outing?" Amy had taken Melody on many walks in the woods in her youth and let her join in the field trips for her vertebrate field ecology class. Ringnecks were her favorite snakes because the tiny harmless serpents meant an ecosystem was thriving with a clean water table.

"No, sorry. Just a roadkill garter snake," Melody replied smiling.

"Well, we have to get back out then. And we have to talk about you and your dad coming to Alaska with my environmental science class," said Amy, returning the smile. "Is your dad home?" Melody nodded.

"Yeah, he is out on the porch," said Melody, her face immediately changing into a perplexed sadness. Amy noticed immediately.

"What is wrong, Mel?" she asked.

"I don't know…" replied Melody, looking at the floor. "He is out there with Mr. Byrne from the paper. I think he is dating someone…?" The inflection in her voice was that of an observational question.

"He is?" Amy said, startled. Having known Clark as long as she had, it was obvious to her that there was an intense attraction between him and Sarah Reistad. Her surprise was that Clark had actually gone through with participating in the budding romance. She had assumed that he was still trapped behind the emotional perimeter fencing erected and guarded by his grief. Apparently, she was wrong, she told herself. But was she too late? Melody walked with Amy through the living room and into the threshold of the doorway to the porch, standing behind the two seated men.

"Dad, you've got a guest," said Melody. "Ms. Biancini, how do you take your coffee?" Melody called behind her as she walked back into the kitchen leaving Amy Biancini standing in the threshold. Richie Byrne turned and smiled at her, giving her a single wave of his hand that looked like a drunken salute. Amy waved back and silently made her way around the opposite side of her seated friend and slid the companion wicker recliner until it was level with Clark and

Richie. The three looked like frumpy, disheveled, disillusioned parents on the sideline of a middle school soccer game, wanting to be anywhere in the world except where they were at that precise moment. No one spoke right away, then Amy broke the silence.

"You can't get involved with her, Clark," said Amy softly, staring straight ahead at the songbird feeder along with the two men. Clark stiffened as he heard her. This must have been why she seemed so out of sorts the other day in the elevator—old-school jealousy. Clark had learned time and again that we all live under the delusion that we will someday reach an age of emotional maturity where the schoolyard adolescent jealousy suddenly disappears one day when we are older. This time, Amy was his minder of how foolish that sentiment seemed. Now it was clear the toll his romance with Sarah would take on their friendship. But it had already just about ruined his job, he thought, so why not go for broke emotionally?

"Listen to her, Clark, this is a wise woman," said Richie, nodding heavily and stretching his arm to point at Amy over Clark's head. His hand curled from a pointed finger into a high five attempting to get Amy to return the gesture and slap his hand. She stared intently at Clark, then looked at Richie.

"Listen, I know you think I'm being crazy or petty, but I just spent yesterday afternoon and some of this morning with Alvim Matsumoto's parents." Amy turned to look out the window again and balance the tears that were filling her lower eyelids. "They are ready to talk on the record with you about the coercion and abuse Alvin went through when Sarah recruited him. In fact, it was more of a kidnapping than a recruitment. She also engaged in various intimidation tactics against them if they tried to leave the base. They said it was more like a prison, and Sarah kept Alvin from them even though they all lived on the base. They said she only let them see him once every few days and always supervised any outside visits." Amy waited for Clark's reaction. He didn't speak but his face melted into an even more troubled expression if that were possible.

"Look Clark, get out of this while you still can," said Richie in the way an older brother would give counsel. "If there is one thing I know it's that you can spot a broad who is bad news, and believe me brother, this one is. Once we find the ledger system they built then this whole operation is going to get shut down in one way or another and you don't want to be anywhere near it. Plus, she is under your skin and down your pants because she needs a certain street cred that your reporting would provide her with. She knows you are way too smart to be manipulated with your eyes wide open no matter how she presents the facts and their alternatives, so she went for the only thing that could cloud your judgment…your balls."

Melody, still eavesdropping out of sight in the kitchen, winced at the imagery. Amy, equally disgusted by Richie's frank but graphic description, swallowed hard and audibly.

"Rich, she is buying a major share in the paper's parent company, and she already has a seat on our board because of it," said Clark, countering Amy's and Richie's suggestions. "I can drop the story, in fact, I probably better. But don't you think she is at best operating a little faster and more efficiently than most government operations? She's been able to harness some momentum with her research. At worst, she is misguided and has grandiose ideas to make money in the private sector with some government-funded genetic research." Clark didn't even believe his own words as he heard them escaping from his mouth. Yet, to acknowledge the truth in anything either Richie or Amy were saying would slam a bank vault-sized door on the euphoria and ecstasy Sarah had brought back into his life. He wanted all of it to go away.

"Clark, there is something else you should know," Amy said, followed by a deep sniff. "The Matsumotos and a bunch of other families are all planning to leave the base and try to bring charges against Sarah and Crisprgen for fraud, coercion, and abuse. Do you really want to be on the wrong end of that headline and romantically linked to a woman who is about to be called out as a corporate villain?"

"'Veteran Decorated Reporter Accused of Ethics Violation for Handling of Kidnapping Perp's Profile'. That makes a great headline," added Richie with a wheezy laugh. Amy ignored him and continued her persuasive debriefing.

"Clark, the Matsumotos are afraid and they think their lives are in danger," said Amy, staring at him intently to make sure he was listening.

"So…ok, I get it. Their son just died by his own hand, of course, they are going to have highly emotional reactions. If there is any accurate info to be found that supports what you're saying or what they are saying, it needs to come from the other families. They would be clear-headed and maybe more measured in their descriptions. Can we speak to the others and get them on the record?" Clark asked. Richie shook his head from side to side with a slight smile.

"Well that's going to be tough," he muttered.

"Well, that's not going to happen," said Amy dismissively.

"Why not? Who are the other families?" asked Clark.

Amy looked at Richie, who seemed as if he already knew what she was about to say.

"The LaRoccas and the Mackouls," Amy replied.

***

The cool air-conditioned space between the sets of glass doors at the entrance to the newspaper office felt like walking into a freezer as Elizabeth Cranford stepped out of the Jersey July heat from her morning jog. You don't realize how hot the day is when exercising in the summer until you cross into an air conditioned space. Then you wonder how you made it more than five steps in the searing humidity outside. Elizabeth's Lycra sport bra, drenched with sweat suddenly felt like an ice pack causing the intercostal muscles between her ribs to spasm and contract. She ascended the grand curved staircase in the glass atrium lobby as quickly as she could before the raging sweat made her shiver even further. When she reached the top, she ducked into her office and grabbed her backpack with a change of clothes and towels before beelining for the ladies' room. This was a borderline religious morning routine for her. She had done this almost every working day of her career, usually dodging her former editor, Sean Caldwell, who always managed to put a crimp in the joy she got from running with a snarky misogynistic remark or lousy assignment. But one thing she almost never encountered in those early morning hours when only her anally retentive boss always lurked was her colleague Clark. Clark had found ways to stay out of the office as much as he could, reiterating constantly to Elizabeth and his other subordinates that a reporter's work was in the field, and they should try to be out in that field as much as possible. And if Clark wasn't in the field on a genuine or fabricated assignment, he seldom made it into the building before 9:30 AM when the morning editorial meeting started. Which is why, as Elizabeth stripped off her soaked Lycra leggings and sports bra in the handicapped stall and started to towel herself dry, she realized that she had seen Clark sitting in his office with his back to the door, staring out the floor-to-ceiling glass windows. Perhaps she had imagined it. After all, the runner's high calls up all kinds of racing thoughts as a jogger's heart rate returns to normal. She looked at her watch, the screen was showing how many steps she had jogged compared to the weekly average and had a line showing her descending heart rate. She clicked the button to return to the home screen8:05 AM. Clark couldn't possibly be in the office this early.

Upon finishing changing her clothes, she put the final touches of her red lipstick, pressing her lips together in a smudging motion a few inches from the mirror. She owed Clark an apology and they both knew it. The endorphins from her run made her feel good and ready. At 8:09, she walked silently down the main corridor where the newsroom was at one end and the editor's offices ringed the center cubicle area like a picture frame. There wasn't a sound to be heard. As she approached Clark's office door, she paused and made sure she didn't make a sound. She stood in the doorway silently observing him as he sat facing away from the door and staring out the window blankly. He seemed to be a shell of the man she once knew. That man would have thrown himself in front of a moving New Jersey Transit train for her, and he would have been able to stop it dead with one arm. But that man was gone, and a train was always coming. Deep down she felt that she bore some responsibility for the sad wrecked heap in front of her, though intellectually she told herself that couldn't be true. She was city editor now because of Clark's mentorship, support, and friendship and there was no way she was going to let there be any bad blood between them. She stood in silence trying to find the gumption to somehow break the ice.

"The story is on your desk, and I emailed you a copy," said Clark in a low voice without looking up. He knew she was standing behind him and didn't offer a greeting or even turn around to make eye contact. He was more pissed than she had realized.

"Thanks," she replied and pulled the second chair in the room so she could sit next to him and also look out the window. No one spoke for what seemed like an eternity. Then Clark broke the silence, speaking again without turning his head or looking at his colleague.

"She got under my skin, Liz," he said softly, sounding dejected. There was an element of defeat in his tone. Elizabeth understood immediately that he was talking about Sarah Reistad. However, her apology needed to come first before they talked about her.

"Clark, listen, about the other day and your story…I—" she stammered. Clark cut her off.

"Oh, don't worry about that," he said abruptly. "That argument we had just means you've officially become an editor, and therefore by definition, we will be adversaries whenever I turn in a story." His deadpan delivery gave Elizabeth pause. It would be very easy for Clark to dismiss her now that she was his editor, something she feared could happen when she took the job. As she felt her body stiffen, she looked to see Clark smiling at her broadly. He was kidding. She smiled back and gushed a sigh of relief. "That won't be the last fight we have Liz, dear. What did you think when you signed up to be my editor? Did you think I was going to be easy?" He laughed and reached out his arm with the palm of his hand turned up, beckoning for Elizabeth's. She gently grabbed his hand.

"Now about this, Ms. Reistad..." Elizabeth sang in a sassy black woman matriarchal tone. Clark turned his head down. "Before I go and wipe your tears, I want you to know that it was not cool that you had Allele escort me out so you could keep playing footsie upstairs with—"

"I didn't tell anybody anything! I wondered why you never came in for the interview!" blurted Clark.

"Yeah, I don't think that's how it happened," said Elizabeth, agreeing with Clark.

Clark looked even more dejected if it were possible. "Liz, the story is on your desk." Liz put her arm around him and sat closer.

"What did you write? Are you going to tell me about it?" she asked, sounding supportive in the way a mother would talk to a seven-year-old boy with tears streaming down his face.

"I wrote it all," Clark muttered. "All of it." He was exasperated.

"Ummm…" Liz burst out laughing. Clark looked at her in hurt shock, then he couldn't resist laughing also.

"Liz, come on," Clark chuckled and shook his head.

"Has this woman got you this bent outta shape?" asked Elizabeth sympathetically. She had never seen him like this.

"Yeah," Clark had to stop laughing for a moment so he could speak. "Well, Liz, it's all there. I think you'll be happy—I've got the Matsumotos on the record revealing coercion, intimidation, theft of intellectual property, hell, its virtual indentured servitude. Then, I've got Sarah on the record extensively describing the Passport Project, which is an ethical atom bomb, but I've also got sources in Washington that say she is operating way out of the bounds of legal and ethical science and are seeking an injunction to shut her down. There is also a dispute about whether this was a government project and that the closure of Fort Monmouth was mistakenly privatized, and Sarah was a corporate raider." Clark sighed as he finished speaking.

"Wow, that's a lot," Elizabeth nodded. "You should take one for the team more often, Clark!" She laughed uproariously. "Sorry!" she giggled. "It had to be said." She covered her mouth as she laughed. Clark, never one to be above satire, shook his head, respecting the humor. "Listen…I know what you are about to say. You are about to look all forlorn and say Liz… you don't understand…" she aped a gruff male voice. "She was the first one that got…. to me since… Mare…" Then she made weeping tears motions and pretended to rub her eyes. Clark was actually flattered that she had the insight into his psyche to detect exactly what he was thinking and about to say. At his age, why feel hurt by something like that?

Elizabeth continued. "Listen, you gotta see it like I see it." She was now firm but friendly. "You were her mark from the beginning. She was running a PR campaign that was working because she knew exactly how to get to you. Then, I also think she is a little off her rocker, a little too intense and dreamy, right? And she probably believed everything she told you, from her megalomaniac sensibility to evolving the human race right down to how you made her feel." Elizabeth paused. Clark looked down again. "Clark, you were a gopher on the train tracks and the train came…that's all. No man I know could have stood up to a woman like Sarah coming on strong. Plus, you were ripe to bust loose and get your feet wet a little bit. You're back in the saddle! There's no shame in that!" Elizabeth squeezed his shoulders in a hug.

"Yeah, I just never pictured my rebound chick to be a criminal evil genius," muttered Clark.

"Well, you had to start somewhere…" Elizabeth squeezed him tighter, and they both laughed uproariously, then sat silent for a while.

"Liz, if you run the story I put on your desk all hell is going to break loose around here. This crazy lady is practically buying the paper's parent company, and she bulldozed right over you in requesting I write the story and then ejecting you from the corporate campus. There is going to be blowback. I understand if you need to hold it. If you really want to avoid any problems then I can take it to another paper or wire. There is no reason for you to catch the shit that will inevitably roll downhill. Believe me, I won't feel weird about it or anything. and I'm not being cryptic or facetious. You don't need a lethal conflict in your first month as city editor." Cark was genuine in giving Elizabeth an out. He knew what would happen if she ran the story, and he didn't want to put her in that position.

"Oh Clark, I'm a big girl. This is what I signed up for. Plus, when it comes to reporting, you are an easy guy to defend because you've always been right. I have watched you shred every story subject, every cranky editor, advertiser or thought leader who ever accused you of impropriety. But I just gotta say…" She started to speak slower.

"You gotta say what?" asked Clark.

"I just gotta say that it would be a little easier if our subject were not in a position of leverage with ethical violation accusations because you got all lovey dovey…" Elizabeth careened her head away and tilted it upward in a fake expression of disapproval.

"Well, yeah…There's that…sorry," Clark said with a smirk. He wasn't sorry, but he still didn't want to put Elizabeth in a bad position. "But wouldn't that make her look bad too? I mean do you think Sarah could face her board—the board that I met—and admit that she had a fling with the reporter who was supposed to be writing a deep dive profile? Wouldn't that be embarrassing?"

"She doesn't seem to be the type of person to be embarrassed by anyone knowing who has done a deep dive on her." Elizabeth made air quotes when she said deep dive. Clark rolled his eyes. "Clark, you told me something once when that outrageous pharma CEO was coming after me, remember? You explained that people who are extremely intelligent and successful often have personality deficits of some kind or another, usually some mania or narcissism, and most importantly, you taught me that some people aren't capable of being embarrassed, and they are the most dangerous. I think Sarah Reistad is all three of those things. She is extremely smart and seems like an obvious narcissist and would not be embarrassed in the slightest if she needed to tell her board or our editor-in-chief that you made her squeal.

People like her don't play by the same rules as everyone else. They have different perspectives, and you can't try to find any logic in it. It's neither good nor bad, it just is. You told me that, Clark." Elizabeth finished talking. Clark smiled. He had told her that, many years ago.

"Yeah, well, I'm pretty sure that my story is going to kill any blossoming romance that was happening. Liz, you gotta understand, I never got involved with a subject before…"

"Never?" Elizabeth shot back with a smile.

"Well… not until after the article was published." Clark laughed. "Nah, this is going to kill it. And I guess that's ok."

"Yeah, it's a lot easier to just publish a hit job on her than have a down to earth conversation and tell her it's not going to work out, and you just want to be friends. Oh sorry…reporter and source kinda friends?" Elizabeth was loving giving Clark the gruff counsel he had provided her all these years as she had navigated the perils of dating.

"Yeah, honestly it is. I don't think it's a cop out. She knew exactly what she was doing, and she could tell that I was pretty hooked because I didn't see it coming." He looked down.

"Uh-huh," Elizabeth nodded.

"And to be truthful, I forgot how raw and shitty the cycle of infatuation and crash and burn can be. I'm too old to be moping around over romance. I'm too old for this shit." he paused and looked at the ceiling. "I'm too old for a broken heart." Elizabeth turned and looked at him directly.

"This woman did not break your heart, Clark. This woman made you feel alive again for a few days and if all of that showed you that you are ready to get back in a relationship with someone and out of your dungeon of self-pity— which you tell yourself is grief—then she did you a favor. Your heart was broken when Mare died, and in a way, it's always going to be broken. Dating or a relationship will help minimize that, but you are going to have to work at it. I'm actually proud that you let yourself go with the flow," Elizabeth counseled.

"How are you so wise about all this?" Clark asked, appreciative of her insights.

"When I was 19, I was about to get engaged, and my boyfriend never made it home from Iraq. Over time, you learn to go forward. There is no one right way, other than to just keep moving, and that's what you are doing." Elizabeth lowered her voice for emphasis. Colleagues were starting to come into the newsroom for the workday. Clark nodded. "I'm not going to cut your story, Clark. Fact check it, yes, but cut it, no. Fuck Sarah! She can live with the fallout and so can I."

"Well, then we better brace for impact..." Clark said softly.

Chapter 10

Elizabeth, Amy and Clark were seated in Amy's Prius. Elizabeth was in the passenger seat, and Clark sat in the back. Amy and Elizabeth had bonded, and they had been correct in their concern for their complicated friend and mentor. Amy glanced in the rear view mirror and saw the mighty Clark Westfield, whom she had known as a spry and physically perfect specimen of a 17 year old man, a 25-year-old bulldog reporter, a 45-year-old two-time Pulitzer Prize winning world renowned investigative reporter and now, a 50-year-old widow. She had seen Clark during some dark times, the darkest of which was after his wife's passing. But he had never looked like this. This was different. He looked, well, heartbroken was the only word that seemed to fit.

They were on their way to the Matsumoto boy's funeral. It was going to be a huge memorial service on the field at Maplewood high school where Amy taught and Alvin had attended. The students were shaken by his well-publicized disappearance and his suicide. He had been a shy, quiet 15-year-old who most students didn't know. So, when his disappearance hit the papers, he had taken on an almost mythic folk hero stature with a viral surge on social media with students expressing support, organizing searches and handing out missing fliers. They never knew he had been recruited by a consumer genetics company that was really a front for secret government research.

The mood in the car was solemn. A young man was dead after taking his own life during great turmoil. Clark kept re-imagining seeing Mrs. Matsumoto on all fours on the ground, sobbing hard with a long line of gooey spit speckled with vomit stretching from her gaping mouth to the floor. The scene played like a video loop in Clark's head. Alvin's parent's devastation weighed heavily on the three occupants of the Prius. But the scene in the rearview mirror of Clark's brokenness weighed heavier on Amy. She hated seeing him like this. He was too good a friend and too good a man. "I could be very good for him," she thought to herself.

Elizabeth turned to Amy at the steering wheel. "I had a thought," she said. "Amy, why don't you write a testimonial obituary of Alvin? Write as his teacher about the student you knew and the meaning we should find in his death."

"Wow…I'd really like that," replied Amy, turning and smiling warmly at Elizabeth. Clark continued to stare out the window. His chest felt heavy. Beyond the malfeasance and deadly shenanigans of Crisprgen, and beyond the third degree burns left on Clark's heart by Sarah Reistad, lay a simple and horribly depressing truth: the human race was collapsing with inevitable major crises on the horizon and the gap between the privileged and the poor was about to get drastically deeper and wider.

"Why bother at all?" he thought to himself. Deep down it hurt. Sarah was the type of woman that you want to believe is real. She says and does all the right things; doing all the work by leading you on while delivering overwhelming deep hitting flattery and sexual acrobatics. Rare women like Sarah knew how to make a man feel like he was being visited and cared for by angels. And every man who found himself on the lofty updrafts of these feminine seraphim will eventually, and abruptly, be forced to swallow a hard truth - that these women don't exist—at least not in real life. Their warm light and promise of eternal affection and sexual fulfillment was actually a confluence of Clark's vulnerability and desire to be loved rather than lonely, combined with a few healthy squirts of her own agenda.

"I should have known better," he thought. "There are no fucking angels." Clark's heart felt heavy.

The car stopped in a parking space in the lot behind the school adjacent to the football field.

"Sorry ladies, I am going to have to run in and use the restroom. I'll meet you in the seats on the field. Save me one," said Clark as he exited the car and trotted towards the door.

"Sure, Clark, go through that door and down the hall past the office; the bathrooms are on the right!" called Amy as she and Elizabeth casually got out of the car and walked towards the rows of chairs that had been set up for students and parents. Clark entered the hallway that was lit only with the sunlight that streamed through the windows. His pace quickened as he got closer to the bathroom. He pushed the heavy industrial aluminum door open and glided over to the urinal. Urination was often a Defcon 5 situation for guys in their 50s, and Clark was no exception. He found the closest one and managed to unzip just in time. Despite the urge and pressure on his bladder, his stream was weak and peeing was a long unpleasant experience. He closed his eyes and tilted his head back. This was one of the less dignified gifts of middle age.

As he stood there, he smelled something usually not encountered in a men's bathroom—lavender. The strong scent of gentle, warm, lavender was overpowering the typical men's room ammonia soaked stench of 10 urinal pucks. Sarah wore lavender and used it in a shampoo. It smelled like her. He then realized she was standing right behind him. A vague sensation quickened in his heart and his adrenaline surged. He felt her hand reach under his ass cheeks and attempt to gently grab his genitalia from behind. He could hear her stifling a giggle. The smell of lavender got stronger and then he could feel her breath on the back of his neck.

"Is someone else in here with me? Trying to perhaps use the exact urinal that I'm using?" Clark said facetiously while tilting his head up towards the ceiling, playing along and pretending not to know she was behind him cupping his balls as he stood there peeing. Sarah notched her chin onto his shoulder where his trapezius muscle connected to his collar bone and let it rest with the full weight of her head and neck. She was still giggling intermittently. "You do realize I'm mid–stream, right?" said Clark, now a bit surprised at how her flirtatious aggression was unfazed by his active urination. It occurred to Clark that Sarah must not have read or seen the story he had turned in to Elizabeth and ran this morning at 6 AM. If she had, she might not have been giggling with a loose grip on his balls.

Clark finished peeing, tucked himself back in his pants, and drew the zipper. Sarah's hand didn't move. Clark turned around and met her gaze straight on. Her expression was warm yet piercing, with gentle longing. It occurred to him that he had never met a woman so enigmatic with such intense appeal, yet possessing such baggage and questionable ethics. And yet, there he was, standing in a high school men's room staring into the eyes of a genius billionairess that ran the world's largest consumer genetic testing company while trying to hoard government secrets and create another evolutionary branch of humanity. All while nonchalantly holding his crotch like a meat hook and giggling like a child. Somewhere his late wife, Mary Lynn was wetting her angel pants in Heaven laughing at this…

Sarah took a step back and pulled Clark by his crotch so he had to walk with her, never breaking her stare. Clark opened his stance and waddled in an exaggerated fashion, letting Sarah pull him along the bathroom floor. She moved backwards towards a stall, the vinyl and aluminum door clanging loudly as she knocked it open. She then backed into the stall, pulling Clark with her, and sat down on the toilet with the lid closed. She unbuckled his belt, opened his pants, and started to fellate him. Clark shut the stall door behind him and leaned against it. What was the protocol for this situation? After a few minutes, the suspense got to him and he spoke.

"Umm, hey Sarah," he stammered, not wanting to interrupt but knowing it was necessary because they were in a high school bathroom, after all. "I don't think we should risk getting caught in here," he managed to say. Sarah looked up at him and shook her head from side to side in a no motion, completely unbothered. Why couldn't he have met this woman when he was 25? "Well, it's one thing if being charged with a felony doesn't bother *you*, but I need to come clean about a story I filed last night. I'm pretty sure you are going to hate me after you read it." The guilt from his article's sharp criticism of the woman seated in the stall with him was made worse by her zealous approach and the slobbering from her current activity.

Sarah looked up at him and mumbled: "Already read it….it's great!" she said with muffled syllables caused by the obstruction of Clark in her mouth.

"What do you mean you read it?" asked Clark. "The one from last night? Really?" Sarah nodded and remained intent on her activity. If she read last night's article, would she really be approaching the circumstances of her current situation with such vigor? Clark gently put his hand on her forehead breaking her rhythmic momentum and then lifted her chin so she made eye contact before he took one step back, disengaging his genitals from her mouth. She looked up at him with a childish frown. While a nice gesture, nothing Sarah was doing would have any effect until he cleared the air…or at least his conscience. Sarah took a break in the action and looked up at him, still seated.

"I read your article, Clark," said Sarah with a friendly smile. "I thought it was wonderful!"

"The article from this morning?" asked Clark incredulously.

"Yes, you ask a lot of great questions," she said matter of factly. Clark paused. His article had extensive quotes from medical ethicists about the morality of a designer human genome, the inequality that would result and the aggressive tactics by Sarah and Crisprgen to recruit and hire smart young people.

"You aren't upset?" asked Clark, somewhat baffled and guarded as he believed Sarah was playing him in some way.

"Does it look like I'm upset with you?" she said seductively while still seated on the toilet. She moved her hand up his thigh and tried to put him back in her mouth. He took another step back, disrupting the action.

"I kinda thought you would never talk to me again," Clark reflected out loud. His mind was churning. He was pinned up against the wall of a bathroom stall, refusing a blowjob from a woman who was trying to re-engineer the human race, and she didn't seem the least bit perturbed that he had written a piece that raised deep legal, social and ethical questions about what she was doing. Something didn't add up.

"Clark, why would I be upset? Your piece wasn't inaccurate, and the attitudes you examine that question our work are all perfectly legitimate. You're a smart one, that's why I'm so into you." Sarah stood up and leaned against him pressing him against the back of the stall door. She leaned in to kiss him and Clark drew his head back avoiding her. She remained in place an inch from his chin.

"I'm not sure I understand." sighed Clark. With Sarah, it seemed that no matter what emotion she triggered, it was never the one that remained after her manipulations.

"You reacted in the precise way I thought you would," Sarah said in almost a whisper, tilting her head to one side for dramatic effect while looking Clark in the eyes. "You were smart enough to grasp the sheer science of what we do and its implications for humanity while illustrating some of the questions and discrepancies the Passport Project raises. You had an intellectual understanding and an empathy for those affected, which originates from the purity of your heart and spirit. You really are all that, Clark Westfield." Sarah kissed his forehead as she stopped talking. Clark was baffled. He had assumed that the story he filed would have been a relationship killer, and he had sweated about alienating Sarah and living with the aftermath. Yet, it seemed to have only drawn him in further into her hypnotic web. "Clark, you being honest about how you feel about our work is fantastic—nobody ever really tells me the truth about what they think or their misgivings and fears. Instead, they couch it in cryptic minimalist language and talk about 'longitudinal population health data' and macroeconomics. No one ever just says it like it is, at least no one with the true capacity to understand the work and who would spend enough time making sure they understand it. You did both, and for that I am genuinely appreciative." Her voice was just above a whisper.

"I kinda assumed you'd be…pissed," muttered Clark.

"Any great leap forward for humanity is going to arrive through a cloud of reticence and trepidation. That's by no means unhealthy. Don't you think I factored it in?" Sarah was now talking more matter of factly. "I knew you were smart, Clark. From both reading your columns all my life and from the fact that you had been tagged early in the homeland security records."

"I was? What records was I tagged in?" Clark was now legitimately ensnared in the manipulation loop.

"Oh sure, you were on their radar since your first federal standardized tests in 8th grade. You were a deliberate find for me, Clark. I'm just happy that you were working at a daily paper in Newark rather than Saskatchewan." Sarah let a giggle escape.

"What do you mean by deliberate?" asked Clark.

"What I mean is that when it comes to both the Transcendence Project and the Passport Project, I have to hand select exactly who will play which role. It's too important not to," she continued. "We need an all-star team of the smartest ones, from all disciplines and all perspectives. We need scientists, we need creatives—"

"Blacksmiths, artists, philosophers, plowmen…I get it," said Clark semi-sarcastically. Sarah continued.

"And someone is going to have to explain what we are doing to the public as it unfolds. Answer their questions, get the right sources on the record, etc."

"And you want me to do the explaining?" Cark interrupted.

"I needed the smartest journalist I could find who could not only read between the lines but who had the courage to tell it like it is. I started out thinking it could be you, hoping it would be, and you've proven me correct at every turn." Sarah kissed his forehead again. Clark was silent for a few moments then said the first thing that came to mind.

"I'm not understanding why you would think my investigative piece about you and your work is to your benefit. Honestly Sarah, I wrote it in the hopes of galvanizing the readers and drawing some scrutiny from whatever government agency that needs to deal with the implications of—"

"With the implications of what my evil genius plot might unleash?" Sarah interrupted, smiling. "Clark, by writing the article that you did, you've given an air of elevated credibility to the Passport Project, legitimizing it in the eyes of all the other power players and thought leaders that I'm eventually going to have to bring into the fold, not to mention the private sector funding I'm going to need. But more importantly, as time goes on and you write more about it, you'll see the urgent necessity of what we are doing, and you'll be grateful that you qualified for the Passport. As your readers and the public are swayed by your gradual change in tone and opinion, it will become more normalized in the eyes of the public."

Clark unlatched the stall door and stepped out of the tiny compartment. He backed into the row of sinks that lined the restroom walls. Sarah stood up and slowly shuffled towards him in a flirtatious manner.

"Clark, you are exactly the right person to be the documentarian for this fork in humanity's evolution. Who better to write about such a turning point for the human race? And I'll never interfere with anything you write because if I can win you over then I am doing my job correctly." Sarah maintained her hypnotic eye contact.

"But you are a majority owner in the paper's parent company, you can change whatever you want," Clark managed to blurt out.

"If I do this right, I'll never need to change anything," said Sarah gently. She was now close to his face again. She held his limp arms at the wrists. Clark felt like a toddler, unsure of what to do in a crowded room. "Clark, I'm never going to change what you write! I bought into the paper to have access to you and your readers. You are exactly who I need telling this story, and your readers are exactly the gene pool we need to draw from in order to perfect the genome for the Passport. I've got big plans for you, Clark. Journalism isn't what it used to be, and I think you can restore some of its integrity while exposing some of the unsavory corruption that lurks everywhere in our decaying society. I might as well tell you now that I plan on making you managing editor, and there are some mergers and acquisitions on the horizon so you'll run multiple papers from multiple regions…all under you. You'll be the official spokesperson for the Passport Project."

Sarah smiled as if pleased with herself. Clark stood still in silence. He didn't know what to think or say.

"So you planned all this?" was the only response he could complete.

"Yes, of course, all important projects have a plan." Sarah laughed again. "Well, I planned everything except for one thing—"

"And what was that?" asked Clark.

"Falling in love with you," Sarah replied and rested her head on his chest. The words shot through Clark like an electric shock. He stood still holding Sarah, then dropped his arms to digest what he had just heard her say. He turned and leaned on the sink, running the water and throwing some on his face for a distraction. When in doubt, he thought, go for a laugh.

"Do you love me enough to enroll me in the Transcendence Project?" he asked with rhetorical humor as he toweled off his face. He rubbed his eyes and looked in the mirror, then wheeled around to look at Sarah and saw only the empty stall and an otherwise empty restroom. As he heard the heavy wooden door close with a dull thud, he realized that she was gone.

***

Clark stood at the edge of the Maplewood high school football field. The principal of the school was speaking, referencing how Alvin Matsumoto succumbed to "the disease of depression." The Matsumoto family, Alvin's two parents and what Clark assumed must have been a younger sister about 14 years old, sat in the first row. All three family members wore sunglasses. About 200 white formal lawn chairs were arranged on a green outdoor artificial turf carpet under a white canvas wedding tent. If one were unaware of the tragedy that had brought everyone to this field, they would have easily mistaken the elegant set design for a scholarship ceremony or graduation.

Clark stood behind the seated cluster of humanity feeling the irony of the moment. The woman who had arguably been the catalyst for this sad assembly had just told Clark that she was in love with him and was going to give him a promotion and a raise in salary. As attractive as that path sounded back in the men's restroom stall, he told himself that any path forward that included Sarah Reistad would undoubtedly be rife with tragic scenes such as this. Her version of progress factored in funerals as simply the cost of doing business, a cost she paid perhaps directly, perhaps tangentially, but always indifferently as she brought her grand ambitions to reality. And yet, Clark felt alive and exuberant around her. She was the only person—hell the only thing— that had made him feel somewhat human in the past five years. And that is precisely what made her so dangerous.

He could see Amy seated directly behind Mr. and Mrs. Matsumoto. Seated at the end of their row, Clark recognized several of the Crisprgen board members, among them Mrs. Katherine O'Halloran, who was in reality, Lt. Col. Kelly Pram. Sarah was nowhere to be seen. The principal concluded his remarks and introduced Suki Matsumoto, who as Clark had presumed, was Alvin's sister. Suki rose from her seat and approached the podium. As she adjusted the microphone to her short stature, Clark felt a large hand on his shoulder.

"Westfield, you're killing me. This whole thing is unbearable to watch, especially as she drags you around like a dog toy." The voice belonged to Richie Byrne. Why would he be at the Matsumoto boy's funeral? "Don't sit down yet, we gotta go somewhere and talk now that you are finished in the boy's room with your…ahem…new girlfriend." Rich smirked and turned away in an exaggerated expression rousing Clark. "I would have barged in and pissed at the urinal while you were grunting in the stall and totally busted on you, but I couldn't have Reistad IDing me. She and I go waayyy back." Richie's beat was national defense and Washington politics, and his years-long affair with Lt. Col. Kelly Pram could easily have caused them to cross paths.

"Did you meet her through Ms. O'Halloran?" Clark asked, giving a quick pointing gesture towards Lt. Col Kelly Pram who was seated at the funeral as Katherine O'Halloran.

"I sure did!" replied Richie in his jovial tone. "Kell brought me to a secret dinner as part of her cover and—"

"You mean as her date," interrupted Clark, not missing a chance to jab his friend.

"Yeah, as her date, but also as ex-military. She wanted a second set of eyes on what Sarah was selling," said Richie.

"Selling? I thought she was recruited in high school for the intelligence communities 'utility genius program' or whatever the fuck they call it. What do you mean 'selling'?" asked Clark.

"She was recruited, that's how she got to Kelly. But Kell didn't work with her or operationalize her. That was some other team. But they called her and said they had someone they wanted to use to launch a major project but they were afraid she had the potential to go rogue, so they wanted her to meet Kelly and explain the contract work she was doing, and Kelly could evaluate her with key questions."

"And you attended this meeting?"

"Please, it was a dinner, and yes, I did. Kelly wanted it to be informal so I posed as her husband, and we all went to dinner."

"Did Sarah bring anyone? Like, did she have a boyfriend?" asked Clark in a quickened tone.

"Good God, you are pathetic. She really got to you, didn't she?" said Richie, shaking his head and chuckling. Clark scowled, embarrassed at the truth. "No, she didn't bring a boyfriend, she has never been married, and to our knowledge in her file, she has no romantic attachments of any kind. I figured she liked girls, not that I care, but back then she wore a lot of flannel if you know what I mean." Richie chuckled and Clark looked back at him bewildered. "So, we go through dinner and basically we learn that Sarah is a master genius in genetics, and she has been assigned to the government's intelligence unit to collect info and conduct science on genetically modified agriculture and livestock. That was her day job with the Department of Agriculture, but she was really working for the Seed Bank."

"The Seed bank?" Clark shook his head bewildered.

"Yeah, the bank in Alaska that has all our Agriculture Intel and seed samples from every plant on earth? Historically, it was created because we thought the Chinese or Russians would hurt our crops and cattle, but in the last decade, it has become a ground zero for climate change contingency planning. I'll take you there someday." Clark nodded wide eyed. "Anyway, she was doing all these plant genetics, and she wanted to meet with the Pentagon about some discovery she said she'd made. Long story short, she had figured out a genetic modification to a fungus that could take out our entire corn crop and the world's rice. She wanted to present it to the Joint Chiefs!" Richie laughed and rolled his eyes. "So we realized that we needed to bring her into the Department of Defense genetics program before she sold any of her research to China. She has really delivered for the Passport Project, but she is in fact also going rogue."

"Are you sure? She hasn't really done anything yet…" Clark protested.

"In addition to her retaining the last critical data, which I've explained, she also took off with the records logs for the Transcendence Project. We have no idea who she gave the TA65 CRISPR-CAS 9, and I fear she was too generous," explained Richie.

"But if she gave those things back…" Clark stammered. Some small voice inside was telling Clark that if he could talk Richie down, that maybe it would all be okay. But, he knew better.

"Yeah, we could probably work something out, but I came here to brief you on a new development. The Mackouls are dead." Richie paused and looked at Clark. "All three—the parents and the boy, Greg. The parents died first in a staged automobile accident, and when Greg found out he took his own life, just like the Matsumoto kid."

"Jesus!" muttered Clark.

"Yeah, the Mackoul kid pinned a note to his chest explaining that Sarah was manipulating him romantically and he had realized that she was ruthless, but leaving meant putting his family in jeopardy. When the parents found him, they took off and that's when they had their auto accident." Richie made air quotes with his hands. Clark sighed. "So

Kelly is evacuating the Matsumotos immediately after the funeral. That's why we've got a perimeter." Richie waved his hand in a circle pointing around the field. Clark looked and saw 6 or 7 men in black trench coats wearing sunglasses and earpieces with a squiggly cable. They were US Marshals. At the end of the football field were three enormous black SUVs with completely black tinted windows.

"Are they gonna arrest Sarah?" asked Clark. He felt his voice waver just a touch.

"Arrest? Hell no, why would we do that? Like you said, she hasn't done anything yet. The LaRoccas and the Mackouls—those were professional hits. She didn't run them off the road, and we aren't certain she was the one who ordered them. We need to know if she is working with a syndicate or a cabal, even one inside the intelligence community. But you are missing the point—she was also romantically manipulating Greg Mackoul and very likely the Matsumoto kid. You were in some genius company with those guys. I guess Sarah really liked the smart ones."

Clark felt queasy. His face grew pale, and his eyes got red and swelled.

"Oh, I'm sorry buddy. You were really in deep weren't you? Well, look at it this way—you got back in the saddle! So for you it served a purpose and now you can re-enter the human race!" Richie patted Clark on the back and rested his hand on his shoulder in the way men do when they genuinely support each other. "Look Clark, if it makes you feel any better, I would have done the same thing, even if I knew she was bad. I mean, why refuse free sex, right?" Richie chuckled again in an attempt to cheer him up. Clark scowled again.

"It wasn't about the sex, Richie," Clark muttered.

"I know, buddy. It was her intense flattery and emotional affirmations that made her so irresistible. That's also what makes her so dangerous. I'm joking about the sex, Clark, but in reality I would have done the exact same thing for the exact same reasons. Guys like us are defenseless when a pretty woman comes on strong and aims her flattery towards a unique spot, usually a spot that we hide because it's too painful. The reality is simply that they are great at spotting men's vulnerabilities. How do you think I got involved with Kelly?" Richie shook his head as he finished speaking. "Speaking of Kelly, she needs to speak with you. You gotta get her attention before she is wheels up with the Matsumotos. She sent me to find you and make sure you got to her. She is sitting in row 3 with—"

"Yeah I know, she is next to Alvin's parents. OK, I'll go talk to her" Clark sighed. It was all such a letdown— he had one of the greatest investigative story breaks of his career, the kind that could garner Watergate level hysteria. Shit, it might even win him two more Pulitzers! But none of that could change the direction of the shadow crossing his heart as the hope and excitement of a new love was sunsetting. After losing his wife five years prior, he thought he would never fall in love again and had resigned himself to gradually deteriorating into a lonely old man, possibly paying for sex if he ever wanted any ever again. Sarah had melted all of that like butter in a microwave, and Clark had really fallen for her. It felt epiphanic to admit that to himself. Richie had given him an off ramp in the way only bros could. Maybe he was right, maybe it was about getting back in the saddle. Clark could live with that idea. It would at least reconcile him intellectually. He turned back to thank Richie, but the stocky ex-Navy veteran reporter had disappeared.

*****

Clark crept to the back row of chairs on the football field, trying to be inconspicuous. He could see Lt. Col Kelly Pram sitting across the opposite side of the podium where the green astroturf carpet started to protect the field from the hundreds of aluminum chairs, and the white canvas wedding tent did not reach. Clark was in the blazing sun and heat, and he would have to find a spot to sit down anyway, so he crept up three rows until he was under the shade the tent provided. He looked again at Lt. Col Pram, and found her slightly shaking her head in a no motion. Clark realized she was telling him not to go any further. She tilted her head at a 45-degree angle towards the school, possibly indicating that she would meet Clark there. She stood up, expressionless, and started to walk towards the aisle. She turned and walked down the aisle, exiting the shady comfort of the tent and walked towards the school, eventually disappearing under the bleachers. Clark walked towards the school to follow after her from the opposite side of the seated crowd. He stepped into the darkness under the empty bleachers at the far end of the football field, at least 50 yards away from any spectators, and let his eyes adjust to the absence of light. After a few seconds, he heard the low baritone of Lt. Col. Kelly Pram's voice.

"You've done well, Westfield," said Lt. Col Pram with her signature inseparable overtone of military authority in her voice. "Frankly, you did better than we all thought you would."

"We? Did well with what? Where the hell are you?" Clark still couldn't see who he was talking to.

"You actually succeeded in obtaining the info we needed from Sarah Reistad." Lt. Col. Pram stepped forward and as his eyes adjusted to the light, he could see she was about five feet in front of him.

"I'm not sure I follow," said Clark trepidatiously. Intelligence officers were a crafty bunch.

"Well, you got Sarah to disclose enough for us to find Greg Mackoul and his CRISPR sequences that she was harvesting. It was genius to couch it under the idea of an interview." Lt. Pram gave a phony smile to match the equally phony flattery.

"I was interviewing her," Clark retorted, somewhat baffled. "That was all genuine, and I was doing my job. Did you read the article?" Clark's head was spinning with stress, confusion and exhaustion. "Listen, Kell, I don't have time for your games. Two high school kids are dead by suicide and their parents may have been murdered. I'm reporting on this so let's stop the cryptic cloak and dagger shit. If you wanted to feel like you are in a James Bond movie then you should have studied acting. But please, let me do my job and simply report this story." Clark's anger was obvious in his tone.

"Let you do your job and simply report? That's rich Westfield." Lt. Col. Pram chuckled and laughed contemptuously. "What part of your job involves fucking your interview subjects? Let's see…by our count it was eleven times in three days? Quite impressive! And what part of good interviewing skills includes getting blown in a bathroom stall as one of the action steps?" Her sarcasm was biting and hurtful, but it stung disproportionately in such close proximity to the harsh realities Clark had swallowed over the last 24 hours. "Seriously Westfield, I don't care what you do. If your editor sanctions you sleeping with sources, you are profiling then you've got the best job in the world. We had the whole base wired and bugged so you got a lot out of her, enough where we at least have what we need with the CRISPRs she was hoarding. We still need some more things, like the database of recipients for the TA-65 CRISPR, but we will find it. Don't worry, you can hang in there a while longer. We need someone on the inside to determine who she is working with on the outside."

"What do you mean hang in a while longer? I wrote my story. This is done. You guys are managing a rogue asset. It's not my problem, and I don't work for you." Clark felt his temperature rising and tremors of frustration. He also wanted to be as far away from Sarah as possible from now on.

"Well, you know what they say, fake it until you make it, right?" Lt. Pram smirked. "She is going to embed herself in the ownership company of your paper so she has access to the databases that curate for your subscribers. Their reading habits, search words, social media and shopping behaviors the millions of profiles of your readers will help her identify not just smart people but anyone that has any specific traits needed for a CRISPR sequence that she will then try to sell commercially. She's already in love with you, Westfield. This is going to be the easiest assignment you've ever had." Her smirk endured. Clark sighed loudly.

"I don't work for you," he said again. "And I won't be working for Sarah Reistad at the paper." He shook his head with frustration.

"Look, I've got to get back to the memorial, as I have my marshals guarding the Matsumoto's. I'm evacuating them immediately afterward, and they will be placed in protective custody. You should proceed to do business as usual. Don't rock the boat. Don't draw any suspicion from Sarah as she comes on board. I'll be in touch about setting up monitoring on her so we can determine who she's got on the outside."

"What monitoring? Kelly fuck off! I DON'T WORK FOR YOU and I don't care what other business you have with her!" Clark's voice was growing louder.

He turned in a huff of frustration and started to walk away towards the parking lot. He never took well to being manipulated. But more importantly, he had forgotten what a broken heart felt like. It had been since before he met his wife more than 25 years ago that he had felt that crushing malaise of nothingness that engulfs your tear ducts, the pit of your stomach and your entire spirit when a romantic relationship runs aground. Sarah Reistad had reminded him of what that unbearable pain and powerlessness felt like and he wanted to be as far away from it as he could. He realized that with the new Sarah romance a total bust, he was back to square one as a middle aged widower and alone again. That reality was worse than losing her. He suddenly felt a pang of grief so sudden and deep it caused him to completely lose his composure. He quickened his pace. Ironically, the pain in his recently sprained ankle radiated like wildfire as he walked just like it had on the day he met Sarah.

He walked back to the car with an air of disgust. His mind was racing like a strobe light. He was angry with himself for letting her get so deep under his skin, and he resented Lt. Col

Pram's premise that he should just stick it out, business as usual, and collect information for Naval intelligence. She had done the same thing to Richie Byrne. Was Richie still a journalist? Did it matter? Once the paper was bought and the sale went through, it would all be one big controlled racket anyway. Nothing that he or Elizabeth had worked on all these years would matter on the other side of that merger. Maybe Clark had run out of road. Maybe it was time to pack it in and leave the newsroom for good. His gait was slow and heavy as he walked into the parking lot. He saw Amy Biancini and Elizabeth Cranford standing in front of Amy's Prius, pointing at the rear door which was opened. They looked like they were having an intense conversation as Clark approached. He didn't want to stick around the memorial any longer. He wanted to go home and puke. Elizabeth motioned for him to come over and walk quicker.

"Clark, come here. You've got to see this," Elizabeth said. Amy stood next to her with an open three ring binder, flipping the pages and shaking her head. As Clark got close enough to see what was in the backseat, Amy shot him a concerned look. "I'd ask where you were but I know better," remarked Elizabeth while pointing in the back seat. There, on the warm vinyl seat cushion were two large file boxes. In scrawled black magic marker were the words "Telomerase Rosters" and the other ones simply said "CRISPR CAS-9

Curation Records." Clark stopped in front of the two women and said nothing.

"Clark, at least one of these boxes has a few binders with biopic profiles," said Amy, still flipping through the pages without looking up. "This seems to be the medical files and dossiers on everyone who got the TA-65 CRISPR and the dates and names of whoever signed off on it. Looks like in the first two years, the approvals came from a ranking official from the Department of Homeland Security, three different ones, but then after a certain date, every one of them has Sarah Reistad's signature."

"That must have been when she went rogue," said Clark. "Ladies, can we leave as quickly as possible? I'm not feeling very good." The two women looked at Clark with concern and compassion. He looked like he had been thrown down a flight of stairs. Amy handed Elizabeth the binder and walked around the back of the car and started to get into the driver's seat. Elizabeth started to get into the back seat, pausing to move the boxes more behind the driver's seat so she could sit down. Clark got in the front seat and collapsed with his head in his hands.

"Oh my God! Clark these are all files from Crisprgen and records from the various programs," said Elizabeth as she shuffled through the boxes in the back seat. "Wow, Clark, you gotta see this This is the note that Alvin Matsumoto wrote before he died." Her words were followed by an eerie silence and more shuffling of papers. "And here is the one Greg Mackoul wrote. Both say that Sarah was in a controlling and personal relationship with them. This directly implicates her in their suicide. Clark this is basically a thorough documentation of Crisprgen pattern of coercion and intimidation of the students and families they recruited."

"Both suicide notes are in those boxes?" asked Clark without turning around. He was still entranced and distracted.

"Yup, both are here," replied Elizabeth.

"OK editor…after all these years of helping me with stories and watching the different moves I've had to make, what's the move here?" asked Clark. Elizabeth shook her head in a yes motion. She knew the answer. It was the only answer. She stared straight ahead confidently as she answered.

"The Board meeting that will vote on the merger with Sarah's hedge fund is soon. We better publish both notes and our findings in their entirety."

***

Amy Biancini sat in the overstuffed leather armchair in the Managing Editor's office at the Newark Examiner. Across from her behind a big oak desk sat Elizabeth Cranford. She had a stack of several pages in front of her and gently turned one page over and put it into the adjacent stack. When it came to crucially important articles, she still preferred to print them out on paper and read through the paragraphs. Something about the smell of the chemicals used to bleach the typing paper and the weight of the words in her hands made it seem more real, more tangible. She put the last typewritten page face down on the stack and looked up at Amy, letting out a sigh.

"I think we are ready to file," Elizabeth said, mustering a smile as she finished Amy's obituary tribute to her student. Amy nodded in response.

"Good. If it's okay with you, I came by this morning to ask if I could see the note Alvin left. I realized I'd rather have it so I am reminded of the aggravating factors surrounding his death," said Amy.

"OK, sure, it's somewhere here in this box," Elizabeth put one hand on the cardboard box and moved it slightly towards Amy until it was on the edge of the desk. Amy stood up and lifted the box onto her lap.

"I guess after you publish this story you'll need to keep these files, right? Kinda like evidence in a police station locker." asked Amy, only half joking.

"Well, the best defense against accusations of libel is truth, right?" said Elizabeth rhetorically. "Clark taught me something a long time ago. When you have a story that involves some big reveals and will damage the public perception of certain stakeholders, you need to make several sets of copies of all notes and materials. The originals stay in the office, then you make a set of copies that you keep at home and ones you put in a place only you and your editor know about. That way if anything disappears or is tampered with, you are covered and you have proof." At that moment, Clark strolled through the door and sat in the second chair across from Elizabeth's desk.

"Hi ladies!" he said in a peppy tone. "Liz, here you go," he said as he tossed Elizabeth a small brass colored key with an orange cap on the handle. It was the size and type of key that you got when you rented a small locker at an airport or a bus terminal. Liz turned it over in her hands with a slight smile, reading the number stamped in black ink.

"2112? Ok that's easy to remember," she said. "And where is the locker?"

"It's in Newark Penn Station," said Clark. "OK, Aim, I am going to need to keep the originals at my house. I've got a basement full of a lifetime of investigations I'm sure the national news museum would want archived after my death." Clark chuckled and moved the cardboard box even closer to Amy on the desk. "Can you take these for now?" Amy nodded.

"I assume after the story is published the records become property of the Pentagon. They spent dozens of years and tens of millions of dollars on those records, presumably not to have them stuffed unsecured into the back of your Prius. Be ready to hand them over when there is a knock on your door," Elizabeth said sternly. Amy held the box on her lap. "Aim, we couldn't have done this story without you. I feel like you should share the by line with Clark and I on the main story."

"Well thanks, but this amount of data on every corner of genomics would be invaluable to me. I'm going to look through here and see if any of the Crisprgen work validates my conclusions. You couldn't buy this kind of data or reference material. So meticulous too!" Amy stood up, holding the box. Elizabeth stood up from behind her desk and hobbled around to give Amy a hug. Clark stayed seated. "OK, I'm leaving Good luck to you two. Clark, I can drop this box off at your house on my way home. I can't wait to see the story when it's posted!" Amy walked out of Elizabeth's office. Elizabeth watched her walk down the hall then turned to Clark.

"You know…." Elizabeth said slowly.

"Don't say it. At least not what I think you are about to say," said Clark looking down at his phone. Elizabeth sighed loudly.

"I was going to say..." Elizabeth paused. "That she is a rare type of person, and she cares for you very deeply."

Clark snorted.

"Yes, she is a great friend," he said abruptly. "Liz, we have to get the story posted. The board meeting is this afternoon." Elizabeth nodded.

"Ok, I'll get it down to legal, and we can have them work in sections."

"Legal?!?" Clark erupted. "We don't have time for legal! Liz. You know we don't have time!"

"Yeah, but Clark, you know the rules, especially for a story like this. We are publishing the suicide notes left by two minors, and I would think that even you would want some legal advice on how to do that without breaking the law or getting sued." Elizabeth was surprised that Clark would think of publishing without getting clearance from the paper's general counsel. After all, every time he received a cease and desist letter, or with the dozens of lawsuits that had been filed over the decades because his investigations upset someone, it was the legal department that always managed to defuse the situation for him.

"Liz, listen to me." Clark's tone was direct and heavy. "That board meeting is in 90 minutes. They are going to vote on whether or not to approve the expanded investment from the parent company, making Sarah one of the major shareholders and all the editorial influence that comes with it. We have a story that links her to four murders and two suicides as well as coercion, bordering on kidnapping. The board needs to know this before they vote!" He was surprised that Elizabeth was willing to even risk publishing the story after the board vote.

"Clark, you know as Managing Editor I can't post a story like this without fact checking or having the legal department give it a green light." Clark started to feel pangs of rage flood his face. Elizabeth sat with a half-smile, which enraged Clark even more. He sat silently, trying to find his next words. Elizabeth then spoke slowly and softly. "But if someone were to load this up in the preview queue, and accidentally publish it on the paper's website, then that person would have made an error, and I would have to find them and admonish them." Elizabeth pretended to flip through papers on her desk in front of her. Clark realized she was being facetious and tacitly telling him to do exactly that. Now she sounded more like his protégé.

"Right, and if the draft version got loaded up onto our social media channels and emailed out to all our subscribers then our social media editor, Mr. John Oates, would be mad at whoever gave him an uncleared draft," added Clark.

Elizabeth nodded and looked Clark in the eye. This was a green light to do exactly that.

"Yes, and that person would be extremely hard to find," she continued with her faux nonchalance. "In fact, I bet a year from now they would still have no idea who did it and jumped the gun." She was pleased with herself. As Clark's mentor, the longtime editor Steve Miller used to say, when there is a need to bend the rules, always look at what is NOT said. If no one was telling Clark not to simply post the story, then that's exactly what he was going to do.

Elizabeth continued shuffling papers on her desk. "I'll go to jail for you when it comes to fact checking on this Clark, I know we are airtight on the details. But if you are going to go with this early, you gotta leave me out of it."

As she looked up to see if he understood her proposition, he was already gone.

Clark knew that if he posted the story too early someone in management would call Elizabeth and ask if it had been reviewed by the lawyers. She would have to pretend she didn't know and it was 100 percent certain the general counsel would immediately take it down off the web site. That's why Clark couldn't put it up too early. Timing was everything. He saw John Oates at the far end of the hallway.

"Oates! Stop! You got a second?" he panted as he jogged up to the social media director. "I need a favor…like a really big favor." He stopped to catch his breath. "Liz and I just finished a big story, and I need it posted on our social channels like right now."

John Oates rolled his eyes.

"You know we can't publish the big breaks until after midnight right? Why not just wait until then? Then we can put some ad money behind it,?" The social media editor was trying to be helpful. Clark couldn't hold back.

"Listen Oates, and listen very carefully. The newspaper Board of Directors is going to vote this afternoon on whether to allow a major infusion of capital into the newspaper from this woman called Sarah Reistad. In exchange, she will get a seat on the board and will also be allowed to curate and merge all of our subscriber data with the genetics database of her company Crisprgen." Clark paused to catch his breath and continued panting.

"So? We sell our data to a lot of companies," Oates replied, not seeing the urgency.

"Yeah, well, this woman is linked to at least four murders, and she hijacked a top-secret government genetics research program. We can't let it happen." Clark stopped speaking and saw that Oates was completely unimpressed by what he was hearing and needed more convincing. "Oh, and I got to uh…know her a little… as I was writing her profile, and she plans on outsourcing the paper's social media to some firm that her nephew has with his college buddies." Now the expression on Oates' face changed as the corners of his mouth became a snarling frown. And in the way that men do when they are looking out for one another, he slowly fist-bumped Clark and said:

"Get me the story. It's going up now…"

***

Melody Westfield padded down the stairs of her home in her fuzzy bunny slippers to answer the door. There stood Amy Biancini with a large box.

"Hi Amy! Come on in," said Melody as she opened the storm door to let her in. Amy brought the box into the house, walked over to the dining room table and placed it down with a thud. "What's in the box? Looks like a lot of files. Are they for my dad?"

"These files are the records from Crisprgen. Make sure your dad hides them in a safe place," said Amy. "There is information in here that can change the fate of humanity." Melody made an expression like she thought Amy was kidding. "I'm serious, Mel. This is decades of research that has discovered and cataloged CRISPR CAS-9 snippets for every trait imaginable, including immunity and longevity. It's also got a ledger of a bunch of humans that are going to be living a hell of a lot longer than anyone ever has. Oh, and at least four people have died so far over all this." Amy flashed a sarcastic smile. Melody peered into the open top of the box and lifted out the three ring binder that was on the top.

"What do you mean living a lot longer than anyone else?" asked Melody as she opened the binder and began casually flipping through the pages.

"Well, we've known there is an enzyme that can allow cells to live longer and keep dividing and replacing themselves which increases life span, but now there is a CRISPR sequence that has been identified, which if given to someone would cause them to make the enzymes themselves automatically..." explained Amy.

"And they would get eternal life!" exclaimed Melody with childlike exuberance.

"Well, not eternal life, but they would live much longer than anyone now or before them, perhaps even a couple hundred years."

Melody's eyes opened wide.

"Wow! So who are these people? And why did they get this magic genetic elixir?" Melody asked as she continued to flip the pages.

"Well, if you look at this page," Amy helped Melody find the page where the list started. "These are the people that were selected— supposedly the first people picked were those who had made extraordinary scientific discoveries or had a unique intellect. But thank god I think it is going to get shut down. It's a mess; there is no oversight and no clear criteria."

"But the people on this list already had this operation or whatever?" asked Melody as she ran her finger down each line on the page, studying the list further. "How do they get this operation again?"

"Oh, it's not an operation, it's a simple injection and a harmless adenovirus carries the DNA and installs it into living cells, essentially making an edit to your genetic code. In this case, the edit causes you to produce this enzyme and Viola! Next thing you know you are 250 years old." Amy smiled and sighed at the outrageous irony that emerges when the spectacular becomes routine.

"So…everyone on this list got this magic injection and are going to live hundreds of years?" Melody asked again without looking up. Amy nodded.

"You got it. But when you think about it, Mel, who would want to live hundreds of years? I mean, I'm sure you could stay relatively healthy I guess, but in a few decades everyone you loved and knew would be gone, and you'd have to grieve every single one of them. You'd watch the world go through all kinds of tragedies, possibly some Armageddon type event like a nuclear war or a comet hitting the Earth…and you'd have to just deal with it all," Amy mused. Melody looked up at her with an expression of deep and obvious concern. "What?" Amy asked her when she saw that she wanted to say something. Melody turned the three ring binder around and handed it to Amy who took it from her. It was open to the end of the list of those who had gotten the TA-65 CRISPR. Melody ran her finger down the lines of names to the last two names on the page and looked up at Amy. Amy looked down and felt a jolt go through her spine. With an overtone of shocking disbelief, she was able to voice a few words.

"Oh dear…." she gasped.

***

Clark sat in the soft plush chairs in the office of the national politics editor of the newspaper. He had come in here countless times over the years to rant to Richie Byrne that the legal department had cut a key detail out of one of his stories. Richie would usually take his time to talk him off the ledge. Clark would reciprocate by finding him a lead or two on stories that intertwined with his beat. Richie's office and the very chair in which Clark sat had been a two way street of journalistic therapy between the two men.

"So you just put it up? You didn't even wait for legal?" Richie asked Clark who sat gripping a cup of coffee so tightly it had started to spill over the sides. As Clark nodded in response, he kept his eyes on the hallway through the glass wall. He could see board members trickling in for the afternoon meeting. One by one they arrived. They were dignified, rich elites who only saw their role of making decisions about what the citizens of New Jersey should read, see, and know, as perfunctory. Clark's knee moved up and down as if he were tapping his foot to some phantom jazz music only he could hear.

"I couldn't wait, Rich - you know they would have tied it up for three days," said Clark. "They gotta know before the vote this afternoon. I'll take the fallout. Elizabeth won't fire me."

He was practically speaking out loud, trying to convince himself that posting his story before the board meeting was the right move.

"Listen, I'm not saying you did the wrong thing, because God knows you and I have pulled some shit in our day," said Richie. "But, Clark, you do know that because you didn't follow the right procedure, you essentially waived any insurance protection you had. If your new girlfriend decides to shove a libel suit up your ass, you are on your own. The paper can't protect you."

"That's fine. I can substantiate everything, and I'll handle anything she throws at me. It's all there. And if I really get in a jam, then you are going to call your side dish in Naval Intelligence and either get her on the record, or get her to find me someone who can." Clark looked around nervously. He had posted the story an hour ago but had heard nothing from anyone about it. This was the very definition of unease.

"Kelly? Don't bring her into this, Clark. Don't even joke. Right now she is happy with you but when she isn't she bites back. You'll see." Richie rolled his eyes as if he spoke from personal experience. "Hey Clark, I'm going through the site now and trying to find your article and read it. Where did you post it?"

"I posted it on my page - click my name and it should be the first article that comes up," said Clark without looking up. Richie shook his head again.

"I'm not finding it, brother," Richie sighed as he kept scrolling. Clark got up and moved around the desk so he could face Richie's computer and find the article for him. Every reporter had their own page with their articles archived. He opened his and scrolled. The Crisprgen investigative story was nowhere to be found.

"Fuck! OK, something is wrong," muttered Clark as Richie wheeled his chair back to give him more space. Just then Elizabeth appeared in the doorway with a gravely concerned look.

"Clark, I got a call from the legal department, they took your article down and they asked to see us together," she said.

"Fuck that! The board meeting is about to start, and they took it down!!!?? Holy shit, Liz!" Clark's voice was now rising in volume. "Liz, what are we going to do?!? The board has to be informed before they vote. We can't go see the legal department now— stall them for a while. I have to figure out how to make sure the board members know." Clark frantically scrolled and clicked at the web site hoping that his article would magically appear. "Fuck it, I'll just post it again," he exclaimed. More board members were walking in, some had two or three people walking with them who appeared to be personal staff, or others vying for their attention in transparent attempts at brown nosing.

"Well, it doesn't matter now since the board members are arriving, and they aren't going to dive in and read a three-thousand-word article as the meeting is starting," said Richie. "Liz you are opening the meeting, right? Don't you have to deliver a quarterly report? Can't you tell jokes or something?"

"No, I can't do that," replied Elizabeth. "But I've got an idea…Clark, hand me the flash drive with your story on it." She grabbed the tiny thumb drive from Clark and quickly turned and exited Richie's office. The two men looked at each other, then Clark said:

"I'm going in there. I'll ask to speak or something, then I'll just tell the board that we are about to run this story, and I'll do it before they vote to add her," Clark said, rushedly.

Richie and Clark got up abruptly from their chairs and jogged down the hallway into the boardroom, which was a large conference room in the middle of the newsroom with glass walls. Anyone in the newsroom and on the three levels that ringed the outside could see everything that was going on in the boardroom and every face. Because this was an important vote, junior reporters and staff had lined up on the outside, some sitting on the stairs and some leaning over the balconies. This was a big moment for the paper, and they all knew it. As Clark and Richie crossed the center of the newsroom to enter the boardroom, a junior staffer made a loud sideline whistle with his thumbs and shouted, "Yeah! Westfield and Byrne!" Then several dozen staff waiting and watching broke into spontaneous applause. Clark gave a friendly wave over his head, smiled, and kept walking. That made him feel good, and he needed it.

As Clark and Richie entered the boardroom, the board members' faces lit up and they stood. Some started clapping as well. Clark had addressed this board over a hundred times in his tenure about upcoming story breaks and other issues with which the paper was dealing. Some of the board members were there when Clark had started. Nowhere was the mutual respect thicker than the space between Clark Westfield, Richie Byrne, and the board of directors at the Newark Examiner. Elizabeth smiled at the reception the two dinosaurs were enjoying as they walked around the room and shook hands with several members. She took her place at the podium at the dais in the front of the room and lifted the microphone.

"Welcome, everyone!" she said in a tone so congenial she was charismatic. "We should get started. Today is an important day, and we have several matters on the agenda. We have a funding discussion and a board seat to vote on." Elizabeth glanced around the room as the board members opened the folders placed in front of them and began shuffling papers and turning pages. Sarah Reistad was nowhere to be found. Clark stood behind the last row of chairs out of sight of those who were turned the other way, looking at Elizabeth. He got her attention and made a big expansive shrug with his hands outstretched while mouthing the word Sarah, indicating he was asking where she was. Elizabeth tried to discreetly shake her head to indicate she didn't know, but as she was leading the meeting she took care not to draw any attention to herself or the exchange. She looked around at the Newark

Examiner newspaper's Board of Directors. They were wealthy, powerful people who she had met as a rookie when Clark would read her story summaries and promotions to them at the start of their quarterly meetings. Perhaps Elizabeth could take the gamble that because they met her as a college graduate and watched her ascend to Managing Editor, she had built up enough capital with her integrity that they would understand and believe what she was about to do…

"Ladies and gentlemen of the board, I want to start in a somewhat unorthodox way," she said, trying not to let her voice waver. "Many of you were here 20 years ago when I walked in this office with Steve Miller to be Clark Westfield's intern. Over the years you approved my graduate school tuition, you started the African American history magazine section for February and you underwrote the book my team put together on the 1967 Newark riots. I guess I just want to convey my gratitude to you all, and I say that to remind myself that I'm here because you all believed in me. On the subject of gratitude, I owe my entire professional training and adult education in journalism and in life - to this man," she said, pointing to Clark in the back of the room. A room full of heads turned. Clark realized Elizabeth was throwing him the ball. He would be happy to take the heat off her and explain the upcoming story and his investigation.

"Clark Westfield is the best teacher a woman could ever ask for. I say that because he tells a woman what she needs to know in this job and what to expect. He's also, after winning two Pulitzer Prizes in his career, still the grandmaster of investigative reporting. Before we start to vote on the new investor proposal, I'd like to have Clark say a few words and give a preview of an upcoming story, about which it's our fiduciary responsibility to alert you to." Elizabeth looked at Clark with a nervous glance. This had to work.

"Hello everyone," said Clark addressing a room full of familiar faces that had both had his back or tried to shank him professionally in various ways. "Before you vote on an investment from Sarah Reistad's investment group and a partnership with her company Crisprgen, you need to know that she has violated federal law by compromising highly classified programs, stolen patents, coerced families into fraudulent work contracts and we have reason to believe she is linked to a series of murders involving smart students she recruited…" The room murmured and looked at one another in disbelief. Elizabeth loaded the flash drive into the laptop computer that controlled the video projection at the front of the room. She opened Clark's story and projected it on the screen. Clark smiled. Liz had really come through for him. She turned and looked at him and gave a smile. Clark had gotten ten times the return on his mentorship of Liz. He had finally been blessed with a sister. As Clark looked back in appreciation, Elizabeth Cranford's warm angelic expression of profound partnership turned to abject terror. Clark then felt a cold, sharp pain ripping into his side two inches higher than his belt. The pain shot up in intensity as he realized he had been stabbed. He smelled lavender and felt Sarah Reistad's warm breath on his ear.

"Neanderthals also know how to fight!" she shrieked in his ear. She wrapped her legs around him and pulled Clark to the ground. One of Sarah's hands was on the knife handle and one was around Clark's throat trying to choke him. She rolled Clark over so she was on top, pinning him down. "Did you really think that you were going to be able to stop what is about to happen? The smart ones always go first. The Neanderthals *were* the smart ones. We went first! You joined us!" She looked absolutely psychotic as her eyes darted and flickered, and foam started to collect in the corners of her mouth. It was starting to get hard for Clark to breathe. Sarah was trying to kill him, and she was succeeding.

Clark struggled to breathe as Sarah sat on his chest with her elbow on his throat, then suddenly, her head smacked to one side as she was struck with the hand grip end of an ornately carved steel walking cane with a stainless-steel golden retriever head the size of a golf ball. Spittles of blood from Sarah's head landed on Clark's forehead and cheek. She fell over, completely unconscious from a massive blow to the head. Elizabeth leaned down to Clark, she was holding the cane. Clark smiled.

"Thanks, Liz..." he whispered. She smiled.

"No…thank her," said Elizabeth pointing to Clark's left. He turned his head despite the discomfort of his slashed torso. There stood Lieutenant Colonel Kelly Pram. Clark managed to speak.

"What are you doing here? And thanks for saving my life." Lt. Col Kelly Pram smiled and knelt down as two U.S. Marshals and two security guards each took a portion of Sarah's body and lifted her off Clark and into custody.

"Well, your girl Liz did the hitting, I just tossed her my cane," said Kelly Pram smiling.

"Clark, I'd like you to meet the newest board member, Katherine O'Halloran," said Elizabeth.

"Are you kidding me?" asked Clark, realizing that Lt. Col Kelly Pram was the board member from Crisprgen that Sarah was installing at the newspaper. At Crisprgen she was Katherine O'Halloran, and now Katherine O'Halloran was going to be on the board of directors of The Newark Examiner.

"Lt. Col Pram is going to join our board, and she can ensure the investment goes through. If Sarah wakes up, she will be arrested for attempted murder and likely other charges. Everything is going to be fine. We need to get you to a hospital." Elizabeth squeezed Clark's hand. Lt. Col. Kelly Pram leaned down close to Clark so she could speak directly in his ear.

"Clark, you can't publish that story," said Kelly Pram, looking at him compassionately but sternly. Clark felt as if he had been stabbed a second time. He understood exactly what was happening.

"Fuck you," he croaked. "Fuck you! You aren't gonna kill it!" he said louder. Federal Marshals were corralling the several dozen board members and staff away from Clark, Elizabeth, and Lt. Col Pram. They were going to need each person in the room and the entire board to sign a federal non-disclosure agreement not to share their knowledge of the Crisprgen story.

"Clark, it's an issue of national security," said Kelly Pram. "We can't have our Passport Project and Transcendence Projects known to the public. It will cause mass hysteria and the revelation of all the CRISPR gene patents will cause uncontrolled social disorder. We have to seize the story. But I'm now the senior board member at Crisprgen, and I am on the newspaper's board as the parent company representative. I will be approving the investment merger. As a thank you for your troubles, I put a line item in there for you and Elizabeth to receive a sizable bonus that has at least seven figures, and I also fattened each of your salaries. I think you'll be happy. That's how this works from now on. When we need you and you come through like this, we reward you. No one ever has to know." Lt. Col. Kelly Pram smiled.

"Come on Clark, we need to get you to the hospital," said Elizabeth as she moved to make way for two EMT's who had entered the room with a stretcher. As they rolled Clark over and he groaned with pain, he looked at Lt. Col Kelly Pram.

"You fucking asshole…!!" he barked. He would have been livid under any circumstances if the government interfered with his story, but he had risked his life for this investigation and had his heart broken in the process. It was too high a price to pay to walk away with nothing. "I don't work for you. Keep your fucking money…" Clark coughed and slightly choked on his spit.

"Like I said... I will make it worth your while," said Lt. Col. Pram again.

"You gotta run my story," Clark pleaded, gasping through the pain of being stabbed as the EMT's strapped him onto the thick yellow plastic transport board with side grips on it. The EMTs with their light blue latex gloves snapped the transport board perfectly in place on the gurney.

"Give me just one second to finish setting this IV," said the female EMT as she expertly and frantically unwrapped a syringe. The EMT removed the intravascular needle at the top and screwed it onto the IV hose line fixture which was coiled and taped to a large bag of saline marked Field Plasma. "We don't want you losing too much blood on us, so you need some plasma before we get on the way to the hospital," she said. Her nonchalant demeanor comforted Clark, who despite the searing and immobilizing pain from the stab wound figured she had seen hundreds of stabbings in her tenure and would sound way more tense if this were really life threatening.

The other EMT taped large sheets of gauze over the wound. Clark felt the pressure inside his abdomen increasing. He could still feel Elizabeth holding his hand as the first responder team began pushing him backward out of the room. He looked to his right to see Sarah being loaded onto a second stretcher, completely unconscious and lifeless. Lt. Col Pram tapped one of the U.S. Marshals placing Sarah on the gurney and made a circular motion with her index finger extended pointing to Sarah's wrist. The marshal nodded and lifted a pair of handcuffs from his belt compartment and strapped one manacle tightly around her left wrist. He snapped the other cuff around the aluminum rail of the gurney, so she was now handcuffed to the stretcher. The EMT finished setting Clark's IV and was taping the hose to his wrist to secure the flow. She looked up and got the attention of Lt. Col. Pram and the federal marshal that was securing the unconscious Sarah as a small trickle of blood ran down the side of her face and onto the gurney pillow.

"Don't do that please!" blurted the EMT. "I need to prepare her for transport, and I need to set up an IV for her and administer clotting agents with that head wound."

"Sarah Reistad is now in custody of the Department of Homeland Security, and we will be remanding her into a federal detention facility," said Lt. Col Pram without looking up. She made another circular motion with her hand and the two federal marshals began wheeling her stretcher forward towards the conference room door.

"Hey! We have to take her to the hospital," called the EMT, clearly frustrated that the Marshals and Lt. Col. Pram were ignoring her. "There are two ambulances outside at the door, put her in the one without the driver, we need to…"

"She is now in federal custody," said Lt. Col. Pram again without making eye contact or directly addressing the EMT who was supervising the situation. "We will have a Marshall return your gurney. Please make sure Mr. Westfield is given immediate attention. We will contact the hospital ahead of time and tell them they have an urgent priority triage coming in." The two Federal Marshals and Lt. Col. Pram then deftly glided the stretcher with an unresponsive Sarah Reistad out the conference door and down the hallway.

"Clark, stay with me, I'm not leaving you," said Elizabeth. "I'm going to ride with you in the ambulance," she said to the EMT.

"Ma'am, you will need to drive your own car, it is standard procedure not to have any witnesses or bystanders in the vehicle," said the EMT. Her tone was stern while she seethed at Kelly Pram for ignoring her.

"I'm not asking," said Elizabeth, giving the EMT a look that let her know she wasn't going to take no for an answer. The EMT shook her head in defeat and turned to take her place at the front of the gurney and guide it out the conference room doors. Elizabeth walked alongside still holding Clark's hands.

"Liz…" Clark managed to whisper. Elizabeth leaned down and put her ear close to Clark's mouth. "Thanks…" he managed to gasp. She kissed his forehead and squeezed his hand.

"I know," she said gently. "Don't try to talk, just breathe. There will be plenty of time later to talk about gratitude." The stretcher slightly bumped against the rear of the ambulance causing Clark to yelp in pain.

"Easy," said the EMT as she pushed the button so the springs could retract the wheels and the responders could lift the stretcher into the back of the ambulance. The EMT turned and extended her arm to help Elizabeth up over the bumper to hop in. Once the three of them were in the back, the driver hurried around and started the engine and a full blare of the sirens. The staff of the Newark Examiner stood on the sidewalk and curb watching the scene. Some were visibly shaken and had tears running down their faces. There was no sign of Lt. Col Pram, the team of Federal Marshals, or any other emergency vehicles, and no sign of Sarah Reistad.

"Liz, you gotta send the story to the New York Times, they will take it as a special," Clark said groaning. "Send it to

TIME magazine…We've still got the story, it's gotta get out. Don't let me die over a story that doesn't get published."

"You aren't going to die, this is mostly a deep muscle injury," said the EMT as she administered a blood pressure cuff. "The knife missed everything important and didn't perforate your thorax or you wouldn't be able to speak right now, and you aren't going to bleed to death now that we have you on the plasma," she reassured him. Elizabeth sighed with relief and then leaned down to speak softly in Clark's ear.

"When you came to lecture my class when I was in high school, you said that an investigative reporter has to be ready to die for the truth if that's where the story takes you," she said with a warm smile.

"Yeah, well, I guess this is what I meant." Clark laughed and winced in pain. Elizabeth put her hand on his forehead.

I'm going to call Melody and tell her to meet us at the hospital," she said.

"Call Amy too…" wheezed Clark. Elizabeth suddenly started to look fuzzy, and Clark had the sensation he was floating, then total blackness.

***

"OK, he seems to be waking up," said a man's voice. Clark opened his eyes and was almost blinded by intensely bright overhead lights. As his vision came into focus, he saw a middle-aged Indian man in scrubs and a white coat leaning over him. Sanjeesh Patel, M.D. was embroidered on his lapel above the medical symbol of two snakes wrapped around a cross and the screen printed the words "St. Michael's Hospital/ Emergency Department. "Mr. Westfield, I'm Dr. Patel, can you see me? Do you know what day it is?" asked the doctor in a heavy Indian accent.

"Yeah, I know what day it is," Clark said, realizing he had a tight and sophisticated wound dressing on his side and that most of the pain was gone. "Did the story run?" he asked, looking around the room.

"I don't know anything about a story," said Dr. Patel, smiling. "But I know you are a very lucky man. Another quarter inch to the middle of your back and that blade would have punctured your descending aorta and you would have bleed out before anyone could dial 911. Another quarter inch higher and it would have punctured your lung, and you would have drowned in your own blood. Luckily, the blade barely made it through your intercostal muscles in your abdominal wall and it only grazed the outside of your right kidney. It's nothing serious and will heal right up. But you are going to have to rest for a few days. Most people who get mugged and attacked don't live to talk about it. They told me they caught the mugger if that's any consolation."

"Mugged? I wasn't mugged," said Clark, confused in a raspy voice. "What happened to the story? Where's Liz?" Clark glanced around the room.

"I still don't know anything about any story, but there are two women here and they have been patient and eager for you to wake up. I'll let them say hello and then I'll be back in a bit to talk about aftercare," said Dr. Patel. He turned towards the door and smiled. "He is all yours…" And then Dr. Patel left the hospital room. Clark looked up to see Melody and Amy standing on each side of the bed. Melody leaned down and hugged her father as best she could as he lay in the hospital bed.

"Dad, oh my god…I was so worried when Elizabeth called," said Melody, choking back tears. "Thank God you are going to be fine," Clark hugged his daughter with the arm free from any IVs. Melody and Clark held an embrace for several seconds. He felt Amy's hand grab his and interlock her fingers with his. She leaned down and joined in the hug as Clark fought to keep his composure.

"They are telling everyone you got mugged, and they put us under a gag order not to talk about Sarah or Crisprgen," said Amy.

"Where is Liz," he asked wearily. "What about the story?"

"Liz is downstairs at the cafeteria with Richie—they have been waiting here the whole time as well.. I'll go tell them you are awake and talking," said Melody, kissing her dad on his forehead and wiping away a tear. "Amy is here with you; I'll be right back," she said as Amy nodded and Melody quickly scurried out of the hospital room.

Clark looked up at Amy as the two found themselves alone. Beeping sounds of biometric monitors and EKGs swirled around them with occasional broken static crackling through the overhead public address speakers.

"Hey, Aim," said Clark, managing a smile and squeezing her hand. "That was pretty close, wasn't it?" She looked at him with the attachment and devotion that can only coalesce between two kindred souls.

"Yeah, it sure was," said Amy, sniffing back a sob. She leaned down and kissed his cheek. "I don't know what I would have done if I had lost you, Clark Westfield. You and I still have a long way to go together." Amy smiled reassuringly.

"Yeah, well, not if Elizabeth gives in and doesn't run our piece," said Clark. "Amy you gotta talk to her and if she won't listen, you gotta help me get it out on the wire somehow. Call Richie. He will talk to her. Can you believe Sarah fucking stabbed me? And now Pram is killing the story, making it all a worthless effort. They broke my heart, tried to kill me, and stole my story. I almost died for nothing, and those two women ruined me." Amy's face didn't change from the look of affectionate devotion she harbored for her Clark.

"Well, I wouldn't say those two women ruined you," said Amy warmly. Clark made a scoffing sound showing his incredulity. Amy leaned down close to Clark's face. "I would argue those two women gave you the ability to be with two other women who care about you and love you very much, and I mean Melody and me."

"How so? Was it the First Amendment suppression or the assault with a deadly weapon?" said Clark sarcastically. Amy shook her head.

"Neither. Lt. Col. Pram gave you all the research records from Crisprgen which has a ledger of everyone who got the TA-65 longevity CRISPR-Cas 9 for the Transcendence project through an injection of a simple adenovirus that delivers the mechanism to edit each cell's DNA. There were two unknown coded names on the list who got the full gene replacement therapy that extends life indefinitely. Apparently, I was one of the unknown study subjects in the early days of the trials and Sarah injected me without me knowing, telling me it was a routine blood draw." explained Amy. Clark raised his eyebrows.

"Ok, well, congratulations," said Clark as Amy said nothing but held his gaze. "Who was the other one? Do we know?" Amy sat down on the bed next to him.

"Clark," Amy said softly. She leaned down closer to his ear so he could feel her breath as she whispered. "You and I are going to grow old together…really old…."

<u>**Clark Westfield will return very soon**</u>
<u>**in his next adventure "The Seed Bank"!!**</u>

Acknowledgements:

First, a heartfelt note of love and appreciation to my wife and children, for their encouragement, wit, satire and patience.

Second, thank you to the real life Smart Ones who had the patience to answer endless questions and explain the complexities of gene therapy - Fred Porter and Rick Johnstone.

Third - to my beta readers for their feedback and encouragement - you make the book better when you spend time reading and discussing it - Patti Maloney and Sandro LaRocca.

Fourth - to everyone at Exit 135 Productions. Your genius insights, skills, strategic brilliance and perseverance are what keep me writing. Thank you for believing in me.

Fifth - I'd like to thank the transportation planners, analysts and building engineers of the Garden State Parkway for creating exits 135 and 137, my two personal exit ramps for peace and serenity, and giving me inspiration that became my personal lifelong toll for traveling your shitty highway. At least I made something good out of it.

The Adventures of Clark Westfield

So now you know the truth… …now what?

Clark Westfield and his adventures are the author's attempt to come to terms with various dimensions of the human spirit and the surprises our world brings. Both the author and his characters are concerned about the problems of the world and Tom hopes that by inviting you along into exciting adventures like Clark Westfield's reporting job, that you will be motivated to solve those problems also..

The Adventures of Clark Westfield…

As one of the last of the golden generation of investigative reporters, middle aged Clark grew up in New Jersey in the 1970's and 1980's. Like most smart kids, he was a sponge for pop culture and world events. Clark's passion for journalism was religious in its devotion, and the pursuit of the news as a way to find truth was a vocation he held with deep conviction. After decades of breaking crucial stories about the highest levels of power and politics, Clark's success has made him a celebrity reporter and a star in the industry. His writing has won two Pulitzer Prizes among countless additional accolades.

And while his career trajectory eventually eclipsed any imposter syndrome, it hasn't helped clarify the world any further. People in power still behave badly. Corruption still rises to the institutional level, and people still hurt one another intentionally. But humans are inherently flawed creatures, and accepting the world as it is can be a daunting process for deep thinkers.

Clark's adventures will take you through situations unique to our point in our natural history, as well as scenarios that have always threaded humanity in fundamental ways. As he explores the major news topics that are the set design for modern times, he continuously uncovers very uncomfortable questions and even more uncomfortable truths. Joining Clark on his adventures gives you a spot on his team of deft investigative journalists whose sole purpose, drive and passion are asking the right questions.

The Cassandra Unit

Clark has to interview a murderer up for parole. The case has haunted him since he found the files as a child and he opportunistically used his father's name to access the first interview. The murderer persuades Clark to investigate the mine which was the crime scene. The secrets and twists Clark discovers are as complicated and unpredictable as the network of abandoned iron mines in Harriman St. Park. Clark is caught in a threeway trap and must choose between preserving his father's reputation, possibly letting a child murderer go free, and keeping the job he spent his life perfecting.

Do No Harm

Clark witnesses a young woman die from an opioid overdose at the Point Pleasant, NJ boardwalk. As he explores the circumstances surrounding her death, he finds indifference in the police and community, a corporate genocide unfolding in broad daylight and tens of thousands of bereaved parents. Clark sees once again how the system of societal checkpoints and safeguards that are supposed to protect us - doctors, police, government oversight - is broken, leaving the grieving parents no recourse. Clark soon finds himself in the dark underbelly of the opioid crisis which has turned an idyllic New Jersey shore town into a dystopian drug wasteland where those still living must devise their own ways to cope...legal or not....

The Smart Ones

Clark is following the cases of several missing students gifted with extreme intelligence. Reluctantly, he accepts an assignment to profile a consumer genetics agency that is engaged in research in the old Fort Monmouth army base in New Jersey. Clark gets caught up in the whirlwind of technology, ethics, and temptation. Clark is drawn to the founder, an enigmatic woman genius who is collecting and curating a main database of genetic code from millions of people and cataloging epigenetic markers. After identifying and harvesting the good genes, CRISPR-Cas9 technology can add them to one's genome to increase disease prevention, longevity and human potential. But as Clark explores the profound changes gene therapy will bring to the human race, the smart persons creating this brave new world begin to meet various tragic ends, and he simultaneously uncovers something far deeper and more sinister.

The Seed Bank

Clark is in Alaska touring the Ft. Richardson Strategic Air Command air force base (Elmendorff) and investigating a murdered climate scientist. He is shown the botanical research and massive inventory of one of the military's official seed banks. It's a vault inside a mountain that catalogs all the seeds in the world by geography, curated, owned and operated by the military high command. As he investigates the murder he is thrown headfirst into the maelstrom weather experiments and shadow databases containing troubling climate news. As Elizabeth fights an emergency injunction brought by the newspaper's advertisers, Clark enlists the help of a local sovereign tribal nation and finds himself at a crossroads for our climate future and in his own personal life.

Blood Among Brethren

When Clark is called to report on a suicide of an all star high school athlete with no apparent cause he winds up investigating the Catholic Church abuse vortex and finds a global protection racket for perpetrator clergy reaching the highest levels of the Vatican. Additionally, he finds an ex-special forces military chaplain who is a tough Irish priest that uses his Bronx street smarts to deal with problems in his own way. But amidst the dirty, secret settlements the Church is paying out to victims, and deep in the labyrinth of crevices under the trafficking system built to protect predator priests, there is a new, violent and deadly element of justice slicing through centuries of institutionalized corruption. And all around there are dead priests with bloody collars.

For more info and to join Clark's news team, go to:
www.adventuresofclarkwestfield.com

Social Media Handles: @TomAlbright135
https://www.facebook.com/profile.php?id=100062921876252

TikTOk: @clarkwestfield2112